Also edited by Robert Shapard and James Thomas
Sudden Fiction: American Short-Short Stories

Also edited by James Thomas
Best of the West: New Stories from the
Wide Side of the Missouri
(An Anthology Series)

Also by James Thomas
Pictures, Moving (Stories)

SUDDEN FICTION
INTERNATIONAL

SUDDEN FICTION
INTERNATIONAL

Sixty Short-Short Stories

EDITED BY

ROBERT SHAPARD and JAMES THOMAS

Introduction by Charles Baxter

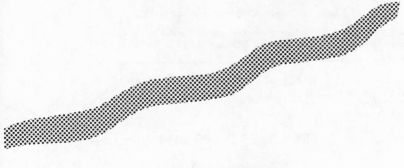

W'· W · NORTON & COMPANY · New York · London

The comments of authors and translators in the *Afternotes* (pp. 296–337) are the sole property of the authors and translators and may not be quoted further, except briefly for review purposes, without permission.

The Acknowledgments on page 338 are an extension of the copyright page.

The text of this book is composed in 10½/14 Janson, with display type set in Corvinus Skyline. Composition and manufacturing by The Maple-Vail Book Manufacturing Group. Book design by Lynn Fischer.

Library of Congress Cataloging-in-Publication Data

Sudden fiction international: sixty short-short stories / edited by
    Robert Shapard and James Thomas ; introduction by Charles Baxter.—
1st ed.
        p.   cm.
    1. Short stories.   I. Shapard, Robert, 1942–
II. Thomas, James, 1946–
PN6120.2.W675   1989
808.83′1—dc19   89–3134

ISBN 0-393-02718-X

W. W. Norton & Company, Inc.
500 Fifth Avenue, New York, N. Y. 10110
W. W. Norton & Company Ltd.
37 Great Russell Street, London WC1B 3NU

BOMC offers recordings and compact discs, cassettes and records. For information and catalog write to BOMR, Camp Hill, PA 17012.

For their editorial assistance in shaping this book,
we are indebted to our associates:

Tom Hazuka

Jonathan Maney

Revé Shapard

Denise Thomas

We would also like to thank the many writers, editors, and friends around the world who helped make this book possible through their invaluable contributions and recommendations. For their direct assistance we'd like to note in particular Stephanie Adkins, Cristina Bacchilega, Diana Baker, Ginger Bohn, Kristin Brucker, Joseph Chadwick, Karen Donahue, Huma Ibrahim, Kathy Matsueda, and Tahl Tyson; Carol Houck Smith of W. W. Norton, who sailed this ship of a book through high seas; and, finally, for putting out the fire that nearly consumed the copyedited manuscript, special thanks to the Miami Township Fire Department.

Contents

CONTENTS

Contents

Contents

Contents

CONTENTS

A Note from the Editors

In 1986 we edited an anthology of American short-short stories called *Sudden Fiction*, which has proved so popular that it is still being discovered, not only at local bookstores but in courses at over two hundred colleges and universities. Moreover, it is being translated into German, Spanish, Italian, Japanese, and Chinese. Why such interest? The recent flowering of the short-short form has been heralded as the birth of a new sub-genre of fiction, one that is sometimes like the larger short story, but often more tantalizing, protean, and highly charged.

As we collected American stories for that anthology, we noted the new visibility of short-shorts in translation. Borges, Babel, Dinesen, Calvino, Colette, and Kawabata—all were coming home to us now, more often and in better translation. So we decided to think of a volume that would be international, and began to ask writers and editors who had helped with *Sudden Fiction* for their suggestions. Responding with generosity, they sent recommendations, lists of translators and publishers, titles of collections, and often stories themselves. Best of all, they gave us direct introductions to writers in many countries.

Sometimes the route to our international contributors was circuitous. We tracked one translator of Chinese fiction through several American universities before we met him, at last, in a coffee shop in San Francisco. "Short-short stories are very popular in China," he told us. We were elated. But not everything panned out so well. An editor in Seoul wrote us that "Not too many short-shorts are being written here. We Koreans are long-winded." Later a visiting Central American playwright jotted down the names and addresses of a dozen compatriots on a hotel napkin. He smiled and said, "Once you know one writer in my country, you know them all." We photocopied his jottings, and wrote more letters. By return mail we received more books in Spanish, stories in English typed on crinkly lightweight paper, and the names of still more authors. Meantime, packets poured in from Europe and the British Isles—tides of photocopies; from Asia came paperbacks smelling of clove (or was it glue?); and there was air mail with exotic stamps from Brazil and Morocco and other farflung places.

After two years of collecting, it was time to take stock, to select from the bounty and choose those stories we felt were most compelling and represented the greatest variety. The result is the book you have in your hand. Some of the writers are known to the world, others are well-known in their own countries, and still others are new talents yet to be widely recognized. When our final selection was made, we asked these writers, and sometimes their translators, to talk about the stories. They do so, under brief biographies, in our Afternotes section. Finally, and above all, such a richly various offering needs a single, clear-eyed look at the form, and this you will find in the introduction by Charles Baxter, author of two collections of stories, *Harmony of the World* and *Through the Safety Net*, and a novel, *First Light*.

We hope you enjoy this voyage around the world of sudden fiction.

Introduction

Imagine, for a moment, that you have fallen asleep while reading a great book. Suppose that the book is *War and Peace* or *Crime and Punishment* or *Moby-Dick;* it doesn't matter, as long as the book carries with it a crushing weight of cultural prestige. But somehow, toward the middle, your attention flags, or you're not up to the challenge, or you're tired and irritable because you've just had a first-class quarrel with the person who is now sulking in another part of the place you call home. Whatever the cause, you've fallen asleep. The huge book you've been reading falls to the floor. Because it's a big book, it makes a resounding thud when gravity finally has its way with it. The sound shocks you awake. You look up, dazed. You feel guilty (again). You have failed, at least temporarily, the Test of Literature. Something is wrong (you have always known it) with your attention span. Perhaps you are one of those famous victims of television. Maybe you pick up the big prestigious book and push onward into it. But maybe you don't.

At this point, I must make a sort of confession: I, too, have fallen asleep over several famous authors. And I have woken up feeling that the fault must be mine, and wondering, vaguely, about the convention of length in literature. I have enjoyed and admired the works of these authors, but upon intermittent reflection I have had the nagging thought that the length of their works is arbitrary or, worse, artificial. As it happens, in the tradition of Western literature we have come to believe that, at

17

least with the novel, length is synonymous with profundity (this is a confusion of the horizontal with the vertical, please notice) and that most great literature must be large. But what if length, great length, *is* a convention not always necessary to the materials but dictated by an author's taste or will, a convention that runs parallel to expansionism, empire-building, and the contemplation of the heroic individual? What if length is a feature of writing that is as artificial as an individual prose style? Perhaps length has something to do with the relation between author and reader, then; length might be a kind of pact, an agreement between reader and writer, to do something for a long time, like living within a marriage. Or it may simply be evidence of the writer's interest in domination.

I am sneaking up on the subject of the very short story, but I have to do so by negation, by talking about what novels do, because whatever the novel form does is more or less what very short stories do not do. One of the qualities that we associate with the novel form is the drama of prolonged moral choice. This drama usually concentrates on an individual and a milieu. In the novels we were all assigned to read in high school, someone comes of age, or must make a decision about a marriage, or accumulates or loses a fortune, or runs through some sequential seductions, or bargains with the forces of light and darkness. Even Don Quixote, crazed by his reading, makes choices. He chooses to be a certain kind of knight. An unusual tragicomedy is the result. And Ahab chooses to be a certain kind of sea captain.

Many of these novels come to us with their moral questions already formed: should Lily marry the awful Rupert, who, despite his repulsive manners and scheming ways, sits on top of a pile of money and who will therefore rescue her from her virtuous and shabby gentility? Moral dilemmas of this kind have given the novel form its characteristic power to compel readerly attention for three hundred years. Gatsby and Raskolnikov and Jane Eyre are all figures of circumstance and moral choice. As a literary form, the novel, especially the long novel, tends to turn crucially on moments when fears and desires have caused characters to make decisions that will have consequences far into the future. Their plot construction often depends on what Henry James might have called "the finer discriminations" and what we might call psychology, in its broadest sense: the particular emotional coloration of individual choices and situations.

And, as a friend of mine once remarked, reading a long novel is like having a relationship with somebody; it's not just another one-night stand.

This world of remarkable individuals making moral decisions across a long span of time is often what passes for profundity in literature. Greatness, we in America especially think, often has to do with sheer *size*, with the expansion of materials. But one is entitled to have occasional doubts. Even Chekhov, in a letter to his friend Suvorin, thought that Dostoyevsky's novels were too long. He believed that Dostoyevsky's novels were immodest and pretentious. It is partly a matter of vision, of where you think reality takes place. The world of large individuals making large decisions is not the distinctive feature of the stories you hold in your hand. Some other world is making its way into literature in these brief, reticent, meticulous stories. That world is both strange and familiar.

With these stories laid out like a miniature world's fair of fiction, the reader, wandering from one moment to the next from India to Canada and then, perhaps, back to China, might well ask what these stories have in common apart from the fact that they are enlightening, entertaining, and, obviously, very short. All right: they're short—so what? We don't expect people who are of similar height to be alike simply because they come up to

19

the same mark on the wall. Apples and oranges are about the same size, but they are, well, apples and oranges. So why should a story that measures out from three to five pages have any-thing—anything at all—in common with another story written out of a different cultural experience two, three, or ten thou-sand miles away?

If there are qualities that these stories have in common, those qualities have to do with the kind of story a writer can tell in a very short space. Think of the shortest story you know. Per-haps it's just an anecdote. The chances are that the story has to do with a sudden crisis, in which a character does not *act* so much as *react*. This is an important distinction. When a char-acter reacts, the situation is larger and more powerful than that character is. Furthermore, the situation was there before the character was. Reactions are not decisions, exactly, or choices; they tend to be automatic. Perhaps they are unconscious choices. But they tell us more about the way people as a whole behave than the way that particular individual behaves. In the conven-tional short story, the protagonist usually has a choice of some kind, or at least an illusion of choice. That condition may lead to a moment of insight. But *these* stories are not dramas of moral choice or psychological inclination. They have more to do with hilarity and panic-states.

When individuals or groups must act without *any* apparent choices available to them, their actions tend to be ritualistic. By "ritualistic" I mean a whole class of reactions that people per-form without thinking, or at least without thinking clearly enough to feel that they have chosen deliberately or are clearly respon-sible for what they have done. Such characters are governed in moments of crisis by intractable chains of cause and effect. Stress is applied immediately and efficiently to these characters; one might almost call this the fiction of sudden stress.

But out of this apparent determinism come little unexpected

explosive moments. In these moments there are visions of tremendous clarity. This is as true of Bessie Head's "Looking for a Rain God" (from Botswana) as it is of Leslie Norris' "Blackberries" (from Wales). In Bessie Head's account of a terrible African drought, the narrative focus has moved away from the individual to the community and from choice to ritual. The individual colorations of psychology do not matter very much in a period of drought and possible famine. Mokgobja, the character who does what might have been unthinkable and does so thanks to recovered ritual, could have been anyone in the community. In these stories, there are no prolonged agonizing reappraisals, disquisitions on psychology, and few epiphanies. The situations don't permit it because time and space have both run out simultaneously. If you're living through a period of famine-producing drought, you do the only thing you can think of to do. Or, as in "Blackberries," if you're poor, and you bring home blackberries in your cap, something in the family inevitably gives way.

It is as if a shift has occurred in these stories away from the imperial character of the nineteenth century novel toward ritual, spontaneity, humor, and forgiveness—all characteristics of reduced geographies. People often discuss time in relation to very short stories. "Short" is usually taken to mean "brief." But what about space? What if very short short stories are products of mass societies in which crowding is an inescapable part of life? The novel is, spatially, like an estate; the very short story is like an efficiency on the twenty-third floor. As it happens, more people these days live in efficiencies than on estates. The result may be that we will start to see a shift in the imperial self of the traditional novel to the *we* and the *they* of communal stories. We will have stories taking place on baseball fields (Stuart Dybek's "Death of the Right Fielder"), in drainpipes ("The Grass-Eaters" by Krishnan Varma), or a spot smaller than the head of a pin ("All at One Point" by Italo Calvino). These stories tell us something about the scale of our lives, not so much that diminishment has occurred but that intimacy and community have increased. It is as if all the borders, to all other realms, have moved closer to us, and we ourselves are living in tighter psychic spaces. A beautiful example of this fiction-of-proximity is R. K. Narayan's "House Opposite."

If everything has moved closer, what kinds of compensations can we expect? What we find, if these stories are part of the evidence, are the virtues of quickness: humor, surrealism, and some skepticism. The skepticism has to do with explanations. We are all getting tired of the Village Explainers. Explanations don't seem to be explaining very much anymore. Authoritative accounts have a way of looking like official lies, which in their solemnity start to sound funny. If you don't know the whole truth, you might as well keep whatever you have to say short. You might as well puncture the pretense of sheer size. Writers begin to offer us permutational fiction, fiction of the "What if . . . " variety and the "If . . . then" mode, like Margaret Atwood's "Happy Endings" and Paulé Bartón's "Emilie Plead Choose One Egg" and, from the master of the permutational, Jorge Luis Borges' "August 25, 1983." Paulé Bartón's story has the if/then structure of parable, while Borges, who all but invented the story form that sounded authoritative but which explored only the labyrinth of explanations, shows us how explanations do not free us, but snare us, instead.

In a similar way, given the brief span of these stories, wild possibilities turn into probabilities and even inevitabilities, as in the bizarre but perfectly logical South African story "Arrest Me" by Denis Hirson, or in the bewildered bureaucratese of Donald Barthelme's "The School," and in the abrupt take-it-or-leave-it style of Peter Carey's "The Last Days of a Famous Mime." What I admire about these stories and so many others in this book is that they are antidotes to Dead Seriousness. It is as if the titanic ego of fiction itself has been brought down to a human scale. These stories are sleek and efficient, modest without being cringing, and they have not a particle of nostalgia. They avoid the kitsch of spectacle and the kitsch of aggression. Unhypnotized by power and glamour, they do not narrate the fantasies of sexual and capital acquisitions (because they cannot); instead, they tell us what we already knew, that the truth was always in front of us, over there, in the corner, or here, squarely in front of us, in the immediate details of our lives. If anyone doubts the power of detail, let that person read Yuan Ch'iung-Ch'iung's "A Lover's Ear," with its delicate and completely memorable obsessional eroticism and its startling little drop of blood. What these stories tell us is that intelligent intensity has nothing to do with scale. It has to do with the quality of a person's attention. Such stories might be considered the appropriate literary technology for a time of diminished resources.

Quite a few critics have been worried about attention spans lately and see very short stories as signs of cultural decadence, bonbons for lazy readers, chocolates stuffed with snow. But many of the wonderful stories gathered in this volume compel quite a lot of attention, and the duration of that attention doesn't seem as important as its quality. And it's not as though we need to blame television (again) for this worldwide and longstanding interest in very short stories. No one ever said that sonnets or haikus were evidence of short attention spans. The short-attention-span argument seems to have been invented by Anglocentric critics who are nostalgic for the huge Victorian novel as the only serious form of literature; and talking about the short attention span is a form of blaming-the-reader.

As for time, these stories not only speed it up, they also, and more often, slow it down. I will use for my example the first story in this book, Dino Buzzati's "The Falling Girl." You will discover when you read this story that the girl of the title, Marta, jumps off the roof of a skyscraper at twilight; the rest of the story chronicles her long, lyric, and increasingly slow journey downward. I will not spoil the story for you if I tell you that, like an arrow in Zeno's paradox, she never reaches the ground. People in the apartment building watch her go by, have conversations with her, perhaps even fall in love with her. The relentless ongoing progress of time and sequencing is suddenly suspended. Time slows down, seems ready (perhaps out of love for Marta) to stop altogether. Time and Dino Buzzati collaborate in saving Marta from her inevitable death; the vertical drop is turned into the horizontal, like a stroll from the top floor to the ground through the air.

Again and again in these stories we have such moments of suspension, a kind of temporal pause often associated with poetry, a widening of the moment. What the detail is to the world of facts, the moment is to the flow of time. Even in the stories of ritual, such as "Looking for a Rain God," there is a similar stop-time effect. Why is this happening? My guess is that in the world we are going to inhabit, moments and details are going to be increasingly important. If human beings are not always in control, then we get comedy on the one hand and expanded moments on the other.

This is also a response to a feeling of information sickness, data-nausea, of being surrounded by information at every moment. What is wanted is not larger, huger chunks of data (we can leave that dream to science), but an effect of elegance and simplicity. Some of these small stories may in fact be the first reaction in literature to the computer. The computer has made quite a few people sick of information, since they must manipulate this information all day long. But we can still have stories that see into the future with tenderness and clarity, and by simple means, such as two beams of light, as in Kawabata's "The Grasshopper and the Bell Cricket," one of the most beautiful stories in this collection and one of the best stories written by anyone anywhere. The stop-time effect here is created by the most simple means, and the reader can see, from the pivot-point of this story, the lives of Kiyoko and Fujio in both directions, both past and future, as if the story itself were a kind of lighthouse.

What we see in this story, and so many others like it, is an ability to end the tale with a suggestion—a play of light—rather than an explicit insight. The history of Anglo-American writing of the last seventy years puts a kind of critical pressure on the writer to provide discursive epiphanies, but in cultures less obsessed than ours with the secular Calvinism of private revelation and guilt about the frivolity of story-telling, the truth is allowed to stand in a much more contradictory or playful condition.

Looking over what I have written, I have the liberating feeling that the form of the very short story is far more mysterious, more multi-faceted, than I have made it out to be. But this simply means that this form is not about to be summarized by any one person's ideas about it. I suspect that these stories appeal to readers so much now because the stories are on so many various thresholds: they are between poetry and fiction, the story and the sketch, prophecy and reminiscence, the personal and the crowd. As Stuart Dybek has said, no one is sure what they are or even what to call them. Which means that, as a form, they are open, and exist in a state of potential. Unpredictable, funny, and certainly memorable, these stories may be *wrong* for the serious world of Big-Time Fiction, but they are right for all the right reasons. Length is not always seriousness; sometimes it simply has to do with how much information a story requires. With the noise of the contemporary world increasing exponentially hour by hour, and people trying to drown you with words alone, these stories have managed a neat trick: they put up *and* shut up.

Charles Baxter

SUDDEN FICTION
INTERNATIONAL

DINO BUZZATI

The Falling Girl

arta was nineteen. She looked out over the roof of the skyscraper, and seeing the city below shining in the dusk, she was overcome with dizziness.

The skyscraper was silver, supreme and fortunate in that most beautiful and pure evening, as here and there the wind stirred a few fine filaments of cloud against an absolutely incredible blue background. It was in fact the hour when the city is seized by inspiration and whoever is not blind is swept away by it. From that airy height the girl saw the streets and the masses of buildings writhing in the long spasm of sunset, and at the point where the white of the houses ended, the blue of the sea began. Seen from above, the sea looked as if it were rising. And since the veils of the night were advancing from the east, the city became a sweet abyss burning with pulsating lights. Within it were powerful men, and women who were even more powerful, furs and violins, cars glossy as onyx, the neon signs of nightclubs, the entrance halls of darkened mansions, fountains, diamonds, old silent gardens, parties, desires, affairs, and, above all, that consuming sorcery of the evening which provokes dreams of greatness and glory.

Seeing these things, Marta hopelessly leaned out over the railing and let herself go. She felt as if she were hovering in the air, but she was falling. Given the extraordinary height of the skyscraper, the streets and squares down at the bottom were very far away. Who knows how long it would take her to get there. Yet the girl was falling.

At that hour the terraces and balconies of the top floors were filled with rich and elegant people who were having cocktails and making silly conversation. They were scattered in crowds, and their talk muffled the music. Marta passed before them and several people looked out to watch her.

Flights of that kind (mostly by girls, in fact) were not rare in the skyscraper and they constituted an interesting diversion for the tenants; this was also the reason why the price of those apartments was very high.

The sun had not yet completely set and it did its best to illuminate Marta's simple clothing. She wore a modest, inexpensive spring dress bought off the rack. Yet the lyrical light of the sunset exalted it somewhat, making it chic.

From the millionaires' balconies, gallant hands were stretched out toward her, offering flowers and cocktails. "Miss, would you like a drink? . . . Gentle butterfly, why not stop a minute with us?"

She laughed, hovering, happy (but meanwhile she was falling): "No, thanks, friends. I can't. I'm in a hurry."

"Where are you headed?" they asked her.

"Ah, don't make me say," Marta answered, waving her hands in a friendly good-bye.

A young man, tall, dark, very distinguished, extended an arm to snatch her. She liked him. And yet Marta quickly defended herself: "How dare you, sir?" and she had time to give him a little tap on the nose.

The beautiful people, then, were interested in her and that filled her with satisfaction. She felt fascinating, stylish. On the flower-filled terraces, amid the bustle of waiters in white and the bursts of exotic songs, there was talk for a few minutes, perhaps less, of the young woman who was passing by (from top to bottom, on a vertical course). Some thought her pretty, others thought her so-so, everyone found her interesting.

"You have your entire life before you," they told her, "why are you in such a hurry? You still have time to rush around and busy yourself. Stop with us for a little while, it's only a modest little party among friends, really, you'll have a good time."

She made an attempt to answer but the force of gravity had already quickly carried her to the floor below, then two, three, four floors below; in fact, exactly as you gaily rush around when you are just nineteen years old.

Of course, the distance that separated her from the bottom, that is, from street level, was immense. It is true that she began falling just a little while ago, but the street always seemed very far away.

In the meantime, however, the sun had plunged into the sea; one could see it disappear, transformed into a shimmering reddish mushroom. As a result, it no longer emitted its vivifying rays to light up the girl's dress and make her a seductive comet. It was a good thing that the windows and terraces of the skyscraper were almost all illuminated and the bright reflections completely gilded her as she gradually passed by.

Now Marta no longer saw just groups of carefree people inside the apartments; at times there were even some businesses where the employees, in black or blue aprons, were sitting at desks in long rows. Several of them were young people as old as or older than she, and weary of the day by now, every once in a while they raised their eyes from their duties and from typewriters.

In this way they too saw her, and a few ran to the windows. "Where are you going? Why so fast? Who are you?" they shouted to her. One could divine something akin to envy in their words.

"They're waiting for me down there," she answered. "I can't stop. Forgive me." And again she laughed, wavering on her headlong fall, but it wasn't like her previous laughter anymore. The night had craftily fallen and Marta started to feel cold.

Meanwhile, looking downward, she saw a bright halo of lights at the entrance of a building. Here long blacks cars were stopping (from the great distance they looked as small as ants), and men and women were getting out, anxious to go inside. She seemed to make out the sparkling of jewels in that swarm. Above the entrance flags were flying.

They were obviously giving a large party, exactly the kind that Marta dreamed of ever since she was a child. Heaven help her if she missed it. Down there opportunity was waiting for her, fate, romance, the true inauguration of her life. Would she arrive in time?

She spitefully noticed that another girl was falling about thirty meters above her. She was decidedly prettier than Marta and she wore a rather classy evening gown. For some unknown reason she came down much faster than Marta, so that in a few moments she passed by her and disappeared below, even though Marta was calling her. Without doubt she would get to the party before Marta; perhaps she had a plan all worked out to supplant her.

Then she realized that they weren't alone. Along the sides of the skyscraper many other young women were plunging downward, their faces taut with the excitement of the flight, their hands cheerfully waving as if to say: look at us, here we are, entertain us, is not the world ours?

It was a contest, then. And she only had a shabby little dress while those other girls were dressed smartly like high-fashion models and some even wrapped luxurious mink stoles tightly around their bare shoulders. So self-assured when she began the leap, Marta now felt a tremor growing inside her; perhaps it was just the cold; but it may have been fear too, the fear of having made an error without remedy.

It seemed to be late at night now. The windows were darkened one after another, the echoes of music became more rare, the offices were empty, young men no longer leaned out from the windowsills extending their hands. What time was it? At the entrance to the building down below—which in the meantime had grown larger, and one could now distinguish all the architectural details—the lights were still burning, but the bustle of cars had stopped. Every now and then, in fact, small groups of people came out of the main floor wearily drawing away. Then the lights of the entrance were also turned off.

Marta felt her heart tightening. Alas, she wouldn't reach the ball in time. Glancing upwards, she saw the pinnacle of the skyscraper in all its cruel power. It was almost completely dark. On the top floors a few windows here and there were still lit. And above the top the first glimmer of dawn was spreading.

In a dining recess on the twenty-eighth floor a man about forty years old was having his morning coffee and reading his newspaper while his wife tidied up the room. A clock on the sideboard indicated 8:45. A shadow suddenly passed before the window.

"Alberto!" the wife shouted. "Did you see that? A woman passed by."

"Who was it?" he said without raising his eyes from the newspaper.

"An old woman," the wife answered. "A decrepit old woman. She looked frightened."

"It's always like that," the man muttered. "At these low floors only falling old women pass by. You can see beautiful girls from the hundred-and-fiftieth floor up. Those apartments don't cost so much for nothing."

"At least down here there's the advantage," observed the wife, "that you can hear the thud when they touch the ground."

"This time not even that," he said, shaking his head, after he stood listening for a few minutes. Then he had another sip of coffee.

Translated by Lawrence Venuti

STUART DYBEK

Death of the Right Fielder

After too many balls went out and never came back we went out to check. It was a long walk—he always played deep. Finally we saw him, from the distance resembling the towel we sometimes threw down for second base.

It was hard to tell how long he'd been lying there, sprawled on his face. Had he been playing infield his presence, or lack of it, would, of course, have been noticed immediately. The infield demands communication—the constant, reassuring chatter of team play. But he was remote, clearly an outfielder (the temptation is to say out*sider*). The infield is for wisecrackers, pepper-pots, gum-poppers: the outfield is for loners, onlookers, brooders who would rather study clover and swat gnats than holler. People could pretty much be divided between infielders and outfielders. Not that one always has a choice. He didn't necessarily choose right field so much as accept it.

There were several theories as to what killed him. From the start the most popular was that he'd been shot. Perhaps from a passing car, possibly by that gang calling themselves the Jokers who played 16 inch softball on the concrete diamond with painted bases in the center of the housing project, or by the Latin Lords who didn't play sports period. Or maybe some pervert with a telescopic sight from a bedroom window, or a mad sniper from a water tower, or a terrorist with a silencer from the expressway overpass, or maybe it was an accident, a stray slug from a robbery, or shoot-out, or assassination attempt miles away.

No matter who pulled the trigger it seemed more plausible to ascribe his death to a bullet than to natural causes like, say, a heart attack. Young deaths are never natural; they're all violent. Not that kids don't die of heart attacks. But he never seemed the type. Sure, he was quiet, but not the quiet of someone always listening to the heart murmur his family has repeatedly warned him about since he was old enough to play. Nor could it have been leukemia. He wasn't a talented enough athlete to die of that. He'd have been playing center, not right, if leukemia was going to get him.

The shooting theory was better, even though there wasn't a mark on him. Couldn't it have been, as some argued, a high-powered bullet traveling with such velocity that its hole fuses behind it? Still, not everyone was satisfied. Other theories were formulated, rumors became legends over the years: he'd had an allergic reaction to a bee sting, been struck by a single bolt of lightning from a freak, instantaneous electric storm, ingested too strong a dose of insecticide from the grass blades he chewed on, sonic waves, radiation, pollution, etc. And a few of us liked to think it was simply that chasing a sinking liner, diving to make a shoestring catch, he broke his neck.

There *was* a ball in the webbing of his mitt when we turned him over. His mitt had been pinned under his body and was coated with an almost luminescent gray film. There was the same gray on his black, hightop gym shoes, as if he'd been running through lime, and along the bill of his baseball cap—the blue felt one with the red C which he always denied stood for the Chicago Cubs. He may have been a loner, but he didn't want to be identified with a loser. He lacked the sense of humor for that, lacked the perverse pride that sticking up for losers season after season breeds, and the love. He was just an ordinary guy, .250 at the plate, and we stood above him not knowing what to do next. By then the guys from the other outfield positions had trotted over. Someone, the shortstop probably, suggested team prayer. But no one could think of a team prayer. So we all just stood there silently bowing our heads, pretending to pray while the shadows moved darkly across the outfield grass. After awhile the entire diamond was swallowed and the field lights came on.

In the bluish squint of those lights he didn't look like someone we'd once known—nothing looked quite right—and we hurriedly scratched a shallow grave, covered him over, and stamped it down as much as possible so that the next right fielder, whoever he'd be, wouldn't trip. It could be just such a juvenile, seemingly trivial stumble that would ruin a great career before it had begun, or hamper it years later the way Mantle's was hampered by bum knees. One can never be sure the kid beside him isn't another Roberto Clemente; and who can ever know how many potential Great Ones have gone down in the obscurity of their neighborhoods? And so, in the catcher's phrase, we "buried the grave" rather than contribute to any further tragedy. In all likelihood the next right fielder, whoever he'd be, would be clumsy too, and if there was a mound to trip over he'd find it and break *his* neck, and soon right field would get the reputation as haunted, a kind of sandlot Bermuda Triangle, inhabited by phantoms calling for ghostly fly balls, where no one but the most desperate outcasts, already on the verge of suicide, would be willing to play.

Still, despite our efforts, we couldn't totally disguise it. A fresh grave is stubborn. Its outline remained visible—a scuffed bald spot that might have been confused for an aberrant pitcher's mound except for the bat jammed in earth with the mitt and blue cap fit over it. Perhaps we didn't want to eradicate it completely—a part of us was resting there. Perhaps we wanted the new right fielder, whoever he'd be, to notice and wonder about who played there before him, realizing he was now the only link between past and future that mattered. A monument, epitaph, flowers wouldn't be necessary.

As for us, we walked back, but by then it was too late—getting on to supper, getting on to the end of summer vacation, time for other things, college, careers, settling down and raising a family. Past thirty-five the talk starts about being over the hill, about a graying Phil Niekro in his forties still fanning them with the knuckler as if it's some kind of miracle, about Pete Rose still going in head-first at forty-two, beating the odds. And maybe the talk is right. One remembers Mays, forty and a Met, dropping that can-of-corn fly in the '71 Series, all that grace stripped away and with it the conviction, leaving a man confused and apologetic about the boy in him. It's sad to admit it ends so soon, but everyone knows those are the lucky ones. Most guys are washed up by seventeen.

LESLIE NORRIS

Blackberries

r. Frensham opened his shop at eight-thirty, but it was past nine when the woman and the child went in. The shop was empty and there were no footmarks on the fresh sawdust shaken onto the floor. The child listened to the melancholy sound of the bell as the door closed behind him and he scuffed his feet in the yellow sawdust. Underneath, the boards were brown and worn, and dark knots stood up in them. He had never been in this shop before. He was going to have his hair cut for the first time in his life, except for the times when his mother had trimmed it gently behind his neck.

Mr. Frensham was sitting in a large chair, reading a newspaper. He could make the chair turn around, and he spun twice about in it before he put down his paper, smiled, and said, "Good morning."

He was an old man, thin, with flat white hair. He wore a white coat.

"One gentleman," he said, "to have his locks shorn."

He put a board across the two arms of his chair, lifted the child, and sat him on it.

"How are you, my dear? And your father, is he well?" he said to the child's mother.

He took a sheet from a cupboard on the wall and wrapped it about the child's neck, tucking it into his collar. The sheet covered the child completely and hung almost to the floor. Cautiously the boy moved his hidden feet. He could see the bumps they made in the cloth. He moved his finger against the inner surface of the sheet and made a six with it, and then an eight. He liked those shapes.

"Snip, snip," said Mr. Frensham, "and how much does the gentleman want off? All of it? All his lovely curls? I think not."

"Just an ordinary cut, please, Mr. Frensham," said the child's mother, "not too much off. I, my husband and I, we thought it was time for him to look like a little boy. His hair grows so quickly."

Mr. Frensham's hands were very cold. His hard fingers turned the boy's head first to one side and then to the other and the boy could hear the long scissors snapping away behind him, and above his ears. He was quite frightened, but he liked watching the small tufts of his hair drop lightly on the sheet which covered him, and then roll an inch or two before they stopped. Some of the hair fell to the floor and by moving his hand surreptitiously he could make nearly all of it fall down. The hair fell without a sound. Tilting his head slightly, he could see the little bunches on the floor, not belonging to him any more.

"Easy to see who this boy is," Mr. Frensham said to the child's mother. "I won't get redder hair in the shop today. Your father had hair like this when he was young, very much this color. I've cut your father's hair for fifty years. He's keeping well, you say? There, I think that's enough. We don't want him to dislike coming to see me."

He took the sheet off the child and flourished it hard before folding it and putting it on a shelf. He swept the back of the child's neck with a small brush. Nodding his own old head in admiration, he looked at the child's hair for flaws in the cutting.

"Very handsome," he said.

The child saw his face in a mirror. It looked pale and large, but also much the same as always. When he felt the back of his neck, the new short hairs stood up sharp against his hand.

"We're off to do some shopping," his mother said to Mr. Frensham as she handed him the money.

They were going to buy the boy a cap, a round cap with a little button on top and a peak over his eyes, like his cousin Harry's cap. The boy wanted the cap very much. He walked seriously beside his mother and he was not impatient even when she met Mrs. Lewis and talked to her, and then took a long time at the fruiterer's buying apples and potatoes.

"This is the smallest size we have," the man in the clothes shop said. "It may be too large for him."

"He's just had his hair cut," said his mother. "That should make a difference."

The man put the cap on the boy's head and stood back to look. It was a beautiful cap. The badge in front was shaped like a shield and it was red and blue. It was not too big, although the man could put two fingers under it, at the side of the boy's head.

"On the other hand, we don't want it too tight," the man said. "We want something he can grow into, something that will last him a long time."

"Oh, I hope so," his mother said. "It's expensive enough."

The boy carried the cap himself, in a brown paper bag that had "Price, Clothiers, High Street" on it. He could read it all except "Clothiers" and his mother told him that. They put his cap, still in its bag, in a drawer when they got home.

His father came home late in the afternoon. The boy heard the firm clap of the closing door and his father's long step down the hall. He leaned against his father's knee while the man ate his dinner. The meal had been keeping warm in the oven and the plate was very hot. A small steam was rising from the potatoes, and the gravy had dried to a thin crust where it was shallow at the side of the plate. The man lifted the dry gravy with his knife and fed it to his son, very carefully lifting it into the boy's mouth, as if he were feeding a small bird. The boy loved this. He loved the hot savor of his father's dinner, the way his father cut away small delicacies for him and fed them to him slowly. He leaned drowsily against his father's leg.

Afterwards he put on his cap and stood before his father, certain of the man's approval. The man put his hand on the boy's head and looked at him without smiling.

"On Sunday," he said, "we'll go for a walk. Just you and I. We'll be men together."

Although it was late in September, the sun was warm and the paths dry. The man and his boy walked beside the disused canal and powdery white dust covered their shoes. The boy thought of the days before he had been born, when the canal had been busy. He thought of the long boats pulled by solid horses, gliding through the water. In his head he listened to the hushed, wet noises they would have made, the soft waves slapping the banks, and green tench looking up as the barges moved above them, their water suddenly darkened. His grandfather had told him about that. But now the channel was filled with mud and tall reeds. Bullrush and watergrass grew in the damp passages. He borrowed his father's walking stick and knocked the heads off a company of seeding dandelions, watching the tiny parachutes carry away their minute dark burdens.

"There they go," he said to himself. "There they go, sailing away to China."

"Come on," said his father, "or we'll never reach Fletcher's Woods."

The boy hurried after his father. He had never been to

42

Fletcher's Woods. Once his father had heard a nightingale there. It had been in the summer, long ago, and his father had gone with his friends, to hear the singing bird. They had stood under a tree and listened. Then the moon went down and his father, stumbling home, had fallen into a blackberry bush.

"Will there be blackberries?" he asked.

"There should be," his father said. "I'll pick some for you."

In Fletcher's Woods there was shade beneath the trees, and sunlight, thrown in yellow patches on to the grass, seemed to grow out of the ground rather than come from the sky. The boy stepped from sunlight to sunlight, in and out of shadow. His father showed him a tangle of bramble, hard with thorns, its leaves just beginning to color into autumn, its long runners dry and brittle on the grass. Clusters of purple fruit hung in the branches. His father reached up and chose a blackberry for him. Its skin was plump and shining, each of its purple globes held a point of reflected light.

"You can eat it," his father said.

The boy put the blackberry in his mouth. He rolled it with his tongue, feeling its irregularity, and crushed it against the roof of his mouth. Released juice, sweet and warm as summer, ran down his throat, hard seeds cracked between his teeth. When he laughed his father saw that his mouth was deeply stained. Together they picked and ate the dark berries, until their lips were purple and their hands marked and scratched.

"We should take some for your mother," the man said.

He reached with his stick and pulled down high canes where the choicest berries grew, picking them to take home. They had nothing to carry them in, so the boy put his new cap on the grass and they filled its hollow with berries. He held the cap by its edges and they went home.

"It was a stupid thing to do," his mother said, "utterly stupid. What were you thinking of?"

The young man did not answer.

"If we had the money, it would be different," his mother said, "Where do you think the money comes from?"

"I know where the money comes from," his father said. "I work hard enough for it."

"His new cap," his mother said. "How am I to get him another?"

The cap lay on the table and by standing on tiptoe the boy could see it. Inside it was wet with the sticky juice of blackberries. Small pieces of blackberry skins were stuck to it. The stains were dark and irregular.

"It will probably dry out all right," his father said.

His mother's face was red and distorted, her voice shrill.

"If you had anything like a job," she shouted, "and could buy caps by the dozen, then—"

She stopped and shook her head. His father turned away, his mouth hard.

"I do what I can," he said.

"That's not much!" his mother said. She was tight with scorn. "You don't do much!"

Appalled, the child watched the quarrel mount and spread. He began to cry quietly, to himself, knowing that it was a different weeping to any he had experienced before, that he was crying for a different pain. And the child began to understand that they were different people; his father, his mother, himself, and that he must learn sometimes to be alone.

Argentina

JULIO CORTÁZAR

Don't You Blame Anyone

Cold weather always complicates things a bit, in summer you're so close to the world, skin against skin, but now at six-thirty his wife is waiting for him at a store to choose a wedding present, it's late and he realizes it's cold, you've got to put on the blue sweater, just anything that goes well with the grey suit, fall is nothing but putting on and pulling off sweaters, closing oneself in, keeping distances. Without really feeling like it, he whistles a tango while moving away from the open window, rummages for the sweater in the closet and starts putting it on in front of the mirror. It's not easy, maybe because of the shirt that sticks to the wool of the sweater, and he has trouble forcing his arm through the hole; little by little his hand advances until at last a finger appears from the cuff of blue wool, but in the evening light the finger looks wrinkled and bent inwards, like a black nail with a sharp tip. With one quick movement he pulls his arm out of the sleeve and stares at his hand as if it were not his own, but now that it's outside the sweater he sees it's just the same hand as always and he lets it fall at the end of his limp arm, but it occurs to him that maybe it would be better to put

45

the other arm into the other sleeve, just to see whether this way it isn't easier. It doesn't seem so, because as soon as the wool of the sweater gets stuck to the material of the shirt, the lack of habit in beginning by the other sleeve makes the operation twice as difficult, and even though he's begun whistling once again to keep his mind occupied, he feels that his hand barely advances and that without some complementary maneuver he will never succeed in getting it to reach the exit. Better to try all at once, bend the head down to bring it to the height of the sweater's neck, while introducing the free arm into the other sleeve, straightening it and tugging simultaneously at both sleeves and at the collar. In the sudden blue gloom that envelops him it seems absurd to keep on whistling, and he begins to feel something akin to heat on his cheeks even though at least part of his head should by now be outside, but the forehead and his entire face remain covered and the hands are barely halfway up the sleeves. Hard as he might pull, nothing comes out into the open, and now it occurs to him that maybe he's made a mistake in that sort of ironic anger with which he started the task all over again, and that he has stupidly forced his head into one of the sleeves and one hand into the sweater's collar. If this were so, then his hand would have to come out easily, but even though he pulls with all his strength he can't manage to advance either hand, but now instead it seems that his head is about to emerge because the blue wool tightens itself with almost irritating strength against his nose and mouth, stifles him more than he could possibly have imagined, forcing him to breathe deeply while the wool becomes wet against his mouth, it will probably run and stain his face blue. Luckily at that very moment his right hand comes out into the open, into the cold outside, at least there is an outside even if the other hand is still trapped inside the sleeve, maybe it's true that his right hand was inside the sweater's collar, that's why what he thought was the collar is pressing so tight on his face, stifling him more and more, and the hand instead has been able to emerge easily. Anyway, just to be sure, all he can do is go on forcing himself through, breathing in deeply and letting out the air little by little, even though it's silly because nothing prevents him from breathing perfectly except that the air he's gulping in is mixed with fluff from either the collar or the sleeve of the sweater, and there's also the taste of the sweater, that blue taste of the wool which is probably staining his face now that the dampness of his breath mingles increasingly with the wool, and though he can't see it because if he opens his eyes his eyelashes bat painfully against the sweater, he's sure that the blue is wrapping itself around his wet mouth, into his nostrils, over his cheeks, and all this fills him with anxiety and he wishes he could once and for all put on the sweater, without even taking into account the fact that it must be late and that his wife must be getting impatient outside the store. He tells himself that the most sensible thing to do is to concentrate on his right hand, because that hand outside the sweater is in touch with the cold air of the room, it's like a sign telling him it won't be long now, and it can help him, it can climb up his back until it holds onto the sweater's waist with the classic movement which helps one put on any kind of sweater by pulling energetically downwards. Unfortunately, in spite of the hand feeling around on the back searching the woollen edge, it seems that the sweater is completely rolled up around the collar and the only thing the hand can find is the shirt which is becoming more and more wrinkled, even dangling in part out of the trousers, and it's of little use to move the hand forward and try to pull at the sweater from the front because on his chest he can only feel the shirt, the sweater must have barely passed the shoulders, and is probably there, rolled up and taut as if his shoulders were too wide for this sweater, which really proves that in fact he has made a mistake and that he has put one hand up the collar and the other

47

up a sleeve, so that the distance from the collar to one of the sleeves is exactly half the distance of one sleeve to the other, and that explains his head being slightly bent to the left, on the side of the hand still imprisoned in the sleeve, if it is in fact the sleeve, and that instead his right hand outside can move about freely in the air, even though it hasn't managed to pull down the sweater still rolled up at the top of his body. Ironically, it occurs to him that if there were a chair nearby he'd be able to rest and breathe more easily until he's managed to get the whole sweater on, but he has lost his sense of direction after having turned in circles so many times with that sort of euphoric gymnastics which initiates any putting-on of an article of clothing and which has something of a surreptitious dance step, irreproachable in anyone's eyes because it responds to an utilitarian end and not to culpable choreographic tendencies. After all, the real solution would be to take off the sweater, seeing that he hasn't been able to put it on, and check the correct opening for each hand in the sleeves, and for the head in the collar, but the right hand carries on going and coming in a haphazard way, as if it were ridiculous to give up at this point, and once it even obeys and climbs up to the height of the head and pulls upwards without his understanding in time that the sweater has stuck to his face with the damp glueishness of his breath mingled to the blueness of the wool, and when the hand pulls upwards it hurts as if something were ripping out his ears and wanting to tear out his eyelashes. More slowly then, try using the hand inside the left sleeve, if it is the sleeve and not the collar, and to do that help the left hand with the right hand so that the left hand can either go deeper into the sleeve or draw back and free itself, even though it's almost impossible to coordinate the movements of both hands, as if the left hand were a rat trapped in a cage and from outside another rat were trying to help it escape, unless instead of helping it were biting it, because suddenly the imprisoned hand hurts him and at the same time the other hand grabs hard onto that which must be his hand, his hand which hurts, hurts him so much that he gives up trying to take off the sweater, he prefers to make one last effort to push his head out of the collar, and push the left rat out of its cage, and he tries by fighting with his whole body, leaning forward and then backwards, turning around in circles in the middle of the room, if he is in the middle of the room, because now he thinks that the window was left open and that it's dangerous to carry on turning around in circles blindfolded, he'd rather stop in spite of his right hand going and coming without paying any attention to the sweater, in spite of his left hand hurting more and more as if his fingers had been bitten or burnt, and nevertheless that hand obeys him, contracting little by little the lacerated fingers he manages to grip through the sleeve the sweater's waist rolled up on the shoulder, he pulls downwards with barely any strength left, it hurts too much and he would need the help of the right hand, instead of its useless climbing up and down his legs, instead of pinching his thighs as it's doing now, scratching or pinching him through his clothes without his being able to prevent it, because all his willpower is limited to his left hand, maybe he has fallen to his knees and he feels as if suspended by his left hand tugging once again at the sweater and suddenly it's the cold on his eyebrows and forehead, on the eyes, absurdly he doesn't want to open his eyes but he knows he's out, that cold substance, that delightful substance is the open air, and he doesn't want to open his eyes and he waits one second, two seconds, he allows himself to live in a cold and different time, the time of outside the sweater, he's on his knees and it's beautiful to be like that, until little by little he gratefully opens his eyes freed from the blue spider's web of wool inside, he opens his eyes carefully and sees the five black fingernails hovering over his eyes, and he has just enough time to lower his eyelids and throw himself back, covering himself with the left hand which is his hand, that is all he has left to defend him from inside the sleeve, to pull at the sweater's collar upwards, and the blue web is spun around his face once more, while he picks himself up to run away some place else, to reach at last some place without the hand, without the sweater, some place where there is only fragrant air to envelop him and accompany him and caress him and twelve floors down.

Translated by Alberto Manguel

SPENCER HOLST

On Hope

The monkey leaped on the man's shoulder.

The man shuddered for he knew who it was. He knew exactly which monkey of the ten thousand that roam about on the Rock of Gibraltar, tame and free as pigeons, walking around in the parks and streets.

It was a demon monkey.

It was the one he'd trained to bring him necklaces, who brought him pearls, garnets, and amber from moonlit bedrooms in the big hotels—stolen from women sunk in snoring.

The monkey dangled before his eyes the largest diamond in the world.

The whole thing began several days previously when all on Gibraltar went into an uproar. The Rock of Gibraltar was visited by royalty, by the queen mother, and the princess. A battleship brought them and their entourage, and with them the famous necklace, the largest stone of which was the *Diamond of Hope*, which the princess was to wear at some great state occasion. (There's a curse on the necklace, you know, and misfortune had followed it, and come to whomever possessed it until it became part of the British crown jewels in the middle of the nineteenth century.)

On the very first night the royal party was in, the monkey returned to his gypsy master with the necklace. The necklace, of course, was valueless. It couldn't possibly be sold. Gibraltar would be swarming with police searching for it.

The gypsy was annoyed with the monkey, irritated at its genius, and terrified of being caught by the police with the gems; and besides, although he had no particular regard for the government—(being a gypsy) he liked the idea of "the princess" and wouldn't dream of stealing her necklace. So he quickly wrapped it up and addressed the package to her and dropped it in an ordinary mailbox. He enclosed a note to her saying something like, "You really ought to guard this more carefully."

The next night the monkey returned again with the necklace.

This time his note implored her to have the police guard the necklace more carefully, and he even gave them advice. He advised them to place the necklace in the center of a cage.

(For a monkey, of course, couldn't get into a locked cage.)

Then the third night, when this story begins, the monkey again brought the gypsy the necklace, and fell at the gypsy's feet, dead. Shot. Very probably the monkey had been fatally wounded by a guard as he was escaping.

The gypsy shuddered at the diamond, and was not surprised at the death of his friend.

The first two times it had been like some freak occurrence, like a weird accident—to unexpectedly discover oneself in possession of part of the British crown jewels! But now . . .

When he received the gems for the third time the whole thing was plunged into meaning. It no longer seemed like an accident. He had been given the necklace. Fate was at work. Now, the necklace was his.

He put it in his pocket.

It never occurred to him (being a gypsy) to doubt the reality of the curse which accompanied the diamond, and he accepted his fate with the stone. Quietly and secretly he buried the animal.

And as he thought about it he was actually a little pleased that he, a gypsy, had been singled out by fate to take the curse off the princess, and the English throne.

He walked down to the shore of the Mediterranean and took off his clothes, and—having nothing in which to put the necklace, he put it on—dove in, and swam.

There was a full moon and the sea was perfectly calm.

Just off Gibraltar there's a very deep place in the Mediterranean. It's called the Gibraltar Trench. Only a mile from shore the sea is a mile deep.

The gypsy was a very good swimmer.

He swam out a mile, over this spot, took the necklace off and dropped it.

At that moment a smile lit his face as he imagined the thousands of Sherlock Holmeses searching for it for the next fifty years.

The man lazily began to swim back toward shore, and the necklace fell down into the depths.

They each had a mile to go—the man had a mile to swim, and the gems had a mile to fall.

The necklace fell much faster than the gypsy swam.

It fell straight down until it got about a hundred feet from the bottom, where it came to rest on the dorsal fin of a shark.

The shark had been sleeping, but the necklace woke it, and it turned round and around wondering what was happening. It decided to go up to investigate.

The shark swam upward even faster than the necklace had fallen.

Meanwhile the man still lazily swam toward the huge "rock," now ablaze as never before with the royal festivities, with a million electric light bulbs—and he thought of the curse. The stone would never bring its misfortune to anyone ever again; it was finished forever, its power over man extinguished for good, buried beneath a mile of water.

Then he looked over his shoulder and saw the necklace floating a foot above the water, moving slowly past him.

(The gypsy did not see the shark's fin, he only saw the necklace glittering in the moonlight, as if floating in the air, not coming toward him, but moving past him, now receding into the distance.)

The man immediately realized that one of two things was true. Obviously, either he was witnessing a miracle (and the whole thing smacked of the miraculous), or he was having a hallucination.

He decided to find out.

Was it a miracle? or, was it a delusion?

He began to shout and wave his arms and splash, and he began to swim after the necklace.

And sure enough the necklace stopped and after a moment began to move toward the man.

The man is swimming toward the necklace. The necklace is moving toward the man.

That is where the story ends.

However, I can't help noticing, at this moment, that at first glance it seems inevitable—you know, that the shark will devour the man.

But I do not believe that result is as inevitable as it seems at first glance; that is, I believe there are several reasons, so to speak, for hope.

1. I do not think a shark has ever been approached like this before, that is, by a man wondering whether the shark is a miraculous manifestation, or whether it is merely a figment of his own imagination. Such a man would smell different.

2. The man is a gypsy animal trainer.

3. The shark is now in possession of the necklace.

Canada

MARGARET ATWOOD

Happy Endings

John and Mary meet.
What happens next?
If you want a happy ending, try A.

A. John and Mary fall in love and get married. They both
    have worthwhile and remunerative jobs which they find
    stimulating and challenging. They buy a charming house.
    Real estate values go up. Eventually, when they can
    afford live-in help, they have two children, to whom
    they are devoted. The children turn out well. John and
    Mary have a stimulating and challenging sex life and
    worthwhile friends. They go on fun vacations together.
    They retire. They both have hobbies which they find
    stimulating and challenging. Eventually they die. This
    is the end of the story.

B. Mary falls in love with John but John doesn't fall in love
    with Mary. He merely uses her body for selfish plea-
    sure and ego gratification of a tepid kind. He comes to
    her apartment twice a week and she cooks him dinner,
    you'll notice that he doesn't even consider her worth the

price of a dinner out, and after he's eaten the dinner he fucks her and after that he falls asleep, while she does the dishes so he won't think she's untidy, having all those dirty dishes lying around, and puts on fresh lipstick so she'll look good when he wakes up, but when he wakes up he doesn't even notice, he puts on his socks and his shorts and his pants and his shirt and his tie and his shoes, the reverse order from the one in which he took them off. He doesn't take off Mary's clothes, she takes them off herself, she acts as if she's dying for it every time, not because she likes sex exactly, she doesn't, but she wants John to think she does because if they do it often enough surely he'll get used to her, he'll come to depend on her and they will get married, but John goes out the door with hardly so much as a good-night and three days later he turns up at six o'clock and they do the whole thing over again.

Mary gets run-down. Crying is bad for your face, everyone knows that and so does Mary but she can't stop. People at work notice. Her friends tell her John is a rat, a pig, a dog, he isn't good enough for her, but she can't believe it. Inside John, she thinks, is another John, who is much nicer. This other John will emerge like a butterfly from a cocoon, a Jack from a box, a pit from a prune, if the first John is only squeezed enough.

One evening John complains about the food. He has never complained about the food before. Mary is hurt.

Her friends tell her they've seen him in a restaurant with another woman, whose name is Madge. It's not even Madge that finally gets to Mary: it's the restaurant. John has never taken Mary to a restaurant. Mary collects all the sleeping pills and aspirins she can find, and takes them and a half a bottle of sherry. You can see what kind of a woman she is by the fact that it's not even whiskey. She leaves a note for John. She hopes he'll discover her and get her to the hospital in time and repent and then they can get married, but this fails to happen and she dies.

John marries Madge and everything continues as in A.

C. John, who is an older man, falls in love with Mary, and Mary, who is only twenty-two, feels sorry for him because he's worried about his hair falling out. She sleeps with him even though she's not in love with him. She met him at work. She's in love with someone called James, who is twenty-two also and not yet ready to settle down.

John on the contrary settled down long ago: this is what is bothering him. John has a steady, respectable job and is getting ahead in his field, but Mary isn't impressed by him, she's impressed by James, who has a motorcycle and a fabulous record collection. But James is often away on his motorcycle, being free. Freedom isn't the same for girls, so in the meantime Mary spends Thursday evenings with John. Thursdays are the only days John can get away.

John is married to a woman called Madge and they have two children, a charming house which they bought just before the real estate values went up, and hobbies which they find stimulating and challenging, when they have the time. John tells Mary how important she is to him, but of course he can't leave his wife because a commitment is a commitment. He goes on about this more than is necessary and Mary finds it boring, but older men can keep it up longer so on the whole she has a fairly good time.

One day James breezes in on his motorcycle with some top-grade California hybrid and James and Mary get higher than you'd believe possible and they climb into bed. Everything becomes very underwater, but along comes John, who has a key to Mary's apartment. He finds them stoned and entwined. He's hardly in any position to be jealous, considering Madge, but nevertheless he's overcome with despair. Finally he's middle-aged, in two years he'll be bald as an egg and he can't stand it. He purchases a handgun, saying he needs it for target practice—this is the thin part of the plot, but it can be dealt with later—and shoots the two of them and himself.

Madge, after a suitable period of mourning, marries an understanding man called Fred and everything continues as in A, but under different names.

D. Fred and Madge have no problems. They get along exceptionally well and are good at working out any little difficulties that may arise. But their charming house is by the seashore and one day a giant tidal wave approaches. Real estate values go down. The rest of the story is about what caused the tidal wave and how they escape from it. They do, though thousands drown, but Fred and Madge are virtuous and lucky. Finally on high ground they clasp each other, wet and dripping and grateful, and continue as in A.

E. Yes, but Fred has a bad heart. The rest of the story is about how kind and understanding they both are until Fred dies. Then Madge devotes herself to charity work until the end of A. If you like, it can be "Madge," "cancer," "guilty and confused," and "bird watching."

F.   If you think this is all too bourgeois, make John a revolutionary and Mary a counterespionage agent and see how far that gets you. Remember, this is Canada. You'll still end up with A, though in between you may get a lustful brawling saga of passionate involvement, a chronicle of our times, sort of.

You'll have to face it, the endings are the same however you slice it. Don't be deluded by any other endings, they're all fake, either deliberately fake, with malicious intent to deceive, or just motivated by excessive optimism if not by downright sentimentality.

The only authentic ending is the one provided here:

John and Mary die. John and Mary die. John and Mary die.

So much for endings. Beginnings are always more fun. True connoisseurs, however, are known to favor the stretch in between, since it's the hardest to do anything with.

That's about all that can be said for plots, which anyway are just one thing after another, a what and a what and a what.

Now try How and Why.

Japan

YASUNARI KAWABATA

The Grasshopper and the Bell Cricket

Walking along the tile-roofed wall of the university, I turned aside and approached the upper school. Behind the white board fence of the school playground, from a dusky clump of bushes under the black cherry trees, an insect's voice could be heard. Walking more slowly and listening to that voice, and furthermore reluctant to part with it, I turned right so as not to leave the playground behind. When I turned to the left, the fence gave way to an embankment planted with orange trees. At the corner, I exclaimed with surprise. My eyes gleaming at what they saw up ahead, I hurried forward with short steps.

At the base of the embankment was a bobbing cluster of beautiful varicolored lanterns, such as one might see at a festival in a remote country village. Without going any farther, I knew that it was a group of children on an insect chase among the bushes of the embankment. There were about twenty lanterns. Not only were there crimson, pink, indigo, green, purple, and yellow lanterns, but one lantern glowed with five colors at once. There were even some little red store-bought lanterns. But most of the lanterns were beautiful square ones which the children had made themselves with love and care. The bobbing lanterns, the coming together of children on this lonely slope—surely it was a scene from a fairy tale?

One of the neighborhood children had heard an insect sing on this slope one night. Buying a red lantern, he had come back the next night to find the insect. The night after that, there was another child. This new child could not buy a lantern. Cutting out the back and front of a small carton and papering it, he placed a candle on the bottom and fastened a string to the top. The number of children grew to five, and then to seven. They learned how to color the paper that they stretched over the windows of the cutout cartons, and to draw pictures on it. Then these wise child-artists, cutting out round, three-cornered, and lozenge leaf shapes in the cartons, coloring each little window a different color, with circles and diamonds, red and green, made a single and whole decorative pattern. The child with the red lantern discarded it as a tasteless object that could be bought at a store. The child who had made his own lantern threw it away because the design was too simple. The pattern of light that one had had in hand the night before was unsatisfying the morning after. Each day, with cardboard, paper, brush, scissors, penknife, and glue, the children made new lanterns out of their hearts and minds. Look at my lantern! Be the most unusually beautiful! And each night, they had gone out on their insect hunts. These were the twenty children and their beautiful lanterns that I now saw before me.

Wide-eyed, I loitered near them. Not only did the square lanterns have old-fashioned patterns and flower shapes, but the names of the children who had made them were cut out in squared letters of the syllabary. Different from the painted-over red lanterns, others (made of thick cutout cardboard) had their designs drawn onto the paper windows, so that the candle's light seemed to emanate from the form and color of the design itself.

The lanterns brought out the shadows of the bushes like dark light. The children crouched eagerly on the slope wherever they heard an insect's voice.

"Does anyone want a grasshopper?" A boy, who had been peering into a bush about thirty feet away from the other children, suddenly straightened up and shouted.

"Yes! Give it to me!" Six or seven children came running up. Crowding behind the boy who had found the grasshopper, they peered into the bush. Brushing away their outstretched hands and spreading out his arms, the boy stood as if guarding the bush where the insect was. Waving the lantern in his right hand, he called again to the other children.

"Does anyone want a grasshopper? A grasshopper!"

"I do! I do!" Four or five more children came running up. It seemed you could not catch a more precious insect than a grasshopper. The boy called out a third time.

"Doesn't anyone want a grasshopper?"

Two or three more children came over.

"Yes. I want it."

It was a girl, who just now had come up behind the boy who'd discovered the insect. Lightly turning his body, the boy gracefully bent forward. Shifting the lantern to his left hand, he reached his right hand into the bush.

"It's a grasshopper."

"Yes. I'd like to have it."

The boy quickly stood up. As if to say "Here!" he thrust out his fist that held the insect at the girl. She, slipping her left wrist under the string of her lantern, enclosed the boy's fist with both hands. The boy quietly opened his fist. The insect was transferred to between the girl's thumb and index finger.

"Oh! It's not a grasshopper. It's a bell cricket." The girl's eyes shone as she looked at the small brown insect.

"It's a bell cricket! It's a bell cricket!" The children echoed in an envious chorus.

"It's a bell cricket. It's a bell cricket."

Glancing with her bright intelligent eyes at the boy who had given her the cricket, the girl opened the little insect cage hanging at her side and released the cricket in it.

"It's a bell cricket."

"Oh, it's a bell cricket," the boy who'd captured it muttered. Holding up the insect cage close to his eyes, he looked inside it. By the light of his beautiful many-colored lantern, also held up at eye level, he glanced at the girl's face.

Oh, I thought. I felt slightly jealous of the boy, and sheepish. How silly of me not to have understood his actions until now! Then I caught my breath in surprise. Look! It was something on the girl's breast which neither the boy who had given her the cricket, nor she who had accepted it, nor the children who were looking at them noticed.

In the faint greenish light that fell on the girl's breast, wasn't the name "Fujio" clearly discernible? The boy's lantern, which he held up alongside the girl's insect cage, inscribed his name, cut out in the green papered aperture, onto her white cotton kimono. The girl's lantern, which dangled loosely from her wrist, did not project its pattern so clearly, but still one could make out, in a trembling patch of red on the boy's waist, the name "Kiyoko." This chance interplay of red and green—if it was chance or play—neither Fujio nor Kiyoko knew about.

Even if they remembered forever that Fujio had given her the cricket and that Kiyoko had accepted it, not even in dreams would Fujio ever know that his name had been written in green on Kiyoko's breast or that Kiyoko's name had been inscribed in red on his waist, nor would Kiyoko ever know that Fujio's name had been inscribed in green on her breast or that her own name had been written in red on Fujio's waist.

Fujio! Even when you have become a young man, laugh with pleasure at a girl's delight when, told that it's a grasshopper, she is given a bell cricket; laugh with affection at a girl's chagrin when, told that it's a bell cricket, she is given a grasshopper.

Even if you have the wit to look by yourself in a bush away from the other children, there are not many bell crickets in the world. Probably you will find a girl like a grasshopper whom you think is a bell cricket.

And finally, to your clouded, wounded heart, even a true bell cricket will seem like a grasshopper. Should that day come, when it seems to you that the world is only full of grasshoppers, I will think it a pity that you have no way to remember tonight's play of light, when your name was written in green by your beautiful lantern on a girl's breast.

Translated by Lane Dunlop

Antigua

JAMAICA KINCAID

Girl

ash the white clothes on Monday and put them on the stone heap; wash the color clothes on Tuesday and put them on the clothesline to dry; don't walk barehead in the hot sun; cook pumpkin fritters in very hot sweet oil; soak your little cloths right after you take them off; when buying cotton to make yourself a nice blouse, be sure that it doesn't have gum on it, because that way it won't hold up well after a wash; soak salt fish overnight before you cook it; is it true that you sing benna in Sunday school?; always eat your food in such a way that it won't turn someone else's stomach; on Sundays try to walk like a lady and not like the slut you are so bent on becoming; don't sing benna in Sunday school; you mustn't speak to wharf-rat boys, not even to give directions; don't eat fruits on the street— flies will follow you; *but I don't sing benna on Sundays at all and never in Sunday school;* this is how to sew on a button; this is how to make a buttonhole for the button you have just sewed on; this is how to hem a dress when you see the hem coming down and so to prevent yourself from looking like the slut I know you are so bent on becoming; this is how you iron your father's khaki shirt so that it doesn't have a crease; this is how you iron your father's khaki pants so that they don't have a crease; this is how you grow okra—far from the house, because okra tree harbors red ants; when you are growing dasheen, make sure it gets plenty of water or else it makes your throat itch when you are eating it; this is how you sweep a corner; this is how you sweep a whole house; this is how you sweep a yard; this is how you smile to someone you don't like very much; this is how you smile to someone you don't like at all; this is how you smile to someone you like completely; this is how you set a table for tea; this is how you set a table for dinner; this is how you set a table for dinner with an important guest; this is how you set a table for lunch; this is how you set a table for breakfast; this is how to behave in the presence of men who don't know you very well, and this way they won't recognize immediately the slut I have warned you against becoming; be sure to wash every day, even if it is with your own spit; don't squat down to play marbles—you are not a boy, you know; don't pick people's flowers—you might catch something; don't throw stones at blackbirds, because it might not be a blackbird at all; this is how to make a bread pudding; this is how to make doukona; this is how to make pepper pot; this is how to make a good medicine for a cold; this is how to make a good medicine to throw away a child before it even becomes a child; this is how to catch a fish; this is how to throw back a fish you don't like, and that way something bad won't fall on you; this is how to bully a man; this is how a man bullies you; this is how to love a man, and if this doesn't work there are other ways, and if they don't work don't feel too bad about giving up; this is how to spit up in the air if you feel like it, and this is how to move quick so that it doesn't fall on you; this is how to make ends meet; always squeeze bread to make sure it's fresh; *but what if the baker won't let me feel the bread?*; you mean to say that after all you are really going to be the kind of woman who the baker won't let near the bread?

COLETTE

The Other Wife

able for two? This way, Monsieur, Madame, there is still a table next to the window, if Madame and Monsieur would like a view of the bay."

Alice followed the maître d'.

"Oh, yes. Come on, Marc, it'll be like having lunch on a boat on the water . . ."

Her husband caught her by passing his arm under hers. "We'll be more comfortable over there."

"There? In the middle of all those people? I'd much rather . . ."

"Alice, please."

He tightened his grip in such a meaningful way that she turned around. "What's the matter?"

"Shh . . ." he said softly, looking at her intently, and led her toward the table in the middle.

"What is it, Marc?"

"I'll tell you, darling. Let me order lunch first. Would you like the shrimp? Or the eggs in aspic?"

"Whatever you like, you know that."

They smiled at one another, wasting the precious time of an

overworked maître d', stricken with a kind of nervous dance, who was standing next to them, perspiring.

"The shrimp," said Marc. "Then the eggs and bacon. And the cold chicken with a romaine salad. *Fromage blanc?* The house specialty? We'll go with the specialty. Two strong coffees. My chauffeur will be having lunch also, we'll be leaving again at two o'clock. Some cider? No, I don't trust it . . . Dry champagne."

He sighed as if he had just moved an armoire, gazed at the colorless midday sea, at the pearly white sky, then at his wife, whom he found lovely in her little Mercury hat with its large, hanging veil.

"You're looking well, darling. And all this blue water makes your eyes look green, imagine that! And you've put on weight since you've been traveling . . . It's nice up to a point, but only up to a point!"

Her firm, round breasts rose proudly as she leaned over the table.

"Why did you keep me from taking that place next to the window?"

Marc Seguy never considered lying. "Because you were about to sit next to someone I know."

"Someone I don't know?"

"My ex-wife."

She couldn't think of anything to say and opened her blue eyes wider.

"So what, darling? It'll happen again. It's not important."

The words came back to Alice and she asked, in order, the inevitable questions. "Did she see you? Could she see that you saw her? Will you point her out to me?"

"Don't look now, please, she must be watching us . . . The lady with brown hair, no hat, she must be staying in this hotel. By herself, behind those children in red . . ."

"Yes. I see."

Hidden behind some broad-brimmed beach hats, Alice was able to look at the woman who, fifteen months ago, had still been her husband's wife.

"Incompatibility," Marc said. "Oh, I mean . . . total incompatibility! We divorced like well-bred people, almost like friends, quietly, quickly. And then I fell in love with you, and you really wanted to be happy with me. How lucky we are that our happiness doesn't involve any guilty parties or victims!"

The woman in white, whose smooth, lustrous hair reflected the light from the sea in azure patches, was smoking a cigarette with her eyes half closed. Alice turned back toward her husband, took some shrimp and butter, and ate calmly. After a moment's silence she asked. "Why didn't you ever tell me that she had blue eyes, too?"

"Well, I never thought about it!"

He kissed the hand she was extending toward the bread basket and she blushed with pleasure. Dusky and ample, she might have seemed somewhat coarse, but the changeable blue of her eyes and her wavy, golden hair made her look like a frail and sentimental blonde. She vowed overwhelming gratitude to her husband. Immodest without knowing it, everything about her bore the overly conspicuous marks of extreme happiness.

They ate and drank heartily, and each thought the other had forgotten the woman in white. Now and then, however, Alice laughed too loudly, and Marc was careful about his posture, holding his shoulders back, his head up. They waited quite a long time for their coffee, in silence. An incandescent river, the straggled reflection of the invisible sun overhead, shifted slowly across the sea and shone with a blinding brilliance.

"She's still there, you know," Alice whispered.

"Is she making you uncomfortable? Would you like to have coffee somewhere else?"

"No, not at all! She's the one who must be uncomfortable! Besides, she doesn't exactly seem to be having a wild time, if you could see her . . ."

"I don't have to. I know that look of hers."

"Oh, was she like that?"

He exhaled his cigarette smoke through his nostrils and knitted his eyebrows. "Like that? No. To tell you honestly, she wasn't happy with me."

"Oh, really now!"

"The way you indulge me is so charming, darling . . . It's crazy . . . You're an angel . . . You love me . . . I'm so proud when I see those eyes of yours. Yes, those eyes . . . She . . . I just didn't know how to make her happy, that's all. I didn't know how."

"She's just difficult!"

Alice fanned herself irritably, and cast brief glances at the woman in white, who was smoking, her head resting against the back of the cane chair, her eyes closed with an air of satisfied lassitude.

Marc shrugged his shoulders modestly.

"That's the right word," he admitted. "What can you do? You have to feel sorry for people who are never satisfied. But we're satisfied . . . Aren't we, darling?"

She did not answer. She was looking furtively, and closely, at her husband's face, ruddy and regular; at his thick hair, threaded here and there with white silk; at his short, well-cared-for hands; and doubtful for the first time, she asked herself, "What more did she want from him?"

And as they were leaving, while Marc was paying the bill and asking for the chauffeur and about the route, she kept looking, with envy and curiosity, at the woman in white, this dissatisfied, this difficult, this superior . . .

Translated by Matthew Ward

United States

MARK HELPRIN

La Volpaia

ecause there was little that Giuliano Debernardi, with his
rigorous high education and his acceptance in ruling circles, could
ever bring himself to say to a priest, he looked away in contempt when a small ancient cleric entered his compartment while
the train was halted, steaming, before its northward passage
through the Alps to Germany. But he was severely startled when
the priest slammed a bottle of red wine down on the little folding table, and said, "Who are you that turns his head when a
man of the cloth comes in?"

"I beg your pardon."

"You heard me. I'm eighty-six years old and I know I'm going
to Heaven. I don't mince words, especially with young intellec-
tuals who imagine that their birth, position, or knowledge make
them better than old men who are priests in unknown mountain
towns." He spoke in a hoarse, energetic voice, breathing hard
and heavy after each declaration. Giuliano Debernardi was indeed
a fop, but not a fool. In a show of courage and precision, he
held to the position the priest had accurately divined.

"At your age, you should be a Cardinal. Why not the principal in a great academy? You are obviously a failure, and you are aggressive to boot. But I am more aggressive."

The priest threw the bottle at him. It nearly struck him in his sternum. "Here, open this. It's too difficult for me. I could have been a Cardinal. I could have risen very far in those directions. I chose not to. It was a decision of strength based on a momentous discovery. Give me the wine. Give it. Give it! I can see that you are lost in your own petty concerns. What are your small fears?"

"I am afraid that my German is not good enough," Giuliano Debernardi said quite bluntly.

"Oh? Do you have a German?"

"Please. I am going to Berlin to work for *Zeitschrift für Sozialwissenschaft*. I will have to write in German. I told them I was fluent. They believed me. I am not fluent."

"That's nothing."

"I don't think it's nothing!"

"You have ignored the compression of the world for foolish concerns such as that. And it shows on your face," he added quickly.

"I have ignored the what? What nonsense. I am part of the world. I see things quite deeply. Don't think that I am superficial just because I don't see with your two eyes. I have my own, you know." He leaned over the table and said, quite fiercely, "A stupid assumption, from a provincial priest."

"You think so?"

"Yes. I do." This priest, thought Giuliano Debernardi, is one of those men who are lacking in power, one of those who cannot act decisively, or bring their wills to bear on others. The train began its climb into the snow-covered mountains.

The priest gestured out the window. He seemed hopelessly behind in the competition with Giuliano Debernardi, who began to pity him.

"Look. What do you see?"

"Nothing."

"Nothing! In that instant in which you saw nothing, I saw enough to speak about for a month. Do you remember what we passed? It was a view across a street in a little town near Feltre. In that blink of an eye were a hundred thousand things."

"I saw nothing unusual—just some people walking, the mountains beyond, a wagon or two, an iron fence, I don't know."

"Did you see Emiglia pass?"

"I don't know who Emiglia is."

"In black, near the lip of the gorge. She is a widow. From the way she walked and held herself, you could extract certain details. In that one frame from which you took nothing, Emiglia walked by."

"What of it? There are widows all over Italy. Here, they go by the thousands. I suppose, since the earthquake, years ago."

"No. The young ones have remarried. Others have affairs, taking a man to bed, drawing from him guilty pleasure."

"How do you know?"

"I have sinned."

"I am not impressed."

"I did not do it," said the priest, with a smile, "to impress you."

"Doesn't this Emiglia have affairs, and take men to bed?"

"No, not Emiglia. It is a case somewhat beyond your wisdom—despite your tailored suit and your splendid briefcase. You did not even *see* her walking by the lip of the gorge, that I know. I did not become a Cardinal because . . ."

"Because you like to drink wine."

"What do you know. Cardinals drink as if they were made of sponge. I did not become a Cardinal because . . . it was too thick near Feltre. There was too much. When you encompass affairs, and rule over things, you cannot even start the task.

73

"Take Emiglia. To you, she was just a flash of black. You did not even see her. She has no affairs. Her husband and six miners rode every day a mile into the mountain, through a tunnel, on bicycles.

"Their way was lit with miner's lamps, and the air was thin and cold. At the tunnel's end, they rose two thousand feet into the heart of the peak. There, they dug silver, under summit ice. With the earthquake, the town was leveled and no one thought of the miners. The mile-long tunnel was shut forever, trapping them in the high chamber." He indicated the enormous mountain, standing astride the rest of the world.

"It isn't that the mountain rides above the town . . . no . . . but," he said slowly, ". . . *their futile movements within the chamber, for time unspecified*. It is difficult to be a young man who has lied to his employer. It is difficult to be an old man who each day just begins to see within an ever-expanding complexity rooted in simple things. It is difficult to be Emiglia, walking by the gorge alone. But none of these things is as difficult, you see, as trying to *draw air through the rock*."

The train dashed into a tunnel. In the darkness, Giuliano Debernardi struggled in panic to loosen his collar. He felt that there was no air. He could not breathe.

The priest was laughing. For there was, of course, no Emiglia, and his timing had been just right.

Czechoslovakia

JOSEF ŠKVORECKÝ

An Insolvable Problem
of Genetics

[From the secret diary of Vasil Krátký,
a third-grade student at the
Leonid Brezhnev High School in K.]

While offering a brotherly hand to many nations, our fatherland also harbours a certain number of dark-skinned African students; some of these undergo preparatory courses in the Czech language in our town. Later they laud the good name of our nation far beyond the borders of our country, but my brother Adolf lost his lifelong happiness because of their overly friendly attitude toward the population.

This is how it happened: for two long years Adolf was secretly in love with the movie star Jana Brejchová and wrote her more than two hundred letters during this time. The interest shown by the film celebrity was not in the least comparable· to my brother's effort, and so Adolf began to pursue Freddie Mourek, whose skinny figure and seemly features resembled somewhat those of the aforementioned actress.

The parents welcomed his decision because Freddie, as the illegitimate daughter of the Secretary of the Party cell at the Lentex linen factory in K., came from a family with an excellent class profile. Nothing but a single flaw disturbed the great impression made by Adolf's girl friend on our family, and that

75

was her given name. One day while at our house, Freddie, to the accompaniment of Adolf's bass guitar, sang a certain loud song in a foreign language. To my father's uneasy inquiry concerning the origins of the song she answered that it was a black American song, whose lyrics protested against discrimination. Father applauded, then extolled briefly the black struggle for equality; then he quite suddenly became very angry, and turning dark red, he began to curse the South African racists. Mother also became angry, and in the resulting friendly atmosphere Father asked Freddie why a girl as thoroughly progressive and an activist of the Young Communist League, would call herself by a name apparently of English origin.

At that Freddie blushed and said that she could now reveal to them the secret of her name because she had just agreed with Adolf to enter into wedlock in a civil ceremony prior to the final matriculation examinations. Father was very heartened by the news as he happens to favour early nuptials for youths finding themselves in their reproductive years, since these are called for by the appropriate authorities in an attempt to prevent population decrease. He then encouraged Freddie to reveal her secret without delay. "My name," she said, "I inherited from my father. He was a certain Frederick Positive Wasserman Brown, a migrant worker from South Carolina, who as a member of General Georgie Patton's Third U.S. Army seduced my mummy in Pilsen, and then had himself transferred to the Far East." "An American?" Father recoiled and turned gloomy. Then he partially recovered: "A migrant worker?" and Freddie, attempting to aid the complete recovery of my father who had earlier lauded so eagerly the heroic struggle of the coloured people, quickly added: "Yes. And besides my father was black." Against all expectations Father's gloom became permanent.

In the following days he began to bring home from the People's Municipal Library books of a certain Lysenko; unable to find in them a satisfactory answer to what he was looking for, he borrowed a volume of the friar Mendel with pictures of various types of peas, white, gray, and black ones. He studied those very diligently, and later when Freddie again sang at our house negro songs in a foreign language, he asked: "Listen, girl, that father of yours, was he a very black black or was he of a lighter hue?" "Very black," said Freddie, who herself is very white, but has eyes which are very black, large and very beautiful. "So black that during the war they used him in reconnaissance, when, completely naked he would in the darkest night penetrate through the German lines, since he was completely invisible." And Father turned once again gloomy and said no more.

However, that evening he advised Adolf to break off without delay his relationship with the black man's daughter. Adolf resisted: "I'm not a racist!" "Neither am I," replied Father. "If Freddie were a dark-skinned girl I would welcome her as a daughter-in-law, because the union with an obvious member of an elsewhere persecuted race would doubtless even further enhance the class profile of our family. But she is white. There arises the danger, that on the basis of the reactionary laws determined by the friar Mendel, she will bear you a black child, and there will be a scandal!" "What scandal? Black or white, it's all the same," Adolf rejoindered, and Father explained: "Nobody will believe that this black child is really yours. Everybody will think that it is the result of the efforts of our guests, the African students, and in that sense they will also slander your wife." And he concluded: "Which is why you will break off the relationship before it is too late."

Adolf turned crimson and ponderous. Then he said: "It is already too late. It is impossible to break off the relationship." A deadly silence prevailed, interrupted only by Mother's moaning and Father's fidgeting. From that day on, Adolf also started to carefully study the writings of the friar Mendel.

No doubt it was too late; it was, I imagine, because Adolf loved Freddie much more than he had ever loved Jana Brejchová, although he almost never sent her any letters. Freddie's mother, the textile worker and Party Secretary, was invited to our house, and I, hidden behind the large portrait of the Statesman, which conceals the hole where Grandfather's wall safe used to stand, overheard Mother emphasizing the terribly tender age of both the children and asking the esteemed Secretary's consent to apply to some sort of a committee in the matter of an absorption (or something that sounded like that). I really could not understand why the Comrade Mother (Mrs. Mourek) got upset to the point of refusing to co-operate with the committee, slammed the door and left, when on other occasions, as a class-conscious woman, she had always shown full confidence in committees, councils, and organs of all kinds.

It did not end there: the Comrade Secretary of the Party Cell at the Lentex linen factory in K. provided us with a further unexpected surprise. Soon after, when Father, Mother, my older sister Margaret, and even Adolf himself began spreading all around town that the father of Freddie was the migrant black Frederick Positive Wasserman Brown, and at the same time introducing the people to the laws of heredity according to which a completely white person can give birth to a black child thanks to the genes of its progenitor (in order to preventively protect the reputation of Freddie in case of a child with other than Czech colouring), Comrade Mourek appeared again, and her squealing voice could be heard from the parlour, expressing herself to the effect that Father, Mother, Margaret, and Adolf were giving the girl (meaning Freddie) a bad name around town and causing trouble, of which she (Comrad Mourek) had had more than her fill throughout her life, the result of some youthful transgression. And although Father, having alertly declared himself the enemy of bourgeois morality, began to explain to her his intentions, he failed nonetheless.

As concerns Adolf, he deteriorated visibly, until finally he spoke about nothing else but the friar Mendel. This aroused the suspicion of the principal of the high school, Comrade Pavel Běhavka, who for several Sundays carefully observed, from his table at the Café Beránek, the entrance to the Catholic church in the town square (adding to his surveillance later on also the chapel of the Czech Protestants, and that of the Czech Evangelical Brethen), to find out whether Adolf, as a result of being converted to the obscurantist faith of the friars, visited the services. He did not, but being psychologically uprooted, he would acquaint everyone at any occasion, even completely strange comrades, with the secret of the background of his fiancée Freddie, as well as with the laws of genetics. Finally, after a large number of arguments, fights, and confrontations, Freddie one day broke up with him. To the accompaniment of his bass guitar they sang together for the last time the protest song "Get Me a New Dolly, Molly!" and then she declared (I overheard it secretly, hidden behind the portrait of the Statesman): "Your indiscretion is getting on my nerves, and I don't intend to put up with it any longer. Also, I would like you to know that I haven't told you everything: for your information, the mother of my father Frederick Positive Wasserman Brown was Japanese, his grandfather, who was brought over from Africa as a slave in chains, was a Pygmy, which, combined with the fact that my mother is one third a Jewish gypsy, leaves me with a very good chance of giving birth to a green dwarf, which your father will not be able to explain to the comrades with or without his Mendel. And it's good-bye forever, my little imbecile!"

Having said that, she left forever; and so my brother, deprived of his life-long happiness by the presence of the African students, did not become a father.

Somewhat later Freddie gave birth to twins: one is a boy and the other a girl, and both are completely pink. However, about that phenomenon, Mendel says nothing at all.

Translated by Michal Schonberg

R. K. NARAYAN

House Opposite

The hermit invariably shuddered when he looked out of his window. The house across the street was occupied by a shameless woman. Late in the evening, men kept coming and knocking on her door—afternoons, too, if there was a festival or holiday. Sometimes they lounged on the pyol of her house, smoking, chewing tobacco, and spitting into the gutter—committing all the sins of the world, according to the hermit who was striving to pursue a life of austerity, forswearing family, possessions, and all the comforts of life. He found this single-room tenement with a couple of coconut trees and a well at the backyard adequate, and the narrow street swarmed with children: sometimes he called in the children, seated them around, and taught them simple moral lessons and sacred verse. On the walls he had nailed a few pictures of gods cut out of old calendars, and made the children prostrate themselves in front of them before sending them away with a piece of sugar candy each.

His daily life followed an unvarying pattern. Birdlike, he retired at dusk, lying on the bare floor with a wooden block under his head for a pillow. He woke up at four, ahead of the rooster at the street corner, bathed at the well, and sat down on a piece of deerskin to meditate. Later he lit the charcoal stove and baked a few chapattis for breakfast and lunch and cooked certain restricted vegetables and greens, avoiding potato, onion, okra, and such as might stimulate the baser impulses.

Even in the deepest state of meditation, he could not help hearing the creaking of the door across the street when a client left after a night of debauchery. He rigorously suppressed all cravings of the palate, and punished his body in a dozen ways. If you asked him why, he would have been at a loss to explain. He was the antithesis of the athlete who flexed his muscles and watched his expanding chest before a mirror. Our hermit, on the contrary, kept a minute check of his emaciation and felt a peculiar thrill out of such an achievement. He was only following without questioning his ancient guru's instructions, and hoped thus to attain spiritual liberation.

One afternoon, opening the window to sweep the dust on the sill, he noticed her standing on her doorstep, watching the street. His temples throbbed with the rush of blood. He studied her person—chiseled features, but sunk in fatty folds. She possessed, however, a seductive outline; her forearms were cushionlike and perhaps the feel of those encircling arms attracted men. His gaze, once it had begun to hover about her body, would not return to its anchor—which should normally be the tip of one's nose, as enjoined by his guru and the yoga shastras.

Her hips were large, thighs stout like banana stalks, on the whole a mattresslike creature on which a patron could loll all night without a scrap of covering—"Awful monster! Personification of evil." He felt suddenly angry. Why on earth should that creature stand there and ruin his tapas: all the merit he had so laboriously acquired was draining away like water through a sieve. Difficult to say whether it was those monstrous arms and breasts or thighs which tempted and ruined men . . . He hissed under his breath, "Get in, you devil, don't stand there!" She abruptly turned round and went in, shutting the door behind her. He felt triumphant, although his command and her compliance were coincidental. He bolted the window tight and retreated to the farthest corner of the room, settled down on the deerskin, and kept repeating, "Om, Om, Rama, Jayarama": the sound "Rama" had a potency all its own—and was reputed to check wandering thoughts and distractions. He had a profound knowledge of mantras and their efficacy. "Sri Rama . . . ," he repeated, but it was like a dilute and weak medicine for high fever. It didn't work. "Sri Rama, Jayarama . . . ," he repeated with a desperate fervor, but the effect lasted not even a second. Unnoticed, his thoughts strayed, questioning: Who was that fellow in a check shirt and silk upper cloth over his shoulder descending the steps last evening when I went out to the market? Seen him somewhere . . . where? when? . . . ah, he was the big tailor on Market Road . . . with fashionable men and women clustering round him! Master-cutter who was a member of two or three clubs . . . Hobnobbed with officers and businessmen—and this was how he spent his evening, lounging on the human mattress! And yet fashionable persons allowed him to touch them with his measuring tape! Contamination, nothing but contamination; sinful life. He cried out in the lonely room, "Rama! Rama!" as if hailing someone hard of hearing. Presently he realized it was a futile exercise. Rama was a perfect incarnation, of course, but he was mild and gentle until provoked beyond limit, when he would storm and annihilate the evildoer without a trace, even if he was a monster like Ravana. Normally, however, he had forbearance, hence the repetition of his name only resulted in calmness and peace, but the present occasion demanded stern measures. God Siva's mantra should help. Did he not open his Third Eye and reduce the God of Love to ashes, when the latter slyly aimed his arrow at him while he was meditating? Our hermit pictured the god of matted locks and fiery eyes and recited aloud: "Om Namasivaya," that lonely hall resounding with his hoarse voice. His rambling, unwholesome thoughts were halted for a while, but presently regained their vigor and raced after the woman. She opened her door at least six times on an evening. Did she sleep with them all together at the same time? He paused to laugh at this notion, and also realized that his meditation on the austere god was gone. He banged his fist on his temples, which pained but improved his concentration. "Om Namasivaya . . ." Part of his mind noted the creaking of the door of the opposite house. She was a serpent in whose coils everyone was caught and destroyed—old and young and the middle-aged, tailors and students (he had noticed a couple of days ago a young B.Sc. student from Albert Mission Hostel at her door), lawyers and magistrates (why not?). . . No wonder the world was getting overpopulated—with such pressure of the elemental urge within every individual! O God Siva, this woman must be eliminated. He would confront her some day and tell her to get out. He would tell her, "Oh, sinful wretch, who is spreading disease and filth like an open sewer: think of the contamination you have spread around—from middle-aged tailor to B.Sc. student. You are out to destroy mankind. Repent your sins, shave your head, cover your ample loins with sackcloth, sit at the temple gate and beg or drown yourself in sarayu after praying for a cleaner life at least in the next birth . . ."

Thus went his dialogue, the thought of the woman never leaving his mind, during all the wretched, ill-spent night; he lay tossing on the bare floor. He rose before dawn, his mind made up. He would clear out immediately, cross Nallappa's Grove, and reach the other side of the river. He did not need a permanent roof; he would drift and rest in any temple or mantap or in the shade of a banyan tree: he recollected an ancient tale he had heard from his guru long ago . . . A harlot was sent to heaven when she died, while her detractor, a self-righteous reformer, found himself in hell. It was explained that while the harlot sinned only with her body, her detractor was corrupt mentally, as he was obsessed with the harlot and her activities, and could meditate on nothing else.

Our hermit packed his wicker box with his sparse possessions—a god's image in copper, a rosary, the deerskin, and a little brass bowl. Carrying his box in one hand, he stepped out of the house, closing the door gently behind him. In the dim hour of the dusk, shadowy figures were moving—a milkman driving his cow ahead, laborers bearing crowbars and spades, women with baskets on their way to the market. While he paused to take a final look at the shelter he was abandoning, he heard a plaintive cry, "Swamiji," from the opposite house, and saw the woman approach him with a tray, heaped with fruits and flowers. She placed it at his feet and said in a low reverential whisper: "Please accept my offering. This is a day of remembrance of my mother. On this day I pray and seek a saint's blessing. Forgive me . . ." All the lines he had rehearsed for a confrontation deserted him at this moment; looking at her flabby figure, the dark rings under her eyes, he felt pity. As she bent down to prostrate, he noticed that her hair was indifferently dyed and that the parting in the middle widened into a bald patch over which a string of jasmine dangled loosely. He touched her tray with the tip of his finger as a token of acceptance, and went down the street without a word.

DAVID MICHAEL KAPLAN

Love, Your Only Mother

I received another postcard from you today, Mother, and I see by the blurred postmark that you're in Manning, North Dakota now and that you've dated the card 1961. In your last card you were in Nebraska, and it was 1962; you've lost some time, I see. I was a little girl, nine years old, in 1961. You'd left my father and me only two years before. Four months after leaving, you sent me—always me, never him—your first postcard, of a turn-pike in the Midwest, postmarked Enid, Oklahoma. You called me "My little angel" and said that the sunflowers by the side of the road were tall and very pretty. You signed it, as you always have, "Your only mother." My father thought, of course, that you were in Enid, and he called the police there. But we quickly learned that postmarks meant nothing: you were never where you had been, had already passed through in the wanderings only you understand.

A postcard from my mother, I tell my husband, and he grunts.

Well, at least you know she's still alive, he says.

Yes.

This postcard shows a wheat field bending in the wind. The

colors are badly printed: the wheat's too red, the sky too blue—except for where it touches the wheat, there becoming aquamarine, as if sky and field could somehow combine to form water. There's a farmhouse in the distance. People must live there, and for a moment I imagine you do, and I could walk through the red wheat field, knock on the door, and find you. It's a game I've always played, imagining you were hiding somewhere in the postcards you've sent. Your scrawled message, as always, is brief: "The beetles are so much larger this year. I know you must be enjoying them. Love, your only mother."

What craziness is it this time? my husband asks. I don't reply.

Instead, I think about your message, measure it against others. In the last postcard seven months ago, you said you'd left something for me in a safety deposit box in Ferndale. The postmark was Nebraska, and there's no Ferndale in Nebraska. In the card before that, you said you were making me a birthday cake that you'd send. Even though I've vowed I'd never do it again, I try to understand what you are telling me.

"Your only mother." I've mulled that signature over and over, wondering what you meant. Are you worried I'd forget *you*, my only mother? In favor of some other? My father, you know, never divorced you. It wouldn't be fair to her, he told me, since she might come back.

Yes, I said.

Or maybe you mean singularity: out of all the mothers I might have had, I have you. You exist for me alone. Distances, you imply, mean nothing. You might come back.

And it's true: somehow, you've always found me. When I was a child, the postcards came to the house, of course; but later, when I went to college, and then to the first of several apartments, and finally to this house of my own, with husband and daughter of my own, they still kept coming. How you did this I don't know, but you did. You pursued me, and no matter how far away, you always found me. In your way, I guess, you've been faithful.

I put this postcard in a box with all the others you've sent over the years—postcards from Sioux City, Jackson Falls, Horseshoe Bend, Truckee, Elm City, Spivey. Then I pull out the same atlas I've had since a child and look up Manning, North Dakota, and yes, there you are, between Dickinson and Killdeer, a blip on the red highway line.

She's in Manning, North Dakota, I tell my husband, just as I used to tell my friends, as if that were explanation enough for your absence. I'd point out where you were in the atlas, and they'd nod.

But in all those postcards, Mother, I imagined you: you were down among the trees in the mountain panorama, or just out of frame on that street in downtown Tupelo, or already through the door to The World's Greatest Reptile Farm. And I was there, too, hoping to find you and say to you, Come back, come back, there's only one street, one door, we didn't mean it, we didn't know, whatever was wrong will be different.

Several times I decided you were dead, even wished you were dead, but then another postcard would come, with another message to ponder. And I've always read them, even when my husband said not to, even if they've driven me to tears or rage or a blankness when I've no longer cared if you were dead or anyone were dead, including myself. I've been faithful, too, you see. I've always looked up where you were in the atlas, and put your postcards in the box. Sixty-three postcards, four hundred–odd lines of scrawl: our life together.

Why are you standing there like that? my daughter asks me.

I must have been away somewhere, I say. But I'm back.

Yes.

You see, Mother, I always come back. That's the distance that separates us.

But on summer evenings, when the windows are open to the dusk, I sometimes smell cities . . . wheat fields . . . oceans—strange smells from far away—all the places you've been to that I never will. I smell them as if they weren't pictures on a postcard, but real, as close as my outstretched hand. And sometimes in the middle of the night, I'll sit bolt upright, my husband instantly awake and frightened, asking, What is it? What is it? And I'll say, She's here, she's here, and I am terrified that you are. And he'll say, No, no, she's not, she'll never come back, and he'll hold me until my terror passes. She's not here, he says gently, stroking my hair, she's not—except you are, my strange and only mother: like a buoy in a fog, your voice, dear Mother, seems to come from everywhere.

Germany

HEINRICH BÖLL

The Laugher

When someone asks me what business I am in, I am seized with embarrassment: I blush and stammer, I who am otherwise known as a man of poise. I envy people who can say: I am a bricklayer. I envy barbers, bookkeepers, and writers the simplicity of their avowal, for all these professions speak for themselves and need no lengthy explanation, while I am constrained to reply to such questions: I am a laugher. An admission of this kind demands another, since I have to answer the second question: "Is that how you make your living?" truthfully with "Yes." I actually do make a living at my laughing, and a good one too, for my laughing is—commercially speaking—much in demand. I am a good laugher, experienced, no one else laughs as well as I do, no one else has such command of the fine points of my art. For a long time, in order to avoid tiresome explanations, I called myself an actor, but my talents in the field of mime and elocution are so meager that I felt this designation to be too far from the truth: I love the truth, and the truth is: I am a laugher. I am neither a clown nor a comedian. I do not make people gay, I portray gaiety: I laugh like a Roman emperor, or like a sensitive

89

schoolboy, I am as much at home in the laughter of the seventeenth century as in that of the nineteenth, and when occasion demands I laugh my way through the centuries, all classes of society, all categories of age: it is simply a skill which I have acquired, like the skill of being able to repair shoes. In my breast I harbor the laughter of America, the laughter of Africa, white, red, yellow laughter—and for the right fee I let it peal out in accordance with the director's requirements.

I have become indispensable; I laugh on records, I laugh on tape, and television directors treat me with respect. I laugh mournfully, moderately, hysterically; I laugh like a streetcar conductor or like an apprentice in the grocery business; laughter in the morning, laughter in the evening, nocturnal laughter, and the laughter of twilight. In short: wherever and however laughter is required—I do it.

It need hardly be pointed out that a profession of this kind is tiring, especially as I have also—this is my specialty—mastered the art of infectious laughter; this has also made me indispensable to third- and fourth-rate comedians, who are scared—and with good reason—that their audiences will miss their punch lines, so I spend most evenings in nightclubs as a kind of discreet claque, my job being to laugh infectiously during the weaker parts of the program. It has to be carefully timed: my hearty, boisterous laughter must not come too soon, but neither must it come too late, it must come just at the right spot: at the prearranged moment I burst out laughing, the whole audience roars with me, and the joke is saved.

But as for me, I drag myself exhausted to the checkroom, put on my overcoat, happy that I can go off duty at last. At home I usually find telegrams waiting for me: "Urgently require your laughter. Recording Tuesday," and a few hours later I am sitting in an overheated express train bemoaning my fate.

I need scarcely say that when I am off duty or on vacation I have little inclination to laugh: the cowhand is glad when he can forget the cow, the bricklayer when he can forget the mortar, and carpenters usually have doors at home which don't work or drawers which are hard to open. Confectioners like sour pickles, butchers like marzipan, and the baker prefers sausage to bread; bullfighters raise pigeons for a hobby, boxers turn pale when their children have nosebleeds: I find all this quite natural, for I never laugh off duty. I am a very solemn person, and people consider me—perhaps rightly so—a pessimist.

During the first years of our married life, my wife would often say to me: "Do laugh!" but since then she has come to realize that I cannot grant her this wish. I am happy when I am free to relax my tense face muscles, my frayed spirit, in profound solemnity. Indeed, even other people's laughter gets on my nerves, since it reminds me too much of my profession. So our marriage is a quiet, peaceful one, because my wife has also forgotten how to laugh: now and again I catch her smiling, and I smile too. We converse in low tones, for I detest the noise of the nightclubs, the noise that sometimes fills the recording studios. People who do not know me think I am taciturn. Perhaps I am, because I have to open my mouth so often to laugh.

I go through life with an impassive expression, from time to time permitting myself a gentle smile, and I often wonder whether I have ever laughed. I think not. My brothers and sisters have always known me for a serious boy.

So I laugh in many different ways, but my own laughter I have never heard.

Translated by Leila Vennewitz

Argentina

JORGE LUIS BORGES

August 25, 1983

I saw by the little station clock that it was a few minutes past
eleven at night. I walked to the hotel. I felt, as on so many other
occasions, the relief and resignation inspired by places we know
well. The heavy gate was open; the building stood in darkness.

I entered the hall where dim mirrors duplicated the potted
plants in the room. Strangely enough, the hotel-keeper didn't
recognize me and handed me the register. I took the pen which
was chained to the desk, dipped it in the bronze inkwell and, as
I bent over the open book, there occurred the first of the many
surprises which that night was to offer me. My name, Jorge
Luis Borges, had already been written on the page and the ink
was still fresh.

The hotel-keeper said, "I thought you'd already gone upstairs."
Then he peered at me more closely and corrected himself. "I'm
sorry, sir, the other looks a lot like you. But you're younger of
course."

"What room is he in?"

"He asked for number nineteen," was the answer. It was as I
feared.

I dropped the pen and ran up the stairs. Room nineteen was

on the second floor and looked on to a poor and badly tended courtyard with a veranda and, I seem to remember, a bench. It was the highest room in the hotel. I tried the handle and the door opened. The lamp had not been switched off. Under the harsh light I recognized myself. There I was, lying on my back on the small iron bed, older, wizened and very pale, the eyes lost on the high stucco moldings. The voice reached me. It wasn't exactly mine; it was like the voice I often hear in my recordings, unpleasant and monotonous.

"How strange," it said. "We are two and we are one. But then, there is nothing really strange in dreams."

I asked bewildered, "Is all this a dream?"

"It is certainly my last dream."

He pointed at the empty bottle on the marble top of the night-table.

"But you have still got plenty to dream before reaching this night. What date is it for you?"

"I don't know exactly," I answered uncertainly. "But yesterday was my sixty-first birthday."

"When you reach this night, your eighty-fourth birthday will have been yesterday. Today is August 25, 1983."

"So many more years to wait," I said in a low voice.

"I have nothing left," he said suddenly. "I can die any day now. I can fade into that which I don't know and yet keep on dreaming of the double. That hackneyed theme given to me by Stevenson and mirrors!"

I felt that to mention Stevenson was a last farewell, not a pedantic allusion. I was he, and I understood. Even the most dramatic moments are not enough to turn one into Shakespeare and coin memorable phrases.

To change the subject I said, "I knew what would happen to you. In this very place, in one of the lower rooms, we began to draft the story of this suicide."

"Yes," he answered slowly, as if collecting vague memories,

3

SUDDEN FICTION INTERNATIONAL

"but I don't see the resemblance. In that draft I bought a one-way ticket to Adrogué, and in the Hotel Las Delicias I climbed to room nineteen, the farthest room of all. There I committed suicide."

"That is why I am here," I said to him.

"Here? But we are always here. Here I am dreaming of you, in the apartment of Calle Maipú. Here I am dying in the room that used to be mother's."

"That used to be mother's," I repeated, trying not to understand. "And I am dreaming of you in room nineteen, on the top floor."

"Who is dreaming whom? I know I am dreaming you but I don't know whether you are dreaming me. The hotel in Adrogué was pulled down many years ago—twenty, maybe thirty. Who knows!"

"I am the dreamer," I answered with a certain defiance.

"But don't you see that the important thing is to discover whether there is only one dreamer or two?"

"I am Borges who has seen your name in the register and has climbed up to this room."

"Borges am I, dying in Calle Maipú."

There was a moment of silence. Then the other said, "Let's put ourselves to the test. Which was the most terrible moment of our life?"

I leant over towards him and we both spoke at the same time. I know we both lied. A faint smile lit the old face. I felt that the smile somehow reflected my own. "We have lied to each other," he said, "because we feel two and not one. The truth is that we are two and we are one."

The conversation was beginning to irritate me. I told him so. And I added, "And you, in 1983, won't you reveal something of the years that lie before me?"

"What can I tell you, my poor Borges? The misfortunes to

94

which you have grown accustomed will keep on happening. You will live alone in this house. You will touch the letterless books and the Swedenborg medallion and the wooden box with the Federal Cross. Blindness isn't darkness—it's a form of loneliness. You will return to Iceland."

"Iceland! Iceland of the seas!"

"In Rome you will say a few lines by Keats whose name, like that of all other men, was written on water."

"I have never been to Rome."

"There are other things as well. You will write our best poem, and it will be an elegy."

"To the death of . . ." I said. I did not dare utter the name.

"No. She will live longer than you." We sat in silence. Then he continued.

"You will write that book we dreamt of for so long. Toward 1979 you will understand that your so-called works are nothing but a series of sketches, miscellaneous drafts, and you will yield to the vain and superstitious temptation of writing your one great book. The superstition that has inflicted upon us Goethe's *Faust*, *Salammbô*, *Ulysses*. To my amazement, I have filled too many pages."

"And in the end you realized you had failed."

"Something worse. I realized it was a masterpiece in the most oppressive sense of the word. My good intentions did not go farther than the first few pages. In the others lay the labyrinths, the knives, the man who believes he is a dream, the reflection that believes itself to be real, the tigers of night, the battles turned to blood, Juan Muraña fatal and blind, Macedonio's voice, the ship made of the fingernails of the dead, old English spoken through so many days."

"I know that museum well," I observed, not without irony.

"And then false memories too, the double play of symbols, the long enumerations, the craft of good prose, the imperfect

symmetries that the critics discover with glee, the not always apocryphal quotations."

"Have you published this book?"

"I toyed—without conviction—with the melodramatic idea of destroying it, perhaps with fire. I finally published it in Madrid under another name. It was described as the work of a vulgar imitator of Borges who had the disadvantage of not being Borges and of having repeated the superficial features of the model."

"I'm not surprised," I said. "Every writer ends by being his own least intelligent disciple."

"That book was one of the roads that led me to this night. As to the others, the humiliation of old age, the certainty of having already lived all those days to come . . ."

"I won't write that book," I said.

"Yes you will. My words, which now are the present, will be barely the memory of a dream."

His dogmatic tone, no doubt the same one I use in the classroom, annoyed me. I was bothered by the fact that we resembled each other so much, and that he should take advantage of the impunity given him by the nearness of death. In revenge I asked him: "Are you really so certain you are about to die?"

"Yes," he answered. "I feel a sort of sweet peacefulness and relief which I have never felt before. I cannot explain it to you. All words require a shared experience. Why do you seem annoyed by what I'm telling you?"

"Because we are far too alike. I hate your face which is a caricature of mine. I hate your voice which apes my own. I hate your pathetic way of building sentences, which is mine."

"So do I," said the other. "That is why I have decided to kill myself."

A bird sang in the street.

"The last one," said the other.

With a gesture he called me to his side. His hand took hold

of mine. I drew back, fearing that both hands would fade into one. He said:

"The stoics have taught us not to regret leaving this life: the gates of prison are at last open. I have always thought of life in this way, but my sloth and cowardice made me hesitate. Some twelve days ago I gave a conference in La Plata on the sixth book of the *Aeneid*. Suddenly, repeating an hexameter, I knew which was the road to take, and I made up my mind. From that moment onwards I felt invulnerable. My fate will be yours, you will receive this sudden revelation in the midst of Virgil's Latin, and you will have forgotten this curious and prophetic dialogue which takes place in two places and two moments in time. When you dream it again you will be the one I am now and I will be your dream."

"I won't forget it and tomorrow I'll write it down."

"It will lie deep inside your memory, beneath the tide of dreams. When you write it, you will believe you are inventing a fantastic story. But it won't be tomorrow. You still have several years to wait."

He stopped talking; I realized he was dead. In a certain sense I died with him. Anxiously I leant forward over the top of the pillow but there was no one there.

I fled from the room. Outside there was no courtyard, no marble staircase, no large silent hotel, no eucalyptus, no statues, no arches, no fountains, no gate of a country building in Adrogué.

Outside were other dreams, waiting for me.

Translated by Alberto Manguel

Poland

SLAWOMIR MROŻEK

The Elephant

The director of the Zoological Gardens had shown himself to be an upstart. He regarded his animals simply as stepping stones on the road of his own career. He was indifferent to the educational importance of his establishment. In his zoo the giraffe had a short neck, the badger had no burrow and the whistlers, having lost all interest, whistled rarely and with some reluctance. These shortcomings should not have been allowed, especially as the zoo was often visited by parties of schoolchildren.

The zoo was in a provincial town, and it was short of some of the most important animals, among them the elephant. Three thousand rabbits were a poor substitute for the noble giant. However, as our country developed, the gaps were being filled in a well-planned manner. On the occasion of the anniversary of the liberation, on 22nd July, the zoo was notified that it had at long last been allocated an elephant. All the staff, who were devoted to their work, rejoiced at this news. All the greater was their surprise when they learned that the director had sent a letter to Warsaw, renouncing the allocation and putting forward a plan for obtaining an elephant by more economic means.

"I, and all the staff," he had written, "are fully aware how

98

heavy a burden falls upon the shoulders of Polish miners and foundry men because of the elephant. Desirous of reducing our costs, I suggest that the elephant mentioned in your communication should be replaced by one of our own procurement. We can make an elephant out of rubber, of the correct size, fill it with air and place it behind railings. It will be carefully painted the correct color and even on close inspection will be indistinguishable from the real animal. It is well known that the elephant is a sluggish animal and it does not run and·jump about. In the notice on the railings we can state that this particular elephant is particularly sluggish. The money saved in this way can be turned to the purchase of a jet plane or the conservation of some church monument.

"Kindly note that both the idea and its execution are my modest contribution to the common task and struggle.

"I am, etc."

This communication must have reached a soulless official, who regarded his duties in a purely bureaucratic manner and did not examine the heart of the matter but, following only the directive about reduction of expenditure, accepted the director's plan. On hearing the Ministry's approval, the director issued instructions for the making of the rubber elephant.

The carcass was to have been filled with air by two keepers blowing into it from opposite ends. To keep the operation secret the work was to be completed during the night because the people of the town, having heard that an elephant was joining the zoo, were anxious to see it. The director insisted on haste also because he expected a bonus, should his idea turn out to be a success.

The two keepers locked themselves in a shed normally housing a workshop, and began to blow. After two hours of hard blowing they discovered that the rubber skin had risen only a few inches above the floor and its bulge in no way resembled an elephant. The night progressed. Outside, human voices were stilled and only the cry of the jackass interrupted the silence. Exhausted, the keepers stopped blowing and made sure that the air already inside the elephant should not escape. They were not young and were unaccustomed to this kind of work.

"If we go on at this rate," said one of them, "we shan't finish by morning. And what am I to tell my missus? She'll never believe me if I say that I spent the night blowing up an elephant."

"Quite right," agreed the second keeper. "Blowing up an elephant is not an everyday job. And it's all because our director is a leftist."

They resumed their blowing, but after another half-hour they felt too tired to continue. The bulge on the floor was larger but still nothing like the shape of an elephant.

"It's getting harder all the time," said the first keeper.

"It's an uphill job, all right," agreed the second. "Let's have a little rest."

While they were resting, one of them noticed a gas pipe ending in a valve. Could they not fill the elephant with gas? He suggested it to his mate.

They decided to try. They connected the elephant to the gas pipe, turned the valve, and to their joy in a few minutes there was a full-sized beast standing in the shed. It looked real: the enormous body, legs like columns, huge ears and the inevitable trunk. Driven by ambition the director had made sure of having in his zoo a very large elephant indeed.

"First class," declared the keeper who had the idea of using gas. "Now we can go home."

In the morning the elephant was moved to a special run in a central position, next to the monkey cage. Placed in front of a large real rock it looked fierce and magnificent. A big notice proclaimed: "Particularly sluggish. Hardly moves."

Among the first visitors that morning was a party of children from the local school. The teacher in charge of them was planning to give them an object-lesson about the elephant. He halted the group in front of the animal and began:

"The elephant is a herbivorous mammal. By means of its trunk it pulls out young trees and eats their leaves."

The children were looking at the elephant with enraptured admiration. They were waiting for it to pull out a young tree, but the beast stood still behind its railings.

". . . The elephant is a direct descendant of the now-extinct mammoth. It's not surprising, therefore, that it's the largest living land animal."

The more conscientious pupils were making notes.

". . . Only the whale is heavier than the elephant, but then the whale lives in the sea. We can safely say that on land the elephant reigns supreme."

A slight breeze moved the branches of the trees in the zoo.

". . . The weight of a fully grown elephant is between nine and thirteen thousand pounds."

At that moment the elephant shuddered and rose in the air. For a few seconds it swayed just above the ground, but a gust of wind blew it upward until its mighty silhouette was against the sky. For a short while people on the ground could see the four circles of its feet, its bulging belly and the trunk, but soon, propelled by the wind, the elephant sailed above the fence and disappeared above the treetops. Astonished monkeys in the cage continued staring into the sky.

They found the elephant in the neighboring botanical gardens. It had landed on a cactus and punctured its rubber hide.

The schoolchildren who had witnessed the scene in the zoo soon started neglecting their studies and turned into hooligans. It is reported that they drink liquor and break windows. And they no longer believe in elephants.

Translated by Konrad Syrop

Zimbabwe / England

DORIS LESSING

Homage for Isaac Babel

The day I had promised to take Catherine down to visit my young friend Philip at his school in the country, we were to leave at eleven, but she arrived at nine. Her blue dress was new, and so were her fashionable shoes. Her hair had just been done. She looked more than ever like a pink-and-gold Renoir girl who expects everything from life.

Catherine lives in a white house overlooking the sweeping brown tides of the river. She helped me clean up my flat with a devotion which said that she felt small flats were altogether more romantic than large houses. We drank tea, and talked mainly about Philip, who, being fifteen, has pure stern tastes in everything from food to music. Catherine looked at the books lying around his room, and asked if she might borrow the stories of Isaac Babel to read on the train. Catherine is thirteen. I suggested she might find them difficult, but she said: "Philip reads them, doesn't he?"

During the journey I read newspapers and watched her pretty frowning face as she turned the pages of Babel, for she was determined to let nothing get between her and her ambition to be worthy of Philip.

At the school, which is charming, civilized, and expensive, the two children walked together across green fields, and I followed, seeing how the sun gilded their bright friendly heads turned towards each other as they talked. In Catherine's left hand she carried the stories of Isaac Babel.

After lunch we went to the pictures. Philip allowed it to be seen that he thought going to the pictures just for the fun of it was not worthy of intelligent people, but he made the concession, for our sakes. For his sake we chose the more serious of the two films that were showing in the little town. It was about a good priest who helped criminals in New York. His goodness, however, was not enough to prevent one of them from being sent to the gas chamber; and Philip and I waited with Catherine in the dark until she had stopped crying and could face the light of a golden evening.

At the entrance of the cinema the doorman was lying in wait for anyone who had red eyes. Grasping Catherine by her suffering arm, he said bitterly: "Yes, why are you crying? He had to be punished for his crime, didn't he?" Catherine stared at him, incredulous.

Philip rescued her by saying with disdain: "Some people don't know right from wrong even when it's *demonstrated* to them." The doorman turned his attention to the next red-eyed emerger from the dark; and we went on together to the station, the children silent because of the cruelty of the world.

Finally Catherine said, her eyes wet again: "I think it's all absolutely beastly, and I can't bear to think about it." And Philip said: "But we've got to think about it, don't you see, because if we don't it'll just go on and *on*, don't you see?"

In the train going back to London I sat beside Catherine. She had the stories open in front of her, but she said: "Philip's awfully lucky. I wish I went to that school. Did you notice that girl who said hullo to him in the garden? They must be great friends. I wish my mother would let me have a dress like that, it's *not* fair."

"I thought it was too old for her."

"Oh, *did* you?"

Soon she bent her head again over the book, but almost at once lifted it to say: "Is he a very famous writer?"

"He's a marvellous writer, brilliant, one of the very best."

"Why?"

"Well, for one thing he's so simple. Look how few words he uses, and how strong his stories are."

"I see. Do you know him? Does he live in London?"

"Oh no, he's dead."

"Oh. Then why did you—I thought he was alive, the way you talked."

"I'm sorry, I suppose I wasn't thinking of him as dead."

"When did he die?"

"He was murdered. About twenty years ago, I suppose."

"Twenty years." Her hand began the movement of pushing the book over to me, but then relaxed. "I'll be fourteen in November," she stated, sounding threatened, while her eyes challenged me.

I found it hard to express my need to apologize, but before I could speak, she said, patiently attentive again: "You said he was murdered?"

"Yes."

"I expect the person who murdered him felt sorry when he discovered he had murdered a famous writer."

"Yes, I expect so."

"Was he old when he was murdered?"

"No, quite young really."

"Well, that was bad luck, wasn't it?"

"Yes, I suppose it was bad luck."

"Which do you think is the very best story here? I mean, in your honest opinion, the very very best one."

I chose the story about killing the goose. She read it slowly, while I sat waiting, wishing to take it from her, wishing to protect this charming little person from Isaac Babel.

When she had finished, she said: "Well, some of it I don't understand. He's got a funny way of looking at things. Why should a man's legs in boots look like *girls?*" She finally pushed the book over at me, and said: "I think it's all morbid."

"But you have to understand the kind of life he had. First, he was a Jew in Russia. That was bad enough. Then his experience was all revolution and civil war and . . ."

But I could see these words bouncing off the clear glass of her fiercely denying gaze; and I said: "Look, Catherine, why don't you try again when you're older? Perhaps you'll like him better then?"

She said gratefully: "Yes, perhaps that would be best. After all, Philip is two years older than me, isn't he?"

A week later I got a letter from Catherine.

Thank you very much for being kind enough to take me to visit Philip at his school. It was the most lovely day in my whole life. I am extremely grateful to you for taking me. I have been thinking about the Hoodlum Priest. That was a film which demonstrated to me beyond any shadow of doubt that Capital Punishment is a Wicked Thing, and I shall never forget what I learned that afternoon, and the lessons of it will be with me all my life. I have been meditating about what you said about Isaac Babel, the famed Russian short story writer, and I now see that the conscious simplicity of his style is what makes him, beyond the shadow of a doubt, the great writer that he is, and now in my school compositions I am endeavoring to emulate him so as to learn a conscious simplicity which is the only basis for a really brilliant writing style.

Love, Catherine.

P.S. Has Philip said anything about my party? I wrote but he hasn't answered. Please find out if he is coming or if he just forgot to answer my letter. I hope he comes, because sometimes I feel I shall die if he doesn't.

P.P.S. Please don't tell him I said anything, because I should die if he knew. Love, Catherine.

GABRIEL GARCÍA MÁRQUEZ

One of These Days

Monday dawned warm and rainless. Aurelio Escovar, a dentist without a degree, and a very early riser, opened his office at six. He took some false teeth, still mounted in their plaster mold, out of the glass case and put on the table a fistful of instruments which he arranged in size order, as if they were on display. He wore a collarless striped shirt, closed at the neck with a golden stud, and pants held up by suspenders. He was erect and skinny, with a look that rarely corresponded to the situation, the way deaf people have of looking.

When he had things arranged on the table, he pulled the drill toward the dental chair and sat down to polish the false teeth. He seemed not to be thinking about what he was doing, but worked steadily, pumping the drill with his feet, even when he didn't need it.

After eight he stopped for a while to look at the sky through the window, and he saw two pensive buzzards who were drying themselves in the sun on the ridgepole of the house next door. He went on working with the idea that before lunch it would rain again. The shrill voice of his eleven-year-old son interrupted his concentration.

107

"Papá."

"What?"

"The Mayor wants to know if you'll pull his tooth."

"Tell him I'm not here."

He was polishing a gold tooth. He held it at arm's length, and examined it with his eyes half closed. His son shouted again from the little waiting room.

"He says you are, too, because he can hear you."

The dentist kept examining the tooth. Only when he had put it on the table with the finished work did he say:

"So much the better."

He operated the drill again. He took several pieces of a bridge out of a cardboard box where he kept the things he still had to do and began to polish the gold.

"Papá."

"What?"

He still hadn't changed his expression.

"He says if you don't take out his tooth, he'll shoot you."

Without hurrying, with an extremely tranquil movement, he stopped pedaling the drill, pushed it away from the chair, and pulled the lower drawer of the table all the way out. There was a revolver. "O.K.," he said. "Tell him to come and shoot me."

He rolled the chair over opposite the door, his hand resting on the edge of the drawer. The Mayor appeared at the door. He had shaved the left side of his face, but the other side, swollen and in pain, had a five-day-old beard. The dentist saw many nights of desperation in his dull eyes. He closed the drawer with his fingertips and said softly:

"Sit down."

"Good morning," said the Mayor.

"Morning," said the dentist.

While the instruments were boiling, the Mayor leaned his skull on the headrest of the chair and felt better. His breath was icy. It was a poor office: an old wooden chair, the pedal drill, a glass case with ceramic bottles. Opposite the chair was a window with a shoulder-high cloth curtain. When he felt the dentist approach, the Mayor braced his heels and opened his mouth.

Aurelio Escovar turned his head toward the light. After inspecting the infected tooth, he closed the Mayor's jaw with a cautious pressure of his fingers.

"It has to be without anesthesia," he said.

"Why?"

"Because you have an abscess."

The Mayor looked him in the eye. "All right," he said, and tried to smile. The dentist did not return the smile. He brought the basin of sterilized instruments to the worktable and took them out of the water with a pair of cold tweezers, still without hurrying. Then he pushed the spittoon with the tip of his shoe, and went to wash his hands in the washbasin. He did all this without looking at the Mayor. But the Mayor didn't take his eyes off him.

It was a lower wisdom tooth. The dentist spread his feet and grasped the tooth with the hot forceps. The Mayor seized the arms of the chair, braced his feet with all his strength, and felt an icy void in his kidneys, but didn't make a sound. The dentist moved only his wrist. Without rancor, rather with a bitter tenderness, he said:

"Now you'll pay for our twenty dead men."

The Mayor felt the crunch of bones in his jaw, and his eyes filled with tears. But he didn't breathe until he felt the tooth come out. Then he saw it through his tears. It seemed so foreign to his pain that he failed to understand his torture of the five previous nights.

Bent over the spittoon, sweating, panting, he unbuttoned his tunic and reached for the handkerchief in his pants pocket. The dentist gave him a clean cloth.

"Dry your tears," he said.

The Mayor did. He was trembling. While the dentist washed his hands, he saw the crumbling ceiling and a dusty spider web with spider's eggs and dead insects. The dentist returned, drying his hands. "Go to bed," he said, "and gargle with salt water." The Mayor stood up, said goodbye with a casual military salute, and walked toward the door, stretching his legs, without buttoning up his tunic.

"Send the bill," he said.

"To you or the town?"

The Mayor didn't look at him. He closed the door and said through the screen:

"It's the same damn thing."

Translated by J. S. Bernstein

PETER HANDKE

Welcoming the Board of Directors

Gentlemen, it's rather cold in here. Let me explain the situation. An hour ago, I called from the city to ask if everything had been prepared for the meeting, but no one answered. I immediately drove here and looked for the porter; he was neither to be found in his booth, in the basement near the furnace, nor in the auditorium. But I did find his wife there; she was sitting in the darkness on a stool near the door, her head bent, her face in her palms, her elbows resting on her knees. I asked her what had happened. Without moving, she said that her husband had left; one of their children had been run over while sledding. That is the reason that the rooms were unheated; I hope you will take this into account; what I have to say won't take long. Perhaps you could move your chairs a bit closer so I won't have to shout; I don't want to make a political speech; I merely want to report on the financial situation of the company. I'm sorry that the windowpanes have been broken by the storm; before your arrival the porter's wife and I covered the spaces with plastic bags to keep the snow from coming in; but as you can see, we weren't entirely successful. Don't let the creaking

111

distract you as I read a statement on the net-balance of this business year; there is no reason for concern; I can assure you that the executive board is unimpeachable. Please move closer if you have difficulty understanding me. I regret having to welcome you here under such circumstances; they are due to the child having sledded in front of the oncoming car; the porter's wife, as she was fastening a plastic bag to the window with string, told me that her husband, who had gone down to the basement for coal, howled; she was arranging chairs in the auditorium for the meeting; suddenly she heard her husband howl from below; she stood riveted to the spot where she heard the scream, she told me, for a long time; she listened. Then her husband appeared at the door, still holding a bucket of coal in his hand; in a low voice, his eyes averted, he told her what had happened; their second child had brought him the news. Since the absent porter has the list of names, I will welcome you as a group and not individually. I said, as a group and not individually. That's the wind. I thank you for coming in the cold through the snow to this meeting; it's quite a walk from the valley. Perhaps you thought you would enter a room where the ice on the windows would have melted and where you could sit by the stove and warm yourselves; but you are now sitting at the table in your overcoats, and the snow which fell from your shoes as you came in and took your seats hasn't even melted; there is no stove in the room, only a black hole in the wall where the stove pipe had been when this room and this empty house were still inhabited. I thank you for coming in spite of all the difficulties: I thank you and welcome you. I welcome you. I welcome you. Let me first welcome the gentleman sitting near the door where the farmer's wife had sat in the darkness; I welcome the gentleman and thank him. Perhaps when he received the registered letter a few days ago informing him of this meeting at which the accounts of the executive board are to be reviewed, he didn't think it imperative to attend since it was below freezing and snow had been falling for days; but then he thought that perhaps everything wasn't as it should be in the company; there was a suspicious creaking in its structure. I said that perhaps he thought that its structure was creaking. No, the structure of the company is not creaking. Pardon me, but what a storm this is. Then he got into his car and drove from the city in the cold through the snow to this meeting. He had to park the car in the village below; a narrow path is the only way up to the house. He sat in the tavern reading the financial section of the paper until it was time to leave for the meeting. In the woods he met another gentleman who was also on his way to the meeting; the latter was leaning on a wayside crucifix holding his hat in one hand and a frozen apple in the other; as he ate the frozen apple snow fell on his forehead and hair. I said that snow fell on his forehead and hair as he ate the frozen apple. As the first gentleman approached him, they greeted each other; then the second gentleman put his hand in his overcoat pocket and brought out a second frozen apple which he gave to the first gentleman; at that the storm blew his hat off and they both laughed. They both laughed. Please move a little closer, otherwise you won't be able to understand me. The structure is creaking. It's not the structure of the company that's creaking; you will all receive the dividends that are due to you in this business year; I want to inform you of that in this unusual meeting. As the two men trudged through the snow in the storm, the limousine with the others arrived. They stood in their heavy black overcoats next to the car, using it as protection against the wind, and tried to make up their minds whether or not to climb up to the dilapidated farmhouse. I said: farmhouse. Although they had their doubts about making the climb, one of them persuaded the others to overcome their fears and reminded them of the grave situation that the company was in; after reading the financial news in the tavern, they left and trudged through the snow to this meeting; they were sincerely concerned about the company. First their feet made clean holes in the snow; but eventually they dragged their feet, making a path in the snow. They stopped once and looked back at the valley: flakes floated down on them from the black heavens; they saw two sets of tracks leading down, one set was faint and almost covered with snow; they had been made by the farmer when he had run down after hearing of the child's accident; he often fell on his face without trying to break his fall with his hands. He often found himself buried in the icy snow; he often dug himself in with his trembling fingers; when he fell, he often licked the bitter flakes with his tongue; he often howled under the stormy skies. I repeat: the farmer often howled under the stormy skies. They also saw the tracks that led to the dilapidated farmhouse, the tracks of the two gentlemen who discussed the situation of the company and suggested that the capital should be increased by distributing new stocks and ate glassy pieces of the green apples as they trudged through the storm. Finally, after night had fallen, the rest of you arrived and entered this room; the first two gentlemen were sitting here, just as they are now, with their notebooks on their knees holding pencils in their hands; they were waiting for me to deliver my welcoming address so that they could take notes. I welcome all of you and thank you for coming; I welcome the gentlemen who eat the frozen apples as they write my words down; I welcome the other four gentlemen who ran over the farmer's son with their limousine as they sped over the icy street to the village: the farmer's son, the porter's son. The structure is creaking again; the roof is creaking, the creaking being caused by the heavy weight of snow; it isn't the structure of the company that's creaking. The balance is active; there are no irregularities in the business management. The beams are bending from the pressure on the roof; the structure is creaking. I would like to thank the farmer for all that he has done for this meeting: for the last number of days he climbed up to the house from the farmstead, carrying a ladder so that he could paint this room; he carried the ladder on his shoulder, holding it in the crook of his arm; in his left hand he carried a pail with whitewash with a broken broom in it. With this he painted the walls after his children had removed the wood that lay piled up to the window sills and had carted it to the farmyard on their sleds. Carrying the pail in one hand and holding the ladder with the other, the farmer walked up to the house to prepare this room for the meeting; the children ran shouting in front of him carrying their sleds, their scarves fluttering in the wind. We can still see the overlapping white rings on the floor where the farmer placed the pail when he climbed the ladder to paint the walls; the black rings near the door where the powdery snow is now coming in are from the pot with the boiling soup which the farmer's wife brought at mealtimes: the three of them sat or squatted on the ground and dipped their spoons in; the farmer's wife stood at the door, her arms crossed over her apron and sang folk songs about snow; the children slurped the soup and rhythmically swayed their heads. Please don't worry: there is no reason for concern about the company; the creaking you hear is in the structure of the roof and is being caused by the weight of the snow which is causing the structure to creak. I thank the farmer for everything he has done; I would address him personally if he weren't down in the village with the child that has been run over. I would also address the farmer's wife and I would thank her, and I would address the children and give them my heartfelt thanks for everything that they have done for this meeting. I thank all of you and welcome you. I beg you to remain seated so that your movement doesn't cause the structure to collapse. What a storm! I said: What a storm. Please remain seated. I thank you for coming and welcome you. It is only the structure that is creaking; I said that you should remain seated so that the roof doesn't cave in. I said that I said that you should remain seated. I said that I said that I said that you should remain seated! I welcome you! I said that I said that I welcome you. I welcome all of you who have come here to be made an end of! I welcome you. I welcome you.

Translated by Herbert Kuhner

JOYCE CAROL OATES

The Boy

There was this boy named Kit, all semester he pestered me
with love, called out Hey good-lookin on the street, after class
he'd hang around eyeing me, Hey teach you're a peach, smart
aleck giggly staring, wet brown eyes, smooth downy skin, didn't
look fourteen but he said he was seventeen which might have
been true. I said, All right damn you, I drove us out to this
place I knew in the woods, a motel meant to be a lodge, fake
logs with fake knotholes, I brought a six-pack of beer along, the
room smelled of damp and old bedclothes, somebody's deodor-
ant or maybe Air-Wick, bedspread that hadn't been changed in
a long time. It's my strategy to praise, actually I mean everything I say, God I wanted him to feel good, there was a lot of
fooling around, getting high, quick wisecracks you roar your
head off at but can't remember five minutes later, we were both
getting excited, Hey let's dance, we got high and fell across the
bed tangling and tickling. I opened his pants and took hold of
him but he was soft, breathing fast and shallow, was he afraid?
but why? of *me?* hey why? I blew in his ear and got him giggling, I teased and said, Okay kid now's your chance, Mommy

ain't anywhere near, kissed and tickled and rubbed against him, God I was hot, down the hall somebody played a radio loud and then a door slammed and you couldn't hear it, now I was flying high and spinning going fast around a turn in the mountains, Oooooo, hair streaming out behind me like it hasn't done in fifteen years, I was crying no I was laughing, wanted to get him hard damn it, big and inside me like a man, then I'd tell him how great he was, how fantastic, it would make me happy too, not just strung out, part-time shitty teaching jobs that I had to drive twenty-three miles one way to get to, thirty miles the other, and pouches under my eyes and a twisty look that scares the nice shy kids. But he never did get hard, it felt like something little that's been skinned, naked and velvety like a baby rabbit, he was squirming like I'd hurt him or he was afraid I might hurt him, finally he said, I guess I don't love you, I guess I want to go home, but I didn't even hear it, I was thinking Oh fuck it the beer's going to be warm, I closed my eyes seeing the road tilt and spin and something about the sky, filmy little clouds that knock your heart out they're so beautiful, Hey let's dance, kid, I said giggling, let's knock the shit out of this room, he was laughing, maybe he was crying and his nose was running, I just lay there thinking, All right, kid, all right you bastards, this is it.

RICHARD BRAUTIGAN

The Weather in San Francisco

It was a cloudy afternoon with an Italian butcher selling a pound of meat to a very old woman, but who knows what such an old woman could possibly use a pound of meat for?

She was too old for that much meat. Perhaps she used it for a bee hive and she had five hundred golden bees at home waiting for the meat, their bodies stuffed with honey.

"What kind of meat would you like today?" the butcher said. "We have some good hamburger. It's lean."

"I don't know," she said. "Hamburger is something else."

"Yeah, it's lean. I ground it myself. I put a lot of lean meat in it."

"Hamburger doesn't sound right," she said.

"Yeah," the butcher said. "It's a good day for hamburger. Look outside. It's cloudy. Some of those clouds have rain in them. I'd get the hamburger," he said.

"No," she said. "I don't want any hamburger, and I don't think it's going to rain. I think the sun is going to come out and it will be a beautiful day, and I want a pound of liver."

The butcher was stunned. He did not like to sell liver to old

119

ladies. There was something about it that made him very nervous. He didn't want to talk to her any more.

He reluctantly sliced a pound of liver off a huge red chunk and wrapped it up in white paper and put it into a brown bag. It was a very unpleasant experience for him.

He took her money, gave her the change, and went back to the poultry section to try and get a hold of his nerves.

By using her bones like the sails of a ship, the old woman passed outside into the street. She carried the liver as if it were victory to the bottom of a very steep hill.

She climbed the hill and being very old, it was hard on her. She grew tired and had to stop and rest many times before she reached the top.

At the top of the hill was the old woman's house: a tall San Francisco house with bay windows that reflected a cloudy day.

She opened her purse which was like a small autumn field and near the fallen branches of an old apple tree, she found her keys.

Then she opened the door. It was a dear and trusted friend. She nodded at the door and went into the house and walked down a long hall into a room that was filled with bees.

There were bees everywhere in the room. Bees on the chairs. Bees on the photograph of her dead parents. Bees on the curtains. Bees on an ancient radio that once listened to the 1930s. Bees on her comb and brush.

The bees came to her and gathered about her lovingly while she unwrapped the liver and placed it upon a cloudy silver platter that soon changed into a sunny day.

Australia

DAVID BROOKS

Blue

It was a summer of fires and shark attacks. No rain for four months. Every day the newspapers brought accounts of foreign wars and preternatural disasters: a planeload of people disappearing over the Bay of Bengal, a volcano in Indonesia, floods ravaging central China. The fish were not biting. All around The Head, for all the dry weather, a strange blue mold grew on people's cheeses, a new and unknown species of mushroom grew from rotten timber and the damp earth under water tanks, and all that could be caught in the Bay were a few blue-spotted, brown, grouperlike fish at first rumored to be poisonous, though many ate them without ill effect.

The rain itself was never properly reported. The editor and staff of the local paper were away at a weekend conference in the capital, and, although the evidence was everywhere, all of us were somehow impressed into relative silence by the majesty of the event. And who, anyway, would have believed it? When asked later what had led to their strange preparations, those who would talk at all spoke of a recurring sensation in the nose and sinuses as if of the ozone after rain, or of a feeling under the tongue as of that left by a bursting cardamom. This reply, while true enough, was usually sufficient to deflect an idle curiosity, though in truth it was the dreams that started us. Not prophetic dreams exactly, and none of us could really say how we got from them the sense that all our floors and our belongings should be bared. One dreamed that he was bathing in an open cage, the swallows darting around him as he scrubbed. Another dreamed of crossing a high, wooden balcony with her lover, and seeing at the other end two women standing in mannequin postures, looking out to sea, their pale green dresses ragged and their long hair bleached in the sun. Another, my brother, dreamed of receiving a long-awaited letter, and taking it to a huge bay window. He smoothed out the great, blank page at the table and tears came to his eyes as he read it, again and again with rapture.

How so many could have interpreted such diverse things in so similar a way I cannot tell. Perhaps the sight or rumor of what others were doing influenced their understandings; perhaps there were dimensions to these signs and portents that none could detect or consciously register. Whatever it was, in Vincentia, in St. Mary's, in Albatross and Mooney Creek and all the small hamlets in between, on hillsides, on neighboring streets, on curves of the highway, roofs came off the houses, the panellings of weatherboard and fibro left the walls, and here a man could be seen showering in a cage of two-by-fours, there a family could be seen in their lounge-room watching the sky over their television, in the manse at Albatross the housekeeper could be seen through the gaps in the bookshelf she was cleaning, staring across to where the SP bookie was tearing the paper from his shopfront, digging away at the putty of the windows, and from the first stirrings of this strange exposure, just after six on Friday, to the time of the shower on Sunday evening, people all down The Head began living out-of-doors in the comfort of their own carpeted rooms, sitting up late by unseasonal hearth fires, making toast as they had once done as children while all the stars of the southern hemisphere attended. True enough, we laughed at ourselves, but we sat there just the same, rugged against the cool night air, listening to the possums, yarning as we hadn't since our honeymoons.

And at last it came by the bucketful. A short, torrential pour which none could have predicted and which all, mysteriously, recognized as the only true and likely culmination of those strange three days of air and light. Children ran about with buckets, the young people danced, and we who are older just sat in a mute amazement: a short, sharp burst of blue carnations, tiny blooms like great, sky-petalled snowflakes in the evening dust. And we knew, all of a sudden, how terribly, terribly thirsty we had been, and we sat there or sang in the phenomenal rain, and something deep within us was drinking, every stem, every petal, every tiny, perfect flower, slaking, in that long, imperfect summer, a deep, deep need for miracles, for something a little more than rain.

India

KRISHNAN VARMA

The Grass-Eaters

or some time several years ago I was tutor to a spherical boy (now a spherical youth). One day his ovoid father, Ramaniklal Misrilal, asked me where I lived. I told him.

Misrilal looked exceedingly distressed. "A pipe, Ajit Babu? Did you say—a *pipe*, Ajit Babu?"

His cuboid wife was near to tears. "A *pipe*, Ajit Babu? How can you live in a pipe?"

It was true: at that time I was living in a pipe with my wife, Swapna. It was long and three or four feet across. With a piece of sack cloth hung at either end, we had found it far more comfortable than any of our previous homes.

The first was a footpath of Chittaranjan Avenue. We had just arrived in Calcutta from East Bengal where Hindus and Muslims were killing one another. The footpath was so crowded with residents, refugees like us and locals, that if you got up at night to relieve yourself you could not be sure of finding your place again. One cold morning I woke to find that the woman beside me was not Swapna at all but a bag of bones instead. And about fifty or sixty or seventy years old. I had one leg over

124

her too. I paid bitterly for my mistake. The woman very nearly scratched out my eyes. Then came Swapna, fangs bared, claws out . . . I survived, but minus one ear. Next came the woman's husband, a hill of a man, whirling a tree over his head, roaring. That was my impression, anyway. I fled.

Later in the day Swapna and I moved into an abandoned-looking freight wagon at the railway terminus. A whole wagon to ourselves—a place with doors which could be opened and shut—we did nothing but open and shut them for a full hour—all the privacy a man and wife could want—no fear of waking up with a complete stranger in your arms . . . it was heaven. I felt I was God.

Then one night we woke to find that the world was running away from us: we had been coupled to a freight train. There was nothing for it but to wait for the train to stop. When it did, miles from Calcutta, we got off, took a passenger train back, and occupied another unwanted-looking wagon. That was not the only time we went to bed in Calcutta and woke up in another place. I found it an intensely thrilling experience, but not Swapna.

She wanted a a stationary home; she insisted on it. But she would not say why. If I persisted in questioning her she snivelled. If I tried to persuade her to change her mind, pointing out all the advantages of living in a wagon—four walls, a roof and door absolutely free of charge, and complete freedom to make love day or night—she still snivelled. If I ignored her nagging, meals got delayed, the rice undercooked, the curry over-salted. In the end I gave in. We would move, I said, even if we had to occupy a house by force, but couldn't she tell me the reason, however irrelevant, why she did not like the wagon?

For the first time in weeks Swapna smiled, a very vague smile. Then, slowly, she drew the edge of her sari over her head, cast her eyes down, turned her face from me, and said in a tremulous, barely audible whisper that she (short pause) did (long

pause) not want (very long pause) her (at jet speed) baby-to-be-
born-in-a-running-train. And she buried her face in her hands.
Our fourth child. One died of diphtheria back home (no longer
our home) in Dacca; two, from fatigue, on our long trek on foot
to Calcutta. Would the baby be a boy? I felt no doubt about it;
it would be. Someone to look after us in our old age, to do our
funeral rites when we died. I suddenly kissed Swapna, since
her face was hidden in her hands, on her elbow, and was roundly
chided. Kissing, she holds, is a western practice, unclean also,
since it amounts to licking, and should be eschewed by all good
Hindus.

I lost no time in looking for a suitable place for her confine-
ment. She firmly rejected all my suggestions: the railway station platform (too many residents); a little-used overbridge (she
was not a kite to live so high above the ground); a water tank
that had fallen down and was empty (Did I think that she was
a frog?). I thought of suggesting the municipal primary school
where I was teaching at the time, but felt very reluctant. Not
that the headmaster would have objected if we had occupied
one end of the back veranda: a kindly man, father of eleven, all
girls, he never disturbed the cat that regularly kittened in his
in-tray. My fear was: suppose Swapna came running into my
class, saying, "Hold the baby for a moment, will you? I'm going
to the l-a-t-r-i-n-e." Anyway, we set out to the school. On the
way, near the Sealdah railway station, we came upon a cement
concrete pipe left over from long-ago repairs to underground
mains. Unbelievably, it was not occupied and, with no prompt-
ing from me, she crept into it. That was how we came to live in
a pipe.

"It is not proper," said Misrilal, "not at all, for a school master to live in a pipe." He sighed deeply. "Why don't you move
into one of my buildings, Ajit Babu?"

The house I might occupy, if I cared to, he explained, was in

Entally, not far from where the pipe lay; I should have no difficulty in locating it; it was an old building and there were a number of old empty coal tar drums on the roof; I could live on the roof if I stacked the drums in two rows and put a tarpaulin over them.

We have lived on that roof ever since. It is not as bad as it sounds. The roof is flat, not gabled, and it is made of cement concrete, not corrugated iron sheets. The rent is far less than that of other tenants below us—Bijoy Babu, Akhanda Chatterjee and Sagar Sen. We have far more light and ventilation than they. We don't get nibbled by rats and mice and rodents as often as they do. And our son, Prodeep, has far more room to play than the children below.

Prodeep is not with us now; he is in the Naxalite underground. We miss him, terribly. But there is some compensation, small though it is. Had he been with us, we would have had to wear clothes. Now, we don't. Not much, that is. I make do with a loin cloth and Swapna with a piece slightly wider to save our few threadbare clothes from further wear and tear. I can spare little from my pension for new clothes. Swapna finds it very embarrassing to be in my presence in broad daylight so meagerly clad and so contrives to keep her back turned to me. Like a chimp in the sulks. I am fed up with seeing her backside and tell her that she has nothing that I have not seen. But she is adamant; she will not turn around. After nightfall, however, she relents: we are both nightblind.

When we go out—to the communal lavatory, to pick up pieces of coal from the railway track, to gather grass—we do wear clothes. Grass is our staple food now: a mound of green grass boiled with green peppers and salt, and a few ladles of very thin rice gruel. We took to eating it when the price of rice started soaring. I had a good mind to do as Bijoy Babu below us is believed to be doing. He has a theory that if you reduce your consumption of food by five grams each day, you will not only not notice that you are eating less but after some time you can do without any food at all. One day I happened to notice that he was not very steady on his feet. That gave me pause. He can get around, however badly he totters, because he has two legs; but I have only one. I lost the other after a fall from the roof of a tram. In Calcutta the trams are always crowded and if you can't get into a carriage you may get up on its roof. The conductor will not stop you. If he tries to, the passengers beat him up, set fire to the tram and any other vehicles parked in the vicinity, loot nearby shops, break street lamps, take out a procession, hold a protest meeting, denounce British imperialism, American neo-colonialism, the central government, capitalism and socialism, and set off crackers. I don't mind my handicap at all; I need wear only one sandal and thereby save on footwear.

So, on the whole, our life together has been very eventful. The events, of course, were not always pleasant. But, does it matter? We have survived them. And now, we have no fears or anxieties. We have a home made of coal tar drums. We eat two square meals of grass every day. We don't need to wear clothes. We have a son to do our funeral rites when we die. We live very quietly, content to look at the passing scene: a tram burning, a man stabbing another man, a woman dropping her baby in a garbage bin.

United States

KENNETH BERNARD

Preparations

I tend to become absorbed with possibilities other people find
absurd. For example, what if the telephone rings while you are
standing naked after a shower? Come quick, your child is
unconscious. She is a block away. She has a chronic illness. You
know what she needs. What do you do? Take the medication
you need and rush over naked? Or take the extra minute to put
on clothes? Which might be a fateful minute: you arrive dressed
but too late. Put it in all its variations—you are making love, in
conference, on the toilet, late for an appointment, about to eat:
somebody needs you at once—the vast majority of mankind would
arrive too late. Yet what good citizen, yourself included, would
hesitate to smile at the man or woman who ran naked through
the street? It simply is not done.

Obviously I am not talking nonsense. But thinking this way
does make nonsense of my life. Looking at friends, I wonder,
"Would you rush naked to my dying side?" It is, of course, like
much else, a metaphor. There are many ways to be naked. How
many, and which, trivial things come between you and life?
Are they really trivial? Are they perhaps life itself (which would

require some serious rethinking)? But people do die. Terrible things do happen. Thus much of my internal life is spent *rehearsing* what I would do in certain circumstances. And I confess that I find myself wanting. I am forced to pay more attention to certain *small* things about myself (you can well imagine what) and take my measure anew. And, in a philosophical way, I am aghast, I mutter, I smile even—how odd life is, what a coward I am, what a solid member of society.

I came to these reflections upon hearing of a certain Ukrainian woman I had seen around, a wife, illiterate. Her husband had heart trouble but was getting along. Friends were visiting, former students, a colleague. She was in the bedroom, changing. There was a loud knock: "Anya! Come quick! It's Fred!" (He was not Russian.) She came out instantly and rushed to the parlor. She was wearing only her underpants. She was fifty-five, much overweight, not pretty. Her breasts hung. Her stomach revealed its folds. Under her arms, at her back, was fat. She went to her husband, knelt, spoke maybe ten words, which no one heard, and he died. Of course, I thought, a peasant. She could do that. It didn't matter. But that was not so. She was, I found out, illiterate only in English, was, in fact, quite educated, had even, in her youth, published a book of poems. And that bothered me, as well as a number of other things. I might as well list them. They have no order.

1. What language did she speak to him in, and did it matter? Did Fred understand Russian? Is it possible that he did not understand Russian, that she nevertheless spoke in Russian, and that it was right that she did so, that is, that Fred heard more and better because he did not understand and died with as much grace as possible? (What language did she use when they made love? There is a question here, but irrelevant.)

2. Obviously, had she put on a bathrobe, her husband would have been dead when she got to him. Would it have mattered,

and if so, how much, and to whom? Not to Fred, certainly. The great evaders of life would no doubt quibble in the matter, missing the point entirely, e.g., she could have put on her bathrobe in transit, so to speak.

3. The people there (some were female)—they must have been shocked, perhaps more so at her nakedness than Fred's death. Did they find her gross? Ludicrous? Obscene? Would it have been easier for them had she been younger, slimmer, firmer, prettier?

4. Did Fred see their disgust at her nakedness? Was he, also, perhaps shocked? Did he appreciate the extraordinary swiftness, I might even say nakedness, of her response? Or would he have preferred to die more decorously, unspoken to by a fat and naked wife in full view of students, colleagues, friends?

5. When Anya finally got up, did she look at any of them? Did she suddenly feel naked? How did she walk out, as she must have, to get dressed (some things we always finish, if we live)? Did any one of them touch her, put an arm over her, perhaps hold her? Did anyone think to cover her, and if so, did she think how *ridiculous*, he is *dying!* May you choke on my flesh!

6. Was she sweating? Or was she cold as ice? Did she smell?

7. What had she looked like when young? Were there children? Why had I, before this incident, thought her a peasant? Why wasn't her English better? What were her poems about? Had they been translated?

8. The incident, I am sure, is etched inside the skulls of those who were privileged to bear witness. Does it remain sharp-edged, uncomfortable, troubling? Do they keep up the relationship? Do they avoid her, drop her? Does she retreat to her *Russians*, her language family? If she had been *completely* naked, could

they have lived, on any terms, with the memory? (What is the memory of those who hear the sounds and see the bodies of the mutilated of the world?)

9. How do they retell the story? What recedes, what becomes highlighted? Do they laugh more with each retelling? Or does the sour taste remain? Do they wonder about their own deaths, who will or will not be present and why? Will they, the next time, be among the dying, the present or the absent?

This woman is a mystery to me. She has something I do not have, and I do not know why. She had come to her dying husband and grasped his heart in her raw hand. It is the nature of civilization, of any culture, in fact, to interpose *things* (clothing, manners, systems of thought) between people and *life*, by which I mean the hidden life that simmers or bubbles beneath the surface like some molten pool out of dim time. The savage, I realize, is no different from me. Reduction is everywhere the law, perhaps the necessary law: there is no game without it. I wear my clothes; the savage carries his feather or magic pebble. We both suffer grievous loss for it; sometimes we even die for it. Only individuals escape, but who they are, how and why, I do not know. But I recognize their superiority, as I recognize the tragic limits and realness of my own *hesitations:* the measure of any civilization is in its hesitations, its pauses, its reservations. Outside of them is wildness, lawlessness, that is as frightening and lonely as it is free. And it is there that Anya is situated.

I have come to bear her a kind of cosmic love. I do not speak to her, but I have made certain modifications in my life to accommodate her existence. They are modest, to be sure, but I think they move in the right direction. For example, I don't sleep as well. It is conscious, on my part. I am deliberately more likely to awaken at a moment's notice. I am not about to go running anywhere *naked*, with my backside, so to speak, unwiped, but I definitely sleep less well. And, oddly, I *dream* much more. Also, I eat differently. For years, it was my custom, when the telephone rang at dinner, to have my wife answer and say we were eating, could they call back. For a while I considered leaving it off the hook at dinner but thought my regular callers might eventually feel rebuffed. But now, when it rings, my wife (who is watching me carefully) says, "Just a moment," and there I am, quickly swallowing my microcosm of food, ready for whatever it is. It is trivial, perhaps even silly, yet I feel *proud*, a little more than proud, possibly a bit mad. If ever I were to die, it would be so comforting to me to have fat Anya, naked, kneeling, hovering over me, sweating like a pig, muttering incomprehensible guttural sweet Russian to me. If I could speak, I would answer, oh, so happily, *"Yes. Yes. I know. You are right. Hold me, Anya."* And it would be all right.

New Zealand / Maori

PATRICIA GRACE

At the River

The morepork *is the native owl of New Zealand, whose night call sounds like "more pork."*

Sad I wait, and see them come slow back from the river. The torches move slow.

To the tent to rest after they had gone to the river, and while asleep the dream came. A dream of death. He came to me in the dream, not sadly but smiling, with hand on heart and said, I go but do not weep. No weeping, it is my time.

Woke then and out into the night to watch for them with sadness on me, sadness from the dream. And waiting, there came a morepork with soft wingbeat and rested above my head. "Go," I said to the bird. "He comes not with you tonight. He is well and strong. His time is not here."

But it cried, the morepork. Its call went out. Out and out until the tears were on my face. And now I wait and I see the torches come, they move slow back from the river. Slow and sad they move and I think of him. Many times have we come to this place for eels. Every year we come at this time. Our children come and now our grandchildren, his and mine. This is the river for eels and this the time of year.

A long way we have travelled with our tents and food stores,

our lamps and bedding and our big eel drums. Much work for
us today preparing our camp. But now our camp is ready and
they have gone with the torches downriver to the best eel place.
And this old lady stays behind with her old kerosene lamp and
the campfire dying, and the little ones sleeping in their beds.
Too tired for the river tonight, too old for the work of catching
eels. But not he. He is well and strong. No aching back or tired
arms he. No bending, no sadness on him or thoughts of death
like this old one.

His wish but not mine to come here this year. "Too old," I
said to him. "Let the young ones go. Stay back we two and tend
our sweet potatoes and corn."

"This old body," he said. "It hungers for the taste of eel."

"The drums will be full when they return," I said. "Let them
bring the eels to us, as they would wish to do."

"Ah no," he said. "Always these hands have fetched the food
for the stomach. The eels taste sweeter when the body has worked
in fetching."

"Go then," I said, and we prepared.

I think of him now as I await their return. "My time is here,"
he said in the dream, and now the bird calls out. And I think
too of the young ones who spoke to him today in a new way, a
way I did not like.

Before the night came they worked, all of them, to make their
torches for the river. Long sticks from the tea-tree, long and
straight. Tins tied at the tops of the sticks, and in the tins rags
soaked in oil. A good light they made as they left tonight for the
river. Happy and singing they went with their torches. But I
see the lights return now, dim. Dim and slow they come and
sadly I await them.

And the young ones, they made their eel hooks. Straight sticks
with strong hooks tied for catching eels. He smiled to see the
eel hooks, the straight sticks with the strong hooks tied.

"Your hooks," he said. "They work for the hands?" But the young ones did not speak, instead bent heads to the work of tying hooks.

Then off, the young ones, to the hills for hare bait as the sun went down. Happy they went with the gun. Two shots went out and we awaited their return. The young ones, they came back laughing. Happy they came with the hare. "Good bait this," they said. "Good bait and good hooks. Lots of eels for us tonight."

But their nanny said to them, "A hook is good for the eel but bad for the leg. Many will be there at the river tonight, your uncles, aunties, big cousins, your nanny too. Your hooks may take a leg in place of an eel. The old way, with the stick, and the bait tied is a safe way and a good way. You waste your time with hooks."

But the young ones rolled on the ground. "Ho, Grandpa," they called, "You better watch your leg tonight. The hook might get your leg, Grandpa."

"And watch your hand, Grandpa, the eel might get your hand."

"Bite your hand off, Grandpa. You better watch out."

Did not like their way of talking to their nanny but he has patience with the young.

"You'll see," he said. "You want to know how to get eels then you watch your grandpa."

They did not keep quiet, the young ones after that. Called out to him in a way I did not like, but he is patient.

"Ah, Grandpa, that old way of yours is no good. That way is old like you, Grandpa."

"You might end up in the river with your old way of catching eels."

Spoke sharply to them then in our own language.

"Not for you to speak in this manner. Not our way to speak

like this. It is a new thing you are doing. It is a bad thing you have learned."

No more talk from these two then, but laughing still, and he spoke up for them.

"They make their torches, the boys, and they make the hooks, and then they go to the hills for hare. They think of the river and the eels in the river, and then they punch each other and roll on the ground. Shout and laugh waiting for the night to come. The funny talk it means nothing."

"Enough to shout and fight," I said. "Enough to roll on the ground and punch each other, but the talk needs to stay in the mouth."

Put my head down then not pleased, and worked at my task of kneading the bread for morning.

Now I wait and stir the ashes round the oven while the morning bread cooks, and on the ashes I see my tears fall. The babies sleep behind me in the tent, and above me the bird cries.

Much to do after a night of eeling when the drum is full. From the fire we scrape away the dead ashes to put into the drum of eels. All night our eels stay there in the drum of ashes to make easier the task of scraping. Scrape off the ashes and with it comes the sticky eel slime. Cut the eels, and open them out then ready for smoking. The men collect green wood from the tea-tree for our smoke drum. Best wood this, to make a good smoke. Good and clear. All day our smoke house goes. Then wrap our smoked eel carefully and pack away before night comes and time for the river again.

But no eels for us this night. No scraping and smoking and packing this time. Tonight our camp comes down and we return. The dim lights come and they bring him back from the river. Slow they bring him.

Now I see two lights come near. The two have come to bring me sad news of him. But before them the bird came, and before the bird the dream—he in the dream with hand on heart.

And now they stand before me, the boys, heads down. By the dim torchlight I see the tears on their faces, they do not speak.

"They bring your nanny back," I say. "Back from the river." But they do not speak.

"Hear the morepork," I say to them. "It calls from the trees. Out and out it cries. They bring him back from the river, I see your tears."

"We saw him standing by the river," they say. "Saw him bend, looking into the water, and then we saw him fall."

They stand, the young ones in the dim torchlight with tears on their faces, the tears fall. And now they come to me, kneeling by me, weeping.

"We spoke bad to him," they say. "They were bad things we said. Now he has fallen and we have said bad things to him."

So I speak to them to comfort them. "He came to me tonight with hand on heart. 'Do not weep,' he said. 'It is my time.' Not your words that made him fall. His hand was on his heart. Hear the morepork cry. His time is here."

And now we weep together, this old lady and these two young ones by her. No weeping he said. But we will weep a little while for him and for ourselves. He was our strength.

We weep and they return. His children and mine return from the river bearing him. Sad they come in the dim light of torches. The young ones help me to my feet, weeping still, and I go toward them as they come.

And in my throat I feel a cry well up. Lonely it sounds across the night. Lonely it sounds, the cry that comes from in me.

ISAK DINESEN

The Blue Jar

There was once an immensely rich old Englishman who had
been a courtier and a councillor to the Queen and who now, in
his old age, cared for nothing but collecting ancient blue china.
To that end he travelled to Persia, Japan and China, and he was
everywhere accompanied by his daughter, the Lady Helena. It
happened, as they sailed in the Chinese Sea, that the ship caught
fire on a still night, and everybody went into the lifeboats and
left her. In the dark and the confusion the old peer was separated from his daughter. Lady Helena got up on deck late, and
found the ship quite deserted. In the last moment a young English
sailor carried her down into a lifeboat that had been forgotten.
To the two fugitives it seemed as if fire was following them
from all sides, for the phosphorescence played in the dark sea,
and, as they looked up, a falling star ran across the sky, as if it
was going to drop into the boat. They sailed for nine days, till
they were picked up by a Dutch merchantman, and came home
to England.

The old lord had believed his daughter to be dead. He now
wept with joy, and at once took her off to a fashionable water-

139

ing-place so that she might recover from the hardships she had gone through. And as he thought it must be unpleasant to her that a young sailor, who made his bread in the merchant service, should tell the world that he had sailed for nine days alone with a peer's daughter, he paid the boy a fine sum, and made him promise to go shipping in the other hemisphere and never come back. "For what," said the old nobleman, "would be the good of that?"

When Lady Helena recovered, and they gave her the news of the Court and of her family, and in the end also told her how the young sailor had been sent away never to come back, they found that her mind had suffered from her trials, and that she cared for nothing in all the world. She would not go back to her father's castle in its park, nor go to Court, nor travel to any gay town of the continent. The only thing which she now wanted to do was to go, like her father before her, to collect rare blue china. So she began to sail, from one country to the other, and her father went with her.

In her search she told the people, with whom she dealt, that she was looking for a particular blue color, and would pay any price for it. But although she bought many hundred blue jars and bowls, she would always after a time put them aside and say: "Alas, alas, it is not the right blue." Her father, when they had sailed for many years, suggested to her that perhaps the color which she sought did not exist. "O God, Papa," said she, "how can you speak so wickedly? Surely there must be some of it left from the time when all the world was blue."

Her two old aunts in England implored her to come back, still to make a great match. But she answered them: "Nay, I have got to sail. For you must know, dear aunts, that it is all nonsense when learned people tell you that the seas have got a bottom to them. On the contrary, the water, which is the noblest of the elements, does, of course, go all through the earth, so that our planet really floats in the ether, like a soap bubble.

And there, on the other hemisphere, a ship sails, with which I have got to keep pace. We two are like the reflection of one another, in the deep sea, and the ship of which I speak is always exactly beneath my own ship, upon the opposite side of the globe. You have never seen a big fish swimming underneath a boat, following it like a dark-blue shade in the water. But in that way this ship goes, like the shadow of my ship, and I draw it to and fro wherever I go, as the moon draws the tides, all through the bulk of the earth. If I stopped sailing, what would those poor sailors who made their bread in the merchant service do? But I shall tell you a secret," she said. "In the end my ship will go down, to the centre of the globe, and at the very same hour the other ship will sink as well—for people call it sinking, although I can assure you that there is no up and down in the sea—and there, in the midst of the world, we two shall meet."

Many years passed, the old lord died and Lady Helena became old and deaf, but she still sailed. Then it happened, after the plunder of the summer palace of the Emperor of China, that a merchant brought her a very old blue jar. The moment she set eyes on it she gave a terrible shriek. "There it is!" she cried. "I have found it at last. This is the true blue. Oh, how light it makes one. Oh, it is as fresh as a breeze, as deep as a deep secret, as full as I say not what." With trembling hands she held the jar to her bosom, and sat for six hours sunk in contemplation of it. Then she said to her doctor and her lady-companion: "Now I can die. And when I am dead you will cut out my heart and lay it in the blue jar. For then everything will be as it was then. All shall be blue round me, and in the midst of the blue world my heart will be innocent and free, and will beat gently, like a wake that sings, like the drops that fall from an oar blade." A little later she asked them: "Is it not a sweet thing to think that, if only you have patience, all that has ever been, will come back to you?" Shortly afterwards the old lady died.

Cyprus

PANOS IOANNIDES

Gregory

y hand was sweating as I held the pistol. The curve of the trigger was biting against my finger.

Facing me, Gregory trembled.

His whole being was beseeching me, "Don't!"

Only his mouth did not make a sound. His lips were squeezed tight. If it had been me, I would have screamed, shouted, cursed.

The soldiers were watching . . .

The day before, during a brief meeting, they had each given their opinions: "It's tough luck, but it has to be done. We've got no choice."

The order from Headquarters was clear: "As soon as Lieutenant Rafel's execution is announced, the hostage Gregory is to be shot and his body must be hanged from a telegraph pole in the main street as an exemplary punishment."

It was not the first time that I had to execute a hostage is this war. I had acquired experience, thanks to Headquarters which had kept entrusting me with these delicate assignments. Gregory's case was precisely the sixth.

The first time, I remember, I vomited. The second time I got sick and had a headache for days. The third time I drank a bottle of rum. The fourth, just two glasses of beer. The fifth time I joked about it, "This little guy, with the big pop-eyes, won't be much of a ghost!"

But why, dammit, when the day came did I have to start thinking that I'm not so tough, after all? The thought had come at exactly the wrong time and spoiled all my disposition to do my duty.

You see, this Gregory was such a miserable little creature, such a puny thing, such a nobody, damn him.

That very morning, although he had heard over the loud-speakers that Rafel had been executed, he believed that we would spare his life because we had been eating together so long.

"Those who eat from the same mess tins and drink from the same water canteen," he said, "remain good friends no matter what."

And a lot more of the same sort of nonsense.

He was a silly fool—we had smelled that out the very first day Headquarters gave him to us. The sentry guarding him had got dead drunk and had dozed off. The rest of us with exit permits had gone from the barracks. When we came back, there was Gregory sitting by the sleeping sentry and thumbing through a magazine.

"Why didn't you run away, Gregory?" we asked, laughing at him, several days later.

And he answered, "Where would I go in this freezing weather? I'm O.K. here."

So we started teasing him.

"You're dead right. The accommodations here are splendid . . ."

"It's not bad here," he replied. "The barracks where I used to be are like a sieve. The wind blows in from every side . . ."

We asked him about his girl. He smiled.

"Maria is a wonderful person," he told us. "Before I met her she was engaged to a no-good fellow, a pig. He gave her up for another girl. Then nobody in the village wanted to marry Maria. I didn't miss my chance. So what if she is second-hand. Nonsense. Peasant ideas, my friend. She's beautiful and good-hearted. What more could I want? And didn't she load me with watermelons and cucumbers every time I passed by her vegetable garden? Well, one day I stole some cucumbers and melons and watermelons and I took them to her. 'Maria,' I said, 'from now on I'm going to take care of you.' She started crying and then me, too. But ever since that day she has given me lots of trouble—jealousy. She wouldn't let me go even to my mother's. Until the day I was recruited, she wouldn't let me go far from her apron strings. But that was just what I wanted . . ."

He used to tell this story over and over, always with the same words, the same commonplace gestures. At the end he would have a good laugh and start gulping from his water jug.

His tongue was always wagging! When he started talking, nothing could stop him. We used to listen and nod our heads, not saying a word. But sometimes, as he was telling us about his mother and family problems, we couldn't help wondering, "Eh, well, these people have the same headaches in their country as we've got."

Strange, isn't it!

Except for his talking too much, Gregory wasn't a bad fellow. He was a marvelous cook. Once he made us some apple tarts, so delicious we licked the platter clean. And he could sew, too. He used to sew on all our buttons, patch our clothes, darn our socks, iron our ties, wash our clothes . . .

How the devil could you kill such a friend?

Even though his name was Gregory and some people on his side had killed one of ours, even though we had left wives and children to go to war against him and his kind—but how can I explain? He was our friend. He actually liked us! A few days before, hadn't he killed with his own bare hands a scorpion that was climbing up my leg? He could have let it send me to hell!

"Thanks, Gregory!" I said then, "Thank God who made you . . ."

When the order came, it was like a thunderbolt. Gregory was to be shot, it said, and hanged from a telegraph pole as an exemplary punishment.

We got together inside the barracks. We sent Gregory to wash some underwear for us.

"It ain't right."

"What is right?"

"Our duty!"

"Shit!"

"If you dare, don't do it! They'll drag you to court-martial and then bang-bang . . ."

Well, of course. The right thing is to save your skin. That's only logical. It's either your skin or his. His, of course, even if it was Gregory, the fellow you've been sharing the same plate with, eating with your fingers, and who was washing your clothes that very minute.

What could I do? That's war. We had seen worse things.

So we set the hour.

We didn't tell him anything when he came back from the washing. He slept peacefully. He snored for the last time. In the morning, he heard the news over the loudspeaker and he saw that we looked gloomy and he began to suspect that something was up. He tried talking to us, but he got no answers and then he stopped talking.

He just stood there and looked at us, stunned and lost . . .

Now, I'll squeeze the trigger. A tiny bullet will rip through his chest. Maybe I'll lose my sleep tonight but in the morning I'll wake up alive.

Gregory seems to guess my thoughts. He puts out his hand and asks, "You're kidding, friend! Aren't you kidding?"

What a jackass! Doesn't he deserve to be cut to pieces? What a thing to ask at such a time. Your heart is about to burst and he's asking if you're kidding. How can a body be kidding about such a thing? Idiot! This is no time for jokes. And you, if you're such a fine friend, why don't you make things easier for us? Help us kill you with fewer qualms? If you would get angry—curse our Virgin, our God—if you'd try to escape it would be much easier for us and for you.

So it is now.

Now, Mr. Gregory, you are going to pay for your stupidities whole-sale. Because you didn't escape the day the sentry fell asleep; because you didn't escape yesterday when we sent you all alone to the laundry—we did it on purpose, you idiot! Why didn't you let me die from the sting of the scorpion?

So now don't complain. It's all your fault, nitwit.

Eh? What's happening to him now?

Gregory is crying. Tears flood his eyes and trickle down over his cleanshaven cheeks. He is turning his face and pressing his forehead against the wall. His back is shaking as he sobs. His hands cling, rigid and helpless, to the wall.

Now is my best chance, now that he knows there is no other solution and turns his face from us.

I squeeze the trigger.

Gregory jerks. His back stops shaking up and down.

I think I've finished him! How easy it is . . . But suddenly he starts crying out loud, his hands claw at the wall and try to pull it down. He screams, "No, no . . ."

I turn to the others. I expect them to nod, "That's enough."

They nod, "What are you waiting for?"

I squeeze the trigger again.

The bullet smashed into his neck. A thick spray of blood spurts out.

Gregory turns. His eyes are all red. He lunges at me and starts punching me with his fists.

"I hate you, hate you . . ." he screams.

I emptied the barrel. He fell and grabbed my leg as if he wanted to hold on.

He died with a terrible spasm. His mouth was full of blood and so were my boots and socks.

We stood quietly, looking at him.

When we came to, we stooped and picked him up. His hands were frozen and wouldn't let my legs go.

I still have their imprints, red and deep, as if made by a hot knife.

"We will hang him tonight," the men said.

"Tonight or now?" they said.

I turned and looked at them one by one.

"Is that what you all want?" I asked.

They gave me no answer.

"Dig a grave," I said.

Headquarters did not ask for a report the next day or the day after. The top brass were sure that we had obeyed them and had left him swinging from a pole.

They didn't care to know what happened to that Gregory, alive or dead.

Translated by Marion Byron Raizis and Catherine Raizis

HERNÁN LARA ZAVALA

Iguana Hunting

In those days we went into the wild to hunt. I had come from the city to stay with my grandparents in Zitilchen for my holidays, and I'd already made some friends. From the low hill that rises south of town, Chidra, the half-breed Mayan, would first go to call for Crispin. When he reached the house, he gave a long whistle and out Crispin came: short, nervous, cunning. Then they came to fetch me. On their way they collected the stones we were to use. They were special stones, almost round, and they rattled in our pockets as we journeyed on.

When they got to our farm Chidra whistled again, and my grandfather would come to the door to let them in. Chidra lived in the wild, and had eaten no food. Not so Crispin. He lived a few streets away and I knew he had had a good breakfast. Both, however, accepted the hot chocolate and rolls my grandmother offered them. While we ate, my grandfather, tall but stooping, joked gravely with us, as was his manner. With Crispin particularly: the old man was very fond of Crispin. He used to call him "don Crispin" and every now and then he'd suggest jobs for him inspired by his diminutive stature and resilient character. He asked him once: "How would you like to join the army when you grow up? Your height would be greatly in your favor." Crispin responded with a dutiful chuckle, revealing the dough between his teeth. In the meantime, Chidra, his mind elsewhere, ate voraciously. My grandfather seldom addressed him. I recall, however, one of his few observations about Chidra. He was talking to Crispin about Padre Garcia's extravagantly mystical sermons: "No," he said, "you're qualified for all sorts of jobs but not that of a priest. You're too much of this world. I would have to think of somebody else for that . . . Chidra, for instance." I don't remember Chidra's reaction.

Although we actually proposed iguana hunting, our expeditions were likely to involve anything. In our forays we spent our time looking for V-shaped branches to make catapults with, or stealing wedges of honeycomb from the hives left out in the fields. Often, as we were walking out of town, we would climb the wall of some orchard to steal oranges or to take a swim in the reservoir. On such occasions I arrived home for dinner clutching my damp underpants in my hand. As soon as my grandmother saw me she'd say: "Have you been swimming in Tomás's reservoir again? The day he finds out you'll be in big trouble and it'll be no use coming to me."

Many were the times we went out to hunt, but it has to be admitted that iguanas were not easy prey. We'd occasionally catch one—and then we'd sell it to a well-known iguana-eater in town—but their natural colors served them all too well. We hunted turtle-doves, lizards, and, on one occasion even an armadillo that Chidra grabbed by the tail. As soon as we were on our own, shooting here and there at the slightest movement in the bushes, Chidra, who in the presence of adults was invariably silent and reserved, could restrain himself no longer. He would tell us the strange occurrences that, according to him, he experienced in his daily walk back home. These tales always provoked Crispin's anger and contempt. Chidra spoke, for instance, about the afternoon when, returning home from town, he had seen a herd of elephants.

"I yelled out for help but nobody came . . ."

"That was when you took coffee for the first time in your bloody life. I don't know how many coffees you had, but it drove you crazy," said Crispin, annoyed.

Chidra, however, would not be swayed. He told us that sometimes when he was on his way home toward midnight he could hear somebody hissing insistently: "pssst . . . pssst . . ." But he never dared turn around to see who it was because he was sure the noises were produced by Xtabay, the evil woman from Mayan mythology. He explained to us that those who turned to see her could not resist her summons since, apart from her feet, her beauty was irresistible. She hid behind the trunk of a ceybo tree and those who responded to her charms woke up next morning with their bodies covered with thorns.

We knew the legend of course. But when Chidra talked about it, he was charged with such conviction that almost every boy in town—Crispin excepted—listened to him enthralled. He told us about a cave in the heart of the wild that led directly to hell. He told us about a wandering Indian, known as Tzintzinito, who was condemned to roam endlessly through the wild.

On one of those mornings Chidra told us that while returning from the camp where his father worked collecting gum, he had seen a naked woman with beautiful long hair bathing in a deep pool. Half joking, half serious, Crispin said:

"Of course you'll tell us she was Xtabay."

"I don't know," answered Chidra. "The woman I saw in the pool had the whitest feet I ever saw. She had long golden hair."

"He's a liar."

"No, I'm not," said Chidra, crossing himself and kissing his thumb.

"When was this?" I asked.

"Yesterday afternoon."

"That's hardly the time Xtabay would come out."

"We'll get him now," said Crispin. "Prove it."

"If you want. But I'd better tell you it's a long way."

"He's afraid," said Crispin.

"Let's go," answered Chidra. "If you're willing, let's go."

Chidra knew the area well. Not only because he lived in the wild but because of his father's work. Chidra was responsible for bringing him food and other necessities every so often. Once in the wild he was the official guide. We left town. We passed the orchards, we passed the hives, we penetrated the wild. We struggled through the undergrowth, parting bushes and trampling weeds. Chidra, confident of his capabilities, moved his head restlessly like a wild animal on a fresh scent.

There was something uncanny about the whole affair. In Zitilchen, days are usually hot and cloudless. That day, however, was humid and gray. When we were in the thickest and most tangled part of the wild we suddenly came across some ancient ruins. Crispin and I were stunned. It was a small abandoned Mayan village but so well kept that it seemed inhabited. We were silent, looking around in awe. After a while Chidra said, "This way. We're nearly there now." Crispin stared at me. I could sense that, like myself, he was afraid as well as fascinated.

Chidra moved forward again, parting the scrub that stood in our way. Nobody thought about the iguanas. Our sole concern was finding out the truth about Chidra's tale. Finally we came to the edge of a large pool. It was a transparent green and its waters were unusually quiet and still. There was nobody around. We found a clearing and hid behind some mangrove trees while we tried to agree what to do. Perhaps there never had been anyone around, except in Chidra's imagination. Crispin wanted to go back to town and repeated constantly that Chidra was a liar. A bloody liar. They had a long argument and were about to come to blows when I saw somebody moving on the other side of the pool. We quickly fell silent, curious to see who it was. A bearded man appeared. We could see him clearly: he was dressed for the bush. He wore glasses and was smoking a pipe. He had a saucepan and as he came to the edge of the pool, he put some soil in the pot and sank it in the water, emptying it some moments later. He was about to leave when a woman, dressed just like him, appeared, bringing a few more utensils to be washed. We couldn't hear what they were saying.

"There she is," said Chidra slowly.

And it was true, she was just as Chidra had described her: a tall, blonde woman. We saw them for just a few minutes; as soon as they finished their washing they left the pool. We stayed on, still waiting, when Crispin broke our silence. He stood up and said, "Shit! I've got a dreadful itching. What the hell is it?" He lifted up his shirt to show us his back.

"Ticks," said Chidra.

"Blast!" said Crispin as he took off his shirt.

"We must be covered in them too," Chidra said to me, looking at his ankles, scratching himself and standing up to take off his own shirt. I did the same. We undressed ourselves in order to shake off the ticks from our clothes. Chidra even had ticks in his armpits, entangled in the wispy hair. We were covered in them. We were still naked when Chidra began to talk about the woman we had briefly seen, full of the fact that this proved he was no liar. He told us again how, the day before, as he was wandering around the mangroves, he had seen a tall, blonde, white woman bathing in the pool. He described her meticulously. He had seen her in her entirety: feminine, naked, almost divine. He was enraptured. Carried away by Chidra's description, I noticed, at first with alarm and then with relief, that all three of us were experiencing the very same sensation.

Our bodies full of ticks, very tired, we got back to Zitilchen well after dark. We reached my grandfather's farm. I waved good-bye to Crispin and Chidra. My eyelids were heavy. My friends walked down the street. I thought about the blonde woman. I felt the ticks all over my body. Thorns. I was exhausted yet Chidra had a long way to go. Once in the house I went straight to my grandmother.

"I'm covered in ticks," I said. "Help me get rid of them."

"What's a few ticks," she answered, "They're not black widows. Come on then, off with your clothes and lie down in bed while I warm up some wax."

Feeling her press me all over with the hot wax, I heard her ask:

"For heaven's sake, there's thousands of them! Where on earth have you been?"

"Today we met Xtabay," I answered, satisfied.

Translated by the author in collaboration
with Andrew C. Jefford

MONICA WOOD

Disappearing

When he starts in, I don't look anymore, I know what it looks like, what he looks like, tobacco on his teeth. I just lie in the deep sheets and shut my eyes. I make noises that make it go faster and when he's done he's as far from me as he gets. He could be dead he's so far away.

Lettie says leave then stupid but who would want me. Three hundred pounds anyway but I never check. Skin like tapioca pudding, I wouldn't show anyone. A man.

So we go to the pool at the junior high, swimming lessons. First it's blow bubbles and breathe, blow and breathe. Awful, hot nosefuls of chlorine. My eyes stinging red and patches on my skin. I look worse. We'll get caps and goggles and earplugs and body cream Lettie says. It's better.

There are girls there, what bodies. Looking at me and Lettie out the side of their eyes. Gold hair, skin like milk, chlorine or no.

They thought when I first lowered into the pool, that fat one parting the Red Sea. I didn't care. Something happened when I floated. Good said the little instructor. A little redhead in an emerald suit, no stomach, a depression almost, and white wet

154

skin. Good she said you float just great. Now we're getting
somewhere. The whistle around her neck blinded my eyes. And
the water under the fluorescent lights. I got scared and couldn't
float again. The bottom of the pool was scarred, drops of gray
shadow rippling. Without the water I would crack open my
head, my dry flesh would sound like a splash on the tiles.

At home I ate a cake and a bottle of milk. No wonder you
look like that he said. How can you stand yourself. You're no
Cary Grant I told him and he laughed and laughed until I threw
up.

When this happens I want to throw up again and again until
my heart flops out wet and writhing on the kitchen floor. Then
he would know I have one and it moves.

So I went back. And floated again. My arms came around
and the groan of the water made the tight blondes smirk but I
heard Good that's the crawl that's it in fragments from the redhead when I lifted my face. Through the earplugs I heard her
skinny voice. She was happy that I was floating and moving too.

Lettie stopped the lessons and read to me things out of magazines. You have to swim a lot to lose weight. You have to stop
eating too. Forget cake and ice cream. Doritos are out. I'm not
doing it for that I told her but she wouldn't believe me. She
couldn't imagine.

Looking down that shaft of water I know I won't fall. The
water shimmers and eases up and down, the heft of me doesn't
matter I float anyway.

He says it makes no difference I look the same. But I'm not
the same. I can hold myself up in deep water. I can move my
arms and feet and the water goes behind me, the wall comes
closer. I can look down twelve feet to a cold slab of tile and not
be afraid. It makes a difference I tell him. Better believe it mis-
ter.

Then this other part happens. Other men interest me. I look
at them, real ones, not the ones on TV that's something else

entirely. These are real. The one with the white milkweed hair who delivers the mail. The meter man from the light company, heavy thick feet in boots. A smile. Teeth. I drop something out of the cart in the supermarket to see who will pick it up. Sometimes a man. One had yellow short hair and called me ma'am. Young. Thin legs and an accent. One was older. Looked me in the eyes. Heavy, but not like me. My eyes are nice. I color the lids. In the pool it runs off in blue tears. When I come out my face is naked.

The lessons are over, I'm certified. A little certificate signed by the redhead. She says I can swim and I can. I'd do better with her body, thin calves hard as granite.

I get a lane to myself, no one shares. The blondes ignore me now that I don't splash the water, know how to lower myself silently. And when I swim I cut the water cleanly.

For one hour every day I am thin, thin as water, transparent, invisible, steam or smoke.

The redhead is gone, they put her at a different pool and I miss the glare of the whistle dangling between her emerald breasts. Lettie won't come over at all now that she is fatter than me. You're so uppity she says. All this talk about water and who do you think you are.

He says I'm looking all right, so at night it is worse but sometimes now when he starts in I say no. On Sundays the pool is closed I can't say no. I haven't been invisible. Even on days when I don't say no it's all right, he's better.

One night he says it won't last, what about the freezer full of low-cal dinners and that machine in the basement. I'm not doing it for that and he doesn't believe me either. But this time there is another part. There are other men in the water I tell him. Fish he says. Fish in the sea. Good luck.

Ma you've lost says my daughter-in-law, the one who didn't want me in the wedding pictures. One with the whole family, she couldn't help that. I learned how to swim I tell her. You should try it, it might help your ugly disposition.

They closed the pool for two weeks and I went crazy. Repairing the tiles. I went there anyway, drove by in the car. I drank water all day.

Then they opened again and I went every day, sometimes four times until the green paint and new stripes looked familiar as a face. At first the water was heavy as blood but I kept on until it was thinner and thinner, just enough to hold me up. That was when I stopped with the goggles and cap and plugs, things that kept the water out of me.

There was a time I went the day before a holiday and no one was there. It was echoey silence just me and the soundless empty pool and a lifeguard behind the glass. I lowered myself so slow it hurt every muscle but not a blip of water not a ripple not one sound and I was under in that other quiet, so quiet some tears got out, I saw their blue trail swirling.

The redhead is back and nods, she has seen me somewhere. I tell her I took lessons and she still doesn't remember.

This has gone too far he says I'm putting you in the hospital. He calls them at the pool and they pay no attention. He doesn't touch me and I smile into my pillow, a secret smile in my own square of the dark.

Oh my God Lettie says what the hell are you doing what the hell do you think you're doing. I'm disappearing I tell her and what can you do about it not a blessed thing.

For a long time in the middle of it people looked at me. Men. And I thought about it. Believe it, I thought. And now they don't look at me again. And it's better.

I'm almost there. Almost water.

The redhead taught me how to dive, how to tuck my head and vanish like a needle into skin, and every time it happens, my feet leaving the board, I think, this will be the time.

Taiwan

YUAN CH'IUNG-CH'IUNG

A Lover's Ear

He noticed that she carried an earpick in her purse. She told him that her ears itched from time to time, and she carried it with her so she could clean her ears whenever she felt like it.

He asked her if she would mind cleaning his ears for him. They also itched from time to time.

The two of them had strong feelings for one another by this time, and they had already done a lot of things together.

In fact, she had used her earpick only on herself, never to clean anyone else's ears. She had always felt that cleaning someone else's ears was the height of intimacy—except, of course, when it was done professionally. Her own mother had been the only other person ever to clean her ears. It seemed to her that if a relationship was lacking either in passion or in trust, there was little chance that one person would clean the other's ears.

She giggled nervously. "Now?" she asked.

They had agreed to meet somewhere else this time, at some open, well-lighted place where there were lots of people. A public place. She had insisted on it. She had told him she didn't want to go to his place or to her place. There was so much passion in their relationship at that point that whenever they were alone they fell immediately into each other's arms. That left them no time to do anything else.

He smiled in return. Taking her hand in his and holding it tightly, he looked her straight in the eye and said softly and a little conspiratorially: "Yes, now." The very same tone of voice he always used when he wanted to do *it*. He would say: "I want to put it in."

She could tell she was blushing. Two women at the next table were just then talking about a man. No more than three paces separated the two tables, so that every word the two women said came through as clear as a bell.

He was sitting opposite her, but fortunately the table was small. She told him to lay his head down on the table, the right side up. His large head took up nearly half the tabletop. Since it was right there in front of her, she could work on his ear with ease. She was able to look straight down into his ear canal. He had fleshy ears and a wide opening to his ear canal. It was strange how you could know absolutely everything about someone you were in love with, how you could see the most private parts of his body, yet surprisingly would never really notice his ears. Since the lighting was on the dim side, she couldn't see all that clearly as she cleaned his ear. She asked if she was hurting him. "No," he said.

When she had finished with the right ear, he turned his head to the other side. Neither of them spoke while she was cleaning his ear, so they could hear every word spoken at the next table. One of the women was saying to the other: "What in the world could have happened? With all that love, I just don't understand it." They were discussing a relationship that had gone sour for no apparent reason. She was concentrating so hard on cleaning his left ear that her eyes began to blur; just then her hand slipped. "Ouch!" he complained tenderly, as though the pain itself were an expression of love. "Oh-oh," she hastened to apologize. "I'm sorry." Drops of blood appeared on the inside wall of his ear. She didn't have the nerve to tell him. "I'm not going to do it anymore," was all she said.

He sat up and felt around in his ear with his pinky. His eyes narrowed as he savored the feeling. He then gave her the oddest look as he said: "That was sort of like putting it in, wasn't it?"

They broke up not long after that.

Their breakup was accompanied by a very unpleasant scene. It took her a long, long time to get over her feelings of loathing for him and pity for herself. Her only reaction to the news that he had gotten married was indifference—not a trace of emotion. He had become totally irrelevant to her life.

From now on, she reflected, his wife can clean his ears for him.

Inexplicably, this thought saddened her—she suddenly felt very, very sad.

Translated by Howard Goldblatt

BARRY YOURGRAU

By the Creek

I come into the kitchen. My mother screams. Finally she lowers her arm from in front of her face. "What are you doing, are you out of your *mind!*" she demands. I grin at her, in my bermudas and bare feet. "It's okay," I tell her in a chambered voice through my father's heavy, muffling lips. "He's taking a nap, he won't care." "What do you mean he won't *care*," she says. "It's his *head*. For god's sake put it back right now before he wakes up." "No," I tell her, pouting, disappointed that her only response is this remonstration, "I'll put it back in a while." "Not in a while, *now*," she says. She moves her hands as if to take the head from me, but then her hands stammer and withdraw, repulsed by horror. "My *god*," she says, grimacing, wide-eyed. She presses her hands to her face. "Go away! Go away from here!" "Mom," I protest, nonplussed. But she shrinks away from me. "Get out of here!" she cries.

I stalk out of the kitchen. Hurt and surprised, I plod heavily up the stairs. I go into my parents' bedroom. I stand at the foot of the bed. My father lies on his back, mercifully unable to snore, one arm slung across his drum-like hairy chest in a pose particular to his sleep. I look at him. Then I back away, stealth-ily, one step at a time, out the door. On silent, bare feet I steal frenetically down the hall, down the front stairs and out the front door. On the street I break into a run but the head sways violently and I slow to a scurrying walk, until I'm in the woods. Then I take my time on the path, brooding, my hands in my bermuda pockets. I come to the creek and stand balancing on dusty feet on a hot, prominent rock. The mid-afternoon sun lays heavy, glossy patches on the water and fills the trees with a still, hot, silent glare. A bumble bee drones past, then comes back and hovers inquiringly. I get off the rock and stoop down, bracing the head with one hand, and pick up a pebble. I get back on the rock and fling the pebble at the creek. It makes a ring in the water. Another ring suddenly blooms beside it. I look around at the path. A friend of mine comes out of the trees. "Hi," I say to him. "Hi," he says, in a muffled, confined voice. He stops a few feet from me. "You look funny," he says. "So do you," I tell him. I make room for him on the rock. "Where's your dad?" I ask him. "In the hammock," he says. "Where's yours?" "We don't have a hammock," I tell him. "He's in bed."

Half an hour later there are half a dozen of us standing great-headed at the side of the creek.

Guatemala

RODRIGO REY ROSA

The Book

The book founders when it goes needlessly into the relation of certain pleasures.

Before the start of the voyage, it tells of a bathroom. It describes the hot water issuing from the tap, and it pauses to recall the sound it made. It speaks of the light coming in through the window and of soapsuds and of the memories that return as he bathes.

Afterward, or even during the bath, someone knocks at the door. He is handed a letter which he reads quickly. He dresses and eats something, packs a valise and takes some money from a box. Then he goes to see the friend who sent him the letter.

They talk a while, he spends the night there, and early the following morning he leaves from a port.

Days later he arrives in a city he calls Ogman. He decides to stop over there, in order to summon up memories of the sound an anchor makes as it drops into the water, and the sound made by the chains that attach a ship to the dock.

The port looks like a market. Without his being aware of it, a boy, or a youth with the face of a boy, dark-skinned, is waiting for him. He calls him by name. Then he leads him far down a narrow alley, until they reach a blue door in a white wall. Surely he is afraid. He mentions many dark eyes and strange smells. They have walked for two hours before arriving at the door, and the author busies himself noting down what he sees: rare plants, dissected snakes, dried roses, and the recently severed heads of goats or sheep, women with everything covered save their eyes, incenses of various hues, and swords and daggers adorned with skins and precious stones. They stop and his guide gives four raps on the door.

There is something different and unexpected in that house. Music sounds continuously. As one listens to it, one becomes confused. The old man who opened the door asks him to sit down at the table, scarcely distinguishable from the floor. Presently he brings a bottle of something dark, along with two identical stone mugs. He fills them and swallows the contents of one, gesturing to the other man to do likewise.

Although at first he was pleased by the interior lighting, it now begins to bother him. When he looks at his host, it seems to him that the man's gaze pierces his skin.

Still neither one of them speaks. Suddenly he feels the need of viewing himself in a mirror; he glances around the room, but sees none.

The old man gets up and goes into the adjoining room. The house has no doors between the rooms—only weighted curtains.

The music is dying away. The light grows feeble: one can sense the arrival of night. From behind the curtain in the next room a voice begins to intone. The rhythm and some of the melody he recognizes, but he is unable to make out the words. He stands up and the voice grows clearer. The curtain moves slightly, as if stirred by the wind. Then it seems to him that he is looking at a girl, and he confuses her silhouette with the shadow of the old man. He takes a step forward, his vision clouds, and the shadow and the silhouette disappear. At that point the book ends.

Translated by Paul Bowles

TALAT ABBASI

Facing the Light

I wish to be fair to you," he says and the head goes up as it always does when he wishes to be fair to her. And in sympathy, in solidarity, the eyebrows and nose rise to the occasion, positioning themselves upwards. And the mouth tightens into a straight line to underline it all. And together they all say the same thing: And now you may thank us, and now you may thank us. And she, bent over her sewing machine, pricks her finger with its needle which she is pretending to thread and snatches up a tissue, wipes off the drop of blood and tosses it in the direction of the maidservant. The woman springs out of the sea of silk and muslin on the Persian carpet, giggles as she catches it, darts across to the wastepaper basket and still giggling, leaps back into the pile of saris. The room is looking like a smuggler's den with trunks and suitcases spilling out hoards of dazzling material. And there is scarcely room to stand let alone sit for rolls of georgette are billowing on the sofa, brocades are draped over chairs and everything is flowing onto the carpet where a clean bedsheet has been spread.

The seasons are changing. Another few days and summer

will be upon Karachi, stretching endlessly like the desert itself from which hot winds are already rising. The brush with cool weather a memory.

So they are right in the midst of sorting out her wardrobe, packing away the heavier silks and satins and unpacking the cool cottons and frothy chiffons and she is instructing the little maidservant—these for washing, these for dry cleaning, that black one throw over to me, I have just the magenta and purple border to liven it up. That petticoat for mending. And this whole lot kicked towards her, all that for throwing out. Yes yes of course that is what she meant—that she could have them all. But no, again no, not this midnight blue chiffon sari, most certainly not. Is she in her senses that she can even ask again? A thousand, twelve hundred rupees for the embroidery alone, for these hundreds of silver sequins—real silver, each one of them, sprinkled all over like stars. And she, whenever she'd worn it, so like a goddess who on a summer night stepping out of heaven had hastily snatched a piece of the star-spangled sky to cover herself with. For after all, that had been the whole idea, she'd designed it herself with herself in mind. And now give it away to a servant? Just like that? Throw it down the drain? Preposterous. How did she dare ask again? How did she dare even think? Yes even if the silver was tarnished, even if every single star had blackened and the sari no more than a shabby rag. Which shouldn't have happened because she herself had packed it away at the end of last season, with these hands, trusting no one, wrapped it up in layer upon layer of muslin, buried it like a mummy, deep inside a steel trunk. Safe, airtight. She'd been so certain the Karachi air couldn't possibly get to it and tarnish the silver. But it had and had snuffed out the stars like candles. And now, on her lap, this veil of darkness, dullness.

And he chooses that precise moment to rap so loudly with his cane on her bedroom door that the midnight blue sari slithers

167

to her feet, an inky shadow. She quickly bends over her sewing machine, pretending to thread the needle. What's he doing here at this time, jamming the doorway of her bedroom? Never home for dinner why here even before tea? "Malik Sahib," announces the woman as though she needs assistance in recognizing her own husband of twenty-two—three—years. And rushes to evict a stack of summer cotton saris which have usurped the sofa. But he makes an impatient gesture with his hands and remains standing and immediately begins to be fair to her. So anxious is he to be fair to her.

"Go to your quarter," she says to the woman, for she cannot allow him to be fair to her in front of the servants. Not when he's going out of his way to be fair to her and she can tell that he's going to outdo himself in fairness today. She can tell by that red flower which has blossomed overnight upon his chest and is now blazing out of his button hole. She can tell by that moustache, till yesterday steel grey, stiff as a rod, today henna red, oiled, curled softly, coaxed gently to a fine point at both edges. Like a pair of wings dipped in a rosy sunset! And as surely as a pair of wings ever did fly she can tell that that moustache will fly tonight.

"But the saris . . ." Such a thrill of excitement has shot through her, lighting up the saucer eyes in the dark face as though car headlights have suddenly flashed in a tunnel. She must stay, she must listen. She mustn't miss a word of this.

"Later."

The woman dares not say another word and hurriedly picks up her slippers at the door.

"Tea in half an hour," she says to the woman so he doesn't spend all evening being fair to her.

The door is closing after her and he is already stretching himself up to his full height—and beyond—in preparation for ultimate fairness to her. Striding over, he will come straight to the point. He will not waste his time blaming her for anything because he realizes that she cannot help herself. And because she will in any case pay for it, regret it all, regrets made more bitter by the remembrance of his own decency throughout, for after all how many men, how many men—but no, straight to the point. Looming over her, smiling, positively beaming down at her in anticipation of her shock at his news, he must tell her that it is too late for regrets. He is leaving. Yes. Leaving and this time it is final. She heard right. She did not imagine it. But in case she thinks she did, he will thump the ground with his cane. Three times he will thump the ground with his cane. And three times the ground reverberates. Final. Final. Final. Yet he will be fair to her. Indeed more than. He will be generous. Large hearted.

And so, his chest is swelling, expanding, the petals on it trembling as it grows larger and larger. In any case, he has a position to maintain and so she will be maintained in the style which she has always been used to and which—stretching himself further up, risking a launch into space in his determination to be fair to her—a man in his position can well afford. Therefore car, house, servants, nothing will change. And looking down at her as at a pebble he has just flung at the bottom of a well he reassures her: car, house, servants . . .

Car, house, servants! Tea in five minutes, she should've said. For—car, house, servants—what more was there? Her fault, her mistake, her stupidity thinking a half hour would be needed, thinking there was so much to say now when not a word had ever been spoken before.

Is she listening? Is she listening?

Noises. Just noises. Two prisoners in neighbouring cells and no one on the other side. Hence the tapping noises. One tap for food, two for money. Short taps, sharp taps, clear taps. And please, not too many. Just enough to pull along, I in my cell, you in yours.

Has she heard? Car, house, serv . . .

The lid crashes down on the sewing machine, the spool of cotton, the thimble, flying to the floor. The other side then! To the far end of the room, to the window, to her big brass bed, there to spread out the sari, all six yards of it, give it another look, every inch of it, one last chance, for surely, surely in the bright light of day, the sun shining directly on it, it would look different. Yes it would, of course it would, everything looks different in the light. So there by the open window, she would see it again, the sparkle of a thousand stars, lost here, in the shadows of the room. It would still be salvaged. Still be saved.

He cannot believe this. Getting up, walking away, right in the middle of his being fair to her. Leaving him talking as though to himself, turning her back to him . . .

Facing the light. The sari laid out on the bed. The curtains drawn aside. The sun streaming through the window, pouring down the skylight onto the bed, warming the brass, setting afire the ruby carpet. Yet here too, that veil of darkness, dullness, will not yield but instead spreads its claim everywhere. For now she sees that same layer of darkness, dullness, on everything. Nothing is safe then, for it is in the air, the very air. Nothing escapes. Nothing remains the same. The toughest metals suffer. Brass blackens. Silver loses its luster. Gold dulls. This bed. These bangles. Constantly being polished and repolished. Even these grilles on this window. Painted how long ago? A month? Two? And already here, there, in patches, the rust is cutting through. Everything is being attacked. As though an unseen force is snaking its way through the city, choosing its victims, the strongest, the most precious, stalking them, ferreting them out as they lie hidden under paint and polish, shrouded in trunks. Strikes them, robs them of their sparkle, their luster, their very light.

. . . as if he isn't there, as if he doesn't exist. Very well then. Out through that door. This instant.

And some things you simply cannot keep polishing and repolishing no matter how precious they are. Too fragile, the fabric. It will have to be discarded, thrown away on that heap of old clothes. She will have it after all. She will. There is no help for it, for it is in the air, the very air. And so, still facing the light, she begins to fold the sari.

United States

PAUL MILENSKI

Lost Keys

The old dziadz was always the first out of the car, heading downstream, fishing as rapidly as the flow of water until he put some distance between him and me. I used to kid him about it in the company of my brother when all three of us went ice fishing together, standing out on early ice, three figures suspended above water on crystal, waiting for red-flagged signals on our tips. "Maybe that's why you never took to trout fishing, Ron, the old dziadz does not like to keep company. Isn't that right, dziadz?"

"Together, you just scare fish on a stream. You need distance. You know that."

"Ron's sociable, that's why he likes it on the ice."

"He's right, dziadz. When I went with you, I felt like a horse left at the gate."

"Either you fish right or you don't."

The old dziadz drove, had his boots on, his pole put together, the crawlers in a shirt pocket. After he parked the car near the stream, he tossed you the keys and he was gone. "I'll catch you later."

Then, in an hour or two, he would appear quietly, instantaneously, like a stag poking its head through the brush, taking you by surprise. "How you doing?"

After his retirement, he slowed down a little. Once he fell on a slippery rock, broke his glasses. Another time, he got caught in the middle of the stream in a swirling current, filled his boots, had to carry half the stream with him to make it to shore. Then, he turned his ankle terribly when he dropped himself from a high bank to the stream bed.

He began to keep the keys. I asked why, and he said, "So you won't have to worry about them."

The last time out it rained. A cold rain, hard and steady. I caught lots of browns, orange-bellied, hook-jawed. They were right in the middle of the stream, in the rain-swollen currents. You had to get in there, fight the swiftness of the water.

We did not meet on the stream as usual. When I returned to the car, he was already there. He was sitting on the wet ground, his back up against a wheel hub. His clothes were soaked, his hair matted down, his curl gone. His lips were blue.

"Did you limit out already?"

I am sure he heard me.

"Did you quit early?"

His voice was barely audible. "I lost the car keys."

He was somewhere on the stream, so he said, reaching into his pockets for a handkerchief to wipe dirt from his eyes because he was whipped by a streamside branch. That's when he realized he did not have the keys.

"Maybe you locked them in the car?"

He said he had already checked, through the foggy windows, the ignition, the car seat, the mat. He had traced his path along the stream, back and forth. No keys.

"I swear I'm losing everything lately."

"One set of keys—that happens."

173

"Now what are we going to do?" He made a face that I'd never seen him make before; there was so much pain in it. His lips were twisted, his eyes almost pressed closed by the compression of his skin.

I suggested we walk to the nearest house, call my brother, ask him to deliver a spare set of keys. He did not like this idea. I said we could hide our equipment under the car or in the brush, bum rides, be driven back later. This was no good. I asked if he wanted to look some more; maybe two of us working together would spot them. No, his looking had been enough.

What was left?

"I deserve to be left out here in the rain."

"What kind of talk is that?"

"I'm losing everything lately."

"I'm not listening to that."

"It's true."

"No it's not. Jesus, one set of car keys."

"I don't even remember taking them out of the ignition. That's the real truth of it."

"Check your pockets again."

"I did."

"Inside your boot. Maybe they fell in there, are hooked over the leg strap."

"I'd feel them there, wouldn't I? Wouldn't I feel them there, rubbing against my leg?"

"Maybe not."

"I would hear them jingle, I think. Wouldn't I hear them when I walked?"

Then, unaccountably, he moved back down to the stream, staring blankly into the water.

I noticed the keys. They were lying near the wheel hub, where he had sat on them, in the indentation from the weight of his body.

I called to him, told him when he came back that he had given them to me, and I had forgotten. But I saw clearly that this did not work. He dropped his head as though it were a burden, spent a lot of time on this our last trip together standing in the rain, continuing to look at the ground, not wanting to be the first to take his pole apart, not wanting to leave.

DENIS HIRSON

Arrest Me

I want to be arrested so that I can read the Bible. Everyone is being arrested, or receiving special visits in the middle of his dreams, or hearing trees shake when there isn't even a breeze. One might at least expect to walk outside in the morning and find the rosebushes with their toes up in the air, freshly dug holes in the ground around them where someone was prospecting for banned books. But ever since they came for my father, our house has been unfairly ignored.

Once again I begin to think of Genesis. Once again the light is divided from darkness, the waters under the heavens are gathered together unto one place and the dry land appears. But there is always some interruption. I have to drive off to the Greek cafe to buy some cat food, or fetch my brother from judo, or the newspaper lands on the lawn covered in blood.

I unfold it, and out fall foaming dog-bites and well-sharpened bicycle spokes, hose-pipes fixed from gas-taps to lovers' mouths, black widow spiders, boxing gloves and bars of soap. Out fall laws and words of the dead. By the middle of the night the grass is still red.

But the house is so quiet. My brother and sister have sunk into sleep. My mother is learning about nerve messages and electricity. Nyanga the schizophrenic cat is up a tree, stalking moonlight. The house is so quiet, standing in its garden in the night. There are only the termites picking at its foundations, and then my mother running a bath.

Suddenly there is a rash of car doors slamming all around our block and I think to myself this is it, they are coming to take me away. I hold my breath waiting for our gate to squeak open, wondering how I am going to get at my toothbrush now that my mother has locked herself into the bathroom. But then the cars grunt and rumble off, there must have been another meeting at the Cripple School across the road.

I want to be arrested so that I can read the Bible, right through from the beginning to the end. I have had enough of this suspension in the cool jasmine air, neither here nor there, the blacks and the others surrounding me with their ancestral bones and their battles, staking out a birthright which is not mine.

I want four pocked walls and a little lock on the door, steps going in the other direction down the corridor. And then at last I will open the Book, and set out across its fine-beaten burning words.

I will learn their ancient shivering heat, the way they heap and flex and infinitely divide. Facet by facet I will follow the contours of their questioning.

And at night I will watch the darkness cover them, letter by letter claiming their white territory, until they each subside and go dumb. And in their silent company I will lay myself down, flat and faithful as a bookmark, waiting for daylight to deliver the next sentence.

England

JEANETTE WINTERSON

Orion

ere are the coordinates: five hours, thirty minutes right ascension (the coordinate on the celestial sphere analogous to longitude on earth) and zero declination (at the celestial equator). Any astronomer can tell where you are.

It's different isn't it from head back in the garden on a frosty night sensing other worlds through a pair of binoculars? I like those nights. Kitchen light out and wearing Wellingtons with shiny silver insoles. On the wrapper there's an astronaut showing off his shiny silver suit. A short trip to the moon has brought some comfort back to earth. We can wear what Neil Armstrong wore and never feel the cold. This must be good news for star-gazers whose feet are firmly on the ground. We have moved with the times. And so will Orion.

Every 200,000 years or so, the individual stars within each constellation shift position. That is, they are shifting all the time, but more subtly than any tracker dog of ours can follow. One day, if the earth has not voluntarily opted out of the solar system, we will wake up to a new heaven whose dome will again confound us. It will still be home but not a place to take for granted. I wouldn't be able to tell you the story of Orion and say, "Look, there he is, and there's his dog Sirius whose loyalty has left him bright." The dot-to-dot logbook of who we were is not a fixed text. For Orion, who was the result of three of the gods in a good mood pissing on an ox-hide, the only tense he recognized was the future continuous. He was a mighty hunter. His arrow was always in flight, his prey endlessly just ahead of him. The carcasses he left behind became part of his past faster than they could decay. When he went to Crete he didn't do any sunbathing. He rid the island of all its wild beasts. He could really swing a cudgel.

Stories abound. Orion was so tall that he could walk along the sea bed without wetting his hair. So strong he could part a mountain. He wasn't the kind of man who settles down. And then he met Artemis, who wasn't the kind of woman who settles down either. They were both hunters and both gods. Their meeting is recorded in the heavens, but you can't see it every night, only on certain nights of the year. The rest of the time Orion does his best to dominate the skyline, as he always did.

Our story is the old clash between history and home. Or to put it another way, the immeasurable impossible space that seems to divide the hearth from the quest.

Listen to this.

On a wild night, driven more by weariness than by common sense, King Zeus decided to let his daughter do it differently: she didn't want to get married and sit out some war while her man, god or not, underwent the ritual metamorphosis from palace prince to craggy hero; she didn't want children. She wanted to hunt. Hunting did her good.

By morning she had packed and set off for a new life in the woods. Soon her fame spread and other women joined her but

Artemis didn't care for company. She wanted to be alone. In her solitude she discovered something very odd. She had envied men their long-legged freedom to roam the world and return full of glory to wives who only waited. She knew about the history-makers and the home-makers, the great division that made life possible. Without rejecting it, she had simply hoped to take on the freedoms that belonged to the other side. What if she travelled the world and the seven seas like a hero? Would she find something different or the old things in different disguises? She found that the whole world could be contained within one place because that place was herself. Nothing had prepared her for this.

The alchemists have a saying, *Tertium non data*. The third is not given. That is, the transformation from one element into another, from waste matter into best gold is a process that cannot be documented. It is fully mysterious. No one really knows what effects the change. And so it is with the mind that moves from its prison to a vast plain without any movement at all. We can only guess at what happened.

One evening when Artemis had lost her quarry, she lit a fire where she was and tried to rest. But the night was shadowy and full of games. She saw herself by the fire: as a child, a woman, a hunter, a queen. Grabbing the child, she lost sight of the woman and when she drew her bow the queen fled. What would it matter if she crossed the world and hunted down every living creature as long as her separate selves eluded her? In the end when no one was left, she would have to confront herself. Leaving home meant leaving nothing behind. It came too, all of it, and waited in the dark. She realized that the only war worth fighting was the one that raged within; the rest were all diversions. In this small place, her hunting miles, she was going to bring herself home. Home was not a place for the faint-hearted; only the very brave could live with themselves.

In the morning she set out, and set out every morning day after day.

In her restlessness she found peace.

Then Orion came.

He wandered into Artemis's camp, scattering her dogs and bellowing like a bad actor, his right eye patched and his left arm in a splint. She was a mile or so away fetching water. When she returned she saw this huge rag of a man eating her goat. Raw. When he'd finished with a great belch and the fat still fresh around his mouth, he suggested they take a short stroll by the sea's edge. Artemis didn't want to but she was frightened. His reputation hung around him like bad breath. The ragged shore, rock-pitted and dark with weed, reminded him of his adventures and he unravelled them in detail while the tide came in up to her waist. There was nowhere he hadn't been, nothing he hadn't seen. He was faster than a hare and stronger than a pair of bulls. He was as good as a god.

"You smell," said Artemis, but he didn't hear.

Eventually he allowed her to wade in from the rising water and light a fire for them both. No, he didn't want her to talk; he knew about her already. He'd been looking for her. She was a curiosity; he was famous. What a marriage.

But Artemis did talk. She talked about the land she loved and its daily changes. This was where she wanted to stay until she was ready to go. The journey itself was not enough. She spoke quickly, her words hanging on to each other; she'd never told anyone before. As she said it, she knew it was true, and it gave her strength to get up and say goodbye. She turned. Orion raped Artemis and fell asleep.

She thought about that time for years. It took a few moments only and she was really aware of only the hair of his stomach

181

that was matted with sand, scratching her skin. When he'd finished, she pushed him off already snoring. His snores shook the earth. Later, in the future, the time would remain vivid and unchanged. She wouldn't think of it differently; she wouldn't make if softer or harder. She would just keep it and turn it over in her hands. Her revenge had been swift, simple and devastatingly ignominious. She killed him with a scorpion.

In a night, 200,000 years can pass, time moving only in our minds. The steady marking of the seasons, the land well-loved and always changing, continues outside, while inside, light years move us on to landscapes that revolve under different skies.

Artemis lying beside dead Orion sees her past changed by a single act. The future is still intact, still unredeemed, but the past is irredeemable. She is not who she thought she was. Every action and decision has led her here. The moment has been waiting the way the top step of the stairs waits for the sleepwalker. She had fallen and now she is awake. As she looks at the sky, the sky is peaceful and exciting. A black cloak pinned with silver brooches that never need polish. Somebody lives there for sure, wrapped up in the glittering folds. Somebody who recognized that the journey by itself is never enough and gave up spaceships long ago in favour of home.

On the beach the waves made pools of darkness around Artemis's feet. She kept the fire burning, warming herself and feeling Orion grow slowly cold. It takes time for the body to stop playing house.

The fiery circle that surrounded her contained all the clues she needed to recognize that life is for a moment in one shape then released into another. Monuments and cities would fade away like the people who built them. No resting place or palace could survive the light years that lay ahead. There was no history that would not be rewritten, and the earliest days were already too far away to see. What would history make of tonight?

Tonight is clear and bright with a cold wind stirring the waves into peaks. The foam leaves slug trails in rough triangles on the sand. The salt smell bristles the hair inside her nostrils; her lips are dry. She's thinking about her dogs. They feel like home because she feels like home. The stars show her how to hang in space supported by nothing at all. Without medals or certificates or territories she owns, she can burn as they do, travelling through time until time stops and eternity changes things again. She has noticed that change doesn't hurt her.

It's almost light, which means the disappearing act will soon begin. She wants to lie awake watching until the night fades and the stars fade and first grey-blue slates the sky. She wants to see the sun slash the water. But she can't stay awake for everything; some things have to pass her by. So what she doesn't see are the lizards coming out for food or Orion's eyes turned glassy overnight. A small bird perches on his shoulder, trying to steal a piece of his famous hair.

Artemis waited until the sun was up before she trampled out the fire. She brought rocks and stones to cover Orion's body from the eagles. She made a high mound that broke the thudding wind as it scored the shore. It was a stormy day, black clouds and a thick orange glow on the horizon. By the time she had finished, she was soaked with rain. Her hands were bleeding, her hair kept catching in her mouth. She was hungry but not angry now.

The sand that had been blonde yesterday was now brown with wet. As far as she could see there was the grey water white-edged and the birds of prey wheeling above it. Lonely cries and she was lonely, not for friends but for a time that hadn't been violated. The sea was hypnotic. Not the wind or the cold could move her from where she sat like one who waited. She was not waiting; she was remembering. She was trying to find what it was that had brought her here. The third is not given. All she knew was that she had arrived at the frontiers of common sense and crossed over. She was safe now. No safety without risk, and what you risk reveals what you value.

She stood up and in the getting-dark walked away, not looking behind her but conscious of her feet shaping themselves in the sand. Finally, at the headland, after a bitter climb to where the woods bordered the steep edge, she turned and stared out, seeing the shape of Orion's mound, just visible now, and her own footsteps walking away. Then it was fully night, and she could see nothing to remind her of the night before except the stars.

And what of Orion? Dead but not forgotten. For a while he was forced to pass the time in Hades, where he beat up flimsy beasts and cried a lot. Then the gods took pity on him and drew him up to themselves and placed him in the heavens for all to see. When he rises at dawn, summer is nearly here. When he rises in the evening, beware of winter and storms. If you see him at midnight, it's time to pick the grapes. He has his dogs with him, Canis Major and Canis Minor and Sirius, the brightest star in our galaxy. Under his feet, it you care to look, you can see a tiny group of stars: Lepus, the hare, his favourite food.

Orion isn't always at home. Dazzling as he is, like some fighter pilot riding the sky, he glows very faint, if at all, in November. November being the month of Scorpio.

Argentina

LUISA VALENZUELA

The Verb *to Kill*

He kills—he killed—he will kill—he has killed—he had killed—he will have killed—he would have killed—he is killing—he was killing—he has been killing—he would have been killing—he will have been killing—he will be killing—he would be killing—he may kill.

We decided that none of these tenses or moods suited him. Did he kill, will he kill, will he have killed? We think he *is* killing, with every step, with every breath, with every . . . We don't like him to get close to us but we come across him when we go clam-digging on the beach. We walk from north to south, and he comes from south to north, closer to the dunes, as if looking for pebbles. He looks at us and we look at him—did he kill, will he kill, would he have killed, is he killing? We put down the sack with the clams and hold each other's hand till he passes. He doesn't throw so much as one little pebble at us, he doesn't even look at us, but afterward we're too weak in the knees to go on digging clams.

The other day he walked by us and right afterward we found

an injured sea gull on the beach. We took the poor thing home and on the way we told it that we were good, not like him, that it didn't have to be afraid of us, and we even covered it up with my jacket so the cold wind wouldn't hurt its broken wing. Later we ate it in a stew. A little tough, but tasty.

The next day we went back to run on the beach. We didn't see him and we didn't find a single injured sea gull. He may be bad, but he's got something that attracts animals. For example, when we were fishing: hours without a bite until he suddenly showed up and then we caught a splendid sea bass. He didn't look at our catch or smile, and it's good he didn't because he looked more like a murderer than ever with his long bushy hair and gleaming eyes. He just went on gathering his pebbles as though nothing were wrong, thinking about the girls that he has killed, will kill, kills.

When he passes by we're petrified—will it be our turn some-day? In school we conjugate the verb *to kill* and the shiver that goes up our spine isn't the same as when we see him passing on the beach, all puffed up with pride and gathering his pebbles. The shiver on the beach is lower down in our bodies and more stimulating, like sea air. He gathers all those pebbles to cover up the graves of his victims—very small, transparent pebbles that he holds up to the sun and looks through from time to time so as to make certain that the sun exists. Mama says that if he spends all day looking for pebbles, it's because he *eats* them. Mama can't think about anything but food, but I'm sure he eats something else. The last breath of his victims, for example. There's nothing more nourishing than the last sigh, the one that brings with it everything that a person has gathered over the years. He must have some secret for trapping this essence that escapes his victims, and that's why he doesn't need vitamins. My sister and I are afraid he'll catch us some night and kill us to absorb everything that we've been eating over the last few

years. We're terribly afraid because we're well nourished, Mama
has always seen to it that we eat balanced meals and we've never
lacked for fruit or vegetables even though they're very expensive in this part of the country. And clams have lots of iodine,
Mama says, and fish are the healthiest food there is even though
the taste of it bores us but why should he be bored because
while he kills his victims (always girls, of course) he must do
those terrible things to them that my sister and I keep imagining, just for fun. We spend hours talking about the things that
he does to his victims before killing them just for fun. The papers
often talk about degenerates like him but he's one of the worst
because that's all he eats. The other day we spied on him while
he was talking to the lettuce he has growing in his garden (he's
crazy as well as degenerate). He was saying affectionate things
to it and we were certain it was poisoned lettuce. For our part
we don't say anything to lettuce, we have to eat it with oil and
lemon even though it's disgusting, all because Mama says it has
lots of vitamins. And now we have to swallow vitamins for him,
what a bother, because the better fed we are the happier we'll
make him and the more he'll like doing those terrible things the
papers talk about and we imagine, just before killing us so as to
gulp down our last breath full of vitamins in one big mouthful.
He's going to do a whole bunch of things so repulsive we'll be
ashamed to tell anybody, and we only say them in a whisper
when we're on the beach and there's nobody within miles. He's
going to take our last breath and then he'll be as strong as a bull
to go kill other little girls like us. I hope he catches Pocha. But
I hope he doesn't do any of those repulsive things to her before
killing her because she might like it, the dirty thing. I hope he
kills her straightaway by plunging a knife in her belly. But he'll
have his fun with us for a long time because we're pretty and
he'll like our bodies and our voices when we scream. And we
will scream and scream but nobody will hear us because he's

187

going to take us to a place very far away and then he will put in our mouths that terrible thing we know he has. Pocha already told us about it—he must have an enormous thing that he uses to kill his victims.

An enormous one, even though we've never seen it. To show how brave we are, we tried to watch him while he made peepee, but he saw us and chased us away. I wonder why he didn't want to show it to us. Maybe it's because he wants to surprise us on our last day here and catch us while we're pure so's to get more pleasure. That must be it. He's saving himself for our last day and that's why he doesn't try to get close to us.

Not anymore.

Papa finally lent us the rifle after we asked and asked for it to hunt rabbits. He told us we were big girls now, that we can go out alone with the rifle if we want to, but to be careful, and he said it was a reward for doing so well in school. It's true we're doing well in school. It isn't hard at all to learn to conjugate verbs:

He will be killed—he is killed—he has been killed.

Translated by Helen Lane

Italy

ITALO CALVINO

All at One Point

*Through the calculations begun by Edwin P. Hubble
on the galaxies' velocity of recession, we can establish
the moment when all the universe's matter was
concentrated in a single point, before it began to
expand in space.*

Naturally, we were all there—*old Qfwfq said*—where else
could we have been? Nobody knew then that there could be
space. Or time either: what use did we have for time, packed in
there like sardines?

I say "packed like sardines," using a literary image: in reality
there wasn't even space to pack us into. Every point of each of
us coincided with every point of each of the others in a single
point, which was where we all were. In fact, we didn't even
bother one another, except for personality differences, because
when space doesn't exist, having somebody unpleasant like Mr.
Pber^t Pber^d underfoot all the time is the most irritating thing.

How many of us were there? Oh, I was never able to figure
that out, not even approximately. To make a count, we would
have had to move apart, at least a little, and instead we all occupied that same point. Contrary to what you might think, it wasn't
the sort of situation that encourages sociability; I know, for
example, that in other periods neighbors called on one another;
but there, because of the fact that we were all neighbors, nobody
even said good morning or good evening to anybody else.

In the end each of us associated only with a limited number of acquaintances. The ones I remember most are Mrs. Ph(i)Nk$_0$, her friend De XuaeauX, a family of immigrants by the name of Z'zu, and Mr. Pber^t Pber^d, whom I just mentioned. There was also a cleaning woman—"maintenance staff" she was called— only one, for the whole universe, since there was so little room. To tell the truth, she had nothing to do all day long, not even dusting—inside one point not even a grain of dust can enter— so she spent all her time gossiping and complaining.

Just with the people I've already named we would have been overcrowded; but you have to add all the stuff we had to keep piled up in there: all the material that was to serve afterwards to form the universe, now dismantled and concentrated in such a way that you weren't able to tell what was later to become part of astronomy (like the nebula of Andromeda) from what was assigned to geography (the Vosges, for example) or to chemistry (like certain beryllium isotopes). And on top of that, we were always bumping against the Z'zu family's household goods: camp beds, mattresses, baskets; these Z'zus, if you weren't careful, with the excuse that they were a large family, would begin to act as if they were the only ones in the world: they even wanted to hang lines across our point to dry their washing.

But the others also had wronged the Z'zus, to begin with, by calling them "immigrants," on the pretext that, since the others had been there first, the Z'zus had come later. This was more unfounded prejudice—that seems obvious to me—because neither before nor after existed, nor any place to immigrate from, but there were those who insisted that the concept of "immigrant" could be understood in the abstract, outside of space and time.

It was what you might call a narrow-minded attitude, our outlook at that time, very petty. The fault of the environment in which we had been reared. An attitude that, basically, has remained in all of us, mind you: it keeps cropping up even today, if two of us happen to meet—at the bus stop, in a movie house, at an international dentists' convention—and start reminiscing about the old days. We say hello—at times somebody recognizes me, at other times I recognize somebody—and we promptly start asking about this one and that one (even if each remembers only a few of those remembered by the others), and so we start in again on the old disputes, the slanders, the denigrations. Until somebody mentions Mrs. Ph(i)Nk$_o$—every conversation finally gets around to her—and then, all of a sudden, the pettiness is put aside, and we feel uplifted, filled with a blissful, generous emotion. Mrs. Ph(i)Nk$_o$, the only one that none of us has forgotten and that we all regret. Where has she ended up? I have long since stopped looking for her: Mrs. Ph(i)Nk$_o$, her bosom, her thighs, her orange dressing gown—we'll never meet her again, in this system of galaxies or in any other.

Let me make one thing clear: this theory that the universe, after having reached an extremity of rarefaction, will be condensed again has never convinced me. And yet many of us are counting only on that, continually making plans for the time when we'll all be back there again. Last month, I went into the bar here on the corner and whom did I see? Mr. Pber^t Pber^d. "What's new with you? How do you happen to be in this neighborhood?" I learned that he's the agent for a plastics firm, in Pavia. He's the same as ever, with his silver tooth, his loud suspenders. "When we go back there," he said to me, in a whisper, "the thing we have to make sure of is, this time, certain people remain out . . . You know who I mean: those Z'zus . . ."

I would have liked to answer him by saying that I've heard a number of people make the same remark, concluding: "You know who I mean . . . Mr. Pber^t Pber^d . . ."

To avoid the subject, I hasten to say: "What about Mrs. Ph(i)Nk$_o$? Do you think we'll find her back there again?"

"Ah, yes . . . She, by all means . . ." he said, turning purple.

For all of us the hope of returning to that point means, above all, the hope of being once more with Mrs. Ph(i)Nk$_0$. (This applies even to me, though I don't believe it.) And in that bar, as always happens, we fell to talking about her, and were moved; even Mr. Pber^t Pber^d's unpleasantness faded, in the face of that memory.

Mrs. Ph(i)Nk$_0$'s great secret is that she never aroused any jealousy among us. Or any gossip, either. The fact that she went to bed with her friend, Mr. De XuaeauX, was well known. But in a point, if there's a bed, it takes up the whole point, so it isn't a question of *going* to bed, but of *being* there, because anybody in the point is also in the bed. Consequently, it was inevitable that she should be in bed also with each of us. If she had been another person, there's no telling all the things that would have been said about her. It was the cleaning woman who always started the slander, and the others didn't have to be coaxed to imitate her. On the subject of the Z'zu family—for a change!—the horrible things we had to hear: father, daughters, brothers, sisters, mother, aunts: nobody showed any hesitation even before the most sinister insinuation. But with her it was different: the happiness I derived from her was the joy of being concealed, punctiform, in her, and of protecting her, punctiform, in me; it was at the same time vicious contemplation (thanks to the promiscuity of the punctiform convergence of us all in her) and also chastity (given her punctiform impenetrability). In short: what more could I ask?

And all of this, which was true of me, was true also for each of the others. And for her: she contained and was contained with equal happiness, and she welcomed us and loved and inhabited all equally.

We got along so well all together, so well that something extraordinary was bound to happen. It was enough for her to say, at a certain moment: "Oh, if I only had some room, how I'd like to make some noodles for you boys!" And in that moment we all thought of the space that her round arms would occupy, moving backward and forward with the rolling pin over the dough, her bosom leaning over the great mound of flour and eggs which cluttered the wide board while her arms kneaded and kneaded, white and shiny with oil up to the elbows; we thought of the space that the flour would occupy, and the wheat for the flour, and the fields to raise the wheat, and the mountains from which the water would flow to irrigate the fields, and the grazing lands for the herds of calves that would give their meat for the sauce; of the space it would take for the Sun to arrive with its rays, to ripen the wheat; of the space for the Sun to condense from the clouds of stellar gases and burn; of the quantities of stars and galaxies and galactic masses in flight through space which would be needed to hold suspended every galaxy, every nebula, every sun, every planet, and at the same time we thought of it, this space was inevitably being formed, at the same time that Mrs. $Ph(i)Nk_0$ was uttering those words: ". . . ah, what noodles, boys!" the point that contained her and all of us was expanding in a halo of distance in light-years and light-centuries and billions of light-millennia, and we were being hurled to the four corners of the universe (Mr. $Pber^t$ $Pber^d$ all the way to Pavia), and she, dissolved into I don't know what kind of energy-light-heat, she, Mrs. $Ph(i)Nk_0$, she who in the midst of our closed, petty world had been capable of a generous impulse, "Boys, the noodles I would make for you!," a true outburst of general love, initiating at the same moment the concept of space and, properly speaking, space itself, and time, and universal gravitation, and the gravitating universe, making possible billions and billions of suns, and of planets, and fields of wheat, and Mrs. $Ph(i)Nk_0 s$, scattered through the continents of the planets, kneading with floury, oil-shiny, generous arms, and she lost at that very moment, and we, mourning her loss.

Translated by William Weaver

RON CARLSON

Bigfoot Stole My Wife

The problem is credibility.

The problem, as I'm finding out over the last few weeks, is basic credibility. A lot of people look at me and say, sure Rick, Bigfoot stole your wife. It makes me sad to see it, the look of disbelief in each person's eye. Trudy's disappearance makes me sad, too, and I'm sick in my heart about where she may be and how he's treating her, what they do all day, if she's getting enough to eat. I believe he's being good to her—I mean I feel it—and I'm going to keep hoping to see her again, but it is my belief that I probably won't.

In the two and a half years we were married, I often had the feeling that I would come home from the track and something would be funny. Oh, she'd say things: *One of these days I'm not going to be here when you get home*, things like that, things like everybody says. How stupid of me not to see them as omens. When I'd get out of bed in the early afternoon, I'd stand right here at this sink and I could see her working in her garden in her cut-off Levis and bikini top, weeding, planting, watering. I mean it was obvious. I was too busy thinking about the races,

194

weighing the odds, checking the jockey roster to see what I now know: he was watching her too. He'd probably been watching her all summer.

So, in a way it was my fault. But what could I have done? Bigfoot steals your wife. I mean: even if you're home, it's going to be a mess. He's big and not well trained.

When I came home it was about eleven-thirty. The lights were on, which really wasn't anything new, but in the ordinary mess of the place, there was a little difference, signs of a struggle. There was a spilled Dr. Pepper on the counter and the fridge was open. But there was something else, something that made me sick. The smell. The smell of Bigfoot. It was hideous. It was . . . the guy is not clean.

Half of Trudy's clothes are gone, not all of them, and there is no note. Well, I know what it is. It's just about midnight there in the kitchen which smells like some part of hell. I close the fridge door. It's the saddest thing I've ever done. There's a picture of Trudy and me leaning against her Toyota taped to the fridge door. It was taken last summer. There's Trudy in her bikini top, her belly brown as a bean. She looks like a kid. She was a kid I guess, twenty-six. The two times she went to the track with me everybody looked at me like how'd I rate her. But she didn't really care for the races. She cared about her garden and Chinese cooking and Buster, her collie, who I guess Bigfoot stole too. Or ate. Buster isn't in the picture, he was nagging my nephew Chuck who took the photo. Anyway I close the fridge door and it's like part of my life closed. Bigfoot steals your wife and you're in for some changes.

You come home from the track having missed the Daily Double by a neck, and when you enter the home you are paying for and in which you and your wife and your wife's collie live, and your wife and her collie are gone, as is some of her clothing, there is nothing to believe. Bigfoot stole her. It's a fact. What

195

should I do, ignore it? Chuck came down and said something like well if Bigfoot stole her why'd they take the Celica? Christ, what a cynic! Have you ever read anything about Bigfoot not being able to drive? He'd be cramped in there, but I'm sure he could manage.

I don't really care if people believe me or not. Would that change anything? Would that bring Trudy back here? Pull the weeds in her garden?

As I think about it, no one believes anything anymore. Give me one example of someone *believing* one thing. I dare you. After that we get into this credibility thing. No one believes me. I myself can't believe all the suspicion and cynicism there is in today's world. Even at the races, some character next to me will poke over at my tip sheet and ask me if I believe that stuff. If I believe? What is there to believe? The horse's name? What he did the last time out? And I look back at this guy, too cheap to go two bucks on the program, and I say: it's history. It is historical fact here. Believe. Huh. Here's a fact: I believe everything.

Credibility.

When I was thirteen years old, my mother's trailer was washed away in the flooding waters of the Harley River and swept thirty-one miles, ending right side up and nearly dead level just outside Mercy, in fact in the old weed-eaten parking lot for the abandoned potash plant. I know this to be true because I was inside the trailer the whole time with my pal, Nuggy Reinecker, who found the experience more life-changing than I did.

Now who's going to believe this story? I mean, besides me, because I was there. People are going to say, come on, thirty-one miles? Don't you mean thirty-one feet?

We had gone in out of the rain after school to check out a magazine that belonged to my mother's boyfriend. It was a copy of *Dude*, and there was a fold-out page I will never forget of a girl lying on the beach on her back. It was a color photograph. The girl was a little pale, I mean, this was probably her first day out in the sun, and she had no clothing on. So it was good, but what made it great was that they had made her a little bathing suit out of sand. Somebody had spilled a little sand just right, here and there, and the sand was this incredible gold color, and it made her look so absolutely naked it wanted to put your eyes out.

Nuggy and I knew there was flood danger in Griggs; we'd had a flood every year almost and it had been raining for five days on and off, but when the trailer bucked the first time, we thought it was my mother come home to catch us in the dirty book. Nuggy shoved the magazine under the bed and I ran out to check the door. It only took me a second and I hollered back *Hey no sweat, no one's here*, but by the time I returned to see what other poses they'd had this beautiful woman commit, Nuggy already had his pants to his ankles and was involved in what we knew was a sin.

If it hadn't been for the timing of the first wave with this act of his, Nuggy might have gone on to live what the rest of us call a normal life. But the Harley had crested and the head wave, which they estimated to be three feet minimum, unmoored the trailer with a push that knocked me over the sofa, and threw Nuggy, already entangled in his trousers, clear across the bedroom.

I watched the village of Griggs as we sailed through. Some of the village, the Exxon Station, part of it at least, and the carwash, which folded up right away, tried to come along with us, and I saw the front of Painters' Mercantile, the old porch and signboard, on and off all day.

You can believe this: it was not a smooth ride. We'd rip along for ten seconds, dropping and growling over rocks, and rumbling over tree stumps, and then wham! the front end of the trailer would lodge against a rock or something that could stop it, and whoa! we'd wheel around sharp as a carnival ride, worse really, because the furniture would be thrown against the far side and us with it, sometimes we'd end up in a chair and sometimes the chair would sit on us. My mother had about four thousand knickknacks in five big box shelves, and they gave us trouble for the first two or three miles, flying by like artillery, left, right, some small glass snail hits you in the face, later in the back, but that stuff all finally settled in the foot and then two feet of water which we took on.

We only slowed down once and it was the worst. In the railroad flats I thought we had stopped and I let go of the door I was hugging and tried to stand up and then swish, another rush sent us right along. We rammed along all day it seemed, but when we finally washed up in Mercy and the sheriff's cousin pulled open the door and got swept back to his car by water and quite a few of those knickknacks, just over an hour had passed. We had averaged, they figured later, about thirty-two miles an hour, reaching speeds of up to fifty at Lime Falls and the Willows. I was okay and walked out bruised and well washed, but when the sheriff's cousin pulled Nuggy out, he looked genuinely hurt.

"For godsakes," I remember the sheriff's cousin saying, "The damn flood knocked this boy's pants off!" But Nuggy wasn't talking. In fact, he never hardly talked to me again in the two years he stayed at the Regional School. I heard later, and I believe it, that he joined the monastery over in Malcolm County.

My mother, because she didn't have the funds to haul our rig back to Griggs, worried for a while, but then the mayor arranged to let us stay out where we were. So after my long ride in a trailer down the flooded Harley River with my friend Nuggy Reinecker, I grew up in a parking lot outside of Mercy, and to tell you the truth, it wasn't too bad, even though our trailer never did smell straight again.

Now you can believe all that. People are always saying: don't believe everything you read, or everything you hear. And I'm here to tell you. Believe it. Everything. Everything you read. Everything you hear. Believe your eyes. Your ears. Believe the small hairs on the back of your neck. Believe all of history, and all of the versions of history, and all the predictions for the future. Believe every weather forecast. Believe in God, the afterlife, unicorns, showers on Tuesday. Everything has happened. Everything is possible.

I come home from the track to find the cupboard bare. Trudy is not home. The place smells funny: hairy. It's a fact and I know it as a fact: Bigfoot has been in my house.

Bigfoot stole *my* wife.

She's gone.

Believe it.

I gotta believe it.

Brazil

EDLA VAN STEEN

Mr. and Mrs. Martins

It rained all week long and Mrs. Martins didn't leave the house even to do her bit of shopping. Often she checked on the weather, looking down at the street crowded with gleaming cars and open umbrellas, feeling no trace of boredom, but merely affirming: what rain! And she would go back to the television.

Despite her polite and smiling manner when greeting the neighbors, she seemed not to have friends, for no one ever visited her. Even so, she neatly combed her short gray hair and applied her lipstick discreetly, ready for any eventuality. No one wrote her letters and she paid her bills on time.

On Sunday she woke up happy—the sun was coming in through the half-open blinds. She dusted the furniture lightly, fried two eggs, and, as usual, put on her best black silk dress and remembered the pearl necklace. Then she bought a bunch of flowers at the corner and headed for the taxi stop, empty at that hour of the morning.

She was one of the first people to enter the cemetery. She walked slowly, reading the familiar inscriptions, for she was afraid of slipping on the stone pavement, which was still wet.

Something new caught her by surprise: "At last your wife's come to keep you company, eh, Mr. Mario?" She read aloud: "Claire Heller de Alencar 1908–1974. We feel your absence." She counted mentally: eight from fourteen, six; zero from six, six. Eight years older than she. Now the sun burned her back and brightened the plants and flowers in the damp beds. It's strange, she thought, men die before women; there are more widows in the world than widowers. Sighing gently, she started up the hill leading to her sepulchre, an austere marble rectangle that rose several centimeters above the ground. The names were written in gilded letters: Abel Martins 1910 space Laura Martins 1916 space. I'm making a point of leaving everything settled, her husband insisted; we have no children, who would bother with us? We must even prepare for living alone.

She climbed the step to the tomb, took a bundle from her handbag, and put it down on the slab. From the package she removed a tool, one of those with a spade on one end and two teeth for mixing the earth on the other, and she calmly began to tend the bed.

"What beautiful flowers." The man approached, hat and newspaper in hand.

Mrs. Martins greeted him without interrupting her task.

"I didn't think this was the season for immortelles," he went on, politely.

"That's true, I was astonished too."

"They're my favorites. They last longer than any others."

"All right then, as long as they have them at the florist's I'll keep on bringing them." She examined the arrangement.

"And you? Which do you prefer?"

"Violets, but they're difficult . . ."

"Next Sunday it's my turn. I'll try to find a few bunches."

Mrs. Martins gathered the withered plants, threw them into the garbage bin, and, using a handkerchief, wiped off the remnants of earth. The rose and purple hues of the immortelles blended harmoniously. She exhaled a sweet and ecstatic expression for both of them and sat on the step next to her husband.

"Do you want part of the paper? I hear that the rains have destroyed some cities in the south. Here's the article. Look at this picture."

"Oh my, and the people?"

"Whole families were found in the branches of trees where they'd tried to escape from the floods. They'd miscalculated the height of the water."

"How horrible."

When they finished reading, they chatted about details of their week until they ran out of subjects.

At noon they ate crackers and apples.

"Is it awful being a widow?"

"I thought it would be worse. But the apartment is what bothers me. It's too big. If I could rent a smaller one, the size of yours . . . I couldn't go out on account of the rain and I felt really alone."

"That's impossible. Everything's all set. Can't you get used to it?"

Mrs. Martins, submissive, didn't argue. She would wait for another opportunity.

"Doesn't the television help?" he inquired, concerned, without turning his head: he knew that entreating look.

"More or less, and for you?" She looked at him curiously: clean collar and suit, polished shoes. A shame he was losing his former posture, his back bending.

He noted her gaze.

"Remember at what loose ends I was at the beginning? But you, you look wonderful, you even seem to have grown younger."

Dozens of people were visiting their dead—movable colors on the landscape. Soon solitude would resume its post there and in those people capable of hearing its very reverberations—as if their souls had found a refuge in the sound they could still emit. Mr. Martins swallowed a deep sob.

"How many installments are left?"

"None."

"What will happen now?"

"We'll just go on waiting."

"Do you think I'll go first?" Mrs. Martins at once regretted the question, so unguarded.

"Would you like to?"

"No, but I feel prepared. If it happens . . ."

"That's why we're practicing." He wanted to embrace his wife, but he refrained.

She thought the moment opportune for her much rehearsed question:

"What if I bought a cat?"

"And who'll take care of it if . . . ?"

"You're right, it's a silly idea. The poor little thing might suffer." She was embarrassed.

An employee sweeps the ground. He wears patched gray overalls. He's of the type that seems to have sprung up from the very ground, so much a part of the surroundings is he.

Mr. Martins hands him an envelope.

"It's so you'll always come take care of this . . . well, we're old, and even if one of us lingers more than the other, this way your dedication will have been rewarded."

"Really, sir, you needn't worry."

"Please, take it."

The employee shifted his shoulders in a rude gesture: why do these two come here every Sunday? The thought was cut off by someone asking for information.

Mr. and Mrs. Martins proceeded to pass the day conversing and simply enjoying one another's presence. Perhaps fragments of their life in common peopled the ample silences.

"Are you really sure about changing apartments?"

"One bedroom and a living room would be enough."

"We'll take care of it tomorrow," he promised.

She smiled, grateful.

"Do you suppose there's one in this neighborhood?" He consulted his watch. "Let's go, it's almost six."

The cool wind caused him to turn up his coat collar before lending his support to Mrs. Martins for the descent.

"We won't have more rain. The weather's calming down."

Slow shadows appear along the cemetery lanes, swelling the line going back.

Mr. and Mrs. Martins part with a kiss, each taking a separate path: Abel misses the feel of an arm on him; Laura must take care not to stumble.

Translated by Daphne Patai

ISAAC BABEL

Di Grasso

A Tale of Odessa

I was fourteen, and of the undauntable fellowship of dealers in theater tickets. My boss was a tricky customer with a permanently screwed-up eye and enormous silky handle bars; Nick Schwarz was his name. I came under his sway in that unhappy year when the Italian Opera flopped in Odessa. Taking a lead from the critics on the local paper, our impresario decided not to import Anselmi and Tito Ruffo as guest artistes but to make do with a good stock company. For this he was sorely punished; he went bankrupt, and we with him. We were promised Chaliapin to straighten out our affairs, but Chaliapin wanted three thousand a performance; so instead we had the Sicilian tragedian Di Grasso with his troupe. They arrived at the hotel in peasant carts crammed with children, cats, cages in which Italian birds hopped and skipped. Casting an eye over this gypsy crew, Nick Schwarz opined:

"Children, this stuff won't sell."

When he had settled in, the tragedian made his way to the market with a bag. In the evening he arrived at the theater with another bag. Hardly fifty people had turned up. We tried selling tickets at half-price, but there were no takers.

That evening they staged a Sicilian folk drama, a tale as commonplace as the change from night to day and vice versa. The daughter of a rich peasant pledges her troth to a shepherd. She is faithful to him till one day there drives out from the city a young slicker in a velvet waistcoat. Passing the time of day with the new arrival, the maiden giggled in all the wrong places and fell silent when she shouldn't have. As he listened to them, the shepherd twisted his head this way and that like a startled bird. During the whole of the first act he kept flattening himself against walls, dashing off somewhere, his pants flapping, and on his return gazing wildly about.

"This stuff stinks," said Nick Schwarz in the intermission. "Only place it might go down is some dump like Kremenchug."

The intermission was designed to give the maiden time to grow ripe for betrayal. In the second act we just couldn't recognize her: she behaved insufferably, her thoughts were clearly elsewhere, and she lost no time in handing the shepherd back his ring. Thereupon he led her over to a poverty-stricken but brightly painted image of the Holy Virgin, and said in his Sicilian patois:

"Signora," said he in a low voice, turning away, "the Holy Virgin desires you to give me a hearing. To Giovanni, the fellow from the city, the Holy Virgin will grant as many women as he can cope with; but I need none save you. The Virgin Mary, our stainless intercessor, will tell you exactly the same thing if you ask Her."

The maiden stood with her back to the painted wooden image. As she listened she kept impatiently tapping her foot.

In the third act Giovanni, the city slicker, met his fate. He was having a shave at the village barber's, his powerful male legs thrust out all over the front of the stage. Beneath the Sicilian sun the pleats in his waistcoat gleamed. The scene represented a village fair. In a far corner stood the shepherd; silent he stood there amid the carefree crowd. First he hung his head; then he raised it, and beneath the weight of his attentive and burning gaze Giovanni started stirring and fidgeting in his barber chair, till pushing the barber aside he leaped to his feet. In a voice shaking with passion he demanded that the policeman should remove from the village square all persons of a gloomy and suspicious aspect. The shepherd—the part was played by Di Grasso himself—stood there lost in thought; then he gave a smile, soared into the air, sailed across the stage, plunged down on Giovanni's shoulders, and having bitten through the latter's throat, began, growling and squinting, to suck blood from the wound. Giovanni collapsed, and the curtain, falling noiselessly and full of menace, hid from us killed and killer. Waiting for no more, we dashed to the box office in Theater Lane, which was to open next day, Nick Schwarz beating the rest by a short neck. Came the dawn, and with it the *Odessa News* informed the few people who had been at the theater that they had seen the most remarkable actor of the century.

On this visit Di Grasso played *King Lear, Othello, Civil Death*, Turgenev's *The Parasite*, confirming with every word and every gesture that there is more justice in outbursts of noble passion than in all the joyless rules that run the world.

Tickets for these shows were snapped up at five times face value. Scouting round for ticket-traders, would-be purchasers found them at the inn, yelling their heads off, purple, vomiting a harmless sacrilege.

A pink and dusty sultriness was injected into Theater Lane. Shopkeepers in felt slippers bore green bottles of wine and barrels of olives out onto the pavement. In tubs outside the shops macaroni seethed in foaming water, and the steam from it melted in the distant skies. Old women in men's boots dealt in seashells and souvenirs, pursuing hesitant purchasers with loud cries. Moneyed Jews with beards parted down the middle and combed to either side would drive up to the Northern Hotel and tap discreetly on the doors of fat women with raven hair and little mustaches, Di Grasso's actresses. All were happy in Theater Lane; all, that is, save for one person. I was that person. In those days catastrophe was approaching me: at any moment my father might miss the watch I had taken without his permission and pawned to Nick Schwarz. Having had the gold turnip long enough to get used to it, and being a man who replaced tea as his morning drink by Bessarabian wine, Nick Schwarz, even with his money back, could still not bring himself to return the watch to me. Such was his character. And my father's character differed in no wise from his. Hemmed in by these two characters, I sorrowfully watched other people enjoying themselves. Nothing remained for me but to run away to Constantinople. I had made all the arrangements with the second engineer of the S.S. *Duke of Kent*, but before embarking on the deep I decided to say goodbye to Di Grasso. For the last time he was playing the shepherd who is swung aloft by an incomprehensible power. In the audience were all the Italian colony, with the bald but shapely consul at their head. There were fidgety Greeks and bearded externs with their gaze fastened fanatically upon some point invisible to all other mortals; there was the long-armed Utochkin. Nick Schwarz had even brought his missis, in a violet shawl with a fringe; a woman with all the makings of a grenadier she was, stretching right out to the steppes, and with a sleepy little crumpled face at the far end. When the curtain fell this face was drenched in tears.

"Now you see what love means," she said to Nick as they were leaving the theater.

Stomping ponderously, Madam Schwarz moved along Langeron Street; tears rolled from her fishlike eyes, and the shawl with the fringe shuddered on her obese shoulders. Dragging her mannish soles, rocking her head, she reckoned up, in a voice that made the street re-echo, the women who got on well with their husbands.

" 'Ducky' they're called by their husbands; 'sweetypie' they're called . . ."

The cowed Nick walked along by his wife, quietly blowing on his silky mustaches. From force of habit I followed on behind, sobbing. During a momentary pause Madam Schwarz heard my sobs and turned around.

"See here," she said to her husband, her fisheyes agoggle, "may I not die a beautiful death if you don't give the boy his watch back!"

Nick froze, mouth agape; then came to and, giving me a vicious pinch, thrust the watch at me sideways.

"What can I expect of him," the coarse and tear-muffled voice of Madam Schwarz wailed disconsolately as it moved off into the distance, "what can I expect but beastliness today and beastliness tomorrow? I ask you, how long is a woman supposed to put up with it?"

They reached the corner and turned into Pushkin Street. I stood there clutching the watch, alone; and suddenly, with a distinctness such as I had never before experienced, I saw the columns of the Municipal Building soaring up into the heights, the gas-lit foliage of the boulevard, Pushkin's bronze head touched by the dim gleam of the moon; saw for the first time the things surrounding me as they really were: frozen in silence and ineffably beautiful.

Translated by Walter Morison

FENG JICAI

The Street-Sweeping Show

"National Cleanup Week starts today," said Secretary Zhao, "and officials everywhere are going out to join in the street sweeping. Here's our list of participants—all top city administrators and public figures. We've just had it mimeographed over at the office for your approval."

He looked like a typical upper-echelon secretary: the collar of his well-worn, neatly pressed Mao suit was buttoned up military style; his complexion was pale; his glasses utilitarian. His gentle, deferential manner and pleasantly modulated voice concealed a shrewd, hard-driving personality.

The mayor pored over the list, as if the eighty names on it were those of people selected to go abroad. From time to time he glanced thoughtfully at the high white ceiling.

"Why isn't there anyone from the Women's Federation?" he asked.

Secretary Zhao thought for a moment. "Oh, you're right—there isn't! We've got the heads of every office in the city—the Athletic Committee, the Youth League Committee, the Federation of Trade Unions, the Federation of Literary and Art Cir-

cles—even some famous university professors. The only group
we forgot is the Women's Federation."

"Women are the pillars of society. How can we leave out the
women's representatives?" The mayor sounded smug rather than
reproachful. Only a leader could think of everything. This was
where true leadership ability came into play.

Secretary Zhao was reminded of the time when the mayor
had pointed out that the fish course was missing from the menu
for a banquet in honor of some foreign guests.

"Add two names from the Women's Federation, and make
sure you get people in positions of authority or who are proper
representatives of the organization. 'International Working
Women's Red Banner Pacesetters,' 'Families of Martyrs,' or
'Model Workers' would be fine." Like an elementary school
teacher returning a poor homework paper to his student, the
mayor handed the incomplete list back to his secretary.

"Yes, your honor, I'll do it right away. A complete list will
be useful the next time something like this comes up. And I
must contact everyone at once. The street sweeping is sched-
uled for two this afternoon in Central Square. Will you be able
to go?"

"Of course. As mayor of the city, I have to set an example."

"The car will be at the gate for you at one-thirty. I'll go with
you."

"All right," the mayor answered absentmindedly, scratching
his forehead and looking away.

Secretary Zhao hurried out.

At one-thirty that afternoon the mayor was whisked to the
square in his limousine. All office workers, shop clerks, students, housewives, and retirees were out sweeping the streets,
and the air was thick with dust. Secretary Zhao hastily rolled
up the window. Inside the car there was only a faint, pleasant
smell of gasoline and leather.

At the square they pulled up beside a colorful assortment of limousines. In front of them a group of top city administrators had gathered to wait for the mayor's arrival. Someone had arranged for uniformed policemen to stand guard on all sides.

Secretary Zhao sprang out of the limousine and opened the door for his boss. The officials in the waiting crowd stepped forward with smiling faces to greet the mayor. Everyone knew him and hoped to be the first to shake his hand.

"Good afternoon—oh, nice to see you—good afternoon—" the mayor repeated as he shook hands with each of them.

An old policeman approached, followed by two younger ones pushing wheelbarrows full of big bamboo brooms. The old policeman selected one of the smaller, neater brooms and presented it respectfully to the mayor. When the other dignitaries had gotten their brooms, a marshal with a red armband led them all to the center of the square. Naturally the mayor walked at the head.

Groups of people had come from their workplaces to sweep the huge square. At the sight of this majestic, broom-carrying procession, with its marshal, police escort, and retinue of shutter-clicking photographers, they realized that they were in the presence of no ordinary mortals and gathered closer for a look. How extraordinary for a mayor to be sweeping the streets, thought Secretary Zhao, swelling with unconscious pride as he strutted along beside the mayor with his broom on his shoulder.

"Here we are," the marshal said when they had reached the designated spot.

All eighty-two dignitaries began to sweep.

The swelling crowd of onlookers, which was kept back by a police cordon, was buzzing with excitement:

"Look, he's the one over there."

"Which one? The one in black?"

"No. The bald fat one in blue."

"Cut the chitchat!" barked a policeman.

The square was so huge that no one knew where to sweep. The concrete pavement was clean to begin with; they pushed what little grit there was back and forth with their big brooms. The most conspicuous piece of litter was a solitary popsicle wrapper, which they all pursued like children chasing a dragonfly.

The photographers surrounded the mayor. Some got down on one knee to shoot from below, while others ran from side to side trying to get a profile. Like a cloud in a thunderstorm, the mayor was constantly illuminated by silvery flashes. Then a man in a visored cap, with a video camera, approached Secretary Zhao.

"I'm from the TV station," he said. "Would you please ask them to line up single file so they'll look neat on camera?"

Secretary Zhao consulted with the mayor, who agreed to this request. The dignitaries formed a long line and began to wield their brooms for the camera, regardless of whether there was any dirt on the ground.

The cameraman was about to start shooting, when he stopped and ran over to the mayor.

"I'm sorry, your honor," he said, "but you're all going to have to face the other way because you've got your backs to the sun. And I'd also like the entire line to be reversed so that you're at the head."

"All right," the mayor agreed graciously, and he led his entourage, like a line of dragon dancers, in a clumsy turnaround. Once in place, everyone began sweeping again.

Pleased, the cameraman ran to the head of the line, pushed his cap up, and aimed at the mayor. "All right," he said as the camera started to whir, "swing those brooms, all together now— put your hearts into it—that's it! Chin up please, your honor. Hold it—that's fine—all right!"

He stopped the camera, shook the mayor's hand, and thanked him for helping an ordinary reporter carry out his assignment.

"Let's call it a day," the marshal said to Secretary Zhao. Then he turned to the mayor. "You have victoriously accomplished your mission," he said.

"Very good—thank you for your trouble," the mayor replied routinely, smiling and shaking hands again.

Some reporters came running up to the mayor. "Do you have any instructions, your honor?" asked a tall, thin, aggressive one.

"Nothing in particular." The mayor paused for a moment. "Everyone should pitch in to clean up our city."

The reporters scribbled his precious words in their notebooks.

The policemen brought the wheelbarrows back, and everyone returned the brooms. Secretary Zhao replaced the mayor's for him.

It was time to go. The mayor shook hands with everyone again.

"Good-bye—good-bye—good-bye—"

The others waited until the mayor had gotten into his limousine before getting into theirs.

The mayor's limousine delivered him to his house, where his servant had drawn his bathwater and set out scented soap and fresh towels. He enjoyed a leisurely bath and emerged from the bathroom with rosy skin and clean clothes, leaving his grime and exhaustion behind him in the tub.

As he descended the stairs to eat dinner, his grandson hurriedly led him into the living room.

"Look, Granddad, you're on TV!"

There he was on the television screen, like an actor, putting on a show of sweeping the street. He turned away and gave his grandson a casual pat on the shoulder.

"It's not worth watching. Let's go have dinner."

Translated by Susan Wilff Chen

BHARATI MUKHERJEE

Courtly Vision

J ahanara Begum stands behind a marble grille in her palace
at Fatehpur-Sikri.

Count Barthelmy, an adventurer from beyond frozen oceans,
crouches in a lust-darkened arbor. His chest—a tear-shaped fleck
of rust—lifts away from the gray, flat trunk of a mango tree.
He is swathed in the coarse, quaint clothes of his cool-weather
country. Jacket, pantaloons, shawl, swell and cave in ardent
pleats. He holds a peacock's feather to his lips. His face is col-
ored in admonitory pink. The feather is dusty aqua, broken-
spined. His white-gloved hand pillows a likeness of the Begum,
painted on a grain of rice by Basawan, the prized court artist.
Two red-eyed parrots gouge the patina of grass at the adventurer's feet; their buoyant, fluffy breasts caricature the breasts of
Moghul virgins. The Count is posed full-front; the self-wor-
shipful body of a man who has tamed thirteen rivers and seven
seas. Dainty thighs bulge with wayward expectancy. The head
twists savagely upward at an angle unreckoned except in death,
anywhere but here. In profile the lone prismatic eye betrays the
madman and insomniac.

On the terrace of Jahanara Begum's palace, a slave girl kneels; her forearms, starry with jewels, strain toward the fluted handle of a decanter. Two bored eunuchs squat on their fleshy haunches, awaiting their wine. Her simple subservience hints at malevolent dreams, of snake venom rubbed into wine cups or daggers concealed between young breasts, and the eunuchs are menaced, their faces pendulous with premonition.

In her capacious chamber the Begum waits, perhaps for death from the serving-girl, for ravishing, or merely the curtain of fire from the setting sun. The chamber is open on two sides, the desert breeze stiffens her veil into a gauzy disc. A wild peacock, its fanned-out feathers beaten back by the same breeze, cringes on the bit of marble floor visible behind her head. Around the Begum, retainers conduct their inefficient chores. One, her pursed navel bare, slackens her grip on a *morchal* of plumes; another stumbles, biceps clenched, under the burden of a gold hookah bowl studded with translucent rubies and emeralds; a third stoops, her back an eerie, writhing arc, to straighten a low table littered with cosmetics in jewelled pillboxes. The Begum is a tall, rigid figure as she stands behind a marble grille. From her fists, which she holds in front of her like tiny shields, sprouts a closed, upright lotus bloom. Her gaze slips upward, past the drunken gamblers on the roof-terraces, to the skyline where fugitive cranes pass behind a blue cloud.

Oh, beauteous and beguiling Begum, has your slave-girl apprised the Count of the consequences of a night of bliss?

Under Jahanara Begum's window, in a courtyard cooled with fountains into whose basin slaves have scattered rose petals, sit Fathers Aquaviva and Henriques, ingenuous Portuguese priests. They have dogged the emperor through inclement scenery. Now they pause in the emperor's famed, new capital, eyes closed, abstemious hands held like ledges over their brows to divert the sullen desert breeze. Their faces seem porous; the late afternoon has slipped through the skin and distended the chins and cheeks. Before their blank, radiant gazes, seven itinerant jugglers heap themselves into a shuddering pyramid. A courtier sits with the priests on a divan covered with brocaded silk. He too is blind to the courage of gymnasts. He is distracted by the wondrous paintings the priests have spread out on the arabesques of the rug at their feet. Mother and Child. Child and Mother. The Moghul courtier—child of Islam, ruler of Hindus—finds the motif repetitive. What comforting failure of the imagination these priests are offering. What precarious boundaries set on life's playful fecundity. He hears the Fathers murmur. They are devising strategems on a minor scale. They want to trick the emperor into kissing Christ, who on each huge somber canvas is a bright, white, healthy baby. The giant figures seem to him simple and innocuous, not complicated and infuriating like the Hindu icons hidden in the hills. In the meantime his eyes draw comfort from the unclad angels who watch over the Madonna to protect her from heathens like him. Soft-fleshed, flying women. He will order the court artists to paint him a harem of winged women on a single poppy seed.

The emperor will not kiss Christ tonight. He is at the head of his army, riding a piebald horse out of his new walled city. He occupies the foreground of that agate-colored paper, a handsome young man in a sun-yellow *jama*. Under the *jama* his shoulders pulsate to the canny violent rhythm of his mount. Behind him in a thick choking diagonal stream follow his soldiers. They scramble and spill on the sandy terrain; spiky desert grass slashes their jaunty uniforms of muslin. Tiny, exhilarated profiles crowd the battlements. In the women's palace, tinier figures flit from patterned window grille, to grille. The citizens have begun to celebrate. Grandfathers leading children by the wrists are singing of the emperor's victories over invisible rebels. Shopkeepers, coy behind their taut paunches, give away their syrupy sweets. Even the mystics with their haggard, numinous faces have allowed themselves to be distracted by yet another parade.

So the confident emperor departs.

The Moghul evening into which he drags his men with the promise of unimaginable satisfactions is grayish gold with the late afternoon, winter light. It spills down the rims of stylized rocks that clog the high horizon. The light is charged with unusual excitement and it discovers the immense intimacy of darkness, the erotic shadowiness of the cave-deep arbor in which the Count crouches and waits. The foliage of the mango tree yields sudden, bountiful shapes. Excessive, unruly life—monkeys, serpents, herons, thieves naked to the waist—bloom and burgeon on its branches. The thieves, their torsos pushing through clusters of leaves, run rapacious fingers on their dagger blades.

They do not discern the Count. The Count does not overhear the priests. Adventurers all, they guard from each other the common courtesy of their subterfuge. They sniff the desert air and the air seems full of portents. In the remote horizon three guards impale three calm, emaciated men. Behind the low wall of a *namaz* platform, two courtiers quarrel, while a small boy sneaks up and unties their horses. A line of stealthy women prostrate themselves and pray at the doorway of a temple in a patch of browning foliage. Over all these details float three elegant whorls of cloud, whorls in the manner of Chinese painting, imitated diligently by men who long for rain.

The emperor leaves his capital, applauded by flatterers and loyal citizens. Just before riding off the tablet's edge into enemy territory, he twists back on his saddle and shouts a last-minute confidence to his favorite court-painter. He is caught in reflective profile, the quarter-arc of his mustache suggests a man who had permitted his second thoughts to confirm his spontaneous judgments.

218

Give me total vision, commands the emperor. His voice hisses above the hoarse calls of the camels. *You, Basawan, who can paint my Begum on a grain of rice, see what you can do with the infinite vistas the size of my opened hand. Hide nothing from me, my co-wanderer. Tell me how my new capital will fail, will turn to dust and these marbled terraces be home to jackals and infidels. Tell me who to fear and who to kill but tell it to me in a way that makes me smile. Transport me through dense fort walls and stone grilles and into the hearts of men.*

> "Emperor on Horseback Leaves Walled City"
> Painting on Paper, 24 cms x 25.8 cms
> Painter Unknown. No superscription
> c. 1584 A.D.
> Lot No. SLM 4027-66
> Est. Price $750

BERNARD MALAMUD

The Model

Early one morning, Ephraim Elihu rang up the Art Students League and asked the woman who answered the phone how he could locate an experienced female model he could paint nude. He told the woman that he wanted someone of about thirty. "Could you possibly help me?"

"I don't recognize your name," said the woman on the telephone. "Have you ever dealt with us before? Some of our students will work as models, but usually only for painters we know." Mr. Elihu said he hadn't. He wanted it understood he was an amateur painter who had once studied at the League.

"Do you have a studio?"

"It's a large living room with lots of light. I'm no youngster," he said, "but after many years I've begun painting again and I'd like to do some nude studies to get back my feeling for form. I'm not a professional painter, but I'm serious about painting. If you want any references as to my character, I can supply them."

He asked her what the going rate for models was, and the woman, after a pause, said, "Six dollars the hour."

Mr. Elihu said that was satisfactory to him. He wanted to talk longer, but she did not encourage him to. She wrote down his name and address and said she thought she could have someone for him the day after tomorrow. He thanked her for her consideration.

That was on Wednesday. The model appeared on Friday morning. She had telephoned the night before, and they had settled on a time for her to come. She rang his bell shortly after nine, and Mr. Elihu went at once to the door. He was a gray-haired man of seventy who lived in a brownstone house near Ninth Avenue, and he was excited by the prospect of painting this young woman.

The model was a plain-looking woman of twenty-seven or so, and the painter decided her best features were her eyes. She was wearing a blue raincoat, though it was a clear spring day. The old painter liked her but kept that to himself. She barely glanced at him as she walked firmly into the room.

"Good day," he said, and she answered, "Good day."

"It's like spring," said the old man. "The foliage is starting up again."

"Where do you want me to change?" asked the model.

Mr. Elihu asked her her name, and she responded, "Ms. Perry."

"You can change in the bathroom, I would say, Miss Perry, or if you like, my own room—down the hall—is empty, and you can change there also. It's warmer than the bathroom."

The model said it made no difference to her but she thought she would rather change in the bathroom.

"That is as you wish," said the elderly man.

"Is your wife around?" she then asked, glancing into the room.

"No, I happen to be a widower."

He said he had had a daughter once, but she had died in an accident.

The model said she was sorry. "I'll change and be out in a few fast minutes."

"No hurry at all," said Mr. Elihu, glad he was about to paint her.

Ms. Perry entered the bathroom, undressed there, and returned quickly. She slipped off her terry-cloth robe. Her head and shoulders were slender and well formed. She asked the old man how he would like her to pose. He was standing by an enamel-top kitchen table near a large window. On the tabletop he had squeezed out, and was mixing together, the contents of two small tubes of paint. There were three other tubes, which he did not touch. The model, taking a last drag of a cigarette, pressed it out against a coffee-can lid on the kitchen table.

"I hope you don't mind if I take a puff once in a while?"

"I don't mind, if you do it when we take a break."

"That's all I meant."

She was watching him as he slowly mixed his colors.

Mr. Elihu did not immediately look at her nude body but said he would like her to sit in the chair by the window. They were facing a back yard with an ailanthus tree whose leaves had just come out.

"How would you like me to sit, legs crossed or not crossed?"

"However you prefer that. Crossed or uncrossed doesn't make much of a difference to me. Whatever makes you fell comfortable."

The model seemed surprised at that, but she sat down in the yellow chair by the window and crossed one leg over the other. Her figure was good.

"Is this okay for you?"

Mr. Elihu nodded. "Fine," he said. "Very fine."

He dipped his brush into the paint he had mixed on the table-top, and after glancing at the model's nude body, began to paint. He would look at her, then look quickly away, as if he were afraid of affronting her. But his expression was objective. He painted apparently casually, from time to time gazing up at the model. He did not often look at her. She seemed not to be aware of him. Once she turned to observe the ailanthus tree, and he studied her momentarily to see what she might have seen in it.

Then she began to watch the painter with interest. She watched his eyes and she watched his hands. He wondered if he was doing something wrong. At the end of about an hour she rose impatiently from the yellow chair.

"Tired?" he asked.

"It isn't that," she said, "but I would like to know what in the name of Christ you think you are doing? I frankly don't think you know the first thing about painting."

She had astonished him. He quickly covered the canvas with a towel.

After a long moment, Mr. Elihu, breathing shallowly, wet his dry lips and said he was making no claims for himself as a painter. He said he had tried to make that absolutely clear to the woman he talked to at the art school when he called.

Then he said, "I might have made a mistake in asking you to come to this house today. I think I should have tested myself a while longer, just so I wouldn't be wasting anybody's time. I guess I am not ready to do what I would like to do."

"I don't care how long you have tested yourself," said Ms. Perry. "I honestly don't think you have painted me at all. In fact, I felt you weren't interested in painting me. I think you're interested in letting your eyes go over my naked body for certain reasons of your own. I don't know what your personal needs are, but I'm damn well sure that most of them have nothing to do with painting."

"I guess I have made a mistake."

"I guess you have," said the model. She had her robe on now, the belt pulled tight.

"I'm a painter," she said, "and I model because I am broke, but I know a fake when I see one."

"I wouldn't feel so bad," said Mr. Elihu, "if I hadn't gone out of my way to explain the situation to that lady at the Art Students League.

"I'm sorry this happened," Mr. Elihu said hoarsely. "I should have thought it through more than I did. I'm seventy years of age. I have always loved women and felt a sad loss that I have no particular women friends at this time of my life. That's one of the reasons I wanted to paint again, though I make no claims that I was ever greatly talented. Also, I guess I didn't realize how much about painting I have forgotten. Not only about that, but also about the female body. I didn't realize I would be so moved by yours, and, on reflection, about the way my life has gone. I hoped painting again would refresh my feeling for life. I regret that I have inconvenienced and disturbed you."

"I'll be paid for my inconvenience," Ms. Perry said, "but what you can't pay me for is the insult of coming here and submitting myself to your eyes crawling on my body."

"I didn't mean it as an insult."

"That's what it feels like to me."

She then asked Mr. Elihu to disrobe.

"I?" he said, surprised. "What for?"

"I want to sketch you. Take your pants and shirt off."

He said he had barely got rid of his winter underwear, but she did not smile.

Mr. Elihu disrobed, ashamed of how he must look to her.

With quick strokes she sketched his form. He was not a bad-looking man, but felt bad. When she had the sketch, she dipped his brush into a blob of black pigment she had squeezed out of a tube and smeared his features, leaving a black mess.

He watched her hating him, but said nothing.

Ms. Perry tossed the brush into a wastebasket and returned to the bathroom for her clothing.

The old man wrote out a check for her for the sum they had agreed on. He was ashamed to sign his name, but he signed it and handed it to her. Ms. Perry slipped the check into her large purse and left.

He thought that in her way she was not a bad-looking woman, though she lacked grace. The old man then asked himself, "Is there nothing more to my life than it is now? Is this all that is left to me?"

The answer seemed to be yes, and he wept at how old he had so quickly become.

Afterward he removed the towel over his canvas and tried to fill in her face, but he had already forgotten it.

NADINE GORDIMER

Terminal

"ven the cat buries its dirt; I carry mine around with me."
She thought of saying it aloud many times in the weeks after
she came home from the hospital. She did not know if he would
decide to laugh—whether they would go so far as to laugh. The
only time the existence of such a contraption had ever been
mentioned by them before the illness happened was a few years
ago, when—exchanging sheets of newspaper as they usually did,
lovely weekend mornings in bed—she had been reading some
article about unemployment and teenage prostitutes, and had
remarked to him, my God, the job the welfare people found for
this girl was in a factory that makes those rubber bag things for
people who have to have their stomachs cut out—no wonder
she went on the streets, poor little wretch. . . .

She remembered that morning, that newspaper, clearly. More
and more of their conversation kept coming back. They had
drifted to talk about the dreariness of industrialization; how early
Marxists had ascribed this to alienation, which would disappear
when the means of production were owned by the workers, but
the factories of the Soviet Union and China were surely just as

dreary as those of the West? And she remembered she had reminded him (they had visited Peking together) that at least the Chinese factory workers had ten-minute breaks for compulsory calisthenics twice a day—and he had said, would you swap that for a tea break and a fag?

The rubber thing that went past on the assembly belt before the sixteen-year-old future prostitute was remote from the two of them, laughing in bed on a Sunday morning, as the life of any factory worker.

Now the contraption was attached to her own body. It issued from her, from the small wound hidden under her clothing. She had moved from their shared bed and he understood without a word. She had been taught at the hospital how to deal with the thing, it was horribly private in a way natural functions were not, since natural functions were—had been—experienced by them both. She was alone with her dirt.

The doctors said the thing would be taken away in time. Six weeks, the first one predicted, not more than three months was what the second one told her. They should have coordinated their fairy story. They said that (after six weeks or three months) everything would be reconnected inside her. The wound that was kept open would be sewn up. She would be whole again, repaired, everything would work. She would go back to her teaching at the music school. She could go back there now— why not?—if she wanted to, so long as she didn't tire herself. But she didn't want to, carrying that thing with her. She had to listen to more stories—from encouraging friends—about how wonderfully other people managed, lived perfectly normal lives. Even a member of the British royal family, it was said. She shut them up with the fairy story, saying, but for me it's only for six weeks (or three months), I don't have to manage. He bought her two beautiful caftans, choosing them himself, and so perfectly right for her, just her colors, her style—in her pleasure she forgot (which she knew later was exactly what he hoped) she would be wearing them to cover that thing. She put on one or the other when the friends came to visit, and her outfit was admired, they said she must be malingering, she looked so marvelous. He confirmed to them that she was making good progress.

They had talked, once, early on. They had talked before that, in their lives, in the skein of their mingled lives—but how impersonal it was, really, then! A childish pact, blood-brotherhood; on a par with that endlessly rhetorical question, d'you love me, will you always love me: if either of us were to be incurably ill, neither would let the other suffer, would they? But when it happens—well, it never happens. Not in that silly, dramatic, clear-cut abstraction. Who can say what is "incurable"? Who can be sure what suffering is terminal, not worth prolonging in order to survive it? This one had a breast off twenty years ago, and is still going to the races every week. That one lost his prostate, can be seen knocking back gin-and-tonics at any cocktail party, with his third wife.

But just before she went into the hospital for the exploratory operation she found the time and place to reaffirm. "If it turns out to be bad, if it gets very bad . . . at any time, you promise you'll help me out of it. I would do it for you." He couldn't speak. She was lying with him in the dark; he nodded so hard the pact was driven into her shoulder by his chin. The bone hurt her. Then he made love to her, entering her body in covenant.

After the operation she found the tube leading out of her, the contraption. They did not talk again; only of cheerful things, only of getting better. The thing—the wound it issued from, that, unlike any other wound, couldn't be allowed to close, was like a contingent love affair concealed in his life or hers whose weight would tear their integument if admitted. They smiled at each other at once, every time their eyes met. It couldn't be borne, after all. There had to be a fairy story. It was told over and over, every day, in every plan they made for next week or next month or next year, never blinking an eyelid; in every assumption of continuing daily life neither believed. There were no words that were not lies. *Did the groceries come. There's been another hijacking. Are you all right in that chair. They say the election's set for Spring. We need new wine glasses. I should write letters. Order coffee and matches. Another crisis in the Middle East. Draw the curtains, the sun's in your eyes. I must have my hair done, Thursday.* If she took his hand now, it was only in the lie of immortality. The flesh, therefore, was not real for them anymore.

There was only one thing left that could not, by its very nature, have become a lie. There was only one place where love could survive: life was betrayed, but the covenant was not with life.

He drove her to the hairdresser that Thursday afternoon and when he came to fetch her he told her she looked pretty. She thanked him awkwardly as a girl with her first compliment. Beneath it ʃhe was overcome—the first strong emotion except fear and disgust, for many months—by an overwhelming trust in him. That night, alone in the room that was now her bedroom she counted out the hoarded pills and, before she washed them down with plain water, set under the paperweight of her cigarette lighter her note for him. "Keep your promise. Don't have me revived."

Ever since she was a child she had understood it as a deep sleep, that's all. Ever since she saw the first bird, lying under a hedge, whose eyes hadn't opened when it was poked with a twig. But one can only be aware of a sleep as one awakens from it, and so one will never be aware of that deep sleep—she had no fear of death but now she had the terror of feeling herself waking from it, herself coming back from what was not death at all, then, could not be. Her eyelids were rosy blinds through which light glowed. She opened them on the glossy walls of a hospital room. There was a hand in hers; his.

229

Haiti

PAULÉ BARTÓN

Emilie Plead Choose One Egg

Emilie was talking with Bélem while looking at the gathered loud of nesting birds. "Which bird going to hatch today's woe, guess that?" Emilie said, she said, "I'll carry that egg to the man who took my donkey for my debt, I'll give him that a breakfast gift!"

"The tax man?" Bélem said.

Emilie said, "That's it, you guessing good today," she said. "Now guess which egg woe is in."

Bélem said, "How can I guess? Look how many eggs there look!"

"Got to make choices in this life," Emilie said, "Each morning a riddle to untie the knot of it, and then use that rope to tie up back luck thinking to any tree here."

Bélem sang, *"Tie up bad luck thinking to a tree here, Fry that woe egg up for the debt man dear,"* then he said, "That makes a good song!" he laughed then.

Emilie she said, "I'll sing it on the way over to his hut, I'll sing it to my donkey too. But now guess which egg!"

But Bélem said, "I sigh. There's too many eggs out there! I

230

tell you my eyes worrying over each one, they look the same all," he said more.

Emilie then, "Got to make a choice hurry! That debt man yawning toward his breakfast table hurry!" Emilie said.

"You asking me something hard here I tell you. You ask a very tight riddle knot, you talking a mystery under just one bird!" Bélem said.

"Got to make a choice! The debt man now sitting at the table now," Emilie said.

Bélem said, "It's like asking does water from the same well taste more better after carried in buckets to your thirsty mouth by a donkey or an ox, which one? It's like asking which of two sticks the same size to knock a lemon down with, which one?" he said.

Emilie said, "Make a choice my friend. You get to taste the drinking water in your throat whoever brings it anyway. You get to squeeze the lemon on your tongue whatever stick knocks it down anyway. That debt man choose my donkey instead my table and chair to take, yes he make that choice one over the other, you know this?"

Bélem said, "O.K. I say all the eggs got woe today's woe in them, how's that if I say that, there I say that!" he said.

Emilie said, "That's no choice, oh my that's no choice! Now the donkey and ox both spilling water, empty gone, now the lemons shriveling up to yellow lizard eyes on the trees, now the debt man thinking greedy want of my table and chair. Which egg will stop all this, friend?" Emilie plead him to choose one egg quick.

But Bélem could not choose, so Emilie hid her table and chair then. Emilie says, "All right Bélem friend, it's all right," she soothes that way.

Bélem he had a wound he felt then somewhere on him, but he couldn't find it. He said, "Emilie, I hurt on me somewhere, can you see the wound?"

Emilie said, "No," she covers the table and chairs with fronds.

Bélem he says, "The salt sea will find this wound on me, it always does when I swim in it, always clean my wound." But Emilie knew the wound of confusion and no-choice was too deep inside for the salt sea to sting it clean for Bélem right now.

Translated by Howard Norman

FERNANDO SORRENTINO

There's a Man in the Habit of Hitting Me on the Head with an Umbrella

here's a man in the habit of hitting me on the head with an umbrella. It is five years to the day since he began hitting me on the head with his umbrella. At first I couldn't stand it; now I've grown accustomed to it.

I don't know his name. I know he's an ordinary man, with a plain suit, graying at the temples, and a nondescript face. I met him one sultry morning five years ago. I was sitting peacefully on a bench in Palermo Park, reading the newspaper in the shade of a tree. All of a sudden I felt something touch my head. It was this same man who now, as I write, automatically and impassively keeps striking me blows with his umbrella.

That first time I turned around full of indignation (I become terribly annoyed when I'm bothered while reading the paper); he went right on, calmly hitting me. I asked him if he were mad. He seemed not to hear me. I then threatened to call a policeman. Completely unruffled, he went on with what he was doing. After a few moments of hesitation—and seeing he was not about to back down—I stood up and gave him a terrific punch in the face. No doubt he is a weak man: I know that despite the force generated by my rage I do not hit all that hard. Still, breathing a tiny moan—the man fell to the ground. At once, making what seemed to be a great effort, he got up and again began hitting me over the head with the umbrella. His nose was bleeding, and I don't know why but at that moment I felt sorry for him, and my conscience troubled me for having struck him that way. Because, after all, the man was not hitting me very hard; he was really striking me quite soft and completely painless blows. Of course, such blows are terribly annoying. Everyone knows that when a fly settles on a person's forehead a person feels no pain; he feels annoyed. Well, that umbrella was a huge fly which, at regular intervals, kept settling on my head. Or, to be more precise, a fly the size of a bat.

At any rate, I could not stand that bat. Convinced that I was in the presence of lunatic, I tried to get away. But the man followed me, in silence, without once letting up his blows. At this juncture, I began running (I may as well point out right here that there are few people as fast as I am). He set out after me, trying without luck to get in a whack or two. The man was gasping and gasping and panting so hard I thought if I kept him running like that my tormentor might sink dead on the spot.

For that reason I slowed to a walk. I looked at him. His face registered neither gratitude nor reproach. He just kept hitting me over the head with his umbrella. I thought of making my way to a police station and saying, "Officer, this man is hitting me over the head with an umbrella." It would have been unprecedented. The policeman would have stared at me suspiciously, asked for my papers, and begun questioning me with embarrassing questions. Probably he would have ended up arresting me.

I thought I'd best go home. I got onto the Number 67 bus. Not once letting up with his umbrella, the man got on behind me. I took the first seat. He stationed himself beside me, holding on to the strap with his left hand while with his right he kept swinging at me with his umbrella, implacable. The passengers began to exchange shy smiles. The driver was watching us in his mirror. Little by little, a fit of laughter, a growing convulsion, seized all the other riders. I was on fire with shame. My persecutor, completely unaffected by the uproar, went on hitting me.

I got off—we got off—at the Puente Pacífico. We continued on down Santa Fe Avenue. Everyone foolishly turned around to stare at us. I felt like saying to them, "What are you staring at, you idiots? Haven't you ever seen anyone whacking a man on the head with an umbrella before?" But it also occurred to me that they probably hadn't. Five or six kids began to follow us, shouting like a pack of wild Indians.

But I had a plan. Arriving home, I tried slamming the door in his face. I didn't manage it. With a firm hand—anticipating me—he grabbed the handle, there was a momentary struggle, and he entered with me.

Since then, he has continued hitting me on the head with his umbrella. As far as I know, he has never slept or had a bite to eat. All he does is hit me. He accompanies me in all my acts— even the most intimate ones. I remember, in the beginning, that the blows kept me from sleeping; I now believe it would be impossible to sleep without them.

Nevertheless, our relations have not always been good. Countless times, in all possible tones, I have asked him for an explanation. It's never been any use; in his quiet way he has gone on whacking me over the head with the umbrella. On several occasions, I have dealt him punches, kicks, and—God help me!—even umbrella blows. He took these things meekly, as though they were all in a day's work. And this is exactly what is scariest about him: his quiet determination, his absence of hatred. In short, his inner conviction of carrying out a secret and superior mission.

Despite his apparent lack of physiological needs, I know when

I hit him he feels the pain, I know he's weak, I know he's mortal. I also know a single shot would free me of him. What I don't know is whether when we're both dead he will go on hitting me on the head with his umbrella. Neither do I know whether the shot ought to be aimed at him or at me. In any case, this reasoning is pointless. I know full well I wouldn't dare kill either him or myself.

On the other hand, it recently occurred to me that I could not live without his blows. More and more frequently now I have a horrible premonition. I am distressed—deeply distressed—to think that perhaps when I most need him, this man will go away and I will no longer feel those soft blows of his umbrella that help me sleep so soundly.

Translated by Norman Thomas di Giovanni
and Patricia Davidson Cran

SIV CEDERING

Family Album

This is their wedding picture. Pappa wears a tuxedo, and
Mamma is wearing a white satin dress. She is smiling at the
white lilies. This is the house Pappa built for Mamma, when
they were engaged. Then this house, then that; they were always
making blueprints together.

Mamma came from Lapland. She was quite poor and dreamed
of pretty dresses. Her mother died when Mamma was small.
Pappa met her when he came to Lapland as a conscientious
objector. He preached in her church. There he is with his banjo.

Pappa was quite poor too; everyone was in those days. He
told me he didn't have any shoes that fit him, one spring, and
he had to wear his father's big shoes. Pappa said he was so
ashamed that he walked in the ditch, all the way to school.

Pappa was one of eleven children, but only five of them grew
up. The others died of tuberculosis or diphtheria. Three died
in a six-week period, and Pappa says death was accepted then,
just like changes in the weather and a bad crop of potatoes. His
parents were religious. I remember Grandfather Anton rocking
in the rocker and riding on the reaper, and I remember Grand-

mother Maria, though I was just two when she died. The funeral was like a party: birch saplings decorated the yard, relatives came from all around, and my sister and I wore new white dresses. Listen to the names of her eleven children:

Anna Viktoria, Karl Sigurd, Johan Martin, Hulda Maria, Signe Sofia, Bror Hilding, Judit Friedeborg, Brynhild Elisabet, John Rudolf, Tore Adils, and Clary Torborg.

We called the eldest Tora. She was fat and never got married. Tore was the youngest son. I remember sitting next to him, outside by the flagpole, eating blood pancakes after a slaughter, and calf-dance—a dish made from the first milk a cow gives after it has calved. Tore recently left his wife and took a new one. He once told me that when he was a boy, he used to ski out in the dark afternoons of the North and stand still, watching the sky and feeling himself get smaller and smaller. This is Uncle Rudolf in his uniform, and this is Torborg, Pappa's youngest sister. Her fiancé had tried to make love to her once before they were married, and—Mamma told me—Torborg tore the engagement ring off her finger, threw it on the floor of the large farmhouse kitchen, and hollered, loud enough for everyone to hear: "What does that whoremonger think I am?" He was the son of a big-city mayor and well educated, but you can bet he married a virgin. Don't they look good in this picture? Three of their five children are doctors. They say that Torborg got her temper from Great-grandfather. When he got drunk he cussed and brought the horse into the kitchen. This is the Kell people from the Kell farm. I am told I have the Kell eyes. Everyone on this side of the family hears ghosts and dreams prophecies. To us it isn't supernatural; it is natural.

Mamma's oldest brother Karl went to America when he was eighteen. There he is chopping down a redwood tree, and there he is working in a gold mine. He married a woman named Viviann, and she visited us in Sweden. Let me tell you, the village had never seen anyone like her. Not only had she been divorced, but she had bobbed hair, wore makeup, and dresses with padded shoulders, matching shoes, and purses. Vanity of all vanities was quoted from the Bible. So of course everyone knew the marriage wouldn't last—besides, they didn't have any children. Uncle Karl is now old and fat, the darling and bene- factor of a Swedish Old Folks Home in Canada. Silver mines help him. This is Mamma's second brother. He had to have a leg amputated. I used to think about that leg, all alone in heaven. This is Aunt Edith. She once gave me a silver spoon that had my name written on it. And this is Aunt Elsa who has a large birthmark on her face. I used to wonder what mark I had to prove that I was born.

Mamma's father was a Communist. He came to Lapland to build the large power plant that supplies most of Sweden's elec- tricity. He told me, once, that he ate snake when he was young and worked on the railroad. His wife Emma was a beauty and a lady, and when the household money permitted, she washed her face with heavy cream and her hair with beer or egg whites. My hair? Both grandmothers had hair long enough to sit on.

I am talking about my inheritance—the family jewelry that I wear in my hair, so to speak, the birthmark that stays on my face forever. I am motherless in Lapland, brought down to size by the vastness of the sky. I rock in the rocker of old age and ride the reaper, while some part of me has already preceded me to heaven. I change one husband for another, and toss my ring, furiously moral at any indignation. I am a pacifist, I am a Com- munist, I am a preacher coddling my father's language and abandoning my mother tongue forever. I eat blood pancakes, calf-dance, snake, and I bring the horse into the kitchen. I build new houses, dream of new dresses, bury my parents and my children. I hear ghosts, see the future and know what will hap- pen. If I step on a crack and break my mother's back, I can say the shoes were too large for my feet, for I know, I know: these are the fairy tales that grieve us. And save us.

PETER CAREY

The Last Days
of a Famous Mime

1.

The Mime arrived on Alitalia with very little luggage: a brown paper parcel and what looked like a woman's handbag.

Asked the contents of the brown paper parcel he said, "String."

Asked what the string was for he replied: "Tying up bigger parcels."

It had not been intended as a joke, but the Mime was pleased when the reporters laughed. Inducing laughter was not his forte. He was famous for terror.

Although his state of despair was famous throughout Europe, few guessed at his hope for the future. "The string," he explained, "is a prayer that I am always praying."

Reluctantly he untied his parcel and showed them the string. It was blue and when extended measured exactly fifty-three meters.

The Mime and the string appeared on the front pages of the evening papers.

2.

The first audiences panicked easily. They had not been prepared for his ability to mime terror. They fled their seats continually. Only to return again.

Like snorkel divers they appeared at the doors outside the
concert hall with red faces and were puzzled to find the world
as they had left it.

3.

Books had been written about him. He was the subject of an
award-winning film. But in his first morning in a provincial town
he was distressed to find that his performance had not been
liked by the one newspaper's one critic.

"I cannot see," the critic wrote, "the use of invoking terror in
an audience."

The Mime sat on his bed, pondering ways to make his performance more light-hearted.

4.

As usual he attracted women who wished to still the raging
storms of his heart.

They attended his bed like highly paid surgeons operating on
a difficult case. They were both passionate and intelligent. They
did not suffer defeat lightly.

5.

Wrongly accused of merely miming love in his private life he
was somewhat surprised to be confronted with hatred.

"Surely," he said, "if you now hate me, it was you who were
imitating love, not I."

"You always were a slimy bastard," she said. "What's in that parcel?"

"I told you before," he said helplessly, "string."

"You're a liar," she said.

But later when he untied the parcel he found that she had opened it to check on his story. Her understanding of the string had been perfect. She had cut it into small pieces like spaghetti in a lousy restaurant.

6.

Against the advice of the tour organizers he devoted two concerts entirely to love and laughter. They were disasters. It was felt that love and laughter were not, in his case, as instructive as terror.

The next performance was quickly announced.

TWO HOURS OF REGRET

Tickets sold quickly. He began with a brief interpretation of love using it merely as a prelude to regret which he elaborated on in a complex and moving performance which left the audience pale and shaken. In a final flourish he passed from regret to loneliness to terror. The audience devoured the terror like brave tourists eating the hottest curry in an Indian restaurant.

7.

"What you are doing," she said, "is capitalizing on your neuroses. Personally I find it disgusting, like someone exhibiting their clubfoot, or Turkish beggars with strange deformities."

He said nothing. He was mildly annoyed at her presumption: that he had not thought this many, many times before.

With perfect misunderstanding she interpreted his passivity as disdain.

Wishing to hurt him, she slapped his face.
Wishing to hurt her, he smiled brilliantly.

8.

The story of the blue string touched the public imagination. Small brown paper packages were sold at the door of his concert.

Standing on stage he could hear the packages being noisily unwrapped. He thought of American matrons buying Muslim prayer rugs.

9.

Exhausted and weakened by the heavy schedule he fell prey to the doubts that had pricked at him insistently for years. He lost all sense of direction and spent many listless hours by himself, sitting in a motel room listening to the air conditioner.

He had lost confidence in the social uses of controlled terror. He no longer understood the audience's need to experience the very things he so desperately wished to escape from.

He emptied the ashtrays fastidiously.

He opened his brown paper parcel and threw the small pieces of string down the cistern. When the torrent of white water subsided they remained floating there like flotsam from a disaster at sea.

10.

The Mime called a press conference to announce that there would be no more concerts. He seemed small and foreign and smelt of garlic. The press regarded him without enthusiasm. He watched their hovering pens anxiously, unsuccessfully willing them to write down his words.

Briefly he announced that he wished to throw his talent open to broader influences. His skills would be at the disposal of the people, who would be free to request his services for any purpose at any time.

His skin seemed sallow but his eyes seemed as bright as those on a nodding fur mascot on the back window ledge of an American car.

11.

Asked to describe death he busied himself taking Polaroid photographs of his questioners.

12.

Asked to describe marriage he handed out small cheap mirrors with MADE IN TUNISIA written on the back.

13.

His popularity declined. It was felt that he had become obscure and beyond the understanding of ordinary people. In response he requested easier questions. He held back nothing of himself in his effort to please his audience.

14.

Asked to describe an airplane he flew three times around the city, only injuring himself slightly on landing.

15.

Asked to describe a river, he drowned himself.

16.

It is unfortunate that this, his last and least typical performance, is the only one which has been recorded on film.

There is a small crowd by the riverbank, no more than thirty people. A small, neat man dressed in a gray suit picks his way through some children who seem more interested in the large plastic toy dog they are playing with.

He steps into the river, which, at the bank, is already quite deep. His head is only visible above the water for a second or two. And then he is gone.

A policeman looks expectantly over the edge, as if waiting for him to reappear. Then the film stops.

Watching this last performance it is difficult to imagine how this man stirred such emotions in the hearts of those who saw him.

France

DANIEL BOULANGER

The Shoe Breaker

Where is Pinceloup?"

"I don't know, sir," replied the clerk.

"Baron," the owner said, as he turned to speak to the client who had just come in, "my staff and I saw him leave early this morning on your behalf."

"What I see," retorted the other, "is that I was counting on my shoes being ready at four o'clock. You assured me they would be. It is now six o'clock and the dinner is at eight. I don't intend to stand here cooling my heels."

"But, sir . . ."

"Don't tell me you're sorry. It is I, my dear man, who am sorry. You can't depend on anyone nowadays."

The baron looked down at his feet and wiggled his toes under the worn calfskin. He'd have to go to the dinner party in his old shoes, bulging from his bunions and bubbled by his corns. Obviously he was comfortable in them, but aren't we always anxious to try out our latest purchase? The pair of dress shoes that he had bought the day before that tortured him so when he first put them on were still walking the streets of Paris, being broken in by a fellow named Pinceloup.

246

"May I make a suggestion?" ventured the owner. "I know the man well. I have used him for more than thirty years, Sir. He has broken in over twelve thousand pairs of shoes for me, following the customers' directives. He figures a morning per pair for normal feet, but an entire afternoon should there by any deformity. Our exceptional patrons . . ."

The baron didn't readily count himself among the latter.

". . . I mean those whom it was nature's whim to deform, and God knows I pity them, will sometimes cost Pinceloup an entire day."

With the tip of his cane, the baron maliciously applied pressure to the corn crowning the big toe of his right foot, swollen by gout.

"Pinceloup is, moreover, a great judge of physiognomy and I shall miss him. He knows at a glance whether to walk pigeon-toed or duck-footed, or to stuff a wad of cotton in the shoe at just the right place, that is to say at the place that . . . Baron, sir?"

"Yes?"

"People like Pinceloup will be hard to come by in the future. Love for one's work is a thing of the past. Love for art is disappearing. But please sit down, he should be here any time now."

"Art?" cried out the baron. "Indeed I shall sit down."

"Pinceloup," the owner continued, "belonged to my father before I took over the business."

This sort of talk the baron savored, and time wore on. The salesmen, meanwhile, were coming and going, carrying piles of boxes, kneeling, wielding their shoehorns, here lacing up an Oxford, there vaunting the quality of the alligator and, over in the women's section, assuming feminine poses as they side-saddled their fitting stools, clamping their knees together like women in bathing suits, not hesitating to look away should gaping thighs offer them the forbidden view. The owner kept a watchful eye on his people without diverting his attention from the baron who, though not a particularly good customer, was a man of great renown. The Petit–Chablis clan, lest one forget, still owned half of the country's railroads, and that is indeed what drew a good part of the clientele.

"Honestly, I can't understand what's keeping him."

"And it's getting dark," the baron sighed.

They were about to give up when the door opened and Pinceloup appeared, green around the gills and dragging at the heels.

"Ah! There you are."

The baron looked at his dress shoes now gracing the shoe breaker's feet. They no longer bore a resemblance to the ones the Baron had purchased, but rather to the good old pair he now wore. His eyes wandered from the one to the other.

"My dear fellow," he exclaimed, putting his hand on Pinceloup's shoulder, "did everything go well?"

"Everything, Baron, sir. There might still be a hint of stiffness in the reinforcement of the outer left heel. I apologize for that."

Am I getting old, Pinceloup wondered. Is the leather less supple due to the new fangled methods of tanning and splicing? Or might the stitching or the lining be too heavy?

"Unshoe him," the owner told a clerk.

"I'd appreciate it," Pinceloup uttered feebly.

"Are you otherwise satisfied?" Baron Petit–Chablis inquired.

With the tip of his cane, he pointed to the already bloated shoes, now emptied of Pinceloup's feet, as well as of the scraps of cardboard, cotton balls, strips of cork, rubber disks and the like.

"They've put in eighteen kilometers," Pinceloup declared. "I advise you to put them on right away while they're still warm. We'll obtain a more generous contact. Talcum powder . . ."

"The talc," shouted the owner.

The talcum powder will save the day, mused Pinceloup.

The baron had himself shod, laced up and helped to his feet.

He shook hands with the owner. At the same time, he extended his left hand which held his cane, trying discreetly to offer Pinceloup a coin. He nearly blinded the poor devil in the process.

The breaker watched the baron as he left with short and hesitant steps.

Seeing him stop in the middle of the street for relief, Pinceloup felt the pain and even a twinge of shame.

"Monsieur," he said to the owner, "I just can't do it any more."

"What's that?"

"I've lost my touch. Look!" They could see the baron limping off.

"I did what I could," Pinceloup muttered as he examined his lacerated feet. His socks were embedded in his flesh and darkened in spots with blood stains.

"Come on now, don't give up for heaven's sake. You're the best breaker in all of Paris, Pinceloup. The main thing in life is to be tops at something. Remember . . ."

"And tomorrow?" interrupted Pinceloup, his sense of honor reviving.

"You'll do two pairs for me. They'll be a snap."

"But I didn't see them on the customers' feet." The owner went to his file and pulled two sheets of vellum.

"Here." He knows that Pinceloup can't read and Pinceloup knows that he knows. If the boss is being mean again, it's because he esteems him, needs him, and can boast that no one else in all of Paris can break in shoes as well as Pinceloup.

"See you tomorrow," Pinceloup murmured.

Since his feet hurt him so, he put on his espadrilles, which he saved for the bad evenings. The boss, despite the fact that it was closing time, asked him to leave through the back service door.

Translated by Penny Million Pucelik
and Marijo Despréaux Schneider

SERGEI DOVLOTOV

Katya

Katya switched on the lights; the window went dark.

It was very early. In the foyer, the windup clock ticked with a deep sound.

Katya pushed her feet into cold house slippers and went to the kitchen. She returned, stood there a while, wrapping herself up in a blue flannelette bathrobe. Then she tore off a page from the day calendar and began to read it slowly with great attention. "Twenty-eighth of February. Thursday. Five hundred and sixty years ago, Abd-ur-rahman Jami was born. The name of this outstanding contributor to Persian culture . . ."

"Egorov, wake up," Katya said. "The water's frozen."

The captain turned uneasily in his sleep.

"Pavel, there's ice in the washbasin."

"Normal," the captain said. "Entirely normal . . . Under conditions of warming, ice arises. While under conditions of cooling—no, not like that. Under conditions of cooling, ice. And from heating, vapor . . . Newton's third law. Of which I'm not entirely persuaded."

"The snowdrifts have reached halfway up the window. Pavel, don't go back to sleep."

"Precipitation," Egorov responded. "Better let me tell you about the dream I just had. It seemed that Marshal Voroshilov presented me with a saber, and with the saber I tickled Major Koyba."

"Pavel, stop behaving like an idiot."

The captain quickly got up, rolled a cold black barbell out of the corner. While doing this, he said, "You train for a century, but you still can't outdrink a whale. And you'll never be as strong as a gorilla."

"Pavel!"

"What's the matter? What happened?"

Egorov moved to her and wanted to put his arms around her.

Katya pulled away and loudly burst into tears. She shuddered and her mouth twisted.

"But why cry?" Egorov asked softly. "Crying is not required. Much less sobbing . . ."

Then Katya covered her face with her hands and spoke slowly—slowly, so the tears would not interfere. "I can't go on."

Now depressed himself, the captain took out a cigarette and lit it in silence.

Behind the window, a gray, frosty morning was spreading. Long bluish shadows lay on the snow.

Egorov dressed slowly, put on a down jacket, and picked up an ax. The snow squeaked under his ski boots.

"But there has to be another life somewhere," Katya thought, "an entirely different life. Somewhere there are wild strawberries, campfires, singing . . . And a labyrinth of paths, crossed with pine tree roots . . . And rivers, and people waiting to cross. Somewhere there are serious white books, the eternally elusive music of Bach, the swish of car wheels . . . While here, it's the howling of dogs. The power saw buzzing from morning till night. And now, on top of everything else, ice in the washbasin."

Katya breathed on the windowpane. Egorov set a log on its

251

end. For some time he looked closely at the little branches. Then he gave the ax a short swing up and let it fall sharply, slanting it a little.

"The Turkish March" came over the radio. Katya imagined a platoon of Turkish soldiers. They trudged through deep snow in heavy turbans, fighting their way from the division of Economic Administration to the machine shop. Their yataghans have frozen to their scabbards, the turbans gone white . . .

"My God," Katya thought, "I'm losing my mind!"

Egorov returned with an armful of firewood and dumped it by the stove. Then he pulled out of his pocket a prison knife with a locking pin, confiscated during a personal search, and began to chip off kindling.

"Once I used to love winter," Katya thought, "but now I hate it. I hate frost in the morning and dark evenings. I hate dogs barking, fences, barbed wire. I hate boots, down vests . . . and ice in the washbasin."

"Be quiet," she said aloud. "I hate your always being right!"

"How's that?" Egorov did not understand. Then he said, "Well, if you'd like, I'll go to Vozhael and get apples and champagne, and we can invite Zhenka Bortashevich and Larissa."

"Your Bortashevich cuts his nails during supper."

"Then Vakhtang Kekelidze. His papa is a count."

"Kekelidze is a vulgarian!'

"Meaning?"

"You don't know."

"Why do you think I don't know?" the captain said. "I know. I know he plays up to you. That's the way Georgians behave. The guy's unmarried. It's unpleasant, of course. Actually, he deserves a punch in the jaw."

"A woman needs it."

"What, exactly?"

"For a man to pay attention to her."

"You need to have a baby," the captain said.

The hoarse, vibrating baying from the kennel grew stronger. One swelling timbre stood out in particular among the other voices.

"Why is it I was never bothered by sea gulls," Katya said, "or wild ducks? I cannot, cannot, cannot endure that barking."

"It's Harun," Egorov said.

"What a horror."

"You haven't heard wolves yet. That's a really terrible business."

The firewood in the stove hissed as it flared up. And there was already a smell of wet snow.

"Pavel, don't be angry."

"What's there to be angry about?"

"Bring some apples from Vozhael."

"By the way, the ice in the washbasin is melting."

Katya came up behind him and put her arms around him.

"You're big," she said, "like a tree in a thunderstorm. I'm afraid for you."

"Fine," he said, "everything will be all right. Everything will be simply wonderful."

"Is it really possible everything will be all right?"

"Everything will be wonderful. If we are good ourselves."

"And is it true the ice is melting in the washbasin?"

"It's true," he said, "it's normal. A law of nature."

In the kennel, Harun began to howl again.

"Wait a second," Egorov said, pulling away from Katya. "I'll be right back. This will just take a minute."

Katya let her hands drop. She went into the kitchen and lifted the heavy cover of the washbasin. Inside, a small piece of ice was melting.

"It really is melting," Katya said out loud.

She went back, sat down. Egorov was still out.

Katya put on a scratchy phonograph record. She remembered some lines from a poem that had been dedicated to her by Lenya Mak, a weight-lifter and unacknowledged genius:

> It's plain I've come at an awkward moment,
> The phonograph has long since stopped, it whispers,
> Better let's wait for a waltz, Katya,
> It's easier for me not to dance this one . . .

In the kennel, a shot rang out. The hoarse canine howl changed to a screech and then stopped.

After a few moments, the captain returned. He walked past the windows. He was carrying something wrapped in a tarpaulin.

Katya was afraid to lift her eyes.

"So, what do you think?" Egorov said, grinning. "It's a bit quieter now, isn't it?"

Katya tried to ask, "What's this? Now what?"

"No problem," the captain assured her. "I'll call over an orderly with a shovel."

Translated by Anne Frydman

Botswana

BESSIE HEAD

Looking for a Rain God

It is lonely at the lands where the people go to plough. These lands are vast clearings in the bush, and the wild bush is lonely too. Nearly all the lands are within walking distance from the village. In some parts of the bush where the underground water is very near the surface, people made little rest camps for themselves and dug shallow wells to quench their thirst while on their journey to their own lands. They experienced all kinds of things once they left the village. They could rest at shady watering places full of lush, tangled trees with delicate pale-gold and purple wildflowers springing up between soft green moss and the children could hunt around for wild figs and any berries that might be in season. But from 1958, a seven-year drought fell upon the land and even the watering places began to look as dismal as the dry open thornbush country; the leaves of the trees curled up and withered; the moss became dry and hard and, under the shade of the tangled trees, the ground turned a powdery black and white, because there was no rain. People said rather humorously that if you tried to catch the rain in a cup it would only fill a teaspoon. Toward the beginning of the seventh year of drought, the summer had become an anguish to live through. The air was so dry and moisture-free that it burned the skin. No one knew what to do to escape the heat and tragedy was in the air. At the beginning of that summer, a number of men just went out of their homes and hung themselves to death from trees. The majority of the people had lived off crops, but for two years past they had all returned from the lands with only their rolled-up skin blankets and cooking utensils. Only the charlatans, incanters, and witch doctors made a pile of money during this time because people were always turning to them in desperation for little talismans and herbs to rub on the plough for the crops to grow and the rain to fall.

The rains were late that year. They came in early November, with a promise of good rain. It wasn't the full, steady downpour of the years of good rain but thin, scanty, misty rain. It softened the earth and a rich growth of green things sprang up everywhere for the animals to eat. People were called to the center of the village to hear the proclamation of the beginning of the ploughing season; they stirred themselves and whole families began to move off to the lands to plough.

The family of the old man, Mokgobja, were among those who left early for the lands. They had a donkey cart and piled everything onto it, Mokgobja—who was over seventy years old; two girls, Neo and Boseyong; their mother Tiro and an unmarried sister, Nesta; and the father and supporter of the family, Ramadi, who drove the donkey cart. In the rush of the first hope of rain, the man, Ramadi, and the two women, cleared the land of thornbush and then hedged their vast ploughing area with this same thornbush to protect the future crop from the goats they had brought along for milk. They cleared out and deepened the old well with its pool of muddy water and still in this light, misty rain, Ramadi inspanned two oxen and turned the earth over with a hand plough.

The land was ready and ploughed, waiting for the crops. At night, the earth was alive with insects singing and rustling about in search of food. But suddenly, by mid-November, the rain flew away; the rain clouds fled away and left the sky bare. The sun danced dizzily in the sky, with a strange cruelty. Each day the land was covered in a haze of mist as the sun sucked up the last drop of moisture out of the earth. The family sat down in despair, waiting and waiting. Their hopes had run so high; the goats had started producing milk, which they had eagerly poured on their porridge, now they ate plain porridge with no milk. It was impossible to plant the corn, maize, pumpkin, and water-melon seeds in the dry earth. They sat the whole day in the shadow of the huts and even stopped thinking, for the rain had fled away. Only the children, Neo and Boseyong, were quite happy in their little-girl world. They carried on with their game of making house like their mother and chattered to each other in light, soft tones. They made children from sticks around which they tied rags, and scolded them severely in an exact imitation of their own mother. Their voices could be heard scolding the day long: "You stupid thing, when I send you to draw water, why do you spill half of it out of the bucket!" "You stupid thing! Can't you mind the porridge pot without letting the porridge burn!" And then they would beat the rag dolls on their bottoms with severe expressions.

The adults paid no attention to this; they did not even hear the funny chatter; they sat waiting for rain; their nerves were stretched to breaking-point willing the rain to fall out of the sky. Nothing was important, beyond that. All their animals had been sold during the bad years to purchase food, and of all their herd only two goats were left. It was the women of the family who finally broke down under the strain of waiting for rain. It was really the two women who caused the death of the little girls. Each night they started a weird, high-pitched wailing that began on a low, mournful note and whipped up to a frenzy. Then they would stamp their feet and shout as though they had lost their heads. The men sat quiet and self-controlled; it was important for men to maintain their self control at all times but their nerve was breaking too. They knew the women were haunted by the starvation of the coming year.

Finally, an ancient memory stirred in the old man, Mokgobja. When he was very young and the customs of the ancestors still ruled the land, he had been witness to a rain-making ceremony. And he came alive a little, struggling to recall the details which had been buried by years and years of prayer in a Christian church. As soon as the mists cleared a little, he began consulting in whispers with his youngest son, Ramadi. There was, he said, a certain rain god who accepted only the sacrifice of the bodies of children. Then the rain would fall; then the crops would grow, he said. He explained the ritual and as he talked, his memory became a conviction and he began to talk with unshakable authority. Ramadi's nerves were smashed by the nightly wailing of the women and soon the two men began whispering with the two women. The children continued their game: "You stupid thing! How could you have lost the money on the way to the shop! You must have been playing again!"

After it was all over and the bodies of the two little girls had been spread across the land, the rain did not fall. Instead, there was a deathly silence at night and the devouring heat of the sun by day. A terror, extreme and deep, overwhelmed the whole family. They packed, rolling up their skin blankets and pots, and fled back to the village.

People in the village soon noted the absence of the two little girls. They had died at the lands and were buried there, the family said. But people noted their ashen, terror-stricken faces and a murmur arose. What had killed the children, they wanted to know? And the family replied that they had just died. And people said amongst themselves that it was strange that the two deaths had occurred at the same time. And there was a feeling of great unease at the unnatural looks of the family. Soon the police came around. The family told them the same story of death and burial at the lands. They did not know what the children had died of. So the police asked to see the graves. At this, the mother of the children broke down and told everything.

Throughout that terrible summer the story of the children hung like a dark cloud of sorrow over the village, and the sorrow was not assuaged when the old man and Ramadi were sentenced to death for ritual murder. All they had on the statute books was that ritual murder was against the law and must be stamped out with the death penalty. The subtle story of strain and starvation and breakdown was inadmissible evidence at court; but all the people who lived off crops knew in their hearts that only a hair's breadth had saved them from sharing a fate similar to that of the Mokgobja family. They could have killed something to make the rain fall.

DONALD BARTHELME

The School

Well, we had all these children out planting trees, see, because we figured that . . . that was part of their education, to see how, you know, the root systems . . . and also the sense of responsibility, taking care of things, being individually responsible. You know what I mean. And the trees all died. They were orange trees. I don't know why they died, they just died. Something wrong with the soil possibly or maybe the stuff we got from the nursery wasn't the best. We complained about it. So we've got thirty kids there, each kid had his or her own little tree to plant, and we've got these thirty dead trees. All these kids looking at these little brown sticks, it was depressing.

It wouldn't have been so bad except that just a couple of weeks before the thing with the trees, the snakes all died. But I think that the snakes—well, the reason that the snakes kicked off was that . . . you remember, the boiler was shut off for four days because of the strike, and that was explicable. It was something you could explain to the kids because of the strike. I mean, none of their parents would let them cross the picket line and they knew there was a strike going on and what it meant. So when things got started up again and we found the snakes they weren't too disturbed.

With the herb gardens it was probably a case of overwatering, and at least now they know not to overwater. The children were very conscientious with the herb gardens and some of them probably . . . you know, slipped them a little extra water when we weren't looking. Or maybe . . . well, I don't like to think about sabotage, although it did occur to us. I mean, it was something that crossed our minds. We were thinking that way probably because before that the gerbils had died, and the white mice had died, and the salamander . . . well, now they know not to carry them around in plastic bags.

Of course we *expected* the tropical fish to die, that was no surprise. Those numbers, you look at them crooked and they're belly-up on the surface. But the lesson plan called for a tropical-fish input at that point, there was nothing we could do, it happens every year, you just have to hurry past it.

We weren't even supposed to have a puppy.

We weren't even supposed to have one, it was just a puppy the Murdoch girl found under a Gristede's truck one day and she was afraid the truck would run over it when the driver had finished making his delivery, so she stuck it in her knapsack and brought it to school with her. So we had this puppy. As soon as I saw the puppy I thought, Oh Christ, I bet it will live for about two weeks and then . . . And that's what it did. It wasn't supposed to be in the classroom at all, there's some kind of regulation about it, but you can't tell them they can't have a puppy when the puppy is already there, right in front of them, running around on the floor and yap yap yapping. They named it Edgar—that is, they named it after me. They had a lot of fun running after it and yelling, "Here, Edgar! Nice Edgar!" Then they'd laugh like hell. They enjoyed the ambiguity. I enjoyed it myself. I don't mind being kidded. They made a little house

261

for it in the supply closet and all that. I don't know what it died of. Distemper, I guess. It probably hadn't had any shots. I got it out of there before the kids got to school. I checked the supply closet each morning, routinely, because I knew what was going to happen. I gave it to the custodian.

And then there was this Korean orphan that the class adopted through the Help the Children program, all the kids brought in a quarter a month, that was the idea. It was an unfortunate thing, the kid's name was Kim and maybe we adopted him too late or something. The cause of death was not stated in the letter we got, they suggested we adopt another child instead and sent us some interesting case histories, but we didn't have the heart. The class took it pretty hard, they began (I think, nobody ever said anything to me directly) to feel that maybe there was something wrong with the school. But I don't think there's anything wrong with the school, particularly, I've seen better and I've seen worse. It was just a run of bad luck. We had an extraordinary number of parents passing away, for instance. There were I think two heart attacks and two suicides, one drowning, and four killed together in a car accident. One stroke. And we had the usual heavy mortality rate among the grandparents, or maybe it was heavier this year, it seemed so. And finally the tragedy.

The tragedy occurred when Matthew Wein and Tony Mavrogordo were playing over where they're excavating for the new federal office building. There were all these big wooden beams stacked, you know, at the edge of the excavation. There's a court case coming out of that, the parents are claiming that the beams were poorly stacked. I don't know what's true and what's not. It's been a strange year.

I forgot to mention Billy Brandt's father, who was knifed fatally when he grappled with a masked intruder in his home.

One day, we had a discussion in class. They asked me, where

did they go? The trees, the salamander, the tropical fish, Edgar, the poppas and mommas, Matthew and Tony, where did they go? And I said, I don't know, I don't know. And they said, who knows? and I said, nobody knows. And they said, is death that which gives meaning to life? And I said, no, life is that which gives meaning to life. Then they said, but isn't death, considered as a fundamental datum, the means by which the taken-for-granted mundanity of the everyday may be transcended in the direction of—

I said, yes, maybe.

They said, we don't like it.

I said, that's sound.

They said, it's a bloody shame!

I said, it is.

They said, will you make love now with Helen (our teaching assistant) so that we can see how it is done? We know you like Helen.

I do like Helen but I said that I would not.

We've heard so much about it, they said, but we've never seen it.

I said I would be fired and that it was never, or almost never, done as a demonstration. Helen looked out of the window.

They said, please, please make love with Helen, we require an assertion of value, we are frightened.

I said that they shouldn't be frightened (although I am often frightened) and that there was value everywhere. Helen came and embraced me. I kissed her a few times on the brow. We held each other. The children were excited. Then there was a knock on the door, I opened the door, and the new gerbil walked in. The children cheered wildly.

CLARICE LISPECTOR

The Fifth Story

his story could be called "The Statues." Another possible title would be "The Killing." Or even "How to Kill Cockroaches." So I shall tell at least three stories, all of them true, because none of the three will contradict the others. Although they constitute one story, they could become a thousand and one, were I to be granted a thousand and one nights.

The first story, "How To Kill Cockroaches," begins like this: I was complaining about the cockroaches. A woman heard me complain. She gave me a recipe for killing them. I was to mix together equal quantities of sugar, flour and gypsum. The flour and sugar would attract the cockroaches, the gypsum would dry up their insides. I followed her advice. The cockroaches died.

The next story is really the first, and it is called "The Killing." It begins like this: I was complaining about the cockroaches. A woman heard me complain. The recipe follows. And then the killing takes place. The truth is that I had only complained in abstract terms about the cockroaches, for they were not even mine: they belonged to the ground floor and climbed up the pipes in the building into our apartment. It was only when I prepared the mixture that they also became mine. On our behalf, therefore, I began to measure and weigh ingredients with greater concentration. A vague loathing had taken possession of me, a sense of outrage. By day, the cockroaches were invisible and no one would believe in the evil secret which eroded such a tranquil household. But if the cockroaches, like evil secrets, slept by day, there I was preparing their nightly poison. Meticulous, eager, I prepared the elixir of prolonged death. An angry fear and my own evil secret guided me. Now I coldly wanted one thing only: to kill every cockroach in existence. Cockroaches climb up the pipes while weary people sleep. And now the recipe was ready, looking so white. As if I were dealing with cockroaches as cunning as myself, I carefully spread the powder until it looked like part of the surface dust. From my bed, in the silence of the apartment, I imagined them climbing up one by one into the kitchen where darkness slept, a solitary towel alert on the clothesline. I awoke hours later, startled at having overslept. It was beginning to grow light. I walked across the kitchen. There they lay on the floor of the scullery, huge and brittle. During the night I had killed them. On our behalf, it was beginning to grow light. On a nearby hill, a cockerel crowed.

The third story which now begins is called "The Statues." It begins by saying that I had been complaining about the cockroaches. Then the same woman appears on the scene. And so it goes on to the point where I awake as it is beginning to grow light, and I awake still feeling sleepy and I walk across the kitchen. Even more sleepy is the scullery floor with its tiled perspective. And in the shadows of dawn, there is a purplish hue which distances everything; at my feet, I perceive patches of light and shade, scores of rigid statues scattered everywhere. The cockroaches that have hardened from core to shell. Some are lying upside down. Others arrested in the midst of some movement that will never be completed. In the mouths of some of the cockroaches, there are traces of white powder. I am the first to observe the dawn breaking over Pompei. I know what this night has been, I know about the orgy in the dark. In some, the gypsum has hardened as slowly as in some organic process, and the cockroaches, with ever more tortuous movements, have greedily intensified the night's pleasures, trying to escape from their insides. Until they turn to stone, in innocent terror and with such, but *such* an expression of pained reproach. Others—suddenly assailed by their own core, without even having perceived that their inner form was turning to stone!—these are suddenly crystallized, just like a word arrested on someone's lips: I love . . . The cockroaches, invoking the name of love in vain, sang on a summer's night. While the cockroach over there, the one with the brown antennae smeared with white, must have realized too late that it had become mummified precisely because it did not know how to use things with the gratuitous grace of the *in vain:* "It is just that I looked too closely inside myself! It is just that I looked too closely inside . . ." From my frigid height as a human being, I watch the destruction of a world. Dawn breaks. Here and there, the parched antennae of dead cockroaches quiver in the breeze. The cockerel from the previous story crows.

The fourth story opens a new era in the household. The story begins as usual: I was complaining about the cockroaches. It goes on up to the point when I see the statues in plaster of Paris. Inevitably dead. I look toward the pipes where this same night an infestation will reappear, swarming slowly upwards in Indian file. Should I renew the lethal sugar every night? like someone who no longer sleeps without the avidity of some rite. And should I take myself somnambulant out to the terrace early each morning? in my craving to encounter the statues which my perspiring night has erected. I trembled with a depraved pleasure at the vision of my double existence as a witch. I also trembled at the sight of that hardening gypsum, the depravity of existence which would shatter my internal form.

The grim moment of choosing between two paths, which I thought would separate, convinced that any choice would mean sacrificing either myself or my soul. I chose. And today I secretly carry a plaque of virtue in my heart: "This house has been disinfected."

The fifth story is called "Leibnitz and the Transcendence of Love in Polynesia." It begins like this: I was complaining about the cockroaches.

Translated by Giovanni Pontiero

BARBARA ALBERTI

Tancredi

In the room where Grandma Santina kept the pictures of her dead children, there were two photos enclosed in a single frame.

These were the photos of Tancredi, Grandma's only son born with two heads.

Grandma's first pregnancy lasted thirteen months, at the end of which she gave birth to a beautiful baby boy who enjoyed good health, despite that anomaly.

Innumerable are the faults of man, and it was useless to seek the one for which God had sent that punishment.

There was some embarrassment when the baby was baptized, and the priest finally gave him the name Tancredi, which resolved every doubt with its ambiguous plural.

Grandma Santini proudly bore her cross.

She nursed the baby with one mouth at each breast, and she didn't complain. She also stifled her complaints because everyone knows that God loves prodigies, and not even in Paradise must there be many two-headed angels.

But Tancredi got through the first months of life without Heaven calling him.

Grandma Santina thought she saw in that delay an invitation to take the initiative.

And it was according to her interpretation of God's will that Grandma left Tancredi's basket in the garden one January night that was too cold for snow. But in the morning the baby was crying, his two mouths agape with hunger, and his faces were red from having taken all that air.

Grandma proceeded to a more explicit attempt, and she gave Tancredi a potion of herbs which an old recipe book recommended to poison wolves.

This time Tancredi had a slight stomach ache. Grandma no longer restrained herself, and threw him out the window. Right at that moment a boat loaded with straw was passing in the river, and Tancredi softly fell into it, opening his four eyes wide with bewilderment.

Grandma had to resign herself to God's will, whose ends, as always, escaped her.

Tancredi grew. And as he grew, the two heads became more and more different.

The right Tancredi had delicate features. His eyes were blue, his hair blond, and because he was timid, he spoke little, but smiled often. The left Tancredi, on the other hand, had a dark complexion, and his eyes flashed. Tough and aggressive, he didn't like to be ordered. And with the hand that belonged to him, the left one, he frequently slapped the right Tancredi who lowered his head, murmuring: "I forgive you."

Both of them disliked being forced to wear the same clothes, because even in the matter of attire they had conflicting tastes. They tried to remedy their predicament with the only possible distinction that fate had granted them, wearing different hats.

The right Tancredi chose romantic hats with wide brims, which partly covered his now perennial frown. The other one wore a dusty beret from which his black curls issued like a goat's tail.

In time everyone realized that even though he had a single body, Tancredi represented two people so different that it was really impossible to treat them in the same way by pretending they both were well-bred, since in fact only one was. When they walked through the village, the right Tancredi removed his hat if he encountered women, priests, even the old ladies who lived in the alley.

The left Tancredi stared straight ahead, his beret lowered over his eyes, and he greeted no one.

Besides, no one greeted him. He was too violent and ill-mannered to merit people's esteem.

Relations between the two heads were not good.

The left Tancredi continually made fun of his right counterpart because he was pious and obedient and always said: "Yes, Mamma."

When they were young and Grandma Santina, once she decided not to kill them, had them kneel down for the rosary, the blond head answered in rapture, while the dark-haired one touched his sex and entertained only hellish thoughts.

The good Tancredi caught butterflies in his right hand, and in them he saw the perfection of the universe. But the other Tancredi skilfully tore them apart with his left hand and crushed them on the good one's face.

In political matters they could never agree. The wicked Tancredi thought that peasants and poor people should be hanged or burned alive, without even fucking their wives and daughters.

The good Tancredi, who held advanced ideas, rather longed for an ordered world in which everyone respected the social inequalities willed by God and by human history. And since he was somewhat of a philosopher, he called his idea "The Sweet

Utopia," and foresaw that at the end of the worldwide renewal, anarchists and Bolsheviks would repent and spontaneously commit suicide to free the earth of evil.

But for both of them the greatest annoyance was that they were unable to dissociate themselves from one another's physical actions. The right head fasted for penance, while the left one gorged himself without dignity or shame; he was dedicated to any pleasure as long as it wasn't spiritual.

And while the dark Tancredi snored, belching in his sleep, the blond couldn't get any rest because he suffered indigestion from those insane meals.

When the left head did something wrong, even though discouraged by the right one, they both had to endure Grandma Santina's lashings, which were intended only for the wicked one, but were a physical reality to both of them.

The worst part of their life together occurred when the irrepressible Tancredi began to frequent Sbrega, a robust whore whose wise hands ultimately received the savings that the chaste Tancredi had accumulated for charity.

During those nights of grievous passion which the dark Tancredi spent with Sbrega, the other one despaired, wept, and closed his eyes, trying not to feel what was happening to him, tormented by the suspicion that he and his twin possessed a single soul.

But at the end of all the violent bucking, a shout of pleasure even escaped from the good head, against his will, against his soul's salvation which he held above everything.

And never once did the right Tancredi complain to anyone about this torture.

Never once did he spy for Grandma Santina, while the wicked one forced him to slip very quietly away toward Sbrega's house, where each time the slaughter of the innocent was repeated.

But when Sbrega and the left Tancredi violated the laws of nature, profaning what must not be profaned, doing what witches do with devils in all the covens of the world, the blond Tancredi had the premonition of what would happen to him in the beyond, and at the instant of that terrible pleasure which could not be repressed, he had a true vision of the Inferno and felt with burning clarity the fiery iron rod with which Satan would penetrate him, mocking his guilt for eternity.

Because of his fear he started to shout deadly threats at Sbrega, who laughed scornfully, content with her sins.

Later, the right Tancredi tried to purify his flesh by inflicting torture on himself. And without informing the left hand, who certainly would not have agreed to it, he slipped a hat pin into his belly with one thrust, in order to prevent the other one from stopping him.

Uttering a cry, the dark Tancredi pulled out the pin. He was so overcome by a dreadful rage that he began to beat the right head, until driven by his unbridled anger, he squeezed the other's throat to strangle him.

The blond head dangled lifelessly. And only then did Tancredi realize, as if after some nasty joke, that he had killed the twin head.

For the first time in his double life, Tancredi burst into sobs without Grandma's beatings. He tenderly raised the inanimate head, caressed it, and said with dismay: "Come on, faker, stop fooling around . . ."

But the other one just focused a dull stare on him. Holding the head in both his hands, which were now his alone, Tancredi sang a sad lullaby after he himself closed his brother's eyes.

A few moments later, when the other head's death reached their single heart, he too died, foregoing his final blasphemy because his brother couldn't hear anything he said, or be annoyed by it.

Translated by Lawrence Venuti

JULIO ORTEGA

Las Papas

He turned on the faucet of the kitchen sink and washed off the knife. As he felt the splashing water, he looked up through the front window and saw the September wind shaking the tender shoots of the trees on his street, the first hint of fall.

He quickly washed the potatoes one by one. Although their coloring was light and serene, they were large and heavy. When he started to peel them, slowly, using the knife precisely and carefully, the child came into the kitchen.

"What are you going to cook?" he asked. He stood there waiting for an answer.

"Chicken cacciatore," the man answered, but the child didn't believe him. He was only six, but he seemed capable of objectively discerning between one chicken recipe and another.

"Wait and see," he promised.

"Is it going to have onions in it?" asked the child.

"Very few," he said.

The child left the kitchen unconvinced.

He finished peeling the potatoes and started to slice them. Through the window he saw the growing brightness of midday.

273

That strong light seemed to paralyze the brilliant foliage on the trees. The inside of the potatoes had the same clean whiteness, and the knife penetrated it, as if slicing through soft clay.

Then he rinsed the onions and cut into them, chopping them up. He glanced at the recipe again and looked for seasonings in the pantry. The child came back in.

"Chicken is really boring," the child said, almost in protest.

"Not this recipe," he said. "It'll be great. You'll see."

"Put a lot of stuff in it," the child recommended.

"It's going to have oregano, pepper, and even some sugar," he said.

The child smiled, approvingly.

He dried the potato slices. The pulp was crisp, almost too white, more like an apple, perhaps. Where did these potatoes come from? Wyoming or Idaho, probably. The potatoes from his country, on the other hand, were grittier, with a heavy flavor of the land. There were dark ones, almost royal purple like fruit, and delicate yellow ones, like the yolk of an egg. They say there used to be more than a thousand varieties of potato. Many of them have disappeared forever.

The ones that were lost, had they been less firmly rooted in the soil? Were they more delicate varieties? Maybe they disappeared when control of the cultivated lands was deteriorating. Some people say, and it's probably true, that the loss of even one domesticated plant makes the world a little poorer, as does the destruction of a work of art in a city plundered by invaders. If a history of the lost varieties were written it might prove that no one would ever have gone hungry.

Boiled, baked, fried, or stewed: the ways of cooking potatoes were a long story in themselves. He remembered what his mother had told him as a child: at harvest time, the largest potatoes would be roasted for everybody, and, in the fire, they would open up—just like flowers. That potato was probably one of the lost varieties, the kind that turned into flowers in the flames.

Are potatoes harvested at night in the moonlight? He was surprised how little he knew about something that came from his own country. As he thought about it, he believed *harvest* wasn't even the correct term. *Gathering? Digging?* What do you call this harvest from under the earth?

For a long time he had avoided eating them. Even their name seemed unpleasant to him, *papas*. A sign of the provinces, one more shred of evidence of the meager resources, of underdevelopment—a potato lacked protein and was loaded with carbohydrates. French-fried potatoes seemed more tolerable to him: they were, somehow, in a more neutralized condition.

At first, when he began to care for the child all by himself, he tried to simplify the ordeal of meals by going out to the corner restaurant. But he soon found that if he tried to cook something it passed the time, and he also amused himself with the child's curiosity.

He picked up the cut slices. There wasn't much more to discover in them. It wasn't necessary to expect anything more of them than the density they already possessed, a crude cleanliness that was the earth's flavor. But that same sense transformed them right there in his hands, a secret flowering, uncovered by him in the kitchen. It was as if he discovered one of the lost varieties of the Andean potato: the one that belonged to him, wondering, at noon.

When the chicken began to fry in the skillet, the boy returned, attracted by its aroma. The man was in the midst of making the salad.

"Where's this food come from?" the child asked, realizing it was a different recipe.

"Peru," he replied.

"Not Italy?" said the child, surprised.

"I'm cooking another recipe now," he explained. "Potatoes come from Peru. You know that, right?"

"Yeah, but I forgot it."

"They're really good, and there are all kinds and flavors. Remember mangoes? You really used to like them when we went to see your grandparents."

"I don't remember them either. I only remember the lion in the zoo."

"You don't remember the tree in Olivar Park?"

"Uh-huh. I remember that."

"We're going back there next summer, to visit the whole family."

"What if there's an earthquake?"

The boy went for his Spanish reader and sat down at the kitchen table. He read the resonant names out loud, names that were also like an unfinished history, and the man had to go over to him every once in a while to help explain one thing or another.

He tasted the sauce for the amount of salt, then added a bit of tarragon, whose intense perfume was delightful, and a bit of marjoram, a sweeter aroma.

He noticed how, outside, the light trapped by a tree slipped out from the blackened greenness of the leaves, now spilling onto the grass on the hill where their apartment house stood. The grass, all lit up, became an oblique field, a slope of tame fire seen from the window.

He looked at the child, stuck on a page in his book; he looked at the calm, repeated blue of the sky; and he looked at the leaves of lettuce in his hands, leaves that crackled as they broke off and opened up like tender shoots, beside the faucet of running water.

As if it suddenly came back to him, he understood that he must have been six or seven when his father, probably forty years old, as he was now, used to cook at home on Sundays. His father was always in a good mood as he cooked, boasting beforehand about how good the Chinese recipes were that he had learned in a remote hacienda in Peru. Maybe his father had made these meals for him, in this always incomplete past, to celebrate the meeting of father and son.

Unfamiliar anxiety, like a question without a subject, grew in him as he understood that he had never properly acknowledged his father's gesture; he hadn't even understood it. Actually, he had rejected his father's cooking one time, saying that it was too spicy. He must have been about fifteen then, a recent convert devoutly practicing the religion of natural foods, when he left the table with the plate of fish in his hands. He went out to the kitchen to turn on the faucet and quickly washed away the flesh boiled in soy sauce and ginger. His mother came to the kitchen and scolded him for what he had just done, a seemingly harmless act, but from then on an irreparable one. He returned to the table in silence, sullen, but his father didn't appear to be offended. Or did he suspect that one day his son's meal would be refused by his own son when he served it?

The emotion could still wound him, but it could also make him laugh. There was a kind of irony in this repeating to a large extent his father's gestures as he concocted an unusual flavor in the kitchen. However, like a sigh that only acquires some meaning by turning upon itself, he discovered a symmetry in the repetitions, a symmetry that revealed the agony of emotions not easily understood.

Just like animals that feed their young, we feed ourselves with a promise that food will taste good, he said to himself. We prepare a recipe with painstaking detail so that our children will recognize us in a complete history of flavor.

He must have muttered this out loud because the child looked up.

"What?" he said, "Italian?"

"Peruvian," he corrected. "With a taste of the mountains, a

mixture of Indian, Chinese, and Spanish."

The child laughed, as if he'd heard a private joke in the sound of the words.

"When we go to Lima, I'll take you around to the restaurants," he promised.

The child broke into laughter again.

"It tastes good," said the child.

"It tastes better than yesterday's," the man said.

He poured some orange juice. The boy kneeled in the chair and ate a bit of everything. He ate more out of curiosity than appetite.

He felt once again that brief defenselessness that accompanies the act of eating one's own cooking. Behind that flavor, he knew, lurked the raw materials, the separate foods cooked to render them neutral, a secret known only to the cook, who combined ingredients and proportions until something different was presented to eyes and mouth. This culinary act could be an adventure, a hunting foray. And the pleasure of creating a transformation must be shared, a kind of brief festival as the eaters decipher the flavors, knowing that an illusion has taken place.

Later, he looked for a potato in the pantry and he held it up against the unfiltered light in the window. It was large, and it fit perfectly in his barely closed hand. He was not surprised that the misshapen form of this swollen tuber adapted to the contour of his hand; he knew the potato adapted to different lands, true to its own internal form, as if it occupied stolen space. The entire history of his people was here, he said to himself, surviving in a territory overrun and pillaged several times, growing in marginal spaces, under siege and waiting.

He left the apartment, went down the stairs and over to the tree on the hillock. It was a perfect day, as if the entire history of daytime were before him. The grass was ablaze, standing for all the grass he had ever seen. With both hands, he dug, and the earth opened up to him, cold. He placed the potato there, and he covered it up quickly. Feeling slightly embarrassed, he looked around. He went back up the stairs, wiping his hands, almost running.

The boy was standing at the balcony, waiting for him; he had seen it all.

"A tree's going to grow there!" said the boy, alarmed.

"No," he said soothingly, "potatoes aren't trees. If it grows, it will grow under the ground."

The child didn't seem to understand everything, but then suddenly he laughed.

"Nobody will even know it's there," he said, excited by such complicity with his father.

Translated by Regina Harrison

The Netherlands

J. BERNLEF

The Black Dog

T here's a fire at Voorthuyzen's bakery on Main Street," his father had said during breakfast. "A large blazing fire," he had added.

Half an hour later he shuffled back, his head lowered. His father had laughed at him. His mother had found it childish that he responded so angrily to his father's joke.

It was Saturday, the first of April. Secretly he had wished his father dead.

Now it was the second of April. You can forget a lot in twenty-four hours. He took the usual Sunday stroll with his father.

Behind the still-closed outdoor wooden swimming pool the sandy land stretched ruggedly toward the pale green backdike. While he dodged through the holes and half-caved-in huts of unknown boys in search of possible treasures, his father whistled softly through his teeth and smoked a Players from a pale blue pack, his shiny black raincoat folded in four over his left arm, for he never trusted the weather report, especially not in April.

At the edge of the dike his father sat staring for a long time in the direction of the three chimney stacks of the electric plant while he, the son, watched the schools of nearly transparent sticklebacks and the scurrying of pitch-black water beetles at the foot of a ditch.

These were always the best hours of the week, all alone with his father, who now took off his glasses and wiped them with a chamois cloth which he removed from a front compartment in his purse. As if he wanted to get a better look at the three upright brick-red chimneys of the power plant.

Sitting on top of the dike in clear weather you could even see the ships slowly sailing through the Connecting Canal on their way to the sea.

These were the best hours of the week because his father didn't do a thing, but just sat there silently and every now and then gave him a short wave whenever he, sitting in a hunched position, would look up from the side of the ditch. He listened to the shrill cries of the peewits and the seagulls in the pasture in front of him. A lightly spotted rabbit jumped clumsily through the short grass.

When his father had finished smoking another Player he made the usual gesture. Time to return. Actually it was only a short walk to the back-dike, but the town's last row of houses still seemed to be far away.

A large black dog ran toward them over the dunes of sand in enormous lopsided leaps. A Bouvier de Flandres. You could tell by the trimmed ears lying flat against his head.

The dog began to jump around them, barking wildly.

"Just keep on walking." His father had barely finished the sentence before he had to use both hands to keep the raving dog at bay. Savagely, with his head shaking, the animal settled his jaws into the black raincoat.

Only now did he notice the flecks of foam flying out of his mouth, the yellowish glare in his eyes and the unusual rigid manner in which the dog fixed his paws, jerking at a flap of the coat with all his might while his father frantically held on to it with both hands. Every now and then the dog's black body trembled as if it were undergoing an electric shock.

He looked around him. A bed spring, a smashed orange crate. Not a person in sight. Nobody who could see them here. Nobody to help his father.

Suddenly the dog let go of the coat. His father lost his balance, stumbled over backwards, and the dog immediately plunged toward him with a wide-open mouth full of foam and threads of bloody slime. Lying on the ground his father gave the dog such a kick with one of this black shoes that the dog tottered a few steps sideways and stood in a daze for a few moments, as if the blow had brought him to his senses.

Then the dog shook his pelt and bent down, the front paws spread out before him, snarling at the ground. His father had jumped up, the shredded raincoat still in his hands. His left hand was bleeding.

A Dodge hobbled over the sandy land loudly blowing its horn. For the first time he dared to do something. He ran toward the stub-nosed car, his thin boy's arms swaying above his head. Come here. Come here. The driver, a man with a thick bald head and red cheeks, leaned out of the lowered side window.

"That dog," he shouted gasping and pointing. "That dog is biting my father to death!"

The man appeared startled by his announcement and accelerated. The car lunged ahead. He ran after the car, which rode in a circle around his father and the dog twice. His father made a motion to the driver. The car then made an abrupt turn and joltingly disappeared in the direction of the main road. And the dog sprung up again with his mouth wide open.

"Go away," his father screamed. "Run. Go home. Hurry up."

He had to. Without even looking he ran from his father who would now surely be bitten to death by the dog.

He began to cross the sandy land, through the Sunday streets, along parks and lampposts, along the closed front doors of friends' homes, the fence of the nursery school, the pharmacy with its brown bottles in the window.

His father, bitten to death by a black wolf-dog. Covered with foam and slime. Bleeding all over.

He ran crying with quivering lips. Everywhere sat silent people across from each other in bay windows.

Panting, he let himself fall against the door of his house. He pressed the bell without letting go. He leaned against the door with such force that when it was opened he slowly glided together with the door's panel into the hallway.

From the open space of the landing above he heard his mother's voice. Who was there? He stumbled up the stairs.

He couldn't utter a word, only shake his wailing head. His mother gathered him up. What is wrong? What had happened?

Finally he sat plopped down in one of the armchairs in the living room. She went to the kitchen and came back with a wet wash cloth which she brusquely rubbed over his face.

"What happened exactly? Quiet down and tell me."

He could only wail, his drawn-up knees pressed against his chest. She could not understand it. Only he knew what he had wished upon his father while walking back from the nonexistent fire that Saturday morning.

"Daddy is dead."

He hardly felt the hard lashing blow on his cheek. His head jerked to the side and bumped against the headrest. It was as if his insides were filling up with ice water. He vaguely heard doors slamming. Then it became silent. In front of him a striped blue wash cloth lay on the carpet.

He let his legs sink to the floor, stood up and walked to the window. The field in front of the door was deserted. Because it was Sunday there were no playing children to be seen. He stood high above the ground and looked out over the lot, the pastures, the canal and the rows of dully shining greenhouses in the distance.

"I'm never going onto the street again," he said loudly.

He turned around. The chairs, the table, the piano, the light rug with the cheerful orange rectangles; he stood in a room that suddenly had nothing to do with home anymore.

Filled with panic he leaped into the side room and grabbed the portrait on his father's desk. His father and mother, arm in arm and laughing, somewhere in a garden.

"That was made when you were not here yet."

Then this could also be possible. That everything would continue as before, the room, the dike, his mother, the school, only his father was not there anymore. A dog which grew ever bigger and blacker while his father got weaker and smaller until he completely disappeared.

He had thought of it first, then he had said it and now it had happened.

From a thin silver frame his father and mother smiled at him. From a time in which he had not existed.

Perhaps that was why he sat behind the desk as if turned to stone, the photo pressed between both hands, when the door opened and he heard his father's voice. As if he still lived. He put the portrait down. With his eyes closed he turned around. He heard his father laughing. Only then did he dare to look.

One of his father's arms was in a white sling. He laughed and leaned with his good arm on the marble mantel shelf. He was really alive. Both of them lived, he and his father, at the same time.

The door opened yet again and his mother entered, a tray in her hands. A teapot, three white cups and three saucers. Three spoons, a sugar pot. He could not keep his eyes from these things.

They went to sit at the table, each at his own place. His father on the left, his mother to his right. Walls and furniture surrounded them. His mother poured the tea. A thin golden-yellow stream that softly splashed into the cups. All three of them stirred their teaspoons at the same time.

He sat at the head of the table peering at a stain on the wallpaper and suddenly everything came to him from the dark spot on the wall as if from out of a hole. The fire in the not burning bakery, the picture from the time he had not yet existed and his bitten-to-death living father, who patted his head with his free hand and said there was no reason to cry.

"They did away with him right away," he heard his father say. "One shot through the head and that was it."

Translated by Frank Scimone

ANN BEATTIE

Snow

I remember the cold night you brought in a pile of logs and a chipmunk jumped off as you lowered your arms. "What do you think *you're* doing in here?" you said, as it ran through the living room. It went through the library and stopped at the front door as though it knew the house well. This would be difficult for anyone to believe, except perhaps as the subject of a poem. Our first week in the house was spent scraping, finding some of the house's secrets, like wallpaper underneath wallpaper. In the kitchen, a pattern of white-gold trellises supported purple grapes as big and round as Ping-Pong balls. When we painted the walls yellow, I thought of the bits of grape that remained underneath and imagined the vine popping through, the way some plants can tenaciously push through anything. The day of the big snow, when you had to shovel the walk and couldn't find your cap and asked me how to wind a towel so that it would stay on your head—you, in the white towel turban, like a crazy king of snow. People liked the idea of our being together, leaving the city for the country. So many people visited, and the fireplace made all of them want to tell amazing stories: the child who happened to be standing on the right corner when the door of the ice-cream truck came open and hundreds of Popsicles crashed out; the man standing on the beach, sand sparkling in the sun, one bit glinting more than the rest, stooping to find a diamond ring. Did they talk about amazing things because they thought we'd turn into one of them? Now I think they probably guessed it wouldn't work. It was as hopeless as giving a child a matched cup and saucer. Remember the night, out on the lawn, knee-deep in snow, chins pointed at the sky as the wind whirled down all that whiteness? It seemed that the world had been turned upside down, and we were looking into an enormous field of Queen Anne's lace. Later, headlights off, our car was the first to ride through the newly fallen snow. The world outside the car looked solarized.

You remember it differently. You remember that the cold settled in stages, that a small curve of light was shaved from the moon night after night, until you were no longer surprised the sky was black, that the chipmunk ran to hide in the dark, not simply to a door that led to its escape. Our visitors told the same stories people always tell. One night, giving me a lesson in storytelling, you said, "Any life will seem dramatic if you omit mention of most of it."

This, then, for drama: I drove back to that house not long ago. It was April, and Allen had died. In spite of all the visitors, Allen, next door, had been the good friend in bad times. I sat with his wife in their living room, looking out the glass doors to the backyard, and there was Allen's pool, still covered with black plastic that had been stretched across it for winter. It had rained, and as the rain fell, the cover collected more and more water until it finally spilled onto the concrete. When I left that day, I drove past what had been our house. Three or four crocuses were blooming in the front—just a few dots of white, no field of snow. I felt embarrassed for them. They couldn't compete.

This is a story, told the way you say stories should be told: Somebody grew up, fell in love, and spent a winter with her lover in the country. This, of course, is the barest outline, and futile to discuss. It's as pointless as throwing birdseed on the ground while snow still falls fast. Who expects small things to survive when even the largest get lost? People forget years and remember moments. Seconds and symbols are left to sum things up: the black shroud over the pool. Love, in its shortest form, becomes a word. What I remember about all that time is one winter. The snow. Even now, saying "snow," my lips move so that they kiss the air.

No mention has been made of the snowplow that seemed always to be there, scraping snow off our narrow road—an artery cleared, though neither of us could have said where the heart was.

China

BAI XIAO-YI

The Explosion in the Parlor

The host poured tea into the cup and placed it on the small
table in front of his guests, who were a father and daughter, and
put the lid on the cup with a clink. Apparently thinking of
something, he hurried into the inner room, leaving the thermos
on the table. His two guests heard a chest of drawers opening
and a rustling.

They remained sitting in the parlor, the ten-year-old daughter looking at the flowers outside the window, the father just
about to take his cup, when the crash came, right there in the
parlor. Something was hopelessly broken.

It was the thermos, which had fallen to the floor. The girl
looked over her shoulder abruptly, startled, staring. It was mysterious. Neither of them had touched it, not even a little bit.
True, it hadn't stood steadily when their host placed it on the
table, but it hadn't fallen then.

The crash of the thermos caused the host, with a box of sugar
cubes in his hand, to rush back from the inner room. He gawked
at the steaming floor and blurted out, "It doesn't matter! It doesn't
matter!"

The father started to say something. Then he muttered, "Sorry, I touched it and it fell."

"It doesn't matter," the host said.

Later, when they left the house, the daughter said, "Daddy, *did* you touch it?"

"No. But it stood so close to me."

"But you *didn't* touch it. I saw your reflection in the window-pane. You were sitting perfectly still."

The father laughed. "What then would you give as the cause of its fall?"

"The thermos fell by itself. The floor is uneven. It wasn't steady when Mr. Li put it there. Daddy, *why* did you say that you . . ."

"That won't do, girl. It sounds more acceptable when I say I knocked it down. There are things which people accept less the more you defend them. The truer the story you tell, the less true it sounds."

The daughter was lost in silence for a while. Then she said, "Can you explain it only this way?"

"Only this way," her father said.

Translated by Ding Zuxin

United States

PAUL THEROUX

Acknowledgments

hanks are due to Dr. Milton Rumbellow, Chairman of the
Department of Comparative Literature, Yourgrau College (Wyola
Campus), for generously allowing me first a small course load
and then an indefinite leave of absence from my duties; to Mrs.
Edith Rumbellow for many kindnesses, not the least of which
has her interceding on my behalf; to the trustees of Yourgrau
College for a grant-in-aid, to the John Simon Guggenheim
Memorial Foundation for extending my fellowship to two years,
and to the National Endowment for the Arts, without whose
help this book could not have been written; to Miss Sally-Ann
Fletcher, of Wyolatours, for ably ticketing and cross-checking a
varied itinerary, and to Miss Denise Humpherson, of the British Tourist Authority, who provided me with a map of the
cycling paths in the areas of England lived in by Matthew Casket; to Mrs. Mabel Nittish for arranging the sublet of my Wyola
apartment and providing me with a folding bike.

As with many other biographers of minor West Country dia-
lect poets, Casket's output was so small that he could feed himself only by securing remunerative employment in unrelated

fields. I am grateful for the cooperation of his former employers—in particular to Bewlence & Sons (Solid Fuels), Ltd., Western Feeds, Yeovil Rubber Goods, and Raybold & Squarey (Drugs Division), Ltd., for allowing me access to their in-house files and providing me with hospitality over a period of weeks; and especially to Mrs. Ronald Bewlence for endlessly informative chats and helping me dispose of a bike, and Mrs. Margaret Squarey, F.P.S., for placing herself entirely at my disposal and sharing with me her wide knowledge of poisons and toxic weeds.

At a crucial stage in my ongoing research, I was privileged to meet Mrs. Daphne Casket Hebblewhite, who, at sixty-two, still remembered her father's run of bad luck. For three months of hospitality at "Limpets" and many hours of tirelessly answering my questions, I must express my thanks and, with them, my sorrow that the late Mrs. Hebblewhite was not alive to read this memorial to her father, which she and I both felt was scandalously overdue. It was Mrs. Hebblewhite who, by willing them to me, gave me access to what few Casket papers exist, and who graciously provided me with introductions to Casket's surviving relations—Miss Fiona Slaughter, Miss Gloria Wyngard, and Miss Tracy Champneys; I am happy to record here my debt for their warmth and openness to a stranger to their shores. Miss Slaughter acceded to all my requests, as well as taking on some extensive chauffering; Miss Wyngard unearthed for me a second copy of Casket's only book, but annotated in his own hand, enabling me to speculate on what he might have attempted in revised form had he had the means to do so, and allowing me the treasured memento of another warm friendship and our weeks in Swanage; Miss Champneys made herself available to me in many ways, giving me her constant attention, and it is to her efforts, as well as those of Ruck & Grutchfield, Barristers-at-Law, that I owe the speedy end of what could have been a piece of protracted litigation. To Señorita Luisa Alfardo Lizardi, who kept

Mrs. Hebblewhite's house open to me after her late mistress's tragic passing and was on call twenty-four hours a day, I am more grateful than I can sufficiently express here.

Special thanks must go to the staff of Broomhill Hospital, Old Sarum, and particularly to Miss Francine Kelversedge, S.R.N., for encouraging me in my project during a needed rest from exhausting weeks of research. Colonel and Mrs. Hapgood Chalke came to my rescue at a turning point in my Broomhill sojourn; to them I owe more than I can adequately convey, and to their dear daughter, Tamsin, my keenest thanks for guiding my hand and for her resourcefulness in providing explanations when they were in short supply. To Dr. Winifred Sparrow, Director of Broomhill, I can only state my gratitude for waiving payment for my five months of convalescence; and to Stones & Sons, Tobacconists, Worsfold's Wine Merchants, and Hine's Distilleries, all of Old Sarum, my deepest thanks for under-standing, prompt delivery, and good will in circumstances that would have had lesser tradesmen seeking legal redress.

I am grateful for the hospitality I received during the weeks I spent at the homes of Mr. and Mrs. Warner Ditchley, Mrs. R. B. Ollenshaw, Dr. and Mrs. F. G. Cockburn, Major and Mrs. B. P. Birdsmoor, and the late Mrs. J. R. W. Gatacre, all of Devizes, as well as for the timely intervention of Miss Helena Binchey, of Devizes, who, on short notice, placed a car at my disposal in order that I could visit the distant places Casket had known as a child. The Rev. John Punnel, of St. Alban's Primary School, Nether Wallop, provided me with safe harbor as well as a detailed record of Casket's meager education; he kindly returned Miss Binchey's car to Devizes, and it was Mrs. Dorothy Punnel who took me on a delightfully informal tour of the attic bedroom in the dorm, which cannot be very different today from what it was in 1892, when, just prior to his expulsion on an unproved charge of lewdness, Casket was a boarder.

I feel lucky in being able to record my appreciation to Pamela, Lady Grapethorpe, of Nether Wallop Manor, for admitting a footsore traveler and allowing him unlimited use of her house; for her introducing him to the Nether Wallop Flying Club and Aerodrome and to Miss Florence Fettering, who expertly piloted him to Nettlebed, in West Dorset, and accompanied him through his visit in the village where Casket was employed as a twister and ropeworker at the gundry. I am obliged also to Miss Vanessa Liphook, of The Bull Inn, Nettlebed, for very kindly spiriting me from Nettlebed to Compton Valence, where Casket, then a lay brother, worked as a crofter at the friary after the failure of his book. It is thanks to the good offices of Miss Liphook, and her indefatigable Riley, that I was able to tour the South Coast resorts where Casket, in his eighties and down on his luck, found seasonal employment as a scullion and kitchen hand; for their faith in my project and their sumptuous hospitality, I am indebted to the proprietors of The Frog and Nightgown, Bognor Regis; The Raven, Weymouth; The Kings Arms, Bridport; Sprackling House, Eype; and The Grand Hotel, Charmouth. To Miss Josephine Slape, of Charmouth, where Casket died of consumption, I owe the deepest of bows for the loan of a bicycle when it was desperately needed; and to the staff of the Goods Shed, Axminster, I am grateful for their speeding the bicycle back to its owner.

To Mrs. Annabell Frampton, of the British Rail ticket office, Axminster, my sincere thanks for being so generous with a temporarily embarrassed researcher; and to Dame Marina Pensel-Cripps, casually met on the 10:24 to London, but fondly remembered, I am grateful for an introduction to the late Sir Ronald and to Lady Mary Bassetlaw, of Bassetlaw Castle, at which the greater part of this book was written over an eventful period of months as tragic as they were blissful. It is impossible for me adequately to describe the many ways in which Lady

Mary aided me in the preparation of this work; she met every need, overcame every obstacle, and replied to every question, the last of which replies, and by far the hardest, was her affirmative when I asked her to be my wife. So, to my dear Mary, the profoundest of thank yous: this book should have been a sonnet.

Lastly, to Miss Ramona Slupski, Miss Heidi Lim Choo Tan, Miss Piper Vathek, and Miss Joylene Aguilar Garcia Rosario, all of the Graduate Section of British Studies, Yourgrau College, my thanks for collating material and answering swiftly my transatlantic letters and demands; to Miss Gudrun Naismith, for immaculately typing many drafts of this work and deciphering my nearly illegible and at times tormented handwriting, my deepest thanks. And to all my former colleagues at Yourgrau (Wyola Campus), who, by urging me forward in my work, reversed my fortunes, my grateful thanks for assisting me in this undertaking.

Afternotes

TALAT ABBASI, born in Karachi, was educated at the London School of Economics, and has lived in the United States for a decade, much of that time in New York. Her stories have appeared in *Ascent*, *Feminist Studies*, *Asian Women's Anthology*, *The Massachusetts Review*, and *Short Story International*.

Commenting on her affinity for the short-short story form, Abbasi writes: "I used to love to watch fireflies at night after the rains, used to sit outside and wait for them. Suddenly in the darkness there would be a glow, moving, alive. It never lit up the sky. But the moment belonged to it. Then it was gone. Then another firefly. Gone again. Another firefly . . .

"More prosaic reasons for my love for short-short stories are the usual ones—temperament and training. I am, on the whole, a person of few words. I studied in a convent in Karachi where the nuns said, 'Economy in everything, including words.' "

BARBARA ALBERTI lives in Rome. A novelist, playwright, and screenwriter, she won the "Premio Inedito" in 1976 for her first novel, *Wicked Memories;* her second, *Delirium*, was published in English in 1980. Translations of her fiction have appeared in *Antaeus*, *Denver Quarterly*, and *Fiction*. Among her film credits are *The Night Porter* and *The Master and Margherita*.

"To comment on 'Tancredi' I can only write another story: This is the story of a Jewish girl over whom a strange destiny hangs—she is doomed to be saved.

"Judith is twelve years old in Nazi Germany. She is not a beautiful little girl, but sort of Woody Allen-ish, awkward, delicate, full of indecisiveness, very nearsighted. She wears large eyeglasses and has a sensitivity that makes her seem the designated victim.

"Being Jewish was important to her, even before the persecution: Judith is a tireless reader of the Bible, who reads and rereads, but always and faithfully the text alone, never a commentary, viewing any gloss a scandal: how can the word of man comment on God's?

"In her vast religiosity, yet to be separated from childish games, Judith is not surprised when the persecutions turn pitiless, when her dearest friends betray her.

"Anne, Judith's twin, who is spiteful and much loved, secretly reads large quantities of novels, and when her family is forced to take shelter in a friend's house, she takes many of them with her. Judith, on the other hand, changes editions: she had always read her grandfather's huge, solemn Bible; now she buys a pocket-size paperback which she can carry with her in any situation.

"Another betrayal—like the thousands described in the Book—and Judith's family is captured. But she, hidden under a box, is forgotten by the aggressors; she alone, she who was ecstatic and resigned, who had tasted the end of every responsibility: first the end of school, this subversion of every rule, and then the wait to be taken away . . . From that moment on, bad luck points at her grazes her seems to strike her. But nothing can touch her, her little Bible hidden in her pocket. To travel to her Uncle Paul's house in Hamburg, she crosses Germany without documents, always in situations of maximum danger, but she is safe: alone, and safe. She will not see her sister again, or her parents, or her little boyfriend, or the people who secretly help her. And yet she has Job's stern rebelliousness: she thinks that some proof has been sent to her; she would never oppose God, not even in exchange for inestimable wealth—she has knowledge of the Book, she is part of the people to whom God dictated it.

"But an extreme misfortune befalls her, the only one she feels unable to confront: she loses her eyeglasses.

"Until then the privilege of salvation was never having to pay any degrading price.

"But now she needs others, in order to read the Bible.

"She is ready to humiliate herself, to take the risk. The danger increases: it is Yom Kippur, and the little loner studies the passers-by at length, before trusting someone and asking timidly, 'Can you read me this passage?'

"In this way she becomes vulnerable—and much too visible.

"Nevertheless, she will reach Hamburg and her Uncle Paul's house.

"At the end of the war, Judith's tears are different from everyone else's. She has to take off her glasses to cry cry cry freely all her odes of salvation her bitter thanksgiving to God bitter as Isaiah the bitterness of the spared.

"She dries her eyes, starts putting her glasses back on, and they fall.

"Desperate, she hurls herself to the floor to search for them: her nearsightedness is worsening, she is virtually threatened with blindness. She cannot distinguish the hand groping across the floor.

"Crack—she treads on them. She lifts her foot.

"Astonished and frightened, she sees the glass fragments perfectly. And the arabesques of the tiles, the window, the face of the radio . . . everything! For the first time, she *sees*. It is a miracle, subdued and mocking. Judith regained her sight."

MARGARET ATWOOD, born in 1939, is the author of more than twenty volumes of poetry, fiction, and nonfiction. Her most recent novels are *The Handmaid's Tale* and *Cat's Eye*. She is married to the novelist Graeme Gibson, and lives in Toronto.

"When I wrote 'Happy Ending'—the year was, I think, 1982, and I was writing a number of short fictions then—I did not know what sort of creature it was. It was not a poem, a short story or a prose poem. It was not quite a condensation, a commentary, a questionnaire, and it missed being a parable, a proverb, a paradox. It was a mutation. Writing it gave me a sense of furtive glee, like scribbling anonymously on a wall with no one looking.

"This summer I saw a white frog. It would not have been startling if I didn't know that this species of frog is normally green. This is the way such a mutant literary form unsettles us. We know what is expected, in a given arrangement of words; we know what is supposed to come next. And then it doesn't.

"It was a little disappointing to learn that other people had a name for such aberrations, and had already made up rules."

ISAAC BABEL was born in 1894 in the Ukraine. As a youth he excelled in the study of languages, including Russian, Hebrew, English, French and German. He served with the military during the Revolution and again during the assault on Petrograd. *Odessa Tales* and *Red Cavalry* are the best known of his story collections; his mastery of the short story form contributed to its popularity in Russia during the 1920s. Babel also wrote screenplays, reminiscences, newspaper articles, and biographical materials; several novels may have been completed but there is no definitive edition of Babel's work—all Soviet editions show some marks of censorship. Political pressures made it increasingly difficult for Babel to write. Arrested in 1939, the manner and date of his death are uncertain.

BAI XIAO-YI is a native of Shenyang, Liaoning Province. His short-short stories have been published in *People's Literature, Novels and Stories, The Journal of Novels and Stories,* and elsewhere. "The Explosion in the Parlor" won the first prize in a short-short story contest jointly sponsored by the Federation of China's Writers and China's Youth Daily.

Ding Zuxin, translator of "The Explosion in the Parlor," writes: "In China, the short-short story has various names, such as 'little short story,' 'pocket-size story,' 'super-short story,' and 'minute-long story.' Among the masses, some people call it a 'smoke-long story' or 'palm-size story.' The more accepted name, however, is simply 'miniature story.'

"The short-short story in China is not an import. People can trace China's earliest short-short stories to the third century B.C. with 'The Story of a Native of Zheng's Buying a Pair of Shoes' by Han Fei, and 'A Good Maid' by Liu Yi-qing in the fifth century. However, most of the short-short stories in those days were myths or fables dealing very little with the life of people in the world.

"The first real short-short story collection is *Curious Stories from an Ancient Study* by Pu Song-ling (1640–1715). It has long been acclaimed as a wonderful short story book, and it contains many superb short-short stories. But no outstanding stories followed, and the short-short story did not continue to flourish.

"China's modern short-short stories began to develop quickly, though, when Western literature was introduced into China on a large scale in the early twentieth century. The influx of Western literary works, especially the works of Chekhov and O. Henry, exerted a great influence, and even today one can still find many Chinese short-short stories written in their styles, or on their models.

"And beginning in 1978, the short-short story in China has witnessed a most flourishing period. Many excellent short-short stories have appeared, occupying a secure position in the field of publication, and quite a few periodicals have emerged which are exclusively devoted to short-short stories. Short-short stories also appear in practically all major dailies, evening papers, and magazines. In 1985, a small short-short story anthology, *Selected Chinese Miniature Story Anthology with Commentaries*, was published in Shanghai, edited by Bo Fang-ming, and its sequel followed in 1987. The two anthologies have played an important role in developing China's short-short stories over the past few years.

"In Taiwan and Hong Kong the short-short story arose earlier, beginning to flourish in the late Sixties. Chun Lin is the most outstanding writer, and her collection, *Chun Lin's Short-Short Stories*, is very popular. Although most short-short story writers in China are young people, not well known or professional, over the past few years such veteran writers as Wang Meng (the present Minister of Culture of the People's Republic of China) and Jiang Zilong have also contributed short-short stories to dailies or magazines."

DONALD BARTHELME (1931–1989), well known to readers of *The New Yorker* and to most readers of American short fiction, was born in Philadelphia. His short stories—frequently under ten pages, often playful, fanciful, self-reflexive—make up many collections, including *City Life*,

Sixty Stories, and *Come Back, Dr. Caligari*. He taught creative writing at the University of Houston.

PAULÉ BARTÓN, who lived his life mainly as a goatherd, was born in Haiti in 1916. After surviving a prison term under the repressive Duvalier regime, he moved from Haiti with his family and finally settled in Costa Rica, where he died in 1974. It was mainly in Jamaica and Trinidad that Bartón collaborated with Howard Norman on the translation of his stories.

"Goats figured in a great variety of Bartón's stories," Howard Norman writes. "They even made cameo appearances to no purpose other than to ambush and butt a character. That's a *purpose*, of course, one with illogical humor. He told 'formal' Ananse (Spider-Trickster) stories. He told 'Cric-cracs,' which he called 'the scary night-time stories.' And he told what might be called more modern stories, such as 'Emilie Plead Choose One Egg.' The latter were often replete with his quirky philosophies, strong-willed women, despairing, often dreamy men. All these stories, with their lilting, syncopated Creole, were deeply imagined. Their plots, even when placed as locally as a shack, felt universal. A single sentence could contain humor and despair. He used the language of 'waking dreams,' by which I mean that the deeper tensions of existence were drawn forth and absorbed fully into the beauty of the language. The humor, poverty, shame and love of his characters is autobiographical.

" 'Emilie Plead Choose One Egg' was read over a radio broadcast in Port-Au-Prince, on the morning that 'Baby Doc' Duvalier's thugs ransacked the station, killing one employee and later beating another senseless. The gentle nature of the tale (it didn't precipitate the act of violence, which no doubt had been planned against the radio station well before that date) seems, even now, in such dread contrast to that brutality."

ANN BEATTIE was born in 1947 in Washington, D.C. Among her works are the novels *Chilly Scenes of Winter* and *Love, Always*, and several collections of stories, including *Jacklighting*, *The Burning House*, and *Where You'll Find Me*.

"I've always resisted explaining my stories because I find it necessary to think that they don't need explaining. But if I could write
poetry—which I certainly cannot—I imagine that 'Snow' might have
been notes for, or an outline of, a poem. I had in the back of my mind
Robert Lowell's 'My Old Flame,' which ends with the image of a snow
plow ('As it tossed off the snow / To the side of the road'). Lowell's
poem is quite understated—and certainly snow plows are ordinary
enough in New England, in winter—so I decided it was okay to bring
in Lowell's plow, in a sense, though I knew at the same time that I'd
have to do something with it: that the snow plow alone wouldn't rever-
berate enough. Thus the ending, which makes apparent, in alluding
to the body, the connection between the real, observable physicality
of things that, nevertheless, is only a cover for our spiritual state.

"I do believe that 'seconds and symbols are left to sum things up,'
and I found when writing this story that it could be very brief indeed.
For what it's worth, there really was an Allen, and the day I saw the
plastic pool cover, after he had died, it struck me instantly as a shroud.
Allen was a writer, retired from *Newsweek*, so he probably would have
agreed with the analogy. Something tells me, though, that he would
also like to remembered as a man who loved dogs, and who didn't turn
the spotlights on outside above the pool when birds nested there in the
spring. Or, since he was so modest, perhaps he would be surprised to
be in a story, or to be discussed in these notes."

J. BERNLEF was born in 1937 in St. Pancras, Holland. His first book
appeared in 1960, and since then about fifty books—novels, short stories, poems, essays, plays and poems—have followed. Bernlef's work
won the prestigious "Constantijn Huyghens Prijs" in 1984, when his
novel *Hersenschimmen* was a bestseller in Holland; subsequently it was
published in Denmark, Norway, Sweden, France, Germany, Switzerland and Poland, and in England and the United States as *Out of
Mind*. In 1987 he received the AKO Literature Prize, the Dutch equiv-
alent of the English Booker Prize, for his novel *Open Secret*. Bernlef
lives in Amsterdam.

" 'The Black Dog' is one of the few autobiographical stories that I
have written. I am not particularly fond of the genre. A writer who

can do nothing else but tell what happened to him in so-called real life is not an important writer.

"That I am not completely unhappy with the story depends on the fact that the story is also about the invention or rather the discovery of lies, which I think is one of the cornerstones of literature. When I discovered that you could use language in such a way that people believe what it described although what it described had never happened, I started out as a storyteller and, later, as a writer of fiction."

KENNETH BERNARD was born in Brooklyn in 1930 and is Professor of English at Long Island University. Both a fiction writer and a playwright, his plays have been produced by the Playhouse of the Ridiculous, under John Vaccaro's direction, and include *The Moke-Eater*, *Night Club*, and *The Magic Show of Dr. Ma-Gico*. He has received a Rockefeller grant and a Guggenheim Fellowship.

"Most of my stories come from a word, a phrase, a sentence at most, occasionally an intonation or a rhythm. I write the story to find out why—that is, why I am struck by this or these words (which are frequently my opening words). I believe that the story is always *in the words* and that by following where they lead, putting one after another, I will, first, *see* the story at some point and, second, know what I must do to reach an end. Sometimes the end of the story is upon me before I am ready for it, and I must be quick to recognize it and stop. All this is to say that I do not *plan* my stories; I let them go on by trust and instinct. Any planning, oxymoronically, comes after, when I have the essentials of the story committed to paper.

"Then I will add, delete, change a few things, *think* (but not too much); rarely do I change the original skeletal structure. And I do not add a lot. My short story work tends always in the direction of leanness (which has other manifestations in my life, e.g. I hate to waste *anything*), of suggestion or even non-statement rather than statement, multiple use of language, and severe understatement. I am much inclined to the multiple ironies of the first person narration (e.g. the relationship between narrator and author and between narrator and reader, the confusion between the assumed autobiographical authority of the 'I' and the awareness of the 'I' as mere strategy), and I seek always the single, sharp, sudden insight—not always easy to paraphrase but obvious, I hope, in its final *presence*.

"As to the story in this collection, 'Preparations,' although there is a brief reference to something specific in my own life right after the opening, the rest of the story moves on to other matters.

"Once I had created the basic situation of the dying husband and the fat Russian wife (I know there are many questions here), the complications of that situation seemed necessary to enumerate, as I say, in no particular order (who could create the philosophical system to give them order?). And I am aware, of course, that a careful reader could add many more items to that list—which, like life, is endless. From that to some generalizations about civilization followed (for me) naturally. I still, at that point, did not know where the story would go. I knew I had not reached any end. I knew only that it was clearly going *somewhere*. When I reached the description of the difference between the Russian woman and the narrator, certain things, certain characteristics of the narrator laid down earlier, for example, cropped up; I remembered something a colleague once told me about eating and telephone calls; and I saw my way clear to the final pitiful (and all too human) irony of the narrator's ignorance and inadequacy. After that, it was a matter of trimming and vanquishing any stray bits of ego."

HEINRICH BÖLL was born in 1917 in Cologne. The political injustice and oppressive cruelties he witnessed during his youth and military service in Nazi Germany were the ground of most of his writings, and his sense of moral outrage often took the form of humor and satire. More than twenty million copies of his books have been sold throughout the world, including the two-volume *Collected Stories* and the novels *Group Portrait with Lady* and *Woman Against a River Landscape*, the latter published shortly after his death in 1985. He was awarded the Nobel Prize for Literature in 1972.

Leila Vennewitz, translator of "The Laugher," writes: "Ever since the appearance in the 1960's of his novel *The Clown* (*Ansichten eines Clowns*), Heinrich Böll's humor has been associated with the humor of all clowns, the essence of which is poignancy. The man in this short story who makes his living as a professional laugher is not himself a clown: he is something sadder than that. Böll's laugher harbors the laughter of the world, of all eras, all races: he does not make people laugh, he merely demonstrates the act of laughter.

"While we smile as we read this story, while we delight in his ability to 'laugh mournfully, moderately, hysterically,' we find ourselves growing sadder and sadder as it winds to its bitter end. Never to have laughed except to earn one's daily bread is pathetic enough; never to have heard one's own laughter prompted by one's own responses to the witty or the comic is surely sadder still. And yet, just as we do at the sight of any clown making a fool of himself, we find ourselves, in the end, laughing."

JORGE LUIS BORGES, born in 1899, grew up in Buenos Aires and Switzerland. As a poet he was associated with Argentinian avant-garde literary movements in the 1920s and early 1930s, but turned to prose in 1938, while recuperating from a head injury. Subsequently he produced such works as *A Universal History of Infamy*, *Fictions*, *The Aleph*, *Dreamtigers*, *Labyrinths*, *Doctor Brodie's Report*, *The Book of Sand*, and *Six Problems for Don Isidro Parodi*. Borges also published biographies, fantasies, and screenplays. He served as Director of the National Library of Argentina until the dictator Juan Perón removed him for political reasons, and was professor of English Literature at the University of Buenos Aires. He died in 1986.

Alberto Manguel, the translator of "August 25, 1983," writes: "For Borges, life has a dreamlike quality. 'The light comes in and clumsily I go, / From my dreams to the sharing of my dreams,' he says in one of his poems. His blindness, that 'constant night,' heightens the impression of being always in a dream. His first 'fiction' (as he calls his stories that pretend to be essays), 'Pierre Menard, Author of *Don Quixote*,' was born from a nightmare caused by high fever, and many of his stories—like 'The Circular Ruins'—explore the world of dreams in search of the secret laws that govern them. In the early seventies he compiled an anthology of dreams which included several of his own. /

"I spoke to Borges in Buenos Aires in May 1982, while the Falkland Islands War was going on. He had just returned from a happy trip to the United States (he had listened to jazz in New Orleans and flown in a balloon in San Francisco) and he found himself back in the midst of an absurd nightmare. Torn between his love for Argentina and his love for England he felt once more betrayed by 'the clumsy fools who rule us.' 'Let us imagine we are dreaming,' he suggested to me. 'Let us imagine we will wake and all this will belong to the past. I will then call you up and say, "I had this curious dream, so absurd, a war with England, just imagine . . ." And you will wait a while and say, "Borges, do you know, I had that very dream myself." ' Then he paused and said, a little wistfully, 'I am so looking forward to that waking-up.'

"August 25 is Borges' birthday. On August 25, 1983, he was eighty-four years old—and a day.

"Later, when asked by journalists why he had not committed suicide on the day of the story, Borges answered: 'Cowardice, I suppose. Or maybe the conviction that taking my life was redundant, because at my age you're almost dead.' "

DANIEL BOULANGER was born in Compiègne, France, in 1922. During his prolific career he has written novels, short stories, children's stories, and film scripts, as well as very short poems which, based on the title of the first volume, he calls "retouches." As a favor to *Nouvelle Vague* director friends (Truffaut, Chabrol, Malle), he has also played bit parts in many films; he is the gangster in *Shoot the Piano Player*, the German general in *King of Hearts* (a very typical Boulanger story), and the cop who kills Belmondo in *Breathless*. In 1973 Boulanger was awarded the "Goncourt de la nouvelle," an honor that has been bestowed only once previously; ten years later he was elected by his peers to the Académie Goncourt.

"The *nouvelle*, or short story, doesn't try to understand, or comfort, or explain. It violates and betrays. It is the art of treachery, of gossip. It doesn't hold its tongue, despite its pretense to silence. It implies all the more because it says so little. It reveals the flaw in beauty, and where the shoe pinches."

Penny Million Pucelik, Boulanger's translator for "The Shoe Breaker," writes: "After his first three volumes of *nouvelles*, Boulanger's stories became increasingly longer. Sixty or seventy short-short stories gave way to eight or ten much longer ones. He admits that many of his

AFTERNOTES

respected critics and friends still claim to prefer the short-short stories. Boulanger's ability to create a universe in a few pages and people it with unforgettable characters like Pinceloup is one of his overwhelming talents. On a trip to France several years ago, I mentioned 'The Shoe Breaker' to him and his reaction was: 'My whole childhood is in that story.'

" 'The Shoe Breaker' was, in general, a joy to translate. Early in the story, however, the baron looks down at his old shoe, 'cuisine d'onions.' In French, *onion* means 'bunion' as well as 'onion,' so his shoes are literally 'cooked (or stewed) with bunions.' Ultimately we settled on 'bulging from his bunions and bubbled by his corns,' but our nine words lack both the recipe and the aroma of his three! I hope that the extremely original and oxymoronic characters are, however, as real, as indelible, and as *sympathique* in English as they are in French."

RICHARD BRAUTIGAN, born in Tacoma, Washington, in 1933, wrote eleven books of poetry, ten novels—including *Trout Fishing in America, A Confederate General from Big Sur, In Watermelon Sugar,* and *The Tokyo-Montana Express.* A short story collection, *Revenge of the Lawn: Stories 1962–1970,* is made up of many short-short stories. He died by his own hand in September, 1984.

DAVID BROOKS, born in Canberra in 1953, received his M.A. and Ph.D. at the University of Toronto. Since returning to Australia in 1980, he has taught at various universities and is currently a lecturer in English at the Australian National University (Canberra). He has published a collection of poetry *(The Cold Front),* stories *(The Book of Sei, Sheep and the Diva)* and essays, and is editor of *The Phoenix Review.*

"My writing of prose fiction began in reaction to my earlier writing of poetry. I had schooled myself in a tradition—more American than Australian—of the poem as an exploration of the self, and developed a sense that each new poem had to register some new level of awareness or further understanding of the self. While it worked for a time, this sense became increasingly solipsistic and repressive. The discovery, in Borges, García Márquez, Calvino, Barthes and others, of kinds of writing I had never before thought legitimate—speculative, fabulous, ironically self-conscious—offered rather suddenly (in a rush of 'free' reading after a doctoral thesis) a chance at play, at joy, which poetry was not at that time offering.

" 'Blue' was one of the first results. A small part of it, doubtless, is the story of my own thirst and my own discovery of prose. And yes, it's very short. When you've tried so often as a poet to get whole stories, ideas, accounts of the self and the world into a small string of images, even three or four pages can seem a vast canvas, an intoxicating freedom.

"But I'm not entirely happy with the term *story* when it comes to things I write—probably not even with the terms *fiction* or *prose*. Many of them are these things clearly enough, and readers, publishers, do seem to need to categorize, but part of the excitement of the discovery I'm talking about is that barriers are breaking down, the distinctions getting harder to defend. I don't just mean that fiction is often a way of telling truths that nonfiction can no longer tell, or that reality itself is a construct—a fiction—though these notions are part of it. I mean also that the writer need no longer feel obliged to listen to the categories (if he / she ever did), and that one can mix 'poetry' and 'prose,' 'narrative' and 'argument,' 'story' and 'essay' at will, enjoying all the time—and this seems to me the real secret—the process of writing as writing, the text itself as landscape, as story, whatever other story one is telling or landscape one is writing about.

"Perhaps the emergence of the very short story owes something to this structural / post-structural meltdown, though such stories have always been there and it may just be the novel, the epic poem becoming unstuck: whatever else they have been, the great novels, the great epic poems have also been great compilations of such things (of textual tropes, gambits as much as little narratives). Find out where the epic poems, the great omniscient narratives have gone—explain where the glue went—and you may have found the seedbed of the short-short story, in the rediscovery of human experience as the vast collection of sudden fictions that it always was."

DINO BUZZATI (1906–1972) lived most of his life in Milan. From 1928 until his death, he worked as an editor and correspondent for the *Cor-*

riere della Sera. His journalism covered such fields as politics, science, and the arts, but also more unusual phenomena like UFO sightings and exorcisms. A painter as well as a prolific writer, Buzzati produced novels, plays, poems, librettos, a children's book, and hundreds of short stories. The novel that won him an international reputation was *The Tartar Steppe* (1940). *A Clinical Case*, his absurdist play, also enjoyed worldwide acclaim; it was translated into French by Albert Camus. His short story collections include *Catastrophe*, *Restless Nights*, and *The Siren*.

Commenting on Italian short fiction, Lawrence Venuti, translator of "The Falling Girl," writes: "The short-short story seems to be a relatively recent invention in Italy. Examples of it surface from time to time in the nineteenth century, but not until the modern period does it really begin to proliferate, bearing all the marks of its contradictory origins.

"Under the influence of the French prose poem and the literary experimentation that accompanied avant-garde movements like Futurism, the Italian short-short is a narrative form that signals a decisive break with realism. The master fantasists of twentieth-century Italian fiction—Tommaso Landolfi, Dino Buzzati, Italo Calvino, among others—put the form through a rich variety of changes: Gothic and fairy tales, sci-fi speculation, parables, absurdist dialogues, dreams. The typical strategy is not so much to abandon realistic storytelling conventions as to implement them with fantastic characters, incidents, or plots. The result, more often than not, issues a seriocomic challenge to realism by probing the conditions of reference and representation.

"At the same time, however, Italian short-shorts display the awareness that they intervene into a real, historically specific situation by joining cultural debates and commenting on social changes. Landolfi's surrealist attacks on rationality, his dismantlings of language, mathematics and interpretation, are often staged as conversations with decayed aristocrats and unemployed university professors. Calvino's Qfwfq rides the New Jersey commuter train into Lower Manhattan. Buzzatian phantasmagoria is filled with topical allusions and frequently cast in journalistic genres: he treats urban crime in 'human-interest' stories, literary celebrity in 'letters to the editor,' advanced technology in scientific 'reports.' And many of Buzzati's fictions were first published in one of Italy's largest daily newspapers, the *Corriere della Sera*, where the fantastic could, however briefly, pass as 'real.'

"It would be more precise to say, then, that Italian sudden fiction has a fantastic mode of address to the world. It is out of this world, but also very much of this world, both an effect of and a calculated response to the social and cultural developments that have characterized Italy during this century.

"My translations negotiate this generic mixture by exaggerating the different fictional discourses it puts to work. I look for discontinuities in the Italian text, the points where fantasy and realism meet, or where the representation suddenly loses its transparency, its illusionistic effect of reality, and becomes opaque, fantastic, fictive. Then I develop a translation strategy which will produce those discontinuities in the English version. In Buzzati's short-shorts, for example, it is often a question of tone: my translations follow very closely the syntax of his plain journalistic prose in an effort to evoke a rather cool detached voice—even when the bizarre and alarming incident is being described. It is this divergence between tone and incident that heightens the black humor of 'The Falling Girl,' one of Buzzati's many commentaries on how the economic boom in post-World War II Italy shaped the culture of the urban bourgeoisie, especially women."

ITALO CALVINO's fictions, ranging from neo-realist to postmodern, have delighted and challenged his readers with lively storytelling and experiments with form. Among his works are: the trilogy *The Cloven Viscount*, *The Baron in the Trees*, and *The Nonexistent Knight*; *Cosmicomics*; *t zero*; *Invisible Cities*; *The Castle of Crossed Destinies*; *If on a Winter's Night a Traveler*; *Palomar*; and the posthumous *Sotto il sole giaguaro* (individual stories translated). His many essays on the art of storytelling and writing have appeared in several collections (*The Uses of Literature*, the posthumous *Six Memos for the Next Millennium*). Born in Cuba of Italian parents in 1923, he lived in San Remo, Rome, and Paris. He died in 1985.

William Weaver, Calvino's translator, writes: "When I read *Cosmicomics*, I quailed. This was the outer space of Calvino's imagination, where his poetry intersected with his scientific bent, his specific interest in astronomy. Trailing after the author, as if clinging to a comet, I entered that vast and, to me, uncharted terrain. For weeks, I read popularizing scientific volumes, studied the Britannica entries on nova and nebula and the constellations and the origin of the planets.

"In all this, Calvino was a constant reference point; and our joint *modus operandi* was gradually established. At a certain point, when I was on the second or third draft of a translation, I would go to him with a list of queries, many of them scientific in nature. Here Calvino was able to explain the puzzling phrases, and often able also to supply the correct English words, since much of his own reading, especially his scientific reading, was done in my language rather than his. Other problems might concern his quotations (*Orlando furioso* cropped up frequently) or elusive references.

"Later, I would show him the final draft, and here again, he sometimes offered useful suggestions. On other occasions, his suggestions were less useful, since his English came more from books than from speech (for that matter, he wasn't a great talker even in Italian). He would take a fancy to a word—frequently a technical or even jargon term, like 'input'—and try to convince me to use it in a translation even though the original Italian word might be miles away.

"We would meet in Rome, then in his house in Paris, then in Tuscany, then again in Rome. Our discussions of words often digressed into talk about other interests: history, travel, movies (we were exact contemporaries and had the same reminiscences of William Powell and Myrna Loy and even favorite character actors of the Thirties, like Franklin Pangborne and Una Merkel). We rarely talked about literature, and almost never about his work, except for the book or story then in the process of translation.

"For me, an important part of translating is getting to know the author (I have translated only one writer from the past: Pirandello). Thinking of *Cosmicomics*, I remember lonely hours, days at the typewriter, in my Rome apartment, my house in Tuscany, even in hotel rooms; but I also remember the relaxed afternoons with Calvino, struggling toward just the right word, the correctly sinuous line of a phrase. I remember those sessions, and I mourn for their loss."

311

PETER CAREY was born in Australia in 1943. His novels include *Bliss*, *Illywhacker*, and *Oscar and Lucinda*, for which he won the Booker Prize in 1988; his story "The Last Days of a Famous Mime" is from his collection *The Fat Man in History*. Another collection is entitled *War Crimes*.

RON CARLSON is the author of two novels, *Betrayed by F. Scott Fitzgerald* and *Truants*, and a short story collection, *The News of the World*. He lives in Tempe, Arizona.

"I will be disingenuous. 'Bigfoot Stole My Wife' was written after the newspaper bearing that same headline had been on my study bulletin board for a year. A friend (newly divorced) sent it to me. I read the article over and over, I guess, and I wondered about that guy, who he was, what he did for a living, and how he found out the bad news. Then, of course, I just started writing one day trying for the right voice. When I write, I always stay wide open and anything that presents itself is allowed into a story. My motto is: 'You want in? Get in, come on, right here, climb right in.' And what climbed in that day was a story my brother had told me about a trailer in a flood which he had been told by a woman he'd been seeing. It was a tough period for my brother. He spent over a year in the company of what we writers call unreliable narrators.

"I'm all for short good writing with no sagging in it at all, but I'm also all for long good writing with no sagging in it at all. Boredom is always the enemy, but I think the boom in short-shorts has more to do with precious page space than with attention spans or anything else. I also suspect they're easier to pass on: all those teachers quickly copying something for class.

"As a writer, when I launch into a story I rarely have a fix on how long it will be."

SIV CEDERING is a fiction writer, poet, photographer, painter, and musician. She has published more than twenty books (including five books for children), and her work has appeared in *Harper's*, *Ms.*, *The New Republic*, *Paris Review*, *Partisan Review*, and *North American Review*.

She has been writer-in-residence at the University of Pittsburgh, University of Massachusetts, and the Interlochen Arts Academy.

"I was born in a small village by the Arctic Circle in Sweden and began to write poetry when I was seven. My family moved to San Francisco when I was fourteen, and I switched to English. For twenty-five years I wrote only in English, but when the distinguished poets/translators Maria Wine and Artur Lundkvist translated two of my poetry books into Swedish, I became interested in Swedish phrasing and wrote again in my native language. The resulting novel came out in 1980, and my second novel a year later.

"I live near the ocean in Amagansett, New York, where I have just finished my first collection of short fiction in English. In addition to writing fiction and poetry in both languages, for adults and children, I am painting and composing music.

"During the last decades I have lived what could be called a very American life, in three major cities (San Francisco, Washington D.C., and New York). I have brought up three American children and have had a chance to get a good look at the business world as well as the art world and family life. Yet I am continuously aware of my relationship to the people from which I come. I don't mean just the generic relationship, but a spiritual one, a shared conscience, a common energy, manifest in a kinship with other things and beings in this world. It is a rootedness that makes you feel at home, no matter where you are. It is this relationship that I address in 'Family Album.' "

COLETTE was born Sidonie-Gabrielle Colette in Saint-Sauveur-en-Puisaye in 1873. *Claudine a l'ecole* was the first of an enormously successful quartet of books about a young country girl who comes to Paris. Though written by Colette, these appear only under her husband's name, Willy. Other works include *La Paix chez les betes*, an album of animal portraits; *Les Heures longues*, sketches about life on the home front; *Dans la foules*, essays on public events; the novels *Cheri* and *La Fin de Cheri*; *La Maison de Claudine*, short stories about Colette's childhood in Burgundy—all told, more than fifty books. Colette always disclaimed any sense of literary vocation, insisting that she became a writer because she was paid to do so. Perhaps her most famous story is "Gigi," written in 1942. She wrote until the end, immensely famous, and by the time she died, on August 3, 1954, her windows, overlooking the garden of the Palais-Royal, had become a Parisian landmark.

Matthew Ward, translator of Colette's story in this volume, writes: "It seems to me that the short-short story is the product of the nature and history of print technology—from the nineteenth century proliferation of newspapers, magazines and journals, to twentieth century technology and today's desk-top publishing. Perhaps there are more of them because there *can* be more of them.

"But when one reads a story such as 'The Other Wife,' what it's called and where it comes from seem utterly beside the point. Colette's story is, quite simply, classic fiction—the swirl of life as we enter the story and the restaurant simultaneously; an unexpected command; a sudden change of mood; a chance moment that throws one's deepest notions of oneself into doubt; doubt, discomfort, envy and curiosity unexpectedly, confusingly welling up over what was meant to be merely a nice lunch; the final irresolution when something essentially, recognizably human has happened, when everything, somehow, has changed. The complete atmosphere, the perfect detail, the finely calibrated mood and tone, it is all there, in sensuous, disquieting, beautiful writing. No matter its length, it has that poetic fullness of language characteristic of any memorable story, and what we learn about short-short stories is that they are limited only by the genius of their author and therefore are, happily, indefinable and unpredictable but always, in Colette's masterly hands, recognizable."

JULIO CORTÁZAR was born in 1914 in Brussels, where his father was an Argentine diplomat; in 1918, his parents returned to Argentina, and Cortázar grew up in Buenos Aires. In 1951, he settled in Paris, where he lived for over thirty years until his death in 1984. His works in English include *Hopscotch*, *The End of the Game and Other Stories*, *62: A Model Kit*, *We Love Glenda So Much and Other Tales*, and *Nicaraguan Sketches*.

Alberto Manguel, the translator for "Don't You Blame Anyone," writes: "One afternoon, sometime in the 1940s, a gangling young man entered the offices of a small literary magazine in Buenos Aires and left a story with the editor. Ten days later, when the young man returned, the editor told him that he had liked the story and that it was already at the printers. The editor was Jorge Luis Borges; the young writer, Julio Cortázar, who found himself suddenly launched on a literary career that would make him one of the most influential writers in Spanish of this century.

"Cortázar was born in Belgium but was brought up in Argentina, and though he left for Paris in the fifties (declaring that Perón's loudspeakers would not let him listen to the music of Bartók in peace) he always remained a *porteno*, a native of Buenos Aires. But Paris was closer to his spirit, especially the Paris of the surrealists, of Breton and Apollinaire. Cortázar shared the surrealist notion that dreams are the true measure of our existence. His stories include in their reality a tiger wandering through a bourgeois apartment, a man entering a hospital for surgery and ending up sacrificed upon an Aztec altar, a man who cannot stop vomiting rabbits, and a hurried husband caught in the death trap of a blue angora sweater.

"When I met him, in 1968, Paris was at the end of the uprising that toppled De Gaulle's reign, and Cortázar saw in the mingling of political and artistic furor a mirror of the essential truth of fiction: 'Poets and artists,' he said, 'lead the revolution, and the others will learn from them. Their motto is the true one: *imagination to power.*' "

ISAK DINESEN, pseudonym for Baroness Karen Blixen, was born in 1885 near Elsinore, Denmark. She married a cousin, Bror Blixen, and went with him to British East Africa, where she remained for seventeen years. The color and detail of that life flavors her memoir *Out of Africa* (1937), later to be a highly successful film. After her divorce she returned to Denmark and began to write—in English—the marvelous stories that made her world famous: *Seven Gothic Tales*, *Winter's Tales*, *The Angelic Avengers*, and *Last Tales*. In the late 1950s, she was repeatedly named as the leading candidate for the Nobel Prize in Literature, but was never awarded it. She died in 1962.

SERGEI DOVLOTOV was born in 1941 and grew up in a bohemian milieu in Leningrad, where his father was a theatrical director and his mother

an actress. None of the short stories he wrote after becoming a jour-
nalist in 1965 were accepted for publication, although in the late Sixties they began to circulate in *samizdat* (underground publication). Later,
he began sending manuscripts to the West, and following severe police
harassment he emigrated, settling in New York in 1978. From 1980 to
1982 he was the editor of the Russian weekly *Novyi Amerikanets (The
New American)*. His books in English translation include *The Invisible
Book, The Compromise*, and *The Zone*.

Although his work presumably circulates unofficially in the U.S.S.R.,
his translator Anne Frydman writes: "He's now very much an *emigré*
writer rather than a Soviet one, having never been published in the
U.S.S.R., though I believe it's about to happen due to the new freedom of the literary journals.

"As a young man, Sergei Dovlotov served as a prison camp guard
in labor camps as part of his military service. In his earliest fiction, he
deals with this experience in a way that brings a new point of view to
Russian prison literature, which goes back very far. This story, 'Katya,'
from the interconnected collection that makes up the fictional part of
The Zone, is one of three stories about the courtship and marriage of a
certain camp officer, Captain Egorov. The dog he shoots, by the way,
whose name is Harun, is a character who has appeared in several other
stories; he's the favorite companion of an Estonian private who teaches
him to obey commands only in Estonian.

"One more note about Dovlotov: he was very influenced by Hemingway's prose, as was his entire generation, and this is one reason
why his work is accessible to translation into English. The other larger
reason is his sensibility."

STUART DYBEK is the author of *Brass Knuckles, Childhood and Other
Neighborhoods*, and lives in Kalamazoo, Michigan.

"A friend, a DJ among other things who ran a jazz show out of East
Lansing, showed me many years ago some very brief stories he'd written. As I remember, the *longest* was three pages, double spaced. This
took place in an era when literary ambition was measured at least in
part by the magnitude of book spines, when writers were supposed to
be concerned with the quest for The Great American Novel, and so I

suppose my friend's short pieces seemed even more compressed than they might now. I know I hadn't read many pieces that short before. They reminded me in their brevity of the vignettes that Hemingway calls 'chapters' in *In Our Time*. I thought they were exciting—extremely fresh—both the DJ's and those Hemingway had written nearly half a century before.

"Of course, a tradition of short prose pieces existed. Continental writers, especially, had been working with the form at least since Baudelaire who, in the preface of *Paris Spleen*, wrote that in his ambitious moments he had dreamed of a poetic prose that was musical and supple and rugged enough to adapt itself to the lyrical impulses of the soul. But neither the DJ nor I were in touch with that yet. The news hadn't reached Connally's, an Irish bar on Chicago's North Side, its decor suggesting that one had entered a shrine of the Kennedys, where we sat on a Sunday afternoon in spring, reading one another's work as we always did when my friend would drive in from Michigan. He'd bring the manuscripts he was working on and a stack of records, and maybe it was merely that juxtaposition, but those little stories he showed me seemed jazzy—tight, rhythmic, incisive like bebop, timed for a world to bloom within the limits of a song on a jukebox.

"And, if the Great American Prose Poem phenomenon of the 1970s is any indication, there must have been a fair number of other writers, holed up in their various versions of Connally's, who were attracted by some aspect of the short prose form—the scale, the novelty, the freshness, the compression, the possibility of a prose as supple as poetry.

"What continues to interest me most about the short-short form is that it so often serves as a vehicle for the exploration of the lyrical possibilities of prose. In this, I think of it as a writer's form, though certainly believe that it can be made to appeal to the mythical 'general reader,' as well."

FENG JICAI was born in 1942 in Tianjin, China, where he lives now with his wife and son. His first career was as a painter, but he had to stop producing "counterrevolutionary" works of art during the Cultural Revolution. He then turned to fiction, but was unable to publish until 1977, after the death of Mao Zedong. He is a prolific author, whose best works depict the contemporary Chinese experience with rare artistry and insight into human nature.

According to his translator, Susan Wilff Chen, the apparent resemblance of "The Street-Sweeping Show" to a real-life incident in which Feng participated aroused a controversy when the story was published in 1982, and it was never reprinted in any of his short story collections. He is now Vice Chairman of the Tianjin branch of the Chinese Writers' Association and Vice Chairman of the Federation of Chinese Writers and Artists.

GABRIEL GARCÍA MÁRQUEZ is the author of several collections of short stories; his novels, international bestsellers, include *One Hundred Years of Solitude*, and, most recently, *Love in the Time of Cholera*. He was awarded the Nobel Prize for Literature in 1982. Born in Aracataca, Colombia, in 1928, he attended the University of Bogotá, and worked as a reporter and foreign correspondent in Rome, Paris, Barcelona, Caracas, and New York. He now lives in Mexico City.

NADINE GORDIMER, the highly acclaimed South African author, was born in Springs, Transvaal, in 1923. Her first publications were *The Soft Voice of the Serpent* and *The Lying Days*. Other works include the story collections *Friday's Footprint*, *Livingstone's Companions*, and *A Soldier's Embrace*, and the novels *A World of Strangers*, *A Guest of Honor*, *Burger's Daughter*, *July's People*, and *A Sport of Nature*.

PATRICIA GRACE was born in Wellington, New Zealand, in 1937. Her two collections of stories are *Waiariki*—the first collection of stories by a Maori woman writer—and *The Dream Sleepers;* her novels include *Mutuwhenua, The Moon Sleeps*, and *Potiki*. She also writes chldren's books in English and Maori. Responding to the question of whether her stories come easily to her or are the result of hard work, she says:

"A Gift or a Labour?

"I write from my own background and experience. I guess one's environment, relationships, ancestry, thoughts, feelings, imaginings, culture, spirituality, etc., are all part of one's background and experience.

"So what I *am* is what has been 'gifted' to me. I try to draw my stories out of myself. The 'drawing out' is where the 'labour' comes in. I keep on revising for the piece as a whole."

PETER HANDKE, Austrian novelist, dramatist, poet, and essayist, was born in 1942. His work first appeared while he studied law at Graz, where such writers as Wolfgang Bauer and Gerhard Roth staged plays and literary events and contributed to the magazine *manuskripte*. His fictions include *Goalie's Anxiety at the Penalty Kick*, *A Sorrow Beyond Dreams*, *A Moment of True Feeling*, *The Left-Handed Woman*, *The Weight of the World*, and *Slow Homecoming*.

BESSIE HEAD was born in Pietermaritzburg, South Africa, in 1937. Of mixed parentage, she was taken from her mother at birth, raised by foster parents until she was thirteen years old, and placed in a mission orphanage. In her loneliness, she drew strength through reading, which she described as "a world of magic beyond your own." Subsequently she taught elementary school in South Africa, worked for *Drum*, and wrote "true romances" for a newspaper. She married in South Africa, in 1961, and had a son. Soon after, she took a teaching job in Botswana, where she also began writing seriously.

Head traveled seldom, claiming she was an "ordinary" woman. But after the publication of the novels *When Rain Clouds Gather*, *Maru*, *A Question of Power*, and *A Collector of Treasures*, as well as *Serowe: Village of the Rainwind*, her first history, she was invited to writers' conferences in the United States, Canada, Europe, and Australia. Her second history, *A Bewitched Crossroad*, was published in 1985. She died in 1986.

"Looking for a Rain God" documents the psychological extremes of human endurance, and was based on a local newspaper report.

MARK HELPRIN is the author of *A Dove of the East & Other Stories* and *Ellis Island & Other Stories*, and two novels, *Refiner's Fire* and *Winter's Tale*. He has been publishing in *The New Yorker* for two decades, and his stories and essays have appeared as well in *The Atlantic*, *Esquire*, *The New Criterion*, *The New York Times*, and *The Wall Street Journal*. He was educated at Harvard, Princeton, and Oxford, and is a fellow of the American Academy in Rome.

"In response to your query, I measured the lengths of the stories in my last collection, in which 'La Volpaia' takes up four pages. The others are 32, 14, 16, 5, 4, 12, 11, and 68 pages long. In the collection before that they are 20, 4, 4, 3, 12, 9, 8, 5, 18, 8, 4, 5, 4, 9, 3, 7, 4, 6, and 38 pages long. This confirms my impression that I wrote more vignettes when I was younger and was either less long-winded or simply could not support the epics I write now. A correlation may exist in how much money one gets for stories of differing lengths and how much money one needs at age 20 and at age 45 (with a family to support), although I hope that is not the case. In music it is the same: you start with songs and proceed to symphonies. In painting you begin with sketches and only later make full canvasses. When you learn to ski jump . . . need I go on? For me, then, it has been a natural progression in which, though I sometimes return to the shorter form, what I write gets longer and longer. When I do write short pieces, it is because they have a different aesthetic, a different feel, and a different effect."

DENIS HIRSON grew up in South Africa and now lives in Paris. His father, a physicist, spent nine years in South African jails for his anti-apartheid activities.

" 'Arrest Me' is a fragment, one among many in my book entitled *The House Next Door to Africa*. I use the word 'fragment' in an archeological sense. Some years after emigrating to France I began sifting through memories of South Africa. After dispensing with a surface layer of anecdotes and moral judgments, I found that my writing began to attain a different density. It was as if the evocation of certain fragments of the past necessitated the use of a more compact mineral language.

"When juxtaposed, these fragments tell a kind of story. Although 'Arrest Me' would seem to me to stand on its own, references made to prison, the father, the house and so on are elucidated or developed elsewhere in *The House Next Door to Africa*."

SPENCER HOLST has lived for many years in New York City with his wife, the painter Beate Wheeler. He has published several collections of very short prose. *Spencer Holst Stories* (1976) received the Rosenthal

Award from The American Academy and Institute of Arts and Letters.

PANOS IOANNIDES, born in Cyprus in 1935, was educated in Cyprus, the U.S. and Canada. He is Head of TV Programmes at the Cyprus Broadcasting Corporation, and has written poetry, plays (which have been staged, broadcast or telecast in many countries), short stories, novels, numerous scripts for radio, and documentary scenarios for television. He has been widely translated, and he has won many national prizes, both for prose works such as his novel, *Census*, and his story collections, *Epics of Cyprus* and *The Unseen View*.

" 'Gregory' is based on an incident which took place during Cyprus' liberation struggle against the British in the late Fifties. I wrote the story in record time, on a rainy, cold winter night in 1963. I was coming down with flu and had a blanket thrown over my shoulders. The idea for the story had dawned on me earlier in the afternoon, following a chance encounter with a former guerilla, one of the men who was responsible for guarding a young English soldier held as a hostage and afterwards executed as a reprisal.

"As for short story writing in general, in my country it has a long tradition; it dominates the literary scene, and comes second only after poetry. The novel and the novelette have developed only recently. The main reason for this is the sad reality that in Cyprus a novelist cannot make his living just by writing; therefore, writing is usually exercised as a sideline during the few fleeting hours available in the daily struggle for survival. So the only forms of literature opportune to pursue for a Cypriot writer have been the short story and verse. Another reason is the absence, until recently, of publishing houses. Before now, writers were obliged to pay from their own pockets the cost of publishing their work, unless they sent stories to newspapers and magazines, both of which were eager to accommodate a short story. A third reason is, I presume, the conditions of anxiety and stress which prevailed following the liberation struggle and then the Turkish invasion of Cyprus in the summer of 1974. The pace of life generally became more asthmatic, which also accounts for writers turning to short forms of writing."

Marion Byron Raizis, the translator of "Gregory," writes: " 'Gregory' possesses the quality of that dramatic tension and sense of immediacy we experience when reading Hemingway's powerful short story 'The Killers.' Despite the technical difficulties presented by the extremely direct style and volatile atmosphere in 'Gregory,' I translated it as a labor of love because I shared, and still do, Panos Ioannides's view about that kind of inter-human relations, and I wanted, just like him, to stress the fact that it is easier to love than to hate a fellow human being.

" 'Gregory' could not have been longer or shorter, I think, because its actual size and form do justice to its artistic function and its humanistic message to all nations."

DAVID MICHAEL KAPLAN is the author of the short story collection *Comfort*. His fiction has appeared in *The Atlantic, Playboy, Redbook, Fiction Network, Ohio Review,* and been broadcast on National Public Radio's *Sound of Writing* series; his stories have also appeared in several anthologies, among them *Best American Short Stories 1986*. He lives in Chicago, where he teaches fiction writing at Loyola University.

"Reading a good short-short is like coming into the theater to see the magic show. We have come to be astonished and delighted and mystified. Miraculous things will happen: the light bulb will float in the air, the elephant will disappear, the bowl of flowers will turn into doves. Our whole world will change! And it's all happening right before our eyes! Nowhere else is the illusion so naked, the mechanics so open to inspection. Quick now, it's happening! We concentrate and look, look and concentrate, trying to spot how the trick is done. Yet if the magician is good, it all happens before we know it, marvelously. And it is something we never even expected. We are left wondering how it was done, yet with little desire to *really* know. The astonishment is enough. A good short-short writer leaves 'em gaping and gasping and clapping for more, and like a good magician, never repeats a trick.

"The well-wrought short-short, in literary terms, is most like a Japanese *haiku:* in a severely restricted and condensed space, a life and a world are suddenly and intensely illuminated, like the quick flaring of a goldfish in a turbid pond. Much is suggested—and then once more the waters are dark. Yet we have seen something important, and feel transfigured.

"I suggest that in an age of anxiety and confusion, when old values are uprooted to be replaced by nothing new, when old explanations prove exhausted and sterile, when all that clamors for our belief is meretricious and jarring, the short-short allows us to feel, for a moment, that transfiguration. When we feel we understand so little of our lives, it allows us to glimpse, for a moment, their possible mystery and meaning. We have become suspicious of large-scale illusions in art and advertising and information. But a small, brief moment of illumination—maybe all we can hope for and all we will really believe in anyway—can feel true. We look again into the pond, and glimpse what is on the bottom (a beautiful shell? a hand sticking from the sand? cloud reflections?). For once something really is there."

YASUNARI KAWABATA was awarded the Nobel Prize for Literature in 1968, the first Japanese to receive this honor. His novels include *The Izu Dancer, Thousand Cranes, The Sound of the Mountain,* and *The Old Capital.* Many of his short-short stories, written over a fifty-year period, are collected in *Palm-of-the-Hand Stories,* translated by Lane Dunlop and J. Martin Holman, including a "palm-sized" version of his novel *Snow Country,* written not long before he committed suicide in Zushi, Japan, on April 16, 1972. His stories focus on the lifelong concerns which also inform his longer works—loneliness, love, the passage of time, and the tension between the traditional and modern in Japanese society. Reflecting the traditional Japanese affinity for the delicate and beautiful, Kawabata is able to endow a small space with spaciousness and to paint an entire portrait with a single brushstroke.

JAMAICA KINCAID is a staff writer for *The New Yorker.* Her stories have appeared in *Rolling Stone* and *The Paris Review,* and her works include *At the Bottom of the River* and *Annie John,* a novel. She was born in St. John's, Antigua.

HERNÁN LARA ZAVALA was born in Mexico City in 1946, but both his parents come from Yucatan where, he writes, "I spent long periods of my childhood, and perhaps because of this so many of my stories are set there." He teaches literature at the University of Mexico and is coordinator of a narrative workshop in Cuernavaca, where he lives with his wife and son. His works include two collections of stories, *De Zitilchén* and *El mismo*, and a novel, *Charras*.

"The very short story is, indeed, part of a long tradition not only in Mexico but in Spain and in most Latin American countries. This form has flourished particularly during the second half of the twentieth century. The very short stories by Gomez de las Serna, Borges, Cortázar, Arreola and Monterroso are considered now as 'classics' of the genre. To me, the core of a good short story is that it contains an inner revelation, a sudden twist—tragic, humorous, moral—that allows the reader to project himself beyond the mere anecdote and the writer to build up a rounded structure.

"As to 'Iguana Hunting,' I never thought in advance about its possible length, as I may do now before sitting down to write a piece of fiction. It was one of the first stories I ever wrote and in a sense it was dictated to me by the muses, or rather from the unconsciousness of childhood which included the Mayan myths, the awakening of sexual life, and the power words have in the minds of young people to evoke sensations yet to be known. Perhaps because of this the story has so many archetypal elements. I wrote it in one go and then proceeded to adjust the details in different drafts. The idea came without much effort, but also without my having clearly in mind just where the twisting point would emerge in the account of childhood experience. The final story turned out to be quite different from the original project."

DORIS LESSING was born in Persia in 1919, moved with her family to Southern Rhodesia (now Zimbabwe) when she was five years old, and has lived in England since 1949. She is the author of more than twenty books—novels, reportage, poems, plays, and short fiction, including *Stories*, a major collection containing much of her short fiction. Recent works include *The Diaries of Jane Somers*, originally published in two volumes by "Jane Somers" (pseudonym), *The Good Terrorist*, and *The Fifth Child*.

CLARICE LISPECTOR was born in the Ukraine, but raised in Brazil, where she died in 1977, three days before her fifty-seventh birthday. Her works have been translated into English, French, German, Spanish, and Czechoslovakian, and include the novels *Close to the Savage* and *The Passion According to G.H.*; a collection of stories, *Family Ties*; and *The Foreign Legion*, stories and chronicles.

"I am incapable of 'relating' an idea or of 'dressing up an idea' with words. What comes to the surface is already expressed in words or simply fails to exist. Upon writing the text, there is always the certainty (seemingly paradoxical) that what confused the writer is the necessity of using words. This is the real trouble. If I could only write by carving on wood or stroking a child's hair or strolling through the countryside, I should never have embarked upon the path of words. I should do what so many people who are not writers do and precisely with the same happiness and the same torment as those who write, and with the same deep, inconsolable disappointments: I should avoid using words. This might prove to be my solution. And as such, it would be most welcome."

Giovanni Pontiero, Clarice Lispector's translator, writes: " 'The Fifth Story' is an admirable example of Lispector's intuitive approach to fiction. Random perceptions have always prevailed in her narratives in preference to tidy plots or conventional character studies. Her highly personal bestiary provides a reliable guide to recurring obsessions in her work: the horror and violence of existence, the perils that lurk beneath the most commonplace domestic chores. In Lispector's world, reality is prone to dramatic metamorphoses: the living have much to fear from the inanimate, rational beings are frequently challenged by lower species, and are often shown to be ultimately inferior."

BERNARD MALAMUD began writing in the 1940s while he taught night classes in New York City at Erasmus Hall High School and Harlem Evening Night School. During the Fifties his stories began to appear in such magazines as *Harper's Bazaar*, *Partisan Review*, and *Commentary*. Malamud taught at Bennington College for more than twenty years. In 1959 he won a National Book Award for "a luminescent collection of stories," *The Magic Barrel*, and in 1967 won both a National Book

AFTERNOTES

Award and a Pulitzer Prize for his novel *The Fixer*. Among his other novels are *The Natural* and *Dubin's Lives*, and other collections include *Idiots First*, *Rembrandt's Hat*, and *The Stories of Bernard Malamud*. He died in New York City in 1986.

PAUL MILENSKI was born in 1942 in Adams, Massachusetts. He has won the Associated Writing Program's Short-Short Fiction Competition, and his work has appeared in many anthologies, including *Sudden Fiction: American Short-Short Stories*.

"I am a metabolizing example of simplicity. I live in a one-bedroom apartment, consume little, walk in the woods daily, search for the center of the earth. I have come to fiction late, laden with ideas and experience, and my life philosophy, which I've always had, matches my art: nothing should be wasted, a little should mean a lot.

"My sudden fictions have not been sketches predating larger pieces; rather, all have been longer pieces in first draft, benefitting thence from cuts and elisions. All my work comes from the heart, as did 'Lost Keys.' I laugh, cry, shake, curse as I write, hold back nothing. I set my stories aside to age for a month, then come back to craft them, reducing the mass of raw feeling into a form, clean and evocative, for the reader. What was mine, thus, becomes with a little luck and lots of hard work, someone else's.

"Worldwide, people know that less is more, that the simple is most long-lasting. Occasionally, these concepts are tested by their contraries, elaborateness and complexity, which become fashionable, then fade, and reappear as curiosities. In literature, excellence is measured by condensation. Even the novel, the longest of genres, is best when character and event are condensed into metaphor. Assuming writers' survival and political needs have been met, there will always be self-sacrificing perfectionists (Chekhov, DeMaupassant, Hemingway, Mishima, García Márquez, Calvino, Borges, and others) who will make the supreme effort to condense their experience.

"I wrote the first draft of 'Lost Keys' in one hour, but only after laboring through twenty longer stories about my father's impending death. The father's questions, about the loss of sensation in aging, insinuate lost opportunities, missing keys to the meaning of life, and so on."

326

SLAWOMIR MROŻEK, born in 1930, is Poland's foremost contemporary satirist and playwright. Best known among his plays are *Tango* and *The Police*, both translated into many languages and widely performed, but his mordant, satirical short stories have been greeted with even greater acclaim. Two volumes of these stories have been published in Konrad Syrop's English translation: *The Elephant* and *The Ugupu Bird*. In 1968, when Mrożek's work was banned in Poland, he left the country for the West. In the 1970s, when political upheavel led to a more liberal period, Mrożek's works were again performed on the Polish stage. Allowed to return to Poland, he nevertheless decided to make his permanent home in Paris.

Of *The Elephant*, translator Konrad Syrop writes: "When the Polish text came into my hands I was enchanted, intrigued, amused, and disturbed at the same time. The poetry of some of the stories captured my imagination, the wit of the satire in all of them made me smile or laugh, while the layers of meaning with their often deliberate ambiguity made me reflect both on human nature and on the absurdities of life under communism.

"Translating the stories into English was for me a labor of love. Some of them presented no difficulty at all, others made me ponder and agonize for hours in the search for a faithful rendering of the author's narrative. Mrożek's economy of expression, and his style, which ranges from the austere to the ornate, depending on the demands of the story, is a challenge to a translator, and one that I found impossible to resist.

"Most of Mrożek's stories can be read and interpreted on at least two levels. 'The Elephant,' for instance, can be taken as a parable about bureaucratic stupidity and the dangers of trying to deceive the public, but is it not also an allegory in which the rubber elephant represents communist doctrine? The effect on the children of discovering the fake does resemble the reaction of naive Stalinists to the revelation that Stalin was not a hero but a monster."

BHARATI MUKHERJEE is the author of two novels, two volumes of short stories, and, with her husband, Clark Blaise, two books of nonfiction. She has been awarded Guggenheim, National Endowment for the Arts, and Woodrow Wilson Fellowships. Her most recent book, *The Middleman and Other Stories*, was selected for the National Book Critics Circle

Award in 1988. Her stories have also appeared in *Best American Short Stories, 1987* and *Editor's Choice*. Born and educated in Calcutta, Mukherjee currently teaches creative writing at Columbia University and City University of New York.

R. K. (Rasipuram Krishnaswamy) Narayan, a Brahmin, was born in 1906. Since the publication of his first novel, *Swami and Friends*, in 1935, he has published travel books, essays, novels, and short stories, including a volume of new and selected stories, *Under the Banyan Tree*. He has also produced modern prose versions in English of India's great epics, the *Mahabharata* and the thirteenth-century Tamil poet Kamban's version of the *Ramayana*. His stories have often appeared in *The New Yorker*.

Leslie Norris was born in 1921 in Merthyr Tydfil, Glamorgan, Wales, and was educated at The City of Coventry College and at Southampton University. He served in The Royal Air Force, and has worked as a local government officer, a schoolteacher, and a university lecturer. He has published many books of poetry, two collections of short stories, and contributes frequently to such magazines as *The New Yorker* and *The Atlantic*. Among his many awards are the Katherine Mansfield Triennial Award, for his fiction, and the Cholmondeley Prize, for his poetry. He is a Fellow of the Royal Society of Literature and a member of Yr Academi Gymreig (The Welsh Academy).

"There is something generally attractive about the tiny piece which says an enormous amount. And I think, too, that at this time, when the written word is losing its popularity in the face of the ominous power of the spoken word, we are probably facing a situation when something which can be absorbed as if it were spoken is somehow more natural.

"My own story probably is the result of these circumstances combined with a very strong oral tradition in Wales. The telling of tales was, when I was young, very common. It seems to me now that I heard very little political or philosophical conversation when I was a boy, but a great deal of anecdote and reminiscence, often artfully organized into something more, in fact a story. Even as young people, in our early teens, we were quite capable of spending an evening telling each other stories: wild adventure, ghost stories, prolonged jokes, that sort of thing. I recall that on a night of heavy rain eight or nine of us, aged between twelve and fourteen, were huddled in the doorway of a lawyer's office, a deep doorway protecting us from the blowing weather, when a policeman passed by. A youngish man, very large and official, he had his great cape swung on his shoulders.

" 'What are you boys up to?' he said.

" 'Telling yarns,' we said . . . that was what our activity was known as.

" 'Move over,' he said, and sitting beside us, he listened to our stories, told his own, and an hour or so later moved on into the night. And naturally these stories were by their very nature brief."

JOYCE CAROL OATES, born in Lockport, New York, is now Roger S. Berlind Distinguished Professor of the Humanities at Princeton University. Poet and critic, as well as fiction writer, she astonishes readers with her variety and the sheer volume of her production. Her most recent work is *American Appetites*. A collection of miniature narratives, such as the one in this volume, appears under the title *The Assignation*.

"Very short fictions are nearly always experimental, exquisitely calibrated, reminiscent of Frost's definition of a poem—a structure of words that consumes itself as it unfolds, like ice melting on a stove. The form is sometimes mythical, sometimes merely anecdotal, but it ends with its final sentence, often with its final word. We who love prose fiction love these miniature tales both to read and to write because they are so finite; so highly compressed and highly charged.

"When a piece of writing comes swiftly and cleanly we are tempted to think that it 'writes itself'; but in fact it can be argued that years and years of preparation have gone into it . . . an entire lifetime, in fact. So though 'The Boy' was, to me, a gift, a means of both expressing and assuaging a private hurt in fictional terms that took less than a day or two to compose, I can't romanticize the process. Chopin is said to have 'heard' his music, then to have spent weeks of misery revising it only to return, in most cases, to the original, by which time what was original and pristine became perfected. This seems to me the ideal method of composition, in which the unsought gift and the fastidiously honed are in equilibrium.

"Of course the form, while being contemporary, is also timeless. As old as the human instinct to combine power and brevity in a structure of words. Consider words as disparate as these:

> There are the seductive voices of the night; the Sirens, too, sang that way. It would be doing them an injustice to think that they wanted to seduce; they knew they had claws and sterile wombs, and they lamented this aloud. They could not help it if their laments sounded so beautiful.
>
> *Kafka*, "The Sirens"

and

> The competitions of the sky
> Corrodeless ply.
>
> *Emily Dickinson*

and

> Western Wind, when wilt thou blow,
> That the small rain down may rain?
> Christ, that my love were in my arms
> And I in my bed again!
>
> *Anonymous*

"As these selections suggest, the rhythmic form of the short-short story is often more temperamentally akin to poetry than to conventional prose, which generally opens out to dramatize experience and to evoke emotion; in the smallest, tightest spaces, experience can only be suggested. Voice is everything, the melting of the ice on the stove, consuming itself as we watch. There are those for whom one of Chopin's brillant little Preludes is worth an entire symphony by one or another 'classic' composer."

JULIO ORTEGA, born in Peru in 1942, has lived in the United States since 1979. He has taught Latin American literature at the Universities of Texas, California, and Brandeis, and currently is a professor at Brown. His poetry, fiction, and essays have appeared in *TriQuarterly*, *Yale Lit*, *Texas Quarterly Review*, *London Magazine*, *World Literature Today*, and other magazines. He is the author of many books in Spanish, and in English of *Poetics of Change* and *García Márquez and the Powers of Fiction*. His first book of short-short fiction, *Diario imaginario*, was published by the Universidad de Antioquia, Colombia.

" 'Las Papas' occurred to me while I was trying to cook for my son in Austin, some years ago. Potatoes originated in Peru, my country, but adapted themselves quite well in many other parts of the world. This metaphor from cultural preservation in exile interested me— cooking is not a melting pot if you care for flavors. *Saber y sabor* (knowledge and flavor) are together in Latin America from the very beginning. In fact, the first poem written in the New World was a Cuban recipe a Spanish cook sent back to Spain.

"From Borges, Cortázar, Juan José Arreola, Luis Loayza, I learned that the short-short story is a figure of articulation—it apprehends a sudden perception. This epiphanic sense is also ironic: the durable intuition can only be instantaneous. Borges thought that simultaneity needs the discourse of the instant. His *The Aleph* is a small sphere in which all objects are present at the same time—and how to communicate that sense of simultaneity is the dilemma of fiction. García Márquez's *One Hundred Years of Solitude*, as well, is based on this metaphor of storytelling.

"I have been writing short-short fiction as an exploration of means and meanings, of articulating images and names. This exercise on notation I have called 'Diario imaginario,' the page being the daily horizon of the *ars combinatoria* of the imaginary. One-page stories are perhaps another measure of time; and a book of short-short fiction is a sort of hour-word that you can turn over in any page into a silent alarm clock."

RODRIGO REY ROSA was born in Guatemala in 1958. His collection, *The Beggar's Knife*, was published in 1985, and his stories have appeared in *El Imparcial* (Guatemala), *Frank Magazine* (Paris), and *The Threepenny Review* (Berkeley).

"I like to believe that stories want to be written, that they must make an effort in order to be heard. They suggest themselves to me constantly, but I have little patience, I am lazy. Now and then, however, when I'm in the right mood, I stop to listen to one and sit down to record it. I think that by now they know I am not patient, so they make themselves short."

JOSEF ŠKVORECKÝ graduated in 1951 from Charles University in Prague and worked as a publisher's editor, a magazine editor, and a freelance writer. His novel *The Cowards*, published in 1958 and immediately banned, marks the beginning of the end of socialist realism in Czechoslovakia. After Czechoslovakia became a Russian colony in 1968, he emigrated to Canada where, "as a loyal subject of Her British Majesty Queen Elizabeth II," he teaches American literature at the University of Toronto. Other novels include *The Bass Saxophone*, *The Engineer of Human Souls*, and *Dvořák in Love*.

"In the days of relaxed censorship in Czechoslovakia—in the mid-Sixties—a kind of sudden fiction thrived in Prague. We called it 'text-appeals' and it somewhat resembled the celebrated jazz-and-poetry readings in San Francisco in the Beatnik Era, only it had nothing to do with poetry, although there was plenty of jazz. We, i.e. a group of writers who secretly yearned to become stage performers, read very short stories from the stage of the Paravan Theatre in Prague once a week, accompanied by the Slava Kunst Jazz Band and by various pretty girls who either sang as the Incognito Quartet (my wife was one of them) or simply walked around the stage in scanty clothing (I didn't permit my wife to do this). The advantage was that whereas every author had to send the text of his short-short story to the censors for approval, nothing could prevent him from losing this approved text and having to reproduce it from memory which, as even the censors knew, is unreliable.

"This particular story, 'An Insolvable Problem of Genetics,' is, unfortunately, not a child of my imagination but something that actually happened to my friend Jan Bich. It is, I think, a sad proof of the even sadder fact that even one who is not is a racist can, under certain circumstances, get in trouble because of race."

FERNANDO SORRENTINO was born in Buenos Aires in 1942. Of his first book of short stories, *Zoological Regression*, he has said he made the error of trying to please hypothetical readers, while in his second collection, *Empires and Servitude*, he began to write the stories he himself would like to read. Among Sorrentino's other story collections are *The Best of All Possible Worlds*, *Stories of the Liar*, and *Sanitary Centennial and Selected Short Stories*.

"I admire precision exceedingly, and, conversely, I don't like ambiguity at all. In my stories, despite the strangeness of many situations, I try to make the images very concrete, very precise."

PAUL THEROUX, born in Medford, Massachusetts, in 1941, is a prolific and highly acclaimed author, whose many books include the story collections *Sinning with Annie and Other Stories*, *The Consul's File*, and *World's End and Other Stories;* novels such as *The Mosquito Coast*, *Half Moon Street*, and *Saint Jack;* and travel books such as *The Great Railway Bazaar: By Train through Asia* and, most recenty, *Riding the Iron Rooster By Train through China*. He has taught at Soche Hill College in Nyasaland (Malawi), at Makerere University in Uganda, and at the University of Singapore, before moving to England in 1971. He now divides his time between London and Cape Cod. In 1984 he was inducted into The American Academy and Institute of Arts and Letters.

"I should say that I have always read the Acknowledgments of a book, and some of them I have found to be immensely more interesting and revealing than the books themselves—nearly often they have a plot, and a little drama, and in the past the typist was always mentioned by name—word processors have eliminated this long-suffering woman who 'painstakingly typed three separate drafts.'

"I am also addicted to Biographical Notes, and indeed wrote a story entitled 'Biographical Notes for Four American Poets' in *Sinning with Annie*."

LUISA VALENZUELA wrote her first short story, "City of the Unknown," when she was seventeen. Her first collection, *Los Hereticos*, was published in 1967. Other works include *Strange Things Happen Here* and *Open Door*.

EDLA VAN STEEN was born in Brazil in 1936. In addition to writing fiction, she has worked in film and theater, and founded and directed an art gallery. Her films and books have been awarded a number of prizes. "Mr. and Mrs. Martins" is taken from a short story collection, *Antes do Amanhecer*. Her most recent collection is *Ate Sempre*.

"For me, each fictional moment has its inner logic. It would be difficult for a short story not to be a short story, for a play not to be a play, a novel not to be a novel. The literary genre takes shape in the act of writing: we sense it. The idea for 'Mr. and Mrs. Martins' came to me at the funeral of an architect friend, in the middle of the cemetery, as I waited for the coffin to be lowered into the grave."

Daphne Patai, van Steen's translator, writes: "I chose 'Mr. and Mrs. Martins' for translation because I was fascinated by its calm and restrained unfolding of a macabre meaning. Its central metaphor—of rehearsal—is not usually associated with death (rehearsals are held for weddings, for performances; not normally for pain or disaster). Though the story is not anchored in space or time, we recognize its 'moment' as that of modern urban bourgeois life, and its interlocking themes as aging, loneliness, and danger, for which the contemporary panacea of 'preparation' is the bizarre solution. The simple and apparently transparent writing, the banal dialogue, leave the reader, at the story's end, with a sense of shock—as if everyday life had slipped away while our attention was elsewhere, and all that is left is the abyss. The story requires of the translator respect for its apparent simplicity and ordinariness, and the selection of a register that conveys these. Anything else would be distortion."

KRISHNAN VARMA was born in Kerala, a southwestern state of India. His stories, in English and Malayalam (an Indian language), have been published in India, the U.S. and Canada.

"Calcutta, the capital of West Bengal, is the largest city of India.

Many awful things have been said about it. Nasty. Frightening. A disaster area. The world's largest slum. The backside of hell. A vision of the end of man . . . I couldn't believe any of it. That's why I went to Calcutta, to see for myself. In 'The Grass-Eaters,' as in some of my other stories, I recapitulate some of the events I saw there."

JEANETTE WINTERSON was born in Lancashire, England, in 1959. Her novels, *Oranges are Not the Only Fruit* and *The Passion*, have received awards, and she has been translated into twelve languages. She was the recipient of the John Llewllyn Rhys Prize for best writer under thirty-five.

"A short story is not a tiny novel, nor is it like an extract from a novel, it has its own rules and limitations and must work perfectly within them. A short story with too much in it is trying to spring out and be a novel, and a story which leaves one unsatisfied, craving for unwritten words, is only an extract. A short story has to be complete.

"Love of language is necessary in a writer and after that, the humility to be disciplined by language. Theoretically, short pieces should be the perfect place for such virtues."

MONICA WOOD was born in 1953 in Mexico, Maine. Her fiction has appeared in such magazines as *Yankee*, *Redbook*, *North American Review*, and *Fiction Network*. She was a high school teacher and counselor before deciding to write full time.

"Two years ago I was at The Virginia Center for the Creative Arts and had the opportunity to swim every day in a usually deserted, pristine indoor pool at the college across the road. One of the visual artists at the Center, Karin Batten, was equally enamored of the pool and was working on a series of big bright paintings of a swimmer in water. In each new painting the swimmer became more obscure, until in the last painting she was indistinguishable from the water.

"On the last day of my stay I went to the pool and became lost in the rhythm of my slow and mediocre swimming—the sound of my breathing and my arms cutting the water seemed for the first time exquisitely matched—and in that moment I flashed back several years to an adult beginners' swimming class I took at my local YWCA. In the class was a terribly heavy woman who, despite her fear of the water, became the star pupil. She was scared and awkward, and came back each week with more courage and much more grace. The water eventually seemed to transform her—she was like an angel, weightless and floating. As I swam in that deserted pool in Virginia, I remembered Karin's paintings and suddenly *knew* (or thought I knew, which for fiction writers is the same thing) what that woman was doing. I got out of the pool, dried myself off, and wrote 'Disappearing.'"

BARRY YOURGRAU has written two collections of short-short stories, *Wearing Dad's Head* and *A Man Jumps Out of An Airplane*, and his work appears in the anthologies *Between C&D* and *Soho Square*. Besides being a writer, Yourgrau performs his stories in theaters, clubs and performance-art spaces, and on radio. He was born in South Africa in 1949 and moved to the United States as a child. He lives in New York and Los Angeles.

"I write short because quite simply that's the way I write. That's how my work comes out.

"There are advantages and special virtues to this particular scale—compression and intensity, variety (as stories accumulate), at the same time a sort of immediate, vivid wholeness to each item—but these don't furnish the conscious motives for my working in the size I do. I really have no conscious motives. I've just found I'm most in tune and expressive working small. Brevity and ardor suit me. If I felt natural working big, I certainly would. But I don't. But I do like to think I can get a lot of big effects anyway—mine just happen to take place in boxes and chambers, as opposed to ballrooms."

YUAN CH'IUNG-CH'IUNG was born in Taiwan in 1950. In addition to short fiction, essays, and poetry (which she writes under a pseudonym), she is one of the most sought-after script writers for daytime TV drama in Taipei. Her first full-length novel has recently been serialized in a Taipei newspaper literary supplement.

Howard Goldblatt, translator of "A Lover's Ear," writes: "Very short fiction has a long tradition in Chinese literature only in the classical language, which is a highly concentrated, difficult-to-master form of writing that often lends itself to numerous interpretations. In vernacular fiction, long stories and much longer novels are the norm. In contemporary Taiwan, where virtually all literary production by established and promising new writers alike appears first in newspaper literary supplements or in one of a dwindling number of literary magazines, the vernacular "more is more" tradition has been continued. Since payment is based upon word count, only the very dedicated or the very rich opt for shorter fiction.

"Very short fiction has been undergoing a resurgence in recent years for a variety of reasons, all tied directly to the literary editors: having perceived a shortening of the attention span of their readers and a need to pack more individual works into a limited space, they have encouraged the production of shorter works by initiating competitions, increasing the amount of payment for shorter works, and refusing to publish all but the best longer fiction, or that by nationally known authors. Several volumes of very short fiction, by individual or various authors, are available in Taiwan; much the same situation exists on the China Mainland.

"Most of Yuan Ch'iung-ch'iung's more recent work, whether long or very short, is of a piece, frequently dealing with young people and more involved with the innner workings of the psyche than external experience. While much of the very short fiction from Taiwan is in the O. Henry tradition of surprise-twist endings and closed-end construction, Yuan's work tends to end (often literally) with a question mark, an unresolved, haunting question or dilemma. Some of her work is slightly bizarre, some is surprisingly (and quietly) erotic; 'A Lover's Ear' has traces of both qualities."

Acknowledgments

TALAT ABBASI: "Facing the Light." Copyright © 1989 by Talat Abbasi. Reprinted by permission of the author.

BARBARA ALBERTI: "Tancredi" from *Memorie Malvage* (Wicked Memories) by Barbara Alberti. Copyright © 1976 by Marsilio Editore (Venice). First published in the English language in *Fiction*. English translation copyright © 1989 by Lawrence Venuti. Reprinted by permission of the translator and the author.

MARGARET ATWOOD: "Happy Endings" from *Murder in the Dark* by Margaret Atwood, published by Coach House Press (Toronto). Copyright © 1983 by Margaret Atwood. Reprinted by permission of the author. This story first appeared in *Ms.* magazine.

ISAAC BABEL: "Di grasso" from *The Collected Stories of Isaac Babel*, edited and translated by Walter Morrison, published 1955, 1974 by New American Library. This story is now in the public domain.

BAI XIAO-YI: "The Explosion in the Parlor." Copyright © 1989 by Bai Xiao-yi. English language translation © 1989 by Ding Zuxin. Reprinted by permission of the translator and the author.

DONALD BARTHELME: "The School" from *Amateurs* by Donald Barthelme, published by Farrar, Straus & Giroux, Inc. Copyright © 1976 by Donald Barthelme. Reprinted by permission of International Creative Management.

PAULÉ BARTÓN: "Emilie Plead Choose One Egg" from *The Woe Shirt, Caribbean Folk Tales* by Paulé Bartón. Copyright © 1980 by Howard A. Norman. English language translation copyright © 1980 by Howard A. Norman. Reprinted by permission of Graywolf Press.

ANN BEATTIE: "Snow" from *Where You'll Find Me* by Ann Beattie, published by Simon & Schuster. Copyright © 1986 by Irony and Pity, Inc. Reprinted by permission of International Creative Management, agent for the author.

KENNETH BERNARD: "Preparations" from *Maldive Chronicles* by Kenneth Bernard. Copyright © 1987 by Kenneth Bernard. Reprinted by permission of P.A.J. *(Performance Arts Journal)* Publications. This story also appeared in *Harper's*.

J. BERNLEF: "The Black Dog" from *Anectodes uit een zijstraat* by J. Bernlef, published 1978 by Em Querido's publishing house (Amsterdam). First published in English in *Ploughshares*. Copyright © 1983 by J. Bernlef. English language translation by Frank Scimone. Reprinted by permission of the author.

ACKNOWLEDGMENTS

HEINRICH BÖLL: "The Laugher" from *18 Stories* by Heinrich Böll, published by McGraw Hill. Copyright © 1966 by Heinrich Böll. English language translation by Leila Vennewitz. Reprinted by permission of Joan Daves, agent for the author.

JORGE LUIS BORGES: "August 25, 1983" from *Black Water: The Book of Fantastic Literature* edited by Alberto Manguel, published by Clarkson N. Potter. English translation copyright © 1983, 1989 by Alberto Manguel. Reprinted by permission of the estate of Jorge Luis Borges, represented by Smith/Skolnick, Ltd.

DANIEL BOULANGER: "The Shoe Breaker" from *les Noces du Merle* by Daniel Boulanger. Copyright © 1963 by Daniel Boulanger, published by Editions de la Table Ronde (Paris). English language translation copyright © 1989 by Penny Million Pucelik and Maryjo Despréaux Schneider. Reprinted by permission of the translators and the author.

RICHARD BRAUTIGAN: "The Weather in San Francisco" from *Revenge of the Lawn* by Richard Brautigan. Copyright © 1963, 1964, 1965, 1966, 1967, 1969, 1970, 1971 by Richard Brautigan. Reprinted by permission of Simon & Schuster, Inc.

DAVID BROOKS: "Blue" from *The Book of Sei* by David Brooks. Copyright © 1985, 1988 by David Brooks. Published by Faber & Faber and reprinted by permission of Curtis Brown on behalf of David Brooks.

DINO BUZZATI: "The Falling Girl" from *Restless Nights*, copyright © 1983 by Dino Buzzati. English language translation copyright © by Lawrence Venuti. Published by North Point Press and reprinted by permission.

ITALO CALVINO: "All at One Point" from *Cosmicomics* by Italo Calvino, copyright © 1965 by Guilio editore s.p.a., Torino. English translation by William Weaver; English translation copyright © 1968 by Harcourt Brace Jovanovich, Inc. and Jonathan Cape, Limited. Reprinted by permission of Harcourt Brace Jovanovich, Inc.

PETER CAREY: "The Last Days of a Famous Mime" from *The Fat Man in History* by Peter Carey, published by Random House, Inc. Copyright © 1981 by Peter Carey. Reprinted by permission of the author, courtesy of Elaine Markson Literary Agency.

RON CARLSON: "Bigfoot Stole My Wife" is reprinted from *The News of the World*, stories by Ron Carlson, by permission of W. W. Norton & Company, Inc. Copyright © 1987 by Ron Carlson.

SIV CEDERING: "Family Album," first published in *The Georgia Review*. Copyright © 1978, 1989 by Siv Cedering. Reprinted by permission of the author and her agent, Joan Daves.

COLETTE: "The Other Wife" from *The Collected Stories of Colette* by Colette. English language translation by Matthew Ward. Translation copyright © 1957, 1966, 1983 by Farrar, Straus & Giroux, Inc. Translation copyright © 1958 by Martin Secker and Warburg, Ltd. Reprinted by permission of Farrar, Straus & Giroux, Inc.

JULIO CORTÁZAR: "Don't You Blame Anyone" from *Cuentos* by Julio Cortázar, published by Alianza, S.A. Copyright © 1956 by Julio Cortázar. First published in

ACKNOWLEDGMENTS

English in *What* magazine (Toronto). English language translation © 1987 by Alberto Manguel. Reprinted by permission of the estate of Julio Cortázar, represented by Carmen Balcells (Barcelona).

ISAK DINESEN: "The Blue Jar" from *Winter's Tales* by Isak Dinesen. Copyright © 1942 by Random House, Inc. and renewed 1970 by Johan Philip Thomas Ingersley on behalf of the Rungstedlund Foundation. Reprinted by permission of Random House, Inc.

SERGEI DOVLOTOV: "Katya" from *The Zone* by Sergei Dovlotov. English language translation by Anne Frydman. Translation copyright © 1984, 1985 by Alfred Knopf, Inc. Reprinted by permission of Alfred A. Knopf, Inc.

STUART DYBEK: "Death of the Right Fielder," first published in *North American Review*. Copyright © 1982 by Stuart Dybek. Reprinted by permission of the author.

FENG JICAI: "The Street-Sweeping Show" from *Chrysanthemums and Other Stories*, translated by Susan Wilf Chen, copyright © 1985 by Susan Wilf Chen, reprinted by permission of Harcourt Brace Jovanovich, Inc. "The Street-Sweeping Show" originally appeared in *Stone Lyon Review II*.

GABRIEL GARCÍA MÁRQUEZ: "One of These Days." Copyright © 1968 in English translation by Harper & Row, Publishers, Inc. English language translation by J. S. Bernstein. From *Collected Stories* by Gabriel García Márquez. Reprinted by permission of Harper & Row.

NADINE GORDIMER: "Terminal" from *Something Out There* by Nadine Gordimer. Copyright © 1984 by Nadine Gordimer. All rights reserved. Reprinted by permission of Viking Penguin, Inc.

PATRICIA GRACE: "At the River" from *Wairiki* by Patricia Grace. Copyright © 1975 by Longman Paul, Ltd. Reprinted by permission of the publisher.

PETER HANDKE: "Welcoming the Board of Directors" from *Begrüssung des Aufsichtsrats* by Peter Handke. Copyright © 1967 by Residenz Verlag. First published in English in *An Anthology of Modern Austrian Literature*, published by Berg Publishers. Reprinted by permission of Residenz Verlag, Salzburg und Wien.

BESSIE HEAD: "Looking for a Rain God" from *The Collector of Treasures*. Copyright © 1977 by Bessie Head. Reprinted by permission of Heinemann Educational Books Ltd. and the author's agent, John Johnson, Ltd.

MARK HELPRIN: "La Volpaia" from *Ellis Island & Other Stories* by Mark Helprin. Copyright © 1981 by Mark Helprin. Reprinted by permission of Delacorte Press/ Seymour Lawrence, a division of Bantam, Doubleday, Dell Publishing Group, Inc.

DENIS HIRSON: "Arrest Me" from *The House Next Door* by Denis Hirson. Copyright © 1987 by Denis Hirson. Reprinted by permission of Carcanet. This story also appeared in *Harper's*.

SPENCER HOLST: "On Hope" from *The Language of Cats and Other Stories* published by the McCall Publishing Company (now E. P. Dutton). Copyright © 1971 by Spencer Holst. Reprinted by permission of the author.

Acknowledgments

Panos Ioannides: "Gregory," first published in *The Charioteer, A Review of Modern Greek Literature*. Copyright © 1989 by Panos Ioannides. English language translation © 1989 by Marion Byron & Catherine Raizis. Reprinted by permission of the author and translators.

David Michael Kaplan: "Love, Your Only Mother" from *Comfort* by David Michael Kaplan. Copyright © 1987 by David Michael Kaplan. Reprinted by permission of Viking Penguin, Division of Penguin Books U.S.A., Inc.

Yasunari Kawabata: "The Grasshopper and the Bell Cricket" from *Palm of The Hand Stories*. Copyright © 1988 by Yasunari Kawabata. English language translation by Lane Dunlop. Reprinted by permission of North Point Press.

Jamaica Kincaid: "Girl" from *At the Bottom of the River* by Jamaica Kincaid. Copyright © 1984 by Jamaica Kincaid. Reprinted by permission of Farrar, Straus & Giroux, Inc.

Krishnan Varma: "The Grass-Eaters," first published in *Wascana Review*. Copyright © 1985 by Krishnan Varma. Reprinted by permission of the author.

Hernán Lara Zavala: "Iguana Hunting" from *De Zitilchen* by Hernán Lara Zavala. English language translation by the author in collaboration with Andrew C. Jefford. Copyright © 1981 by Editorio Joaquín Mortiz. Reprinted by permission of the publisher and the author.

Doris Lessing: "Homage to Isaac Babel" from *A Man and Two Women* by Doris Lessing. Copyright © 1958, 1962, 1963 by Doris Lessing. Reprinted in the United States by permission of Simon & Schuster, Inc. and in Canada by McIntosh & Otis, agents for the author.

Clarice Lispector: "The Fifth Story" from *The Foreign Legion* by Clarice Lispector. Copyright © 1964, 1986 by Clarice Lispector. English language translation © 1986 by Giovanni Pontiero. Reprinted by arrangement with Carcanet Press.

Bernard Malamud: "The Model," first published in *The Atlantic Monthly*. Copyright © 1983 by Bernard Malamud. Reprinted by permission of Russell & Volkening as agents for the author.

Paul Milenski: "Lost Keys," first published in *Calliope*. Copyright © 1984 by Paul Milenski. "Lost Keys" was a PEN Syndicated Fiction Competition winner, 1986. Reprinted by permission of the author.

Slawomir Mrożek: "The Elephant" from *The Elephant* by Slawomir Mrożek. Copyright © 1962 by Grove Press. English language translation copyright © by Konrad Syrop. Reprinted by permission of Grove Press and the translator.

Bharati Mukherjee: "Courtly Vision" from *Darkness* by Bharati Mukherjee. Copyright © 1985 by Bharati Mukherjee. Reprinted by permission of Penguin Books Canada, Limited.

R. K. Narayan: "House Opposite" from *Under the Banyan Tree* by R. K. Narayan. Copyright © 1985 by R. K. Narayan. All rights reserved. Reprinted by permission of Viking Penguin, Inc.

ACKNOWLEDGMENTS

LESLIE NORRIS: "Blackberries" from *The Girl from Cardigan* by Leslie Norris. Copyright © 1988 by Leslie Norris. Reprinted by permission of Gibbs M. Smith Inc., Peregrine Smith Books.

JOYCE CAROL OATES: "The Boy," copyright © 1988 by *The Ontario Review, Inc.* From *The Assignation*, first published by the Ecco Press in 1988. Reprinted by permission.

JULIO ORTEGA: "Las Papas," first published by *The Magazine of the Boston Globe*, as part of the PEN Syndicated Fiction Project. Copyright © 1988 by Julio Ortega. English language translation by Regina Harrison. Reprinted by permission of the author.

RODRIGO REY ROSA: "The Book" from *The Beggar's Knife* by Rodrigo Rey Rosa. Copyright © 1985 by Rodrigo Rey Rosa. English language translation by Paul Bowles. Reprinted by permission of City Lights Booksellers & Publishers.

JOSEF ŠKVORECKÝ: "An Insolvable Problem of Genetics," first published by *Host do domu magazine*, 1966, first English translation in *Prism International*. Copyright © 1983 by Josef Škvorecký. English language translation copyright © 1983 by Michal Schonberg. Reprinted by permission of the author and the translator.

FERNANDO SORRENTINO: "There's a Man in the Habit of Hitting Me on the Head with an Umbrella," first published in *Mundus Artiam*. Copyright © 1970 by Fernando Sorrentino. English language translation by Norman Thomas di Giovanni. Reprinted by permission of the author.

PAUL THEROUX: "Acknowledgments" from *World's End and Other Stories* by Paul Theroux. Copyright © 1980 by Paul Theroux. Reprinted by permission of Houghton Mifflin Company. This story originally appeared in *The New Yorker*.

LUISA VALENZUELA: "The Verb *to Kill*" from *Open Door* by Luisa Valenzuela. Copyright © 1988 by Luisa Valenzuela. English language translation by Helen Lane. Reprinted by permission of North Point Press.

EDLA VAN STEEN: "Mr. and Mrs. Martins" first appeared in *The Literary Review*. Copyright © 1984 by Edla van Steen. English translation by Daphne Patai. Reprinted by permission of the author and the translator.

JEANETTE WINTERSON: "Orion," first published in *Granta*. Copyright © 1988 by Jeanette Winterson. Reprinted by permission of Suzanne Gluck, agent for the author.

MONICA WOOD: "Disappearing," first published in *Fiction Network*. Copyright © 1988 by Monica Wood. Reprinted by permission of the author.

BARRY YOURGRAU: "By the Creek" from *Wearing Dad's Head*. Copyright © 1987 by Barry Yourgrau. Reprinted by permission of Gibbs M. Smith Inc., Peregrine Smith Books.

YUAN CH'IUNG-CH'IUNG: "A Lover's Ear," first published in *Zyzzyva*. English translation and copyright © 1985 by Howard Goldblatt. Reprinted by permission of the translator.